BLOOD
OF THE
OLD KINGS

BLOOD

OF THE

OLD KINGS

SUNG-IL KIM

TRANSLATED BY ANTON HUR

TOR PUBLISHING GROUP

NEW YORK

BLOOD OF THE OLD KINGS

Copyright © 2016 by Sung-il Kim
English translation © 2024 by Anton Hur

Originally published in South Korea as 메르시아의 별 by Onuju.

Designed by Omar Chapa
Map designed by Emily Langmade

A Tor Book
Published by Tom Doherty Associates / Tor Publishing Group
120 Broadway
New York, NY 10271

www.torpublishinggroup.com

Tor® is a registered trademark of Macmillan Publishing Group, LLC.

The Library of Congress Cataloging-in-Publication Data is available upon request.

ISBN 978-1-250-89533-2 (hardcover)
ISBN 978-1-250-89534-9 (ebook)

Our books may be purchased in bulk for promotional, educational, or business use. Please contact your local bookseller or the Macmillan Corporate and Premium Sales Department at 1-800-221-7945, extension 5442, or by email at MacmillanSpecialMarkets@macmillan.com.

First U.S. Edition: 2024

Printed in the United States of America

0 9 8 7 6 5 4 3 2 1

To Narim, the first discoverer of everything that I mean to write

WHIT

HYBERIA

Shaira

Ledon

Kamori

Dehan
Forest

Arland

Finvera Pass

Dalosia

IMPERIAL
HEARTLAND

Imperial
Capital

Farov

Beruvia

Feredan

Bachr

Tanvalia

N

Arpheia

Rammania

S

ESERT

Tythonia

Ebria

ROOK MOUNTAINS

Cassia

Mersian
Wastes

Varata

asra

CALIDIA

Thiops

For King Gwaharad of Kamori,
from his most devoted subject.
May he lead the way to the
liberation of our homeland and
the world that suffers.

BLOOD
OF THE
OLD KINGS

1

LORAN

When she came to, Loran found herself under the scrutiny of a dark red dragon with too many eyes.

The beast had two enormous eyes where you would expect them, flanked by two smaller ones on the left and three more on the right. And all seven of these eyes were trained on Loran, boring into her with an unreadable expression.

More than how the fire-dragon loomed over her like a tower, more than the teeth that looked like swords and spears in a crowded weapons rack, more than the black chains entangled over the scales of its back, and more than the claw pressing down on her chest and holding her in place—it was these two rows of eyes, left and right, that frightened her.

When she tried to get up, the pressure on her chest increased. The claw was thicker than Loran's thigh, sharper than a dagger, and pierced her clothes and flesh.

Loran grimaced and a groan escaped her. The claw lightened a little.

"A princess of Arland."

The dragon's voice was not loud—it was as soft as a human's, yet otherworldly and full of menace. Loran tamped down on her terror and took in her surroundings. The walls of gray basalt looked naturally formed but, at the same time, not. There were blackened spots in places, and large scratch marks. Despite the cavern being inside of a volcano, there was a chill in the air.

She took a deep breath and spoke in a clear voice.

"I am common-born. Not a princess."

Loran tried not to cringe as the dragon's enormous face closed in on hers. It squinted all seven of its eyes and shifted its attention a little downward. It was examining the *t'laran* inked around her neck. She bore clan tattoos like all Arlanders, though since the Empire came the concept of clans had lost its hold over Arland, especially in Kingsworth, where she lived. But the dragon was looking for the royal markings designed in its own image, and her *t'laran* certainly didn't have them. She could smell the sulfur on the dragon's breath as it spoke.

"Not a princess? Do you not know that only those carrying the blood of kings may survive crossing the threshold?"

Loran knew what the legends said, but still she had come.

"Arland is an old country, and the royal blood has spread to many of its people. I have come here in the belief that I, too, have a little of the blood of the old kings."

The dragon made a horrible sound, which Loran realized was laughter.

"To leap into the fire of the volcano on such a whim! But with the demise of your last king, it no longer matters whether you are a princess or a commoner. Whatever blood you have only allows you to stand before me. I, who failed to keep my promise and was defeated by a mere toy, and now lie here tied in the outsiders' chains."

The menace in the dragon's voice had faded. The claw was lifted from her chest. So as not to provoke the beast, Loran got up slowly as she gathered her courage once more.

Fire-dragon of the mountain, guardian of the kings of Arland. More than twenty years have passed since the Empire conquered us, and the people are starving. The prefect kills innocents as if scything grass, falsely accusing them of treason and rebellion. Our country has fallen, but no one rises to lead us. I have come here to beg for your help.

These were the words she had committed to memory before coming here, when standing before the dragon had felt like a daydream. Even once she'd resolved to seek this creature of lore, the more likely outcomes had been that she would fall off the volcano and die, get caught by the pursuing soldiers and die, or disintegrate in lava before she had time to scream. Despite her likely demise, she had rewritten this speech many times, practicing it over and over in a low voice in front of the mirror, just in case.

But what passed her lips now was completely different.

"My husband and daughter were murdered by the Imperial prefect. I am not powerful enough to avenge their deaths. If you help me, I will do anything for you in return."

The dragon did not even bother to shake its head.

"Do the legends say I am a granter of wishes? I may have failed to keep my pact with the king, but there is no longer a king for me to make amends to. Go home. Twenty years have passed since my last good meal." Making a show of it, the dragon licked its lips, its

3

three-pronged tongue red as lava. Then it turned its long neck away from her, nestled its head on its flank, and closed its eyes.

Was that it? A day and night spent scaling the steep mountain face, all just for this? She had thrown herself into the opening of the volcano, ready for a sudden death, but here she was, alive yet empty-handed. Even being eaten by the enraged dragon was an ending she had steadied herself for, but instead, her petition had been refused as if by some clerk at the prefect's office.

Loran thought of her family. All they had done was to compose a mourning song and sing it. To the prefect and the Empire, it was treason. She remembered her husband and daughter, hanging by their necks at the crossroads for the whole world to gawk at. Her eyes squeezed themselves shut.

"*I* shall become King of Arland."

A voice cut through the silence, and her heart pounded. If the dragon hadn't opened its eyes and turned toward her, she wouldn't have thought the words had come out of her own mouth at all.

"Make a new pact—with me," Loran said. "Then I will help you keep your promise with the old king."

The dragon rose on its four legs. The chains around it stretched taut, and the stone floor beneath them rumbled. The scales along its back rose like hackles.

"King? You? Pitiful girl, do you not know the invincible Empire reigns over all lands under the sun? Did you not see their Powered weapons that struck down dragons from the sky? Do you not fear the Star that felled Mersia in a single night? How do you propose to be king? To swear in front of a dragon such a brash oath, one you do not even mean in your heart, is to deserve a burning death!"

4

Deep inside the dragon's mouth, a smoldering blue fire appeared.

Loran had no reply. Aside from her skills as a humble swordmaster with a handful of pupils, she was merely a widow who had only seen thirty-some years, and entirely without means—"brash" was right. But the dragon was wrong that she didn't mean it in her heart. She had meant every word. For it was the only path left to her.

Loran stood her ground. She met the dragon's great eyes until eventually the blue flames in its throat subsided. The dragon asked in a calm voice, "What is your name?"

She had not expected this. Then again, she didn't know what she had expected after declaring she'd become king. "My name is Loran."

The dragon asked again, this time in an almost caring tone, "What were your husband and daughter called?"

Her mouth opened halfway, but the words wouldn't come out. She hadn't spoken their names aloud for some time now. Their names reminded her of the countless times she had uttered them with love. It ached even more than remembering their deaths. The dragon studied Loran's face as she stood silent, then spoke.

"Never have I forgotten the day the Empire's legions swarmed our land like ants," the dragon said. "Their chains bind me, and I have tried to pass my imprisonment in slumber. But sleep only brings dreams, and in dreams, I watch again and again as the king, riding on my back into battle, is slain. Perhaps you suffer as I do."

Loran waited for the dragon to continue.

"If we enter a pact, will you banish the Empire from this land and become king, Princess of Arland?"

"I am not a—"

The dragon hissed and raised a single claw, quieting her.

"Will you become king and break these cursed chains?"

Loran nodded solemnly.

"Then give me your left eye to seal our pact, as the first of your kings did, so that I may see the world through you."

The dragon's claw approached her face. Instinctively, she tried to blink, but she couldn't—she let out a piercing scream as her eye was scooped from its socket.

She wasn't sure how much time passed before she managed to uncurl from where she had fallen, doubled over in pain, and to open her remaining eye. The dragon now had eight eyes. Its new eye felt familiar to Loran, as if she were looking at her own face in the mirror.

The dragon brought its claw to its mouth and broke off one of its fangs. It seemed to grimace, as if this caused it pain, then wrapped its claws around the bloody tooth. It closed all eight of its eyes and spoke words that Loran did not understand but that rang achingly inside her head. Smoke issued from the cage of the dragon's claws. When they opened, there was an ivory-colored sword glowing with a strange light.

"This, too, is a symbol of our pact. This sword shall slay our enemies in my stead."

Pressing the pulsing wound of her eye socket with one hand, Loran reached for the sword with the other, taking hold of the hilt. It gripped back. A wave of heat rippled through her.

"There are many lands in this world. They have almost all been taken by the Empire. In these lands, many died, others were enslaved, and yet others became slave drivers for their new masters.

But there are still those who fight. And there always will be. Now you may count yourself among them."

Loran nodded. The dragon pointed to one of the walls.

"Go there. A path shall open to the valley for the bearer of the sword. That path is unguarded. Even if someone is there, they shall be no match for you, or my fang." The dragon made the strange laughing wail again. "You must succeed. For me, for your vengeance, and for Arland."

Thus spoke the fire-dragon of Arland, guardian of legend, before slowly closing its eyes.

Loran bowed deeply and made her way to the wall indicated by the dragon. The barrier melted like snow in spring, revealing a tunnel just big enough for a single person to pass through. She heard water trickling on the other side. Loran stepped into the passageway, then hesitated, looking back at the dragon.

Without opening its eyes, the dragon said, "Speaking after so long spent in silence has exhausted me. Be on your way. Is the burden on your shoulders not heavy enough? Or the path you must walk not long already?"

Loran gave a final nod, then left the stone chamber. In the dark passage, her sword shone lightly, guiding her, and she whispered though there was no one to hear.

"I am a princess of Arland. And I shall become king."

2

CAIN

Cain had just stepped into the alley that would take him home when the blue light of the streetlamp behind him blinked once before going out completely. A gust of winter cold rustled his old tan coat. The ghost-like shadows that haunted the buildings melted into the dark, and now the only light came from a smattering of candles in the windows above the alley.

The Power generator in this run-down part of the Imperial Capital was low-grade, and old at that, so simply covering the fuses with a thin lead panel could disrupt the lamps for a while. A method commonly used by muggers, but no mugger or thief in this vicinity would dare make a mark of Cain.

Someone must want to talk to him. Perhaps it had something to do with Fienna. Maybe it was going to be violent. Cain pinched a leg of his spectacles but decided against stashing them in their steel case. Whatever was going to happen, he couldn't afford to miss any details.

In the alley ahead, a man appeared, his face hidden by the hood of a black cloak. Another person materialized from the shadows at Cain's right, from the main street he'd just turned off of, and he could hear muffled footsteps farther down the alley from approaching figures he couldn't yet see.

Cain had a concealed dagger in the inner pocket of his coat, his hand unconsciously creeping toward it, but he paused—he could make out at least five shrouded figures blocking his exit from all angles now. This was not a situation he could get out of by force.

"Cain?" an unfamiliar voice asked. "Cain, of the oil shop?"

Cain turned to face the speaker. A tall woman with short hair stood at the entrance of the alley. No weapons were visible on her person, but the iron in her voice and stance made it clear she'd once served in the legions. And like any ex-legionary, she was bound to be carrying at least one weapon, or to even be wearing armor under her coat.

Cain delayed answering as he glanced at the walls of the alley, noting how smooth they were despite their grime, with nary a handhold to aid his escape. He turned his head back down the alley where a man had come to a stop just six or seven steps away, face still in shadow. Not even his nose or mouth was discernible by the light of the stars and the weak candlelight.

"And who wishes to know?" Cain finally answered, wondering if talking could buy him the time he would need.

"You've been asking after that woman all day." This was spoken by the man nearest to him in the alley, behind whom now stood two more hooded figures.

"What woman?"

Cain knew perfectly well the answer to this question—he'd

9

spent hours inquiring after Fienna, inquiring about her *death*. And he'd realized, from the moment the streetlamp had blinked off, why these people were after him. He needed time.

He made as if to backtrack but heard quick footsteps behind him. Five of them, including the ex-legionary, just as he had suspected. No way to fight his way out and no escape.

"The woman pulled from the river today, the one named Fienna."

How polite of them to keep the conversation going. Their accents were not of the Imperial Capital but oddly similar to Arland's. Ledon? Kamori? Eshen? Cain's mind went down the list of provinces and the accents he knew from each of them.

"What river?"

"Is there any other river near but the Apathos? There's no use feigning ignorance."

The extended hiss in the *s* of Apathos betrayed their Kamori origins. Cain was from their neighboring country of Arland, and Fienna had also been an Arlander. It mattered to the people who moved to the Capital which province they came from. Not that anyone in power here could find Arland or Kamori on a map of the Empire.

"I have no idea who that is. I just sell olive oil." This time, Cain let his voice tremble as if he were afraid.

"You went to the dye shop where she worked and asked all sorts of questions about her. We know you're also the one who went to the patrollers."

Cain had been to ten places today, but these were the only two the man mentioned. Did that mean something?

"I was asking after the new awning at the dye shop. And reporting a thief to the patrollers."

"Lies. We know you examined the body at the patrollers' station."

The man didn't note the three cobblers Cain had also visited, because of the new stitching he'd seen on Fienna's shoes. If they didn't know that, they hadn't been following him all day.

Cain made a mental note to return to the dye shop and the patrollers if he survived this encounter. Come to think of it, Fienna had once told him the dye shop owner had regularly accompanied a great merchant, one with a monopoly license, to both Kamori and Arland, before she had her own shop. That might have something to do with all of this.

Fienna had not shown up at the tea shop, their usual meeting place, the night before. And this morning, her body had been fished out of the river by a ferryman's pole.

When they'd last spoken, Fienna had said there was something important she needed to tell him. Everything seemed important to Fienna—it was just one of many things he loved about his friend—but this time, instead of the usual excitement in her voice whenever she related news from their homeland, her tone had been one of fear. Whatever she had wanted to speak with him about, Cain thought, it had led to her death. He had to find out what it was. Which meant he needed to take advantage of the situation he found himself in now.

"Answer us, imbecile!"

That was another odd thing—the lack of strong curses in their words. Local thugs would have been swearing with gusto in one language or another. Aside from the slight Kamori accents and the mild threats, their Imperial was practically genteel. The silence of the remaining four was also beginning to bother him.

The man walked forward menacingly. Cain took a couple of steps back. It was going to be violent, after all. Cain took off his spectacles and quickly slipped them into their case. The candlelights in the windowsills seemed to flicker in his hazy vision.

"But I honestly don't know what you're talking about," Cain said, adopting a whining tone.

"You should've stuck to selling oil." The first man strode toward him and drew back his left fist, as if announcing to the world that he was about to take a swing at Cain. He'd stepped close enough to reveal his face, visible even to Cain's unaided vision, but the man's nose and mouth were covered by cloth. Was this someone Cain knew? Was that why he had covered his face? But Cain wasn't acquainted with anyone from Kamori. And no one who knew Cain would try to intimidate him with such lack of finesse.

The fist came flying and Cain didn't try to duck. The darkness became darker. Cain spun from the force and fell to the ground as the others rushed toward him, their footsteps ringing in the quiet alley, one of their boots catching his eye. Cain, under the pretense of putting up a fight, grabbed at the hem of one of their trousers. A sleek and thin fabric. He tried to tear it but despite its lightness, it held strong. There was only one kind of fabric Cain knew that had this quality.

One of the boots connected with his spine. He involuntarily screamed in pain and arched his back, but curled quickly back into the fetal position, protecting the case that contained his spectacles.

The blows continued. The well-placed kick had apparently been a bit of blind luck, as the subsequent ones only hit the top half of his back and his forearms, which he held up as offerings to protect his stomach and chest. These assailants were not, evidently, used to violence. And the soldier from before? She was watching the beating unfold with her arms crossed, her sharp gaze shifting from the alley entrance to Cain and back again.

He'd known they had no intention of killing him. If they had, the soldier would have dispensed with the interrogation and instead let the sword she had discreetly fastened beneath her coat speak for her. But whatever their intentions, even fools might eventually land a kick to the back of his head that could accidentally kill him.

As the beating got rougher, Cain carefully but firmly bit the inside of his cheek and coughed dramatically, spitting blood onto the alley floor.

The first man, startled, took a step back.

"Wait, wait! Stop, stop it now."

There was fear in his voice. The others stopped kicking Cain and looked at one another. The legionary woman walked calmly to Cain and prodded him with her foot; Cain hoped he seemed badly injured but not fatally so, but the woman saved him the trouble of further acting.

"He's fine. It takes more to kill a man than that."

The man with the soft trousers mopped his brow with his hand.

"If you keep going around making trouble," he said to Cain, "we'll kill you in your sleep."

The five of them left Cain sprawled on the ground and disappeared down the alley. It was quiet now, almost like they'd never been there at all. A bit delirious, Cain laughed, but it came out in a real cough.

Lying there, he wondered. There weren't many Kamori in the Imperial Capital. Certainly not many who could afford to wear Cassian velvet. This neighborhood was full of shadowy figures who wouldn't hesitate to commit worse things than murder for a small price. But the fact that instead such tender-palms should cross paths with him gave him pause.

He rolled to his back and heard a window slam shut above him. Just as he noted it was the one on the third floor to the left, the candle in it went out too. Briefly, he considered coming back the next night to ask them what they had seen.

As he rose from the ground Cain touched his jaw where the first punch had landed. The raw wound was wet, and it stung. If he was lucky, there could be an impression of the ring the man had worn. The streetlamp's blue light came back with a flicker, restoring the long, ghost-like shadows to their proper places on the alley walls.

Cain took the steel case from his inner pocket and put his spectacles back on.

3

ARIENNE

To be a first-year student studying at the Division of Sorcery in the Imperial Academy was to live in fear. The Academy had so many rules it was impossible to remember them all, and you could be punished for any infraction, real or imagined. And not only by the housemaster; the upperclassmen acted as enforcers too. A majority of your first year was spent cowering, terrified of leaving your dorm room except for classes and meals.

But eventually, as you numbed to the terrifying reality of your everyday, it would slowly become clear that this was all bluster. The Academy's harsh reputation was just that: reputation. By the start of your second year, you would realize that you could stay out all day and night, you could partake of anything and everything the Capital had to offer; as long as you were back by morning, there would be no consequences. In everyday life, it would be not so different from the mundane divisions of the Academy where non-sorcerers studied.

Still, the inkling of fear you felt at the start would never quite leave you; it helped you remember that being here was not a choice, and that there were some rules that must not be broken no matter what year you were, or even if you were a professor: You must not try to escape. You must not enter the underground chamber where the Power generator resided.

In her sixth year at the Division of Sorcery at the Eleventh College of the Imperial Academy, Arienne found herself about to break both rules at the same time.

Late in the afternoon, Arienne put her boyfriend, Felix, under a sleeping spell in his room. Making sure nobody was in the hallway, she slipped out of the dormitory through a back window, unnoticed. As far as anyone knew, she was still in that room with him. Arienne felt a slight pang of guilt—confusion and chaos awaited him when he woke up. Maybe he would even be dragged away to the Office of Truth. If *she* hadn't already been dragged there before him.

The sleeping spell wasn't anything her professors had taught her. The Academy never taught them spells—such were *un-Imperial* relics of the past. She had learned it from Kaya, a Bachrian girl one year senior who liked to show off the beautifully crafted scars on her shoulders. Kaya had told everyone that she had learned a smattering of hedge magic from an old grimoire she discovered in the library and subsequently lost, but she later confessed to Arienne that her teacher had been a rogue witch hiding from the Empire, back in her southern home province.

Unlike Kaya, Arienne had not known any spells at all when she took the mandatory admission test at the age of ten. Among the half dozen Arlander children suspected of magic, only she was ordered to the Imperial Capital that year. It was the duty of all sorcerers to enroll in the Imperial Academy. In the fringes of the Empire, where the Office of Truth was unable to administer regular testing, undetected magical children grew up to be feral sorcerers, or so the rumors said. But since Arland was a small province firmly under Imperial rule, she had always known such a life would never be hers, ever since the moment she felt the first violet thrum of magic in her. But still.

Her parents were compensated generously for handing Arienne over without complaint. The villagers put on a grand party for her, as if she were going to the Capital to get a fancy job. There was a cake shaped like an old woman sorcerer wearing a conical hat and a long robe with star patterns, striking a dramatic pose. The baker was repeatedly stroking his bald head, looking pleased with his work. After that day, Arienne never spoke to her parents again.

She had already known what kind of life was waiting at the Imperial Academy, and hated her sorcerer's fate for it. If she had ever tried to escape, she would have been hunted down and killed. Even that would have been no escape from what the Empire had planned for her, for all sorcerers. But things had changed recently. She now had a *chance* at a different fate, something undreamed of till now.

Arienne crossed the courtyard, the hood of her robe pulled low to avoid recognition, and entered the library in the main building. She waited there like a mouse for hours, crouched between the dusty corner shelves no one visited. When the librarian finished reshelving and finally went home close to midnight, Arienne crept out of the library to the other side of the building where the entrance to the basement was. No one stood guard; no one *needed* to stand guard with the eye insignia of the Office of Truth hanging above the iron door, dissuading her from what she was determined to do.

The Office of Truth oversaw sorcerers, along with all things magical. Most Imperial heartlanders thought of them as the sorcerer-engineers who manufactured and operated Power generators. For provincials, they were the inquisitors who would take you away at night if you were found practicing the old faiths. But to all sorcerers, they were the lords and jailers, in life and in death, never to be defied. Arienne knew enough horror stories involving hapless sorcerers and macabre inquisitors to bite her thumbnail in hesitation.

Her heart calmed a little bit at the sight of rust covering the door—and a corner of the Office insignia. Nobody, inquisitor or not, seemed to have been through this door in years. She sighed as she felt inside her sleeve pocket for the key stolen for this occasion.

Arienne had flunked the previous three years at the Academy. She couldn't focus herself on whatever it was the Empire desired of her. Even before coming here, she had known they wouldn't be teaching her spells. But she hadn't expected the sorcery curriculum to consist mainly of weird calisthenics and brainteasers. The Academy wanted her, first and foremost, to keep her body and mind primed for her eventual transformation into a Power generator— the fate of all sorcerers in the Empire upon their deaths. There were also classes on the theory and practice of Power generators, which were not nearly as emphasized unless you wanted to be a sorcerer-engineer. Other subjects, like history, literature, and music, were offered as well, and were taught with the same depth as in other, mundane divisions of the Academy, but such subjects were "academics," which in the Division of Sorcery was code for "things that don't matter." Her third flunking report card had a red note attached saying that she would make a Class Eight generator at best, and such a poor result guaranteed only minimum pension. Nobody cared about her academics scores, which were quite high.

Had this been any other division of the Imperial Academy, her family would have been asked for a large donation, or she would have been expelled. But this was a school for sorcerers, and they were determined to keep her until she died.

Arienne stood before the iron door in the middle of the main hall. The passage leading deep down to the Power generator chamber was said to be rigged with wards and traps. There were rumors of Powered weapons guarding the passage, and the tales first-year students would hear between classes were even more sensational, involving monsters and spirits the Empire had captured in its myriad conquests. Arienne imagined herself hanging by her fingertips over a dark wailing pit lined with hungry bestial eyes, a companion trying to get her to reach out and grab their hand. But as she stood there, about to break one of the deadliest rules of the Imperial Academy, she had no such companion with her. This gave her pause.

Well, she did have an accomplice. Of sorts. The voice that had suggested all this to her. But it had been silent ever since she left Felix in his room.

Arienne slathered both the lock and the key with olive oil from a bottle so slick that half of its label had peeled off. She applied a generous amount to the hinges and the doorframe as well. She tucked the bottle back into her inner pocket and wiped her hands on her student's robe. She smelled spoiled oil and the tang of rust as the key turned in the lock with a muted clang. Oil dripped to the stone floor as she pushed the door open, and every drop seemed to echo in the deep, deep silence. She stared into the unlit stairway that led to the generator chamber, afraid of taking the step that would make everything irrevocable.

Every student in this school knew what fate awaited them. The Power generators that sustained the whole Empire were made from the bodies of dead sorcerers. These generators lit up the cities at night, drew up water from the rivers, and enabled the Empire's weapons to wreak havoc upon the world. In a world conquered by the Empire, sorcerers were no longer astonishing beings that shook the heavens with mysterious spells. They were now more useful dead than alive. And the students at the Imperial Academy's Division of Sorcery were nothing more than living corpses herded together to await their deaths.

Most students numbed to their eventual fate after their third year or so. What the Empire chose to do with their corpses happened after they were dead, after all. Most would be content to live out their lives, as the sorcerer on the lowest pension rank still fared better than the average Imperial citizen.

The day after she had flunked her fifth year, Magnus, an honors student with the most beautiful hair, had offered to tutor her, either out of pity or an inborn friendliness so common to scions of prominent families. Arienne had asked the prodigy sorcerer what spells he could teach her. Naming a handful of minor convenience spells he had learned from his classmates, Magnus looked puzzled as to why he was being asked such things. He reminded her that their formal education was about preparing them for their service after death, and sorting out the students who would serve the Empire in life as sorcerer-engineers or professors, the former of which he aspired to be. He was going to travel the world as an attendant engineer to the best of all the hundred legions. He looked proud when he said it was his birthright and destiny. Arienne refused Magnus's offer with a polite smile. Magnus, taken aback, made an awkward compliment about the tattoos surrounding her neck. She didn't explain to him that they were *t'laran*, clan markings all Arlanders had. After that conversation, she altogether avoided talking about the school, sorcery, or her future.

Arienne didn't have the drive necessary to become an engineer or a professor. Neither did she have the good sense to make peace with her assigned fate. She had no way of escape, and no one to confide in.

But in the winter of her fifth year, just before a new term, she began to hear the voice—the voice that had now returned and was reminding her why she chose to stand in front of this forbidden door.

"Why are you hesitating? Did you not tell me you loathed to become a Power generator? That you feared a meaningless life and endless death above all else? Descend."

The voice was right. She gritted her teeth, then walked down the dusty spiral staircase. The soft brush of her leather slippers against the stone steps echoed against the invisible wards, sounding like a dozen whispers in the dark.

This year, her sixth since entering the Academy, Arienne had placed first in her class. The last time a sorcerer from a province and not an old heartlander family achieved such an honor was twenty years ago. In another division of the Academy, this would have been enough to arouse suspicion, but as a student of sorcery, she was simply congratulated as a late bloomer who would make a decent Power generator after she died. A professor even suggested to her that she might want to take extra courses to be a sorcerer-engineer, citing her academics scores.

Duff, a custodian of the dorms, was as overjoyed as if he'd placed first himself, and bought her a cake. Duff was a burly, middle-aged Ledonite man whose bald head reminded Arienne of the baker who had made the farewell cake back in Arland. He treated young Arienne from his homeland's neighboring province of Arland like a niece, which always made Arienne uncomfortable. As a sorcerer, she was an asset of the Empire. It didn't matter where she was from. A man acting like he was family—when he wasn't even from her province but from a neighboring one—did not sit well with her.

Not to mention, she hadn't exactly placed first on her own. Her marks this year had little to do with her prowess as a student and everything to do with the voice in her head.

When the voice first made itself known, she'd assumed it was a prank being played by one of the other students who had picked up an amusing spell somewhere; her boyfriend, Felix, for one, had been reprimanded a few times for such mischiefs. But the voice was neither male nor female, young nor old. The voice knew all sorts of things that no one should know: stories of Arienne's childhood; the illicit relationship between a professor and a student; the code that briefly dissolved the ward around the safe where the sixth-year exam results were held; the hour of the night in which old Quintus, the guard who kept watch over the safe, would inevitably drift off to sleep; and in the same room, on a dusty shelf, a forgotten wooden case that held the key to the basement . . .

"Young sorcerer, you still recall the unraveling codes I told you?"

"If I forget you can tell me again," muttered Arienne, answering the voice for the first time since slipping out of her dorm.

Her foot unexpectedly landed on an invisible surface instead of a step, making her stumble. A rune glowed in the air beneath her feet, creating pale waves like the surface of a pond reflecting the moon. Inhaling deeply, she backed up from the ward and recited the code of unraveling in one breath.

The mist of her breath turned violet and sparkled. Like the smoke from a hearth being drawn up a chimney, her breath flew down to the pale waves, melting into them and diminishing their glow. She stepped forward, confident the remaining four wards would be just as easy to unravel with the codes the voice had given her.

Once she had topped her class by forging the exam results, Arienne was no longer skeptical of the voice. Whatever its intentions, it clearly existed, and everything it spoke was true.

Magnus, coming in second this year, had kept asking Arienne how she had done it. His smile was cold, as if in recognition of the upstart provincial as a serious contender. Arienne had no desire to entertain any rivalry. She had another, more important matter occupying her mind.

The voice made promises, that it would help her escape the school, teach her real sorcery. The voice had a price, however. She was to sneak into the underground levels of the Division of Sorcery's main hall and extract a Power generator.

Only the Empire's sorcerer-engineers knew how to build the Power generators, and they were granted this knowledge only at the Imperial Academy. It was this monopoly of Power that made the Empire's conquest of the world possible. From the weaker generators that lit the streetlamps and purified the waters to the stronger ones that animated the massive gigatherions for war, each generator was the possession of the Empire. Stealing one was a crime so serious that execution was the *least* amount of punishment one would receive.

The Power generator would be encased in a coffin made of lead to prevent the leakage of Power. Because it contained the remains of a sorcerer, it would be as large as an ordinary coffin. Its weight, however, was bound to be significant, even without the heavy control chains it would also be wrapped in. But the voice had taught Arienne a way to move it, a strange sorcery her books had never even mentioned.

Having cleared all five wards, she had started down a small final staircase when her eyes glimpsed a skeleton lying at the bottom with its neck snapped in two. She stumbled backward in surprise, sitting down on a step. A mouse poked its head through of one of the skeleton's eye sockets and peered in her direction.

Arienne whimpered as the mouse scrambled across the skull and down the frayed student's robe wrapped around the lifeless bones, before leaping off and slipping through a crack in the wall. After a moment, she got to her feet and continued down the stairs, the skull grinning up at her as she approached.

Staring at the skull, she remembered Magnus's face when he found out she had placed first in the exams. She could have a future like Magnus's now, if she worked harder. In contrast, the skeleton served as a reminder of the wholly different future she was likely to meet at the end of her chosen path if she wasn't careful.

Arienne shook away the thought and approached the skeleton.

Just as the voice had said, there was a key in a sleeve pocket of the dead student's robe. There was also a small notebook, scribbled with the kind of things a Division of Sorcery student might be concerned with. The last entry was dated five years ago. Had it been that long since a living soul had entered this space?

Beyond the skeleton, there was another iron door before her, a big old thing that would require much strength to open, even if she managed to unlock it. She took out her bottle of olive oil once more and smeared the key, pouring it onto the keyhole as well.

Like ice gliding on ice, the door opened silently. A narrow corridor waited before her.

"You are almost there," said the voice. *"You will see it when you pass the door at the end of the corridor."*

Arienne whispered, "The Power generator Eldred . . ."

She walked in. The thick iron door closed on its own behind her. The corridor was flooded with light.

4

CAIN

Lukan, the owner of this tavern, was an Arlander like Cain, but most of his clientele were Imperial heartlanders. Before he'd left Arland, Cain had imagined everyone living in the Capital as either functionaries of the prefect's office or rich merchants, but he'd since learned that laborers and the poor existed here as well, that the streets were paved not with gold but with cobblestone, and that the walls were covered not with brocade silk but with chalky lime. And those who came to drink Lukan's cheap swill were precisely those who laid such cobblestones and applied that limewash.

Cain lived not far from here. His room was above the olive oil shop where he worked, in a large market square close to some of the city's many commercial docks, just west of the gates to the affluent old city. It was easier to forget about his past life, in that part of town that people from countless corners of the world called home.

Twelve years ago, in Kingsworth, the provincial capital of

Arland, his parents had been wanted by the prefect's guards on charges of sedition and treason against the Empire. For safety, they had placed their twelve-year-old son in the care of a traveler headed to the Capital. Cain had never heard from his parents again. The traveler had told him that a great purge was happening in Arland and it was no longer safe there. Maybe that was why he had been avoiding Arlanders ever since he had arrived in the Capital.

Lukan, being one of the few Arlanders in the neighborhood, was an exception to this rule. By now, Cain was a man of the Capital through and through, but the smell of Arlander food was something that he hadn't been able to resist.

And Fienna. She had been an exception too—perhaps the greatest exception of his life.

Around midnight, when Cain dragged his beaten, throbbing body into the tavern, Lukan shouted greetings to him in Arlandais, which made a couple of the drunkards raise their heads from the bar to look at both Lukan and Cain. Lukan was skinny, tall, and middle-aged. There were many provincial men who would crop their hair short or iron it straight to look more like the heartlanders, but Lukan was determined to be the opposite, framing his angular Arlander face with shoulder-length, tightly braided hair that was adorned with the occasional blue cord weaved into the strands. Even more well-kept than his hair was his thick beard, which he kept trimmed and also braided with ornamental blue cord. Cain hadn't seen another blue-braided hair and beard like Lukan's since he'd left Arland more than ten years ago. Sliding the tavern's doors open, Cain breathed in the smell of a savory vegetable soup that lingered in the air. Steam hovered like a fog over the boiling cauldron in the fireplace. It was a small establishment, but the tavern was regularly packed—the kind of packed where anyone needing to go to the latrine had to ask three or four others to move aside to make way. Many of the tables and chairs bore the marks of being hastily fixed, casualties of rowdy nights and inept carpentry.

The night was late, but the tavern was still half full. Earlier in the evening, when the patrons were just drunk enough, the mood here would have been boisterous, but by this hour the remaining laggards were either drunk off their feet or drinking silently, kept busy with their own thoughts. The tavern was quiet.

Cain limped toward the end of the cheaply lacquered bar. Every spot where those kicks had landed ached. Behind the bar, Lukan was wearing a collarless tunic even in this cold weather, perhaps to show the complex, traditional clan markings around his neck. Cain's own markings were simplified and thinner, as had been the fashion in Kingsworth ever since the Empire came twenty years ago. Even the Arlander immigrants in the Capital still tattooed their children on their eighth birthday as was tradition, though clans hadn't mattered since the Empire came to Arland and replaced the royal house with their prefect's office. Seated near the end of the bar was a petite, well-dressed woman with her lustrous hair in a neat bun, a glass of spiced wine before her. She wore a black stola with a short hem and a brooch with a small sapphire on her chest.

As Cain approached, the woman shifted her stool a little to the left, giving him room. Cain nodded his thanks and to Lukan, who brought him a bowl of soup, he held up two fingers, a sign Lukan obliged by bringing a small glass filled almost to the brim with brown liquid.

"What happened to your chin?" Lukan asked as he wiped

the bar so vigorously that its wobbling panels almost spilled the woman's drink.

"Hand me a mirror," Cain said, cleaning his steamed-up spectacles with his sleeve before putting them back on.

"Haven't seen you this beat up in ages." Lukan disappeared into the back room and returned with a small mirror.

Cain used it to examine his chin. The tear was rough and broad, big enough that his little finger would barely cover it. Lukan handed him the rag he was wiping the bar with. Cain looked at the rag, then at Lukan's face, and frowned.

"Look, Cain, a wound like that, you've got to stitch it up properly."

This bit of obvious advice was spoken by the bricklayer Fabricius, who sat at a table behind him holding a large mug in one hand and pointing at his own chin with the other. The three others who shared his table, their flushed faces as red as Fabricius's, were also looking in his direction. Cain made a serious face and nodded. He dipped the edge of his sleeve into his drink and cleaned the wound, gritting his teeth at the stinging pain.

He held up the mirror once more. No luck—the ring had not left a clear impression. But he could surmise, tilting the mirror this way and that, that the ring hadn't featured a mounted stone.

Lukan returned to wiping the bar. "You ought to be more careful, your face looks bad enough on a good day."

Cain heard a laugh by his side. The woman in the black stola was holding her drink and looking rather intently at him.

A man like Cain walking in with a gaping wound on his face and being chastised by the tavern owner was all part of the scenery, so it wasn't a strange thing at all to be looked at and talked to.

No. The strange thing here wasn't Cain, but the woman. Her clothes did not let her blend in, and neither did her hairdo or her choice of drink. She was also alone. Most of the people who came to this place wanted to forget the aches and pains of the day's labors by numbing themselves with drink, but not her. Nor was Lukan's a place for courting. Above all else, it was how she was making no effort at all to hide the fact that she did not fit in. He had the feeling that nothing good could possibly come from getting involved with her.

"He's the kind of man who'll go back out there and get hit in the face again if it means a pretty lady like you will smile at him," said Lukan as he put down his rag and topped up Cain's glass.

Cain downed half of it. The smell of earth came up through his throat and into his nose. He hadn't been of drinking age when he lived in Arland, but this smell, at least, was familiar since childhood. The drink taking effect gave him the shivers, and he turned to Lukan, whose dirty rag was now being used to wipe mugs.

"Name a rich Kamori in the Capital."

"You know better than I do who's who in this city," replied Lukan.

"I'm asking anyway."

"How rich?" Lukan held up the mug to the lamplight before stuffing his rag into it once more.

"Rich enough to wear Cassian velvet."

Lukan raised his eyebrows.

"Aside from the Kamori councillor in the Commons? I don't know. An ordinary provincial rich enough for velvet should be well-known, though."

A high-and-mighty in the Imperial Commons Council orchestrating the murder of a lowly dye shop worker? An impossible notion to begin with, but Cain made an effort to remember who the Kamori councillor was. The councillor for Arland was a rich landowner, and Cain knew him only by name. Not even a councillor's shadow would grace the likes of this neighborhood.

"Did you know that Fienna died this morning?"

"Fienna? The friend you always talk about? What happened?" Lukan's tone was serious, but his hands continued to polish his mugs and glasses.

"She drowned in the Apathos."

"Huh." Lukan's hands left the mug he was polishing and rose to stroke his beard. "I do seem to recall there's one rather rich personage from Kamori. Yes, you're probably not aware of her since she's a merchant who comes and goes, not a woman of the Capital in the strictest sense."

As Cain emptied the other half of his glass, Lukan in a low voice told him about a merchant named Gladdis. A woman who sourced local goods from not only Kamori but the whole of the greater Lontaria region to sell in the Capital, which meant she had also been to Arland and Ledon. Cain remembered that Fienna's boss used to travel to that region with a great merchant.

"She has a monopoly license on five types of goods from the three provinces of Lontaria, according to a Kamori boy who comes here from time to time," Lukan said with a note of envy, and then pointed at the bottle he'd poured from. "I think that is one of her imports."

Monopoly licenses didn't grow on trees, being among the most coveted privileges in the world. Such a merchant was guaranteed to have connections in one of the ministries, or even the Senate itself.

The woman sitting next to him had her face turned away, as if considering the bottles of spirit behind the bar, but was clearly eavesdropping. Cain watched her from the corner of his eye as he took in the information about Gladdis. He had a feeling he should avoid meeting her gaze directly. He pressed down on an impulse to run out of the tavern.

"Quite a big name for a provincial," Lukan continued, "rumored to have been a close friend of a senator. Her residence here is more like one house out of many, it's a mansion by the docks. No doubt she keeps a similar place in each of the seven cities of the heartland, as well as in the three provinces of Lontaria."

"Where is she now?"

"Who knows? She stays at that mansion when she's in the Capital. But she only drops by from time to time these years, I'm sure it's just her servants there now." Lukan explained the way to Gladdis's house at the docks.

"Thanks." Cain lifted his glass to finish his drink but there wasn't a drop left.

"So, you think that Kamori merchant killed Fienna?"

"I don't know yet." Cain placed money on the bar and got up. "When I find out, I'll let you know."

The outside air was chilly. Closing the sliding door of the tavern, Cain adjusted his spectacles and glanced back at the bar where he'd been sitting, and his eyes met those of the woman in black. He quickly looked away and made haste down the long and dim alley toward home.

5

ARIENNE

The corridor was blindingly white. It was impossible to tell right from left or up from down. It seemed like the only things that existed were Arienne's body, the old and heavy iron door she had just come through, and a translucent door some distance ahead of her. There was also a drumming in her ears—her own heartbeat. It was the only thing she could hear.

Arienne was afraid. Ahead, somewhere, was the Power generator. Her professors had taught her about the generators for six years across many different courses, but they had never touched on the most important things about them: How did they generate so much of the Power? Could the dead body of a sorcerer go on making the Power indefinitely? If they were generating the Power after death, could they really be said to be dead? Arienne suspected the professors themselves did not know the answers to these questions. They never explained why the people of the Empire accepted the use of Power generators without so much as a frown. People who

would flinch at the sight of a corpse, much less a magically preserved one, had no issue with Powered machines harvesting their
crops and scrubbing their sewers, knowing full well what they were
made of.

The Power generators were inscrutable things. Not wanting to
become one even more desperately than not wanting to die, Arienne
found herself here—in the small hours of the morning, following a
strange, unknown voice, breaking the unbreakable rules.

Upon closer inspection, the door ahead turned out to be a
semitransparent layer. At the tentative touch of her palm, the
layer undulated like the surface of a calm lake and her hand sank
through. The undulation widened until it was large enough for
her entire body to pass through.

After the brilliance of the corridor, it took a moment for her
eyes to adjust to the dimly lit generator chamber. The door that
had been translucent a moment ago was, from the other side, so
black it was almost invisible. Arienne closed her eyes. Instead of
the thumping of her own heart, which had felt so loud just a moment ago, there was a low and uninterrupted hum. The sound of
the Power generator. The poets described it as an endless song, but
it reminded Arienne instead of the deep rumble of the volcano in
her homeland. People there had called it the sound of the sleeping
dragon.

What slept here was not a dragon but the body of a sorcerer.
And not just any sleep but an endless sleep, eternal and yet devoid
of rest, a most uncomfortable and fitful sleep . . . Arienne shivered
in revulsion.

As her eyes adjusted, she took in the room, which was cast in
a cool violet light. Violet was the color of sorcery, and the chamber

was full of the Power. Before her were two coffins of dull metal resting on stone platforms.

The coffin on the left was the source of the faint light that filled the chamber. It was wrapped in chains, and there were runes engraved along the chains that glowed. This was the one powering the Academy. In contrast, the coffin on the right was dark, illuminated only by the glowing runes on its neighbor's chains, maybe a reserve generator or a broken one. Arienne was trying to read the inscriptions on the coffins to determine which of them was Eldred's when the voice spoke.

"The one on the right. The one that is dark and inert. That is the Power generator Eldred."

She turned to the coffin on the right and took a deep breath. Now for the spell to move the coffin—the spell that was stronger and trickier than any she had attempted before. As she began to conjure the necessary images in her mind, the voice spoke again.

"Unchain the coffin and open it first. We only need to take what's inside."

"What? How am I supposed to withstand the Power without the containment box? This isn't what you told me before."

"There's nothing to be done. Lead as an insulator of Power works both ways. Spells do not pass through it. Surely you knew that much before my having to tell you?"

She had come so far. She couldn't turn back now for the fear of some leakage from the generator. Gripping the chains, she managed to drag them off the coffin despite each link being the size of her fist. The sound of iron scraping lead rang throughout the chamber.

The humming from the coffin intensified as the chains were removed. Arienne pushed aside the heavy lid. Violet wisps of smoke rose from the interior, and she quickly covered her nose and mouth. Inside was something like a cocoon, a human shape wrapped in bandages, with red runes that she couldn't read scrawled across them. There was no smell of decay or of embalming oils, just a scent much like burning paper.

Arienne straightened, closed her eyes, and summoned the image of her family home in her mind. A small thatched-roof farmhouse, the kind you'd see anywhere in Arland. Arienne had a room of sorts in the loft right under the roof. A mattress stuffed with fresh straw, a small chest of drawers her mother made from leftover carpentry scraps, and a box for her knitting things. No desk, but there was a little shelf with all ten books she'd owned, written in Imperial. Arienne concentrated on every detail, not letting a single thing slip her attention. Not the touch of the rusty candlestick on the windowsill, the flame flickering on the shrinking candle, the patchwork of rags on the doll her father had made for her, the surprisingly good carpet on the floor, nor the decree of entry for the Imperial Academy that lay folded in half on the mattress.

In her mind, Arienne picked up the decree. This nonexistent folded piece of paper in her imagined loft in her imagined house hovered above the mattress. But the imagined decree, which should've been filled with the Imperial letters, was completely black, a black so dark it began to look like a violet swirl, a hole that looked into the depths of another world. The paper unfolded once. Then twice. Then three times. It became not a square piece of paper but an elliptical hole. Arienne sent the body in the coffin, the Power generator Eldred, into the room in her mind through that very hole and laid it down on the mattress.

She opened her eyes. Her head hurt. The coffin was empty.

The body of the dead sorcerer now lay in the room of her mind. A dizziness overcame her—and a very obvious fact occurred to her like a blow to the head.

"You have done well. Now leave this place. You must escape from this school as swiftly as possible. And—"

"*You* are Eldred! You're the body that's inside my mind right now!" Arienne shouted. There was a sharp pressure in her head, as if it would burst any second.

"Indeed," said the voice, or Eldred.

"You're dead. You're a Power generator! How is a dead person speaking to me?"

"Let's say I'm a ghost, for now."

Tears rose in her eyes, whether from the pain of the headache or some other unknown reason she couldn't say. "Why did you make me do this?"

"Because for the past five years, no one has heard me except you."

Arienne understood. The person who lay at the bottom of the spiral staircase had heard Eldred five years ago—had heard him, had come down to the basement, and had been pushed by Eldred after refusing to help him. No doubt Eldred had allowed them to think they were leaving the basement, getting high enough on the staircase that a fall would break their neck. Eldred must have realized that if that student had been allowed to go back, his secret would be discovered. And a Power generator that had a will of its own and could whisper secrets into someone's mind—an abomination like that would never be left unguarded again by the Imperial Academy, the Office of Truth, or anyone of any consequence in the whole of the Empire. Why was such a thing down here, and who put it there?

Inside the room of her mind, the tightly wrapped cocoon shaped like a human sat up on the edge of the mattress. His face was covered and he could not move freely, but his very manner of sitting exuded utter exhaustion. The hole in the air, through which Arienne had helped him enter the room, now neatly folded in on itself until it became a piece of paper again and fell to the floor. The words "Decree of Entry" in red letters could just about be discerned.

"First, you must leave here. The longer you hesitate, the more certain your capture will be. Now that I've been removed from my chains, things will be set in motion. It's only a matter of time until someone discovers what we have done here. Be reminded that, with me in tow, the Office of Truth inquisitors will be coming for you like they have done for no other runaway sorcerer. That is the price you pay for your chance at freedom."

Arienne wanted to feel regret. That maybe the life of a pensioner, modest as it might be, was a comfortable way to live out a life. Or that she could study harder and become a sorcerer-engineer or professor, or join a legion and travel the world. She liked Felix, Kaya, and the other friends she had made at the school, even Magnus. Perhaps she would raise a family with another sorcerer, or someone she had yet to meet. There was a life for a sorcerer, even in the Empire, one that she could be happy with. But at the end of every such life, no matter how comfortable, was the fate she saw starkly before her: being turned into a Power generator. As long as she was within the confines of the Empire, this fate would be inescapable. And here, inside the room in her mind, was proof of how horrifying an end that would be.

Bile rose in her. It couldn't be stopped—she vomited.

"Hurry. Hurry!"

She didn't want to die. More than that, she didn't want to become what Eldred had become. Now that the identity of the voice was revealed, her determination had only gotten stronger. She stared at what had come up from inside her as she gripped her stomach, and once her fear and disgust melted away, she straightened. Even her headache subsided to a tolerable level.

She retraced her steps, through the white corridor to the iron door, pausing only briefly beside the skeleton at the foot of the stairs.

An escape route out of the school was already in place, and it was unlikely anyone would look for her before the sun rose tomorrow. Even longer before anyone would make the connection between the missing Power generator and her disappearance. In the slums of the western side of the city, there was an estranged uncle who had a tavern. She'd met him only once, when she first came to the Capital, but maybe he would help her if she asked.

The life before her was that of a fugitive from the law—and for the first time in six years, Arienne felt alive.

6

LORAN

In a wide clearing near the center of Dehan Forest, Loran sat on a tree stump. She ripped an Imperial banner into strips and tied one around her head, a fresh eyepatch for her empty left socket. The cool autumn air still smelled vaguely of sulfur, and black smoke rose from the smoldering logs of the guardhouse that had been set ablaze in blue flame.

In the seven days since she'd left the dragon's lair, Loran had used the sword to devastate three legion outposts, each of them manned by a dozen legionaries. The burning rubble before her was all that remained of the third one. It had not been an ordinary fire that consumed her enemy but the breath of the dragon. Loran had named her sword Wurmath, which in Arlandais meant "the dragon's promise."

For Wurmath was a sword that could summon dragonfire. Her worries about possessing only the skills of a mere local swordmaster, a teacher and not a regular practitioner of the blade, seemed absurd now, when the dragon's fire would refuse to go out until there was nothing left to burn. The soldiers would roll around or douse themselves with water trying to extinguish the flames, but this had no effect on the blue tongues that lapped at their skin. Regardless of their efforts, an agonizing death was always the outcome.

These deaths brought Loran not satisfaction or emptiness but another, strange feeling—a kind of anxiety, stemming from realization that nothing would change no matter how many of these outposts she burned. All she was doing was giving the Empire a reason to send more forces—stronger forces—to oppress Arland further.

When the last king of Arland had ridden the back of the fire-dragon into battle against the Empire, Loran was a teenage girl, standing on the city walls beside her mother, witnessing the fate of her country. The Empire's enormous Powered weapon, a so-called gigatherion, looked like a gigantic beetle and flew despite its machine bulk, its power matching the dragon in every way. The dragon's fire had only charred the surface of its iron armor at best. The Empire had dozens, perhaps hundreds of gigatherions, machines designed for battle with dragons or gods, each with its own Power generator. And as for the ultimate Powered weapon, of which only rumors persisted, the Star of Mersia that was said to have reduced the prosperous nation of its namesake into a wasteland overnight . . .

Even without the gigatherions or the Star of Mersia, the Empire's forces had no equal. They had Powered chariots that felled fortress walls like rotten boards, and elite legionaries whose Powered armor gave them the strength of several ordinary men. Their advantage in numbers alone daunted Loran. How long could she fight against the largest army in the world? She was only a lay swordswoman who had become so consumed with grief and thoughts of revenge that she had risked her life to obtain the fang of a dragon and was now aimlessly thrashing it about. Surely this was not the true meaning of becoming king.

Perhaps, she wondered, her sword should've been named "a woman's promise."

Her thoughts were interrupted by approaching footsteps. A low hum accompanied the heavy footfalls, a rumble like the one from the volcano in Arland, the so-called sound of the sleeping dragon. Dehan Forest was at the eastern edge of Arland, on the border with Kamori. Loran looked westward, but the volcano wasn't visible through the dense forest. What she did see, though, was a lookout platform for Imperial soldiers, built into the top of one of the far-off trees. It had been on her left side, which was perhaps why she had missed it in her approach. She was still getting used to seeing with only one eye.

The standard of the Empire came into view at the other side of the clearing; the number "25," the designation of this legion, was barely discernible, but it was unclear whether the animal of the insignia was a bird or lion. The standard-bearer was wearing armor from the neck down, his armor so large that his exposed head looked ridiculously small in comparison. As he entered the clearing, hoisting the banner before him, four more soldiers in similar armor came into view behind him. Loran had seen such armor only once before, when her daughter had begged her to go see a legion parade. This was the armor Powered by the generators, worn only by the Empire's most elite soldiers.

A legionary with opulent gold ornaments on his armor stepped forward and called to Loran.

"You there! We came when we saw the smoke. What's happened here?"

His flawless Imperial marked him as a heartlander. His golden armor decorations looked similar to those that adorned the centurions of the 171st Legion, the one that had occupied Arland and its neighboring lands for the last few years. The Imperial legions toured the provinces, taking turns occupying the many fortresses of the vast Empire. Loran had heard a recent rumor that a shift in the resident legion of Lontaria was at hand. Evidently, it was the Twenty-Fifth Legion's turn to occupy Ledon, Arland, and Kamori.

Behind the troop of five Powered legionaries was a cart of sorts, a box with an open top and four legs. There was no beast drawing it. Loran couldn't see what was inside, but a man behind it had his hands tied and chained to the cart. He was tall, perhaps about forty years old, but seemed like a child next to the suits of Powered armor. His eyes met hers. They were scores of steps apart, but she found herself unable to break his steady gaze.

"You! Are you deaf, woman?!"

The legionary approached her. Loran didn't answer him. She was thinking. If she couldn't win against Powered legionaries, there was no future for her in battle. They were a mountain she had to climb.

"That neck scribble. An Arlander. What are you doing on the Kamori border? You can't be responsible for this yourself?"

Without thinking, Loran covered her clan markings with her

43

hand. The centurion unsheathed his sword, and his helmet, which had been hanging in the back, flipped forward and sealed him in his armor. The other legionaries followed suit, drawing their swords and donning their helmets, as the shields attached to their left forearms also unfolded.

"Lay down your weapons and comply with our questioning. Gwaharad of Kamori is also in our hands."

Gwaharad? She didn't know of any Gwaharad. He must be the man whose hands were tied, and they must think she was here to rescue him.

Loran drew Wurmath from her belt.

"I am Loran, Princess of Arland. I know of no Gwaharad, but it is true that I am responsible for what you see before you." Loran couldn't keep the note of pride from her voice as she taunted, "I did this. Against twelve of your friends."

Wurmath grew hot in her hand. She gripped the hilt and heard a sound like the hiss of heated iron being dropped into cool water. The blade glowed red, sulfuric smoke rising from it. But the armored men continued to approach, not hesitating.

"Destroying a legion outpost is a crime," said the centurion. Then, with a speed she wouldn't have thought possible for something so large, the armored legionary sprang toward her. He was at least eight feet tall, thanks to the armor, and his approach was like that of a falling cliff.

Loran was momentarily stunned but managed to raise Wurmath and block the centurion's short blade just in time. If he'd been using the ordinary shortsword most legionaries wielded, his blade would have been cut in half by Wurmath's heat. But his sword was different. It had a violet light lingering about it.

But it was the centurion, not Loran, who took a step backward in surprise.

"What is this?"

The man named Gwaharad was now in front of the cart watching the fight. At the centurion's signal, the legionaries surrounded Loran in well-drilled movements, leaving only the standard-bearer by the cart with the prisoner. Loran gestured to Gwaharad to duck. He nodded, and quickly slipped back behind the cart.

Loran swung Wurmath in a semicircle, conjuring fire and screams of confusion and pain from the soldiers. When the fires dispersed, only Loran and the centurion were left standing unharmed while the legionaries that surrounded them were screaming in their now red-hot armor. None of the soldiers had fallen to the ground, the sheer bulk of their armor keeping them on their feet while black smoke issued from the joints of their armor and the stench of burning hair filled the air. The screaming soon turned to whimpers, then ceased.

The centurion's armor steamed a little, but he was otherwise unscathed as he watched in horror as his men were cooked alive inside their armor.

"A monstrous trick," he said finally, the same violet light she'd seen on his sword now creating a protective sheen over his armor. The centurion's gold-adorned armor was more than just opulent, Loran gathered.

"It is no trick," she responded. "It is the fire of the dragon that watches over Arland."

The centurion kept his sword trained on her as he considered her words.

"I see you for what you are. You are a worshipper of gods and demons. You curry favor with inhuman things to disrupt the peace and order of the Empire. But see this, enemy of man. What effect has that dragon's fire had on me? On this armor and sword made by the Empire, by man."

"Mighty words for someone who just lost three of his men." But Loran could not think of a way to fight him if his armor truly was impenetrable, even by dragonfire.

The centurion adjusted the grip on his shortsword, and the violet light intensified. The blade seemed to grow.

"That sword may spew the fire of dragons," he said, "but the one who yields it is merely human."

His subsequent thrust was more aggressive than his previous swing, and Loran barely dodged it, much less tried to parry. His sword sliced the edge of her leather armor and bit into the flesh by her ribs. She gritted her teeth. He was more skilled with the sword than she was. True, the Powered armor helped his strength and speed, but that was the kind of academic difference one might argue about in a sword-fighting lesson, not on the field of battle.

"A one-eyed swordswoman with moves like a schoolmarm," sneered the centurion. "Came into a bit of luck with a fancy sword, have we?"

Loran cared less about such mockery and more about the fact that she might die here.

His blade shone violet as he attacked her again, relentless and from all angles. Just dodging and parrying the blows was enough to make her lose her breath. Her opponent's blade grazed her side again.

She could see that the centurion was pleased with himself. The Empire loved nothing more than power and strength, and the subjugation of those they considered inferiors was a point of virtue to them. She remembered her petitions to the prefect in her attempts to save the lives of her husband and daughter, convicted for treason when all they had done was sing. The Empire mocked you if you cried. Stepped on you if you knelt. Spat on you if you begged.

She was goaded to the edge of the clearing, and there was only dense forest behind her. It would be even harder to defend herself there. Either she ended it here or she herself was ended.

And her opponent knew this. He paused in his relentless thrusts and proclaimed, in a loud voice full of pride, "I shall teach you who it was that killed you. I am Marius, high centurion of the Twenty-Fifth Legion!"

He raised his sword above his head.

Her very sight trembled. Not because she feared death, or because she was overwhelmed by Marius's skills. No, this short vertigo came from rage. She was enraged at the man's arrogant glee. Enraged that after having just declared herself a princess of Arland, she allowed herself to be backed into a corner like this. Loran was a princess of this land and its future king. She was not someone to be treated this way by a mere soldier of the Empire.

She knew, in her head, that such thoughts were ridiculous, that she was not a real princess and that the centurion's words were closer to the truth—she was only a "schoolmarm" swordswoman with an interesting sword. But her body, for some reason, refused to acknowledge this. Her arms shook. Blood rushed to her head. The wound covered by her makeshift eyepatch grew hot.

Marius suddenly took a step back. The helmet that covered his head made his expression impossible to see, but his stance was enough to convey his surprise and confusion. His boasts ceased. His sword hovered in the air.

"What—"

Loran threw Wurmath on the ground and charged at Marius like a rising wave. The centurion fell, a lighthouse overwhelmed by the force of an ocean, the metal giant landing on his back with a violent clang. The Powered armor hummed a pitch higher as it tried to get its owner back on his feet, but its efforts were in vain.

Loran, straddling the fallen soldier, brought her face right up to his helmet visor and growled, "You insolent bastard!"

Her right hand slipped under the gap between the chest armor and helmet as her left went for the helmet itself. There was a screech of ripping metal as the helmet gave way and went flying off, the chest armor crumpling like foil from her sheer strength. Marius's bare face and chest were exposed. His thin cotton tunic was drenched in sweat.

Suddenly, her field of vision expanded—she could see out of her left eye. In the widened eyes of the terrified Marius, Loran saw the reflection of a blue flame in her empty eye socket, the same hue as what she had seen inside the dragon's mouth.

"Dr—drag—dragon—"

"I am Loran. Princess of Arland."

Loran plunged her fingers into Marius's chest, which gave way like so much cooked meat to a fork. Dark red blood spurted from Marius's mouth and chest.

She pulled her hand back, the force releasing another spray of blood, and rose. She picked up Wurmath and looked down at the centurion writhing at her feet. Soon, even the surprise and terror that had lit up his eyes were no more.

Loran held up her right hand, the hand that had pierced Marius's chest. Her nails were dagger-like claws, but soon resumed the shape of an ordinary human hand, if a little callused. She touched her left eye and found that her eyepatch had a hole. The blue flame. It must have burned through the patch. She removed it and saw a burnt spot, as if she'd stuck a red-hot poker into it. The sight in her left eye that had briefly returned slowly turned back to black.

She stood there for a moment before remembering the standard-bearer of the Twenty-Fifth Legion and turning quickly toward the cart. The legion standard was lying on the ground now, and Gwaharad was strangling the standard-bearer with the rope that kept him tied to the cart. How had Gwaharad managed to take off the man's helmet?

She approached the cart as the standard-bearer's body grew slack. Gwaharad watched her for a moment in silence, then dropped the rope and turned to run. But the rope pulled tight against the weight of the cart, to which it was still tied, and he fell. Loran stepped forward with her palms up, showing she had no intent to harm.

"By all the sacred groves, what are you?" Gwaharad's voice shook with fear.

Loran hesitated before answering. "My name is Loran, and I am an Arlander. I understand that your name is Gwaharad. Why have you been captured by the Imperials?" She hadn't an inkling as to how a princess should sound. She tried to speak with dignity but without arrogance.

Gwaharad did not answer, only stared at Loran with wide eyes, rubbing at his cheeks with both hands. Loran mirrored him, touching her own face. She felt something hard and smooth and

49

flaky. She rubbed harder, and two red scales, almost an inch in size, fell from her skin. Astonished, she scrubbed at her face—and found it covered from forehead to chin in scales, like a helm with no faceplate. They didn't feel like they grew out of her, more like they had appeared from nowhere and attached themselves to her. Scales continued to fall as she clawed at her hairline and her chin in disbelief.

Gwaharad seemed to find her consternation reassuring. He bowed deeply. "I beg Your Highness's forgiveness for my impudence." There was respect in his voice where before it had held only fear.

"In truth, I am not His Majesty King Gwaharad but his brother, Emere. Circumstances compelled me to pretend to be the king, and I had no intention of misrepresenting myself to a princess of Arland. Again, I beg your forgiveness."

Gwaharad must be the King of Kamori. Which meant Emere, his brother, was something like a prince, arguably the same rank as a princess. Loran suddenly felt silly about this wrangling of made-up titles. Kamori had no real king. Neither did Arland or Ledon, or anywhere else in the world. At least, this was so in the eyes of the Empire. Loran imagined Gwaharad to be someone much like herself. *There are still those who fight. And there always will be.* That was what the dragon in the volcano had said.

As she hesitated, unsure of how to answer, Emere went on. "My brother, the king, will arrive shortly. Your Highness has achieved what I had hoped to by feigning capture." Emere eyed the Powered cart. As Loran wondered what it was carrying, Emere bowed deeply and continued. "I beseech you to meet with the King of Kamori and allow us to share your cause."

Emere's manners were flawless. Loran assented, and she lifted Wurmath to carefully sever the knot that bound his hands.

Emere brought his freed hand to his lips and whistled three times.

The forest rippled. Men and women dressed in green and brown and disguised with leaves and branches slowly emerged from the woods. Their disguises were varied, but they each had an archer's bow on their back. By their orderly walk and uniform expression, Loran could tell this was not a group of ordinary bandits. Soon, about sixty Kamori soldiers had come into the clearing. The blue fire of the burning log guardhouse was still sending up black smoke into the sky. As the soldiers fell into formation, a middle-aged man with long hair came out of the forest. He wore no disguise. Instead, he wore a gold crown and a cloak hemmed with silver thread. Painted on his armor underneath the cloak was a green lion standing on its hind legs. The sword on his belt was black from hilt to scabbard. His expression was benevolent but unsmiling. This must be Gwaharad.

Emere darted through the formation of soldiers and went down on one knee before him. "Your Majesty."

"Very good, Emere," said Gwaharad. "Do you have what we came for at hand?" His gaze briefly shifted toward Loran before returning to his kneeling brother.

"I do, Your Majesty."

"We were going to move once you entered Dehan Forest, but the smoke issuing from here made us reluctant to proceed. Who is this hero?"

"A princess of Arland," said Emere, the words Loran herself found so difficult to use issuing smoothly from his lips. "She single-handedly obliterated this outpost and killed four Powered legionaries."

All eyes turned to Loran. The attention was uncomfortable. Gwaharad brushed past Emere and the ranks of his soldiers, who moved to widen the path for him without any other prompting.

Standing before Loran, Gwaharad held out both his hands.

"I am Gwaharad, King of Kamori. It is gladdening to meet a princess of Arland."

"It is my honor to be in your illustrious presence, Your Majesty." She had never heard of his name before this day, but Loran was prudent.

"Join us. You, Princess, have vanquished the Imperial dogs in this forest and saved many of my people's lives—we are in your debt. And I am eager to hear the story of how you came upon your sword."

Emere gestured and the soldiers moved to the cart, where they began off-loading its cargo, the largest being a metal box wrapped in chains. It looked like a coffin, and heavy even for ten people sharing the burden on their shoulders.

"We must go," said Gwaharad briskly, "before the smoke attracts more of the Imperial soldiers."

Loran nodded in agreement. Though she was exhausted from the fight, her steps felt light as she followed Gwaharad and Emere out of the clearing. There were other people out there standing against the Empire, and she had found them. She was no longer alone.

7

CAIN

It was late morning when Cain stepped inside the olive oil shop at the mouth of the Grocer's End just off the market square. Old Agatha's expression turned grim when she saw him, but the owner of the eatery across the street was at the counter haggling over a tall bottle of oil, so the old woman made no comment about Cain's lateness.

A pile of fresh olives in the corner of the shop gave off an inviting perfume. Though all of the shop's oil was pressed and imported from Dalosia to the north by ship, Agatha kept fresh olives on display at all times. She had Cain throw them out when rot set in, then would buy another pile and the cycle would repeat. All four walls of the shop were lined floor-to-ceiling with shelves, bottles of olive oil both new and long rancid crowded together.

Cain got to work without a word, picking up a large jar of bad oil with both hands, the first of the score he would need to empty that day. It was work he should've finished the day before, but Fienna—the image of her lying in the patrollers' morgue rose in his mind, and he shoved the thought away. The inquiries, as it were, had kept him away from his work.

The customer exited. "Come here," Agatha called.

Pretending not to hear, Cain carried the heavy jar outside. As he stepped back in and lifted a second jar, Agatha said, "In all these years, I've never treated you like some provincial guttersnipe"—on the contrary, she'd been regularly reminding him of that fact for the past five years that he'd worked here—"despite my having brought on some urchin from the street. Because I thought you had a clever look about you, the air of a diligent worker, I taught you the work and paid you almost as much as a heartlander apprentice. But you keep going about town making trouble!"

Cain carefully lowered the second jar to the ground outside the shop and came back for another.

"What could you possibly be doing that such people would darken the doorstep? If it were the city patrollers, I would assume the silly boy had gotten into drunken mischief or whatnot, but this is the Ministry of Intelligence—"

The Ministry of Intelligence?

A muscle jerked in his right arm. Cain almost dropped the oil jar, but kept his voice calm.

"Ministry agents were here? What did they want?"

Had it been Ministry agents who ambushed him in the alley? Cain decided against it. Those men were too clumsy to be the secret eyes and ears of the Empire.

"They wanted to know where you were, that's what. I told them I didn't know, and they left. Look, did you join in a rebellion or something? Is that what you're up to? You were such a hard worker until now, why would you do such a thing?"

"I haven't."

There was no resistance movement in Arland. Or at least, there wasn't anymore. The only Intelligence business Cain could think of involved his parents. He did not know what his parents had done to have been executed for treason all those years ago. All he knew was that they were dead, and that Arland was a distant memory. His life was built from scratch right here in the Capital, in this oil shop and around the market square. He had neither love nor hate for the Empire. It was just a place where he ended up, safer than where he had been. It was the place where Fienna was. Had been. But the Ministry of Intelligence would not care. He put the third jar outside and went back in the shop.

"It's that Fienna's doing, isn't it? What's that little wench got you mixed up in?"

Cain could hear the undercurrent of panic in Agatha's words. But she had good reason to be afraid. Ever since the whole world fell under the reign of the Empire, the Ministry of Intelligence's mission had been to keep the prefects under surveillance and punish even the smallest sign of disorder or rebellion. They never brought in just one suspect for questioning; if their agents were looking for Cain, it meant Agatha was not wholly safe either. But somehow, Cain found it hard to concentrate on the very real danger to his person, the danger of the Ministry taking an interest in him.

"Nothing." He lifted the fourth jar and turned to the door.

"Wake up, you fool! Or you'll end up just like her!"

The feeling of weight on his chest that he had been fighting since he learned of Fienna's death suddenly gripped his heart like a vise. Cain threw the jar he was holding. It shattered, spilling oil and pottery fragments everywhere, and causing his boss to gasp and step away from him to back behind the counter. The rancid scent of spoiled oil filled the shop. Cain gave Agatha a cold stare, then opened the door and left the shop.

His head was swimming with two thoughts, and two thoughts only. *Why did Fienna die? Who killed her?* If he didn't get answers fast, he was going to lose his mind.

Outside the shop, the market square was brimming with colorful tents, full carts and teetering wheelbarrows, and itinerant peddlers from all over the world, their words coming and going in standard Imperial, accented Imperial, and the occasional provincial languages. The smell of sweat, perfume, and cheap food assaulted his nose. As his anxiety threatened to boil over, Cain made his way through the square toward the port, trying to shed every useless memory as he went: the fear on old Agatha's face, the sound of the jar shattering, the smell of oil, the clamor of the square—they faded to nothing. All of his inner focus centered on Gladdis, the Kamori merchant. And on Fienna, drenched with river water, her long braids glistening, so slick in his trembling hands with slime and scum.

Lukan had said Gladdis had a house on the docks. Since she had other bases of operations all over the Imperial heartland, as well as in her homeland Kamori, and since she went back and forth regularly between the Capital and the three provinces of Lontaria, there was little chance he would find her if he went to her house now. But if the man in the velvet trousers was indeed working for Gladdis, Cain knew he would find him there.

Cain could smell a hint of the ocean in the wind. The sun rose over a bell tower in the distance. Once he made a turn at that tower, he'd be at the place Lukan had told him about. The streets were as crowded as the market, but his pace quickened, and he suppressed the urge to break into a run. The answers were ahead. He was sure of it.

When he had first met Fienna, Cain was starving and in tears, ignorant of the language of the Imperial heartland. To a twelve-year-old boy, a seventeen-year-old girl might as well be an adult. Fienna talked to him in Arlandais, brought him an orange and bread and soup, found him a place to sleep. She taught him the language of the Capital and helped him make friends.

From behind, someone was cursing at him; come to think of it, he did feel like he had bumped into something just now. He couldn't even remember what the color of the man's tunic was. Cain did not slow his pace.

Just as he was about to turn a corner, someone grabbed his left arm with a grip so strong he could not easily shake it off. He turned and saw a skinny giant, at least two heads taller than himself, latching on to him and not letting him go. The giant's face was dead serious. Was he the man he had bumped into just now? Cain's eyes grew wide. He couldn't remember. But how could he have not noticed such a tall man passing right by him?

Like an errant child caught by an angry parent, Cain was dragged into an alley by the bell tower. Cain pretended to resist as he discreetly took in his surroundings. A stout man in gray was urgently trying to cross the busy street, his eyes fixed in their direction. The main street was filled with carts on their way to market, but the alley was narrow and shaded. Neither the stout man nor the skinny giant had been among the group that assaulted him the other night, but there was a chance they were part of the same gang.

First things first. He had to do something about this giant if he was ever to have a chance of escape. Without hesitating, Cain drew his dagger and sliced along the giant's forearm in one motion. Blood gushed, and the giant yelled out. Cain swiftly kicked him in the shin, then stomped on the giant's sandaled foot, and when he bent over in agony, Cain delivered a perfectly timed blow to the chin with his left palm. As the giant staggered, Cain plunged his dagger in and out of his foot—the giant was unlikely to come after him now. Cain raced down the alley, glancing back briefly to see that the stout man was still impeded from crossing the street by the river of carts and people.

Cain turned a corner at full sprint. While he knew every little alley and dead end around his market square, he didn't know much about this dockside neighborhood other than the main streets. He could only hope that if he kept running and tried to lose himself in the maze, the people pursuing him would not be able to follow him either.

He was getting out of breath. Finally, he collapsed against a dirty wall, his mouth and throat burning. A drunk with a large bushy beard was sitting against the same wall a stone's throw away, cradling a wine bottle that didn't even have a label. Judging by the worn-out bottoms of his sandals, he was not a fake vagrant.

Only then did Cain notice that his vision was blurry. His spectacles were gone. He didn't know at what point he'd dropped them. When he bumped into someone? When he fought the giant? Or while he was running for his life?

Cain sighed in frustration. At least he was almost sure the two just now were of a different pack than the five from the previous night. He hadn't been anywhere since the assault except Lukan's tavern. Last night's gang was probably hoping their threat had worked, and it wouldn't make sense for them to have people out on a busy street to watch for whether he was coming for them or not. The giant's mannerisms were completely different from those of the ex-legionary woman from the night before. So there was one final option, and that was what they had to be.

He leaped to his feet. Why the Ministry of Intelligence were looking for him and how they knew it was Gladdis's place he was headed to, he didn't know. But what he did know for sure was that he was in trouble.

Slow, determined footsteps rang from the end of the alley. It was the giant from before, blocking the narrow alley as he approached. His clothes were bloodied but he didn't move as if he'd been injured. The foot Cain had sunk his dagger into seemed to support the man's large frame with no pain or trouble, even though the sandal was soaked in blood. Cain sprang toward the other direction, half expecting the stout man in gray to be there, but instead there was the woman in the black stola with the brooch who had sat next to him in the tavern the night before. She was looking at him intently, one of her delicate hands holding up Cain's spectacles.

Cain took the bloody dagger from his inner pocket and tossed it onto the ground, holding up his hands in surrender.

A sack covering his head, Cain was pushed into a chair as his arms were tied behind his back with rough hands. Despite his lack of vision, he took in his surroundings as best he could. A room with a chair. Echoes from a high ceiling, with windows mounted near the top of the wall betraying the noise of the street. A basement. There were maybe three other people there, judging by what he could hear.

Finally, someone spoke.

"My name is Septima."

He assumed this was the woman in the black stola. Soft clicking sounds, as if she was playing with his spectacles, folding and unfolding the legs. He shrugged to show he was listening.

"We work for Intelligence."

This he had already guessed. What he didn't know was why Ministry agents, of all people, had captured him. This particular office of the Empire was tasked with surveilling prefects and rooting out rebels, neither of which Cain had anything to do with.

The sack was whipped from his head. There was just enough light for him to make out the figures in the room, despite the lack of his spectacles. The stout man from before was holding the sack. His arms, sleeves curled up, were covered with hair. Septima stood facing Cain, her arms crossed, her left hand deftly playing with his spectacles. The giant whom Cain had stabbed in the foot was leaning against a wall and giving him a look that simmered with resentment. He had changed out of his bloody clothes. Neither his arm nor foot showed any sign of being cut or stabbed. Cain couldn't help but stare at the giant in amazement.

Noting his gaze, Septima said, "Devadas is an *amrit*," as if he was supposed to know what an "*amrit*" was. Apparently, that word explained his lack of injury. "From Varata."

Cain shrugged. "What is he doing outside an Office of Truth

cell?" The Office had a monopoly on sorcery and didn't tolerate anything outside Imperial generator magic. The first thing the Empire did after conquering a land was unleash their inquisitors to round up local magic users and priests. There were stories around the market square, about old-magic sorcerers from all over the world and their horrible fates. In those stories, the magic users had many different names and powers, but to the Empire they were all sorcerers. This man Devadas would qualify as one, regardless of the term his people had reserved for him.

Septima answered. "Oh, he *was* in a cell, until we got him out on a permanent loan. Sometimes, Intelligence needs more than Truth dogma to protect the Empire."

Until the Office needs him more, Cain thought. All sorcerers, wherever they came from or whatever they were capable of, were obligated to serve the Empire as Power generators in their deaths.

The stout man added, with an unmistakable note of pride, "He's the last of his monastic order."

Devadas let out a low groan. Septima sent the briefest frown in the stout man's direction, and he promptly shut up. Holding Cain's spectacles still in her fingertips, Septima clapped her hands twice. "Now, enough questions from you."

Cain had his run-ins with the patrollers. He had been on the receiving end of interrogation more than a few times. Septima seemed to be the head of this team and chief interrogator. The stout man was probably in charge of beating Cain if he happened to give them the wrong answer; it didn't look like he used any special tools to do it other than his fists. The giant Devadas had the demeanor and build of a proper warrior. He seemed embarrassed to have been ambushed in the alley like that.

Cain looked Septima in the face. His vision unaided, he could barely make out the shape of her eyes. "So, what is it you want from me?"

She didn't answer, and instead asked a question of her own, playing with his spectacles again.

"The dead girl, Fienna. What were you to her?"

"A friend."

"A lover?"

"Not really."

Septima slightly raised an eyebrow, perhaps in surprise.

"Why were you going to the docks?"

The clicks of his spectacle legs in her fingers were starting to annoy him.

"Thousands go to the docks every day, why shouldn't I?"

Septima placed the cold tip of her right index finger on his forehead.

"We ask the questions, not you. What business do you have at Gladdis's house?"

"Didn't you already hear everything at Lukan's?"

The finger went away. Septima nodded, finally answering a question.

"Gladdis is being secretly investigated."

"Why?"

"Treason. We suspect her of conspiring with undesirables in a province. If you go to her and make things loud and unpleasant, we'll have a more difficult time of it. Which is why we stopped you."

This answer only raised more questions for Cain. That they happened to be in the same tavern the other night could not have been a coincidence. But why would they have sought him out in the first place?

"Is Lukan being investigated?"

Septima placed her index finger on his forehead once more.

"You came to the Capital about twelve years ago, correct? When you were twelve? Thirteen? That's around the time there was an insurrection in Arland. And you ran away because your parents were involved in that?"

Cain didn't answer. Septima moved his spectacles over her knuckles, all the while managing to click their legs.

"You don't *have* to say anything to that. The prefect of Arland has all the records. But I don't want to make him skittish over such a small matter, and we don't want to be trapped here while we wait for a reply to our inquiry, do we?"

"Is the prefect of Arland under investigation as well?"

"All prefects everywhere are always under investigation."

The stout man stepped forward, but Septima stopped him with a gesture. "It's fine," she said, "it was a long time ago, and he was a child. And all the instigators were apprehended."

The stout man nodded and stepped behind Cain, seeming disappointed he hadn't been needed to break a finger or throw a punch to Cain's jaw.

Septima continued. "Unless, of course, you *are* involved in seditious activities. After all, you must feel some grudge against the prefect of Arland for what he did to your family."

She was trying to scare him, preparing him for the real interrogation. If she really had suspected him, this whole affair would be going very differently. "Enough about my parents and this nonexistent sedition. You said yourself that I was just a child back then, and

I assume you already know I don't hang around other Arlanders. I'm busy with my life here, so let's dispense with these Intelligence pleasantries and get to the point. What do you want from me?"

Septima let slip a short laugh and nodded. "This morning, I heard you were quite well-known around the market square for being rather *helpful*. That even the district patrollers received your *help* a few times."

"A few times." He shrugged as best he could with his arms tied behind his back. "I've got eyes and ears. Speaking of my eyes, be careful with those."

Septima scoffed, clicking the legs of the spectacles again. "You really need these to see properly, don't you? Lenses are not something street riffraff can afford, even if they work at a moderately successful oil shop. How did you come by these?"

Cain licked his lips. "You already know that I do odd jobs for people in my neighborhood. It was a gift from a glassmaker for a job well done."

Septima raised her eyebrow again. "What did you do for him?"

"*Her* son was being held for ransom by a street gang. The patrollers couldn't be bothered, but I could."

Her hands unfolding the spectacles, Septima floated a faint smile. "So, you are something of an investigator, a problem solver, much like I am. You know how to handle these things."

Cain almost returned the smile in pride. "I'd like to think so."

Septima suddenly leaned toward him. Unable to read her face, Cain felt his muscles tense. She gently placed his spectacles over his eyes. Cain relaxed a little as his vision cleared. Septima's eyes showed a hint of concern.

"Then why were you off to that house like a charging bull when you should've known better? What was she to you, that made you so reckless?" Septima lowered her voice a little. "Do you want me to tell you what might have happened to you if we didn't intervene in time? That house is a vipers' nest. It wouldn't have ended with a little beating in an alleyway. Two of our own informants have gone missing."

"Maybe the Ministry of Intelligence needs better training for its agents."

At this, the stout man grabbed Cain by the throat. Devadas detached himself from the wall and took a step toward them, but Septima raised her hand again, directing them both to stand down. Despite the show of rage, the stout man's grip was measured. He was a professional, and a good actor too. He hadn't volunteered his name, nor had Septima introduced him. Would he give his name, real or fake, when asked? The hand fell from Cain's neck.

Septima continued.

"You're different, right? You never miss a thing? You never forget what you see and what you hear? That's what the patrollers say. You must be very chummy with the sergeant. He even showed you Fienna's body."

Cain didn't answer.

"You must know then that her funeral is tomorrow?"

The words were like a blow to the head. He hadn't known there would be a funeral, much less who would pay for it or who would come. He was ashamed. He lowered his head and shook it.

"Let me make you an offer."

At that, Cain raised his head again. "An offer?"

"There is quite a lot of . . . interference. In Gladdis's case. She has ties to the Senate, you see."

Lukan had also mentioned the rumor that Gladdis was close to an Imperial senator.

"Which is why our office is having so much trouble handling her," Septima went on, a note of distaste in her voice. "Every time we try to do something, an order comes down from above. We could use a little help from the outside."

Cain had a feeling about where this conversation was headed. This could be a valuable chance for him, in his own investigation into Fienna's murder.

"The reason we brought you here," continued Septima, "is to make sure our goals are the same. You want to catch your friend's murderer, correct? If it's revenge you want, work with us. We want the same thing, in the end."

Cain thought for a moment before saying, "So what do you want me to do?"

Septima's eyes narrowed as she smiled. "Fienna was being paid by Gladdis. That much we know. What we don't know yet is why. Find that out for us."

This was something Cain hadn't heard. From what he knew, Fienna had no money coming into her pocket other than her wages at the dye shop. He had even loaned her a small amount recently. Why would Fienna ask him for money if she was receiving pay from a rich merchant like Gladdis?

"We'll give you a clue to start. If Gladdis is indeed the murderer, she will send someone to the funeral to make sure everything has gone to plan. You must find out who this person is."

"If they were watching Fienna, they'll know my face."

"They know our faces even better. And wouldn't they think it strange if you didn't show up to your good friend's funeral?"

Cain nodded. "Fine. If you can answer one more question, I'll do as you tell me."

"Ask."

"Why were you at Lukan's last night?"

Septima glanced at the stout man and then at Devadas as if seeking their opinion. They both shrugged and offered nothing more.

"That's a separate affair," said Septima. "Last month, Imperial outposts were attacked in Arland, the guardhouses burned and dozens of soldiers killed. There are always insurrectionists, this isn't something unprecedented . . . But five Powered soldiers from the legion that had come to relieve the previous one all died near the border with Kamori. Their Power generator is missing as well."

The stout man laughed. "Those sons of whores in the Office of Truth must be scattering like bees from a knocked-down hive, losing a whole legion Power generator like that. Couldn't have happened to a more deserving bunch."

"The Power generator doesn't fall under our purview," said Septima, "but the treason very much does."

"So you're putting every Arlander in the Capital under surveillance?"

"We can't watch every single one of you. We were just going to take a look around. Sometimes, that's enough to smoke out the fidgety ones. Besides, Arland neighbors Kamori, which means there's a slight chance the outpost attack might have something to do with our Gladdis investigation. We think that's unlikely, but of course we can leave no stone unturned. For all we know, maybe it has something to do with Fienna."

Cain's heart skipped a beat. Septima had just lied to him for the first time.

She'd spoken of the incident in Arland casually, not attempting to hide what was going on there, as if it only mattered to her if it had something to do with Gladdis, which she didn't think it did. But that wasn't what she was really feeling. Cain didn't know what had happened in Arland, but he could feel in his bones that the events there weighed heavily on her mind and that they almost certainly had something to do with Gladdis. This was the most profitable moment of the whole interrogation for him.

Septima glanced once more at the stout man and nodded, whereupon the latter began untying Cain from the chair. Adjusting his spectacles, Cain observed them as closely as he could from the corner of his eye. He didn't sense any suspicion from them as yet, but it wouldn't hurt to put a stake in it with another gesture.

"My help will cost you," he said. "I lost my job because of you, and I have no place to live now—"

The stout man scoffed. "That was your own fault."

Septima slipped a hand into her sleeve, took out a small pouch, and set it on Cain's knee.

"Cleaning out rancid oil? We can find a job for you that's just as remunerative. And if you prove yourself to be as good as they say, you can keep working for us. That's the thing about Intelligence—we don't look down on you just because you're a provincial." Septima glanced at the giant Devadas.

Cain nodded and put the coin pouch in his inner pocket. He

stood up and, rubbing his wrists where the ropes had dug into the skin, passed Devadas and walked out of the room.

"Be here tomorrow at midnight," Septima called after him.

The pressure that had gripped his heart in the oil shop came back.

8

ARIENNE

"Next, we go to the Senate."

This was what Eldred, who had been silent since they'd left the school in the small hours of morning, said to Arienne as she dug into a crowd for warmth and anonymity. She had spent the rest of the night walking from the northern part of the Capital where the Academy was, and she was cold and tired. Her uncle, Lukan, wouldn't be opening his tavern until the sun set this coming evening, and she planned to hide in plain sight until then, perusing the market and blending into the crowd until finding her way to her uncle's establishment right before it closed.

"The Senate? Why there?"

Eldred couldn't read her mind; his voice resounded as if from within her own head, but if she wanted to be audible to him, she had to at least mumble in her smallest voice. It was unlikely anyone would make out what she said over the bustle of the market, but she was conscious all the same of the many eyes and ears around her.

"You do know what the Circuit of Destiny is, I assume."

The Circuit of Destiny was a device built by joining together multiple Power generators, and it was said to be able to predict the future. It was one of the greatest treasures of the Empire. In theory, it was her professors at the Imperial Academy who would have been designing and maintaining a machine like this, but in all her years there, she'd never heard it spoken of in an official capacity. Some rumors said that it was housed in the basement of the Senate, others that it was kept in the underground dungeons of the Office of Truth. And still others, of course, claimed that it was just a lie, made up by this Imperial ministry or that to scare the enemies of the Empire.

"I know what they say it is. But it really exists?"

"I have business to attend to with the Circuit."

Of course you had your own agenda, Arienne thought. Eldred had promised her freedom and the chance to learn real sorcery, but for now, getting somewhere safe had to take priority. If she was caught, she would be promptly turned into a Power generator herself for her transgressions, shut away for eternity in a lead coffin, a worse fate than if she'd not run away in the first place. She didn't know what that would mean for Eldred, who was hidden away inside her mind, but he didn't seem as worried as he should be.

"One false move, and I—we!—will be caught. I have to get out of the Capital and as far away from the Imperial heartland as possible." Despite having just said this, she had no idea where she would run.

"Are you not a sorcerer yourself? Running away is easy, and it won't be too late to leave after having dropped in on the Senate. A Phaidian shapeshifter could turn into a bird and fly away. A death priest of Thiops

could become a shadow. A Cassian geomancer could shrink the earth and leap over it. A high amrit of Varata has prodigious strength and is virtually impervious to weapons. You're young, and I know that school of yours teaches nothing worthwhile, but surely you have a few tricks mastered on your own by now?"

Arienne didn't reply. She knew the names of all the provinces from her geography classes, but she didn't recognize the words that presumably referred to old-magic sorcerers of those lands. To her, the feats Eldred listed were only the stuff of storybooks.

"Maybe such spells are too sophisticated for you. In which case I hope you're a fast runner, and a good killer. But there must be something you know how to do."

"I can light fires."

"Pyromancy. The Farovian art. A talent as useful as it is common."

"No, I mean, I can . . . light candles."

"And?" Eldred's voice was filled with suspicion.

"I can make someone who's sleeping go deeper into sleep. That's it. And that other thing you taught me."

In the room inside her mind, Eldred, wrapped in his bandages, raised his head.

"Is that all you've learned during six years of school? I know you failed three of them, but . . ."

Arienne had nothing to say to that. She'd come to think of her division at the Imperial Academy as just storage for warm bodies—a place that trained young sorcerers how to best take care of themselves, ahead of their eventual task of becoming Power generators in death. Their education, if you could call it that, was largely to do with keeping your body and mind in a certain state, with some knowledge of the manufacture and maintenance of generators thrown in for variety. There was no benefit to the Empire for sorcerers to learn combat spells, or really anything that would become useful in an escape situation.

After a silence, Eldred said, *"You can create and maintain a room like this in your mind, so you are clearly a sorcerer of talent. Perhaps not a great one for the ages, but at least a bit better than most. If there is nothing else you have learned, I shall teach you a thing or two. It will help us both with the task ahead."*

A Power generator that should have no thoughts or a will of its own was offering to teach her sorcery, and had actually taught her some already. Were the memories from his life intact? How? And how much of them? The basic facts of the dead sorcerer's life would have been engraved in the lead coffin, per regulation. Arienne regretted not having time to take a closer look before they'd had to flee.

"So. Are you able to learn if you're taught, little one?"

Arienne waited until a passerby was out of earshot.

"Yes. I am."

"Good. For you shall not be of much use to me as things are."

Eldred lowered his head and was silent once more.

Arienne recalled the broken skeleton at the foot of the spiral staircase in the main hall. The remains of someone who hadn't been of much use to Eldred five years ago. Arienne had been only a year into her education at the time but vaguely remembered hearing about a student who had supposedly escaped that year. She could not remember their name, as hard as she tried.

What was Eldred going to do once he got to the Circuit of Destiny? Arienne imagined him standing in a white room, wrapped in bandages, scores of coffins spread out at his feet. She did not actually know what the Circuit of Destiny would look like, or whether the room would indeed be blinding white, like the corridor she'd crossed to reach Eldred, or impossibly black, like the hole through which he'd entered the room in her mind.

Arienne continued to picture the Circuit of Destiny, and in her mind envisioned a tea shop waiter with a silver platter in hand, winding his way around Powered coffins as he approaches Eldred. Arienne is standing by his side, watching him. A folded piece of paper rests on the platter—"Your prophecy, sir," says the man as he presents the note to Eldred with a little bow. Eldred nods and unfolds the paper and reads it. His bandages begin peeling off. He is very thin, his skin as dry as a parchment and looking like it would crumble if she were to reach out and touch him. As Eldred reads the prophecy, a satisfied smile cracks his face. Then, he turns to Arienne and says, "Now I shall have my revenge."

Arienne was surprised by her own imagination. *Revenge.* Why did that word, of all words, come to mind?

But just then, a familiar voice interrupted her thoughts, rising over the noise of the market and coming from the other side of the square.

"Arienne! Arienne!"

It was Duff, the custodian of the dorms, pushing through the crowd to get to her. Following him were students in Academy robes. Arienne suddenly remembered she was still wearing her own robes and was very noticeable to those who would be looking for her.

She hadn't expected to be found out by the Academy this quickly, but seeing as it was just Duff and some students, they must not have reported her to the Office of Truth just yet. Maybe the Academy did not want a public incident on their hands. It occurred

74

to Arienne that there was a slight chance that if she got caught now, all she would have to endure was a scolding and two months' detention in her dorm room. Shivering and bone-tired as she was, the vision of her bed and having no reason to leave it was so tempting it momentarily overwhelmed her senses.

But such a fate would never do—she could not go back to the days of feeling like a living corpse. She would not accept the fate of being wrapped in bandages and enclosed in a cold lead coffin for eternity; she'd pour oil over her body, set herself on fire, and become a handful of ash before allowing herself to be dragged back to that life. That would be a warmer, quicker death.

She turned and ran as fast as she could in the other direction. Duff used his large bulk to push aside the marketgoers, making way for the robed students and paying not an iota of attention to the curses that followed him.

"But think of what a good student you are—"

Duff, although out of breath and panting between words, was getting closer and closer. Something tugged at Arienne's robe, tearing it, but when she looked back it wasn't Duff but a nail on a cart that had snagged her.

"Stop, I say! Let's talk!"

But as he said this, there was a flash of violet light and a crate of apples broke open behind Arienne. The fruit seller stepped back in surprise, and Arienne, glancing over her shoulder, saw Duff step on an apple and lose his balance. He yelled out to the students following him.

"Idiots! Are you trying to catch her or me?"

The exploding crate must have been Titus, a fourth-year who always bragged about how he knew a real combat spell, when all he could do was break a chair leg or a wooden bucket. When she had pointed this out, he argued that he could kill everyone on a speeding carriage if he broke a wheel spoke.

Duff liked his drink and was on the heavyset side. His face had already turned bright red from exertion. Despite this, the distance between them was closing fast. Arienne did not bother to look back anymore and concentrated on running as fast as she could through the crowded market square.

"Why are you running like an ordinary girl? Act like a sorcerer!"

She shouted back at Eldred, "Then why don't you do something yourself!"

Suddenly Arienne's robe was pulled taut from behind and she nearly fell. She looked back to see Duff holding on to a handful of her hem, the length of his body against the ground. The sorcery students, the Academy-prescribed exercises not designed to do anything for their physical performance, were panting as they pushed through the crowd, still a distance away. Duff gave her a murderous look as he caught his breath. "You wicked wench, your running away will kill us all!" His panting words came out as a mist in the cold air.

Duff tried to get up but fell again. Arienne used this opportunity to twist and kick him in the head, almost falling down herself. Duff grunted but held on to her robe. Normally taking off the student's robe would be as easy as throwing off a used towel, but Duff's pull turned the garb into a tight lasso. The exhausted students behind her started to run once more.

"You can do it," Eldred said. *"Cut off your clothes and run, even you can do this."*

She could feel Duff's hot breaths on her heels, and the eyes of the people of the market gathering around them. Instinctively, Arienne focused on the robe she had put on for every day of the past six years, trying to imagine a single thread that might or might not exist, a single thread that held the whole robe together. Then she imagined the words, the words that had never before passed her lips, syllables that she had never even known existed. The incantation escaped her mouth and a strength came to the tip of her tongue. An unseen knife sliced through the imaginary thread.

The front of her robe split like the carapace of an emerging cicada, and she slipped out of it in the white linen dress she wore underneath.

Duff, exhausted, could only grasp at the abandoned robe and try to catch his breath. Arienne fled into the maze-like alleys.

Once she had shaken Duff and the students off, Arienne hid in a dark alley by Lukan's tavern and waited for the customers to leave. It was a good thing she had left behind her school robe, but now she was freezing with only the linen material of her dress to shield her. She was so afraid of being spotted she dared not enter any establishment. She had not eaten all day or slept the night before during her escape from the Academy, and her dress and shoes were filthy from wandering the city's dirty alleys.

Why hadn't she realized that the customers who were going to and from the tavern would pass by her in this alley? They looked her up and down, this loiterer in her unseasonable outfit, some deranged woman who was surely the talk of the tavern by now. *A stupid choice*, thought Arienne grimly.

The Academy must've given up on trying to handle this quietly and reported her to the Office of Truth by now. If the Office noticed the absence of the Power generator, they would eventually realize that Arienne hadn't run away on her own. The inquisitors would be after her then.

She imagined herself tied to a rack and being tortured by the inquisitors. The rack in her imagination was cross-shaped. The inquisitors wore black headcloths and held tongs, the kind used in fireplaces. What the inquisitors would ask and how she would reply, she couldn't think up. How little she knew about the situation she found herself in, a situation ironically of her own making.

The Office of Truth did not generally approve of sorcerers—dead sorcerers were useful as Power generators that would contribute to the glory and prosperity of the Empire, but living ones were rather less controllable. At the Academy, the inquisitors of the Office were spoken of as if they were ghosts. They came silently, and people would disappear, never to be heard from again. Arienne didn't know a single sorcerer who had been taken by the Office of Truth. Somehow, this ignorance spawned even more terrifying imaginings.

To get away from the torture chamber and inquisitors of her imagination, Arienne focused on the old room she had in her mind, entering it and closing the door behind her. Her consciousness was in the room, where it was warm, but the cold of the reality around her body didn't abate one bit, which gave her an odd feeling. Eldred sat on the edge of the bed with his head down, just as before.

She stood before the shelf her mother had made for her and took down a book, an adventure story she had read as a child. She couldn't even remember the name of the main character. She started reading it, her childhood memory coming back as she retraced the daring deeds of an Imperial merchant. But if she had forgotten all about the book, how could she have imagined its contents? Puzzled, she put the book back and noticed there was a book with a yellow leather cover lying on the bed beside Eldred.

The Sorcerer of Mersia. That was the title stamped on the cover. Mersia. The province that had declared its freedom from the Empire only to be extinguished by a legendary Powered weapon. A weapon called the Star of Mersia. But that had been a hundred years ago, and felt more like a myth than a real piece of history today. Had such a book existed in her house? There was a smaller title stamped below the big one, but the gilt had flaked off and it was difficult to make out. Arienne stared at it, trying to make sense of the remaining letters.

Then, in the real world, something tapped her shoulder. She almost jumped out of her skin.

Before her in the dark alleyway, where she was cold and crouched and in only a dirty linen dress, was a man of perhaps twenty-odd years of age, wearing spectacles. Since escaping the school, Arienne hadn't seen a single person wearing spectacles. The man had a fresh wound on his chin and looked serious and a little nervous, but there was an air of curiosity in his gaze as he stared at her.

"Excuse me—"

"Go away!" spat Arienne. "You have the wrong person. Go!"

Her gestures only seemed to elicit further fascination from the man, who studied her as if she were some rare bird he'd come across.

Then he said something unthinkable. It wasn't what he said

really, but how he said it—in Arlandais, a language Arienne hadn't heard or spoken for years.

"*T'lie Arleshe?*"

Arienne was so startled she replied in Arlandais. "*Yehre.*" She glimpsed Arlander clan markings on the man's throat. Her own must be fully visible, without her robe.

The man's serious expression broke into a smile.

"*Aidee. Mia Cain.*"

"*Aidee. Mia Arienne.*"

She forgot the cold wind blowing through the alley. She forgot that she needed to be hiding her real name.

"*T'li bidan.*"

The man named Cain held up a finger, pulled a paper bag from his inner pocket, and handed it to Arienne. He continued speaking to her in Arlandais. She understood most of it, although she hadn't uttered a single word since coming to the Capital. Cain spoke quickly, omitting words and contracting phrases every so often. He was clearly from Kingsworth, the largest city in Arland. Arienne was a little intimidated and could hardly answer him, but Cain's face brightened as he spoke on.

The bag was warm from having come from his inner pocket. When she opened it, the scent of olive oil and bread wafted out from inside.

"*Tandas,*" answered Arienne.

"*Ni yehre.*" Cain gave Arienne's shoulder two light pats and headed into Lukan's tavern.

Arienne devoured the warm, oil-dipped bread. Cain was likely to say something about her to Lukan. Maybe tell him her name. Then would Lukan come out and look for her?

She no longer had a reason to wait until he closed for the night. She turned the corner and walked right into the brightly lit tavern.

Everyone's eyes fell on Arienne as she entered the doors. Half of them were people who had passed her in the alley. They all wore grimy clothes and hard expressions, but compared to Arienne's state of disarray, they were positively genteel. Her face grew red.

Cain was sitting at the bar, watching her approach. Walking over, she sat down next to him, feeling the gazes of the other patrons falling on her back. The warm tavern was humid and smelled of cooking vegetables. She gulped.

Lukan had stopped wiping down the bar and was looking at her as well. His lush beard, his braided hair, the blue cords interweaved into his braids—he looked exactly the same as six years ago.

"Someone you know?" Lukan asked Cain, not recognizing his own niece.

"Only just. Her name is Arienne, and she's an Arlander." Cain nodded at Arienne and said to Lukan, "She looks like she's been cold and hungry for a while, though. Got something for her to eat?"

Lukan glanced quickly at Arienne's *t'laran* and scratched his own neck tattoos as he turned to Cain. Cain tapped his chest. The sound of metallic clinking was heard from it. Only then did Lukan look at Arienne and smile.

"Oh, I didn't notice your *t'laran*. A girl from the old country. I have a relative, something like a niece, who's also named Arienne. I haven't seen her in a while, but she ought to be around your age. She's studying at the . . ." His smile disappeared. He leaned over the bar and stared squarely at Arienne's clan markings, eyes widening in realization and horror. He whispered to her, "What are you doing here?"

Fear was mixed in his voice. Arienne also bent low over the bar and whispered, "I ran away from school this morning. I'll tell you everything soon, but please don't attract any more attention."

Lukan's face hardened. Cain seemed to sense something was wrong as well. He glanced at Lukan and then back at her.

Finally, Lukan managed to get ahold of himself, and without a word, ladled some soup into a bowl for her. It was almost completely broth. Arienne also did not say a word as she gulped it down, feeling its warmth spread through her body. There was a bench in the corner with a gray blanket that was singed in places from lit candles past. Arienne went to the bench and wrapped herself in the blanket as if she had just crawled out of the surf after a shipwreck.

Time passed. Customers left. Arienne noticed Cain taking note of every person who came and went. Lukan signaled for him to leave as well, but Cain shook his head.

When it was just the three of them, Lukan closed the door and bolted it. He snuffed out every candle and lamp save one.

Before Lukan could say anything, Arienne quickly asked, "Has anyone come looking for me?"

Lukan sighed. "It's the dungeons of the Office of Truth for you and me. They didn't come today, but by tomorrow the inquisitors will certainly be knocking at my door." He shook his head. "To think my only relative so far away from home is a runaway sorcerer."

Cain glanced at Arienne, his eyes gleaming behind his spectacles, but otherwise did not show any surprise.

Lukan poured himself a drink and drank it in one gulp.

"Look," said Arienne, "I'm going to leave the Capital, I just need to hide for a little while, just to rest and—" She gestured to her dirty white shift. She would draw attention anywhere dressed like this. "I have some money, Uncle. I just need some clothes and to prepare myself for travel—"

"Six years without so much as a visit, what makes you think you can make these demands!"

Arienne flinched, tightening her grip on the blanket around her.

"Lukan, be quiet," Cain said in a whisper. Arienne hadn't noticed that Cain was by the doors and had his ear against them.

"Is someone there?" Arienne asked, her grip on the blanket tightening.

Cain shook his head and stared worriedly at Lukan. "I don't think so. But if you shout like that, they'll hear you all the way up there in the Office of Truth, one way or the other."

Lukan sighed. Silence followed.

The situation was getting out of her control. All Arienne had thought of was to ask Lukan for help, to give him some money, get new clothes and travel gear, and escape the city. She had no idea she would be treated like an unkempt fugitive by her own blood, or would accidentally involve a stranger who had nothing to do with her save for their shared homeland. She had made quite a mess, and she was angry at Eldred.

Arienne couldn't trust Cain completely either; all he'd done was give some bread to a person he pitied. To him, it must have been like throwing a coin to a beggar.

But this man looked serious. Cain wasn't blaming Arienne. He wasn't panicking or showing regret, instead just making sure no one was listening in on them.

Arienne looked at Cain again. The man's demeanor made him look older than when she first saw him in the alley. She recognized the type, not from real life, but from the stories she liked to read, a protagonist wise beyond his years, thanks to a hard life on the mean streets. He even had dark, tired eyes behind his spectacles, like many such heroes.

"That one looks useful."

Arienne jumped at the sound of Eldred's voice. With everything happening, she'd almost forgotten she was playing host to a long-dead Power generator. She opened the door inside her mind to see Eldred sitting up, his bandaged face turned in her direction.

"Ask that one for help," he said, referring to the man who'd given her the bread. *"This uncle, while a blood relation, seems only keen on saving his own neck. I would be relieved if he didn't do anything more than report you."*

The tavern was quiet and both men were looking at her, so she couldn't respond.

After inspecting the windows, briefly opening each of them to peer outside, Cain nodded in their direction. Lukan poured himself another drink.

Cain said, coming back to the bar, "Look, she *is* family—"

"*You* don't have family, that's why you would say such a thing," shot back Lukan. "Look at what the one family I have in the Capital is doing right now."

84

Cain turned to her and said, "If you really have no one else, I can try to help you at least."

She didn't know what to say. Cain's offer was like sweet rain in a long drought. After a moment's thought, she said, "I would need a place to sleep for a little while, some clothes, and if you could help me get ready to travel . . ."

"I know a place you can stay for a couple of days. The rest I can get for you tomorrow. I've some business all day and it'll be evening by the time I come back, but you should probably leave at night anyway."

"He's putting himself forward, this is good," said Eldred. *"But you don't know how he's going to turn. Tomorrow I shall teach you a spell that can kill a man in a second."*

It disconcerted Arienne how Eldred could say such horrifying things, when all he had talked about in the Academy were hopes and promises . . . What would happen if she failed to learn the sorcery he was willing to teach? What was he capable of, sitting there in the room inside her mind?

But that was not something to worry about right now. Her priority was to leave the Capital. Arienne nodded at Cain. "Thank you."

Cain shrugged.

Lukan lifted the glass to his lips, but stopped as if he remembered something. He said, with suspicion in his voice, "This girl has the nerve to expect things from me because I'm family. But why are *you* volunteering?"

Cain rolled his eyes behind his spectacles, as if he wasn't sure. "I don't know. But she needs help, right? And I can give it. I know I needed whatever I could get when I first came to this city."

The street hero, just like in the books, Arienne thought again, as she caught a glimpse of sadness briefly disturbing his calm face. Did he have a troubled past as well, just like those heroes?

Lukan emptied another glass and turned to Arienne. "I won't report you." He took out a metal box from under the bar, counted out a handful of silver coins, and shoved them in her direction. "You're going to have to run far if you don't want those Office of Truth bastards to catch you."

And how far could these few coins get her? Arienne grabbed the coins, gratitude, anger, and shame warring inside her.

Lukan must've also been embarrassed at his own stinginess as he cleared his throat and said, "Leave by the back door. Take a good look to see if anyone is watching you. And if the Office inquisitors come looking for me—"

"Tell them she was someone I came in with," interrupted Cain, "and you have no idea who she was because you didn't recognize her after all these years."

"You want me to mention you as well?"

"There are limits to how much you can lie convincingly, I've noticed."

Cain turned to Arienne and took her hand. "This way."

Arienne allowed herself to be led to the door, where Cain peeked out for a moment before stepping out ahead of her. The streetlamps flickered their blue lights, a sign that the Power generator in this neighborhood was old. Was there an end, even for dead sorcerers in lead coffins? It was oddly comforting to think that. Still covered with the blanket, she took off her shoes so they wouldn't make a sound on the cobblestones and walked the cold ground on her bare feet. The door of the tavern closed silently behind them.

9

LORAN

Loran looked around the large room made of white stone. It was, unlike what she expected from an underground cave, dry and warm. Small, compared to the one in the volcano where she'd made the life-altering deal with the dragon, but there were rooms of all sizes down here, like a rabbit warren. Worn reliefs decorated the walls, with scenes of battle, noble gatherings, and peasants harvesting in fields.

Hung on a wall was a tapestry map, newer than anything else in the room. Drawn, Loran walked up to it, Gwaharad following her. On the upper edge of the map were embroidered words: THE WORLD TO BE LIBERATED. It was different from any other world map she had seen in Imperial atlases. Kamori and the rest of Lontaria were depicted in a grand manner, inflated to be as large as the Imperial heartland, whereas many provinces that she knew by name were shrunken or even omitted completely. The bottom of the tapestry read FOR KING GWAHARAD OF KAMORI, FROM HIS MOST

DEVOTED SUBJECT. MAY HE LEAD THE WAY TO THE LIBERATION OF OUR HOMELAND AND THE WORLD THAT SUFFERS. Loran ran her fingers over the tapestry. Cassian velvet, she surmised.

The king of Kamori had his mind on liberating the *world* from the Empire, even when he was struggling to free his own kingdom. In contrast, she still didn't know what to do with the power she had been given. She tried to imagine the world freed, then sighed.

Gwaharad cleared his throat and spoke. "This is the underground palace built by Kamori's first king, Uter. They say he ruled all of the Three Kingdoms except the northern part of Ledon."

Loran noted Gwaharad using the old term for Arland, Kamori, and Ledon, instead of the name the Empire gave them: Lontaria. As long as Loran could remember, it was considered archaic to refer to the region as the Three Kingdoms. The Empire's language and culture had come long before their legions did.

They were surrounded by stone walls, but Gwaharad's voice did not echo.

In the center of the room was a large stone throne, its once-intricate carvings worn down after years of use. Loran had known of King Uter, but he was a legend of so long ago that no one knew how far back. Loran traced the right armrest of the throne with a finger. The parts where countless royal hands had rested over the centuries were especially worn, making it impossible to tell what had been carved in those places.

"The later kings of Kamori did not use this place, and it was eventually forgotten. Until I found it again."

Loran listened. He had a way of speaking that made her wary of interrupting him, even by accident. Loran, since watching the last king of Arland die in battle, had not laid eyes on another king again until now. She had only a vague idea of them being similar to prefects but even grander. Despite her ambition to rid her lands of the Empire and become king, she didn't really know how exactly a king should be.

"We shall give you a room, Princess. Please stay as long as you wish."

"Your Majesty. I do have a question."

"Ask."

"How is it that you became king?"

Gwaharad smiled.

"It's because I am the child of the former king, of course. Kamori may be ruled by the Empire, but our royal bloodline persists. My older sister, the original successor of the royal house, has been dragged to the Capital to sit in their puppet Commons. Instead, I stay here in the kingdom and fight for it. The crown and this palace are all mine, and the people put themselves forward as soldiers to fight with me. Do such things not make me fit to be king?"

"I beg Your Majesty to forgive me, it was not my intention to imply that I doubted your legitimacy. It's just—"

"Just what?"

"I have promised to become . . . King of Arland. But I am not the child of a king, the people do not recognize me, and I have no soldiers to fight the Empire with."

"But you said you were a princess?"

Loran couldn't find the words to explain. Gwaharad pressed further. "On the way back here, you told us that you had made a pact with the dragon of Arland and received the sword. I had assumed that the dragon would have discerned your heritage." Gwaharad eyed Wurmath slung on Loran's side, licked his lips, then looked at her intently. His gaze carried a hint of annoyance. "I knew that the royal line of the Arlanders ended upon the Empire's arrival, but I'd been under the impression that you were a hidden scion that managed to survive . . ."

Loran felt caught in a lie. Her hand moved to her neck, where her *t'laran* were partially covered by her tunic.

The king cleared his throat.

"Kamori's first king, Uter, made war to unite the Three Kingdoms, which was riddled with division among the many tribes, and that is how he ascended to the throne. I have heard that Kinedris of Arland became king by making a pact with the dragon of the volcano to protect her people, just like you have. Who knows whether Uter and Kinedris were leaders of their tribes or the lowliest of peasants before their ascension? Yet, who among us now would dare question their royal blood?"

The words were kind, but Loran did not mistake his tone of disdain for that of an encouragement. A forced smile appeared on Gwaharad's face to erase the expression of annoyance.

"Fight the Empire and let your name be known far and wide. Arlanders everywhere will be sure to acknowledge you."

Despite the obvious disappointment in the way he spoke, Loran felt as if she was shown a way forward. She returned the smile. "I shall."

"My soldiers and I are Kamori, but this battle is for all of the Three Kingdoms. If you fight with us, there will be many chances to make your name. It is already unimaginable that you should have felled four legionaries in Powered armor! The Kamori Liberators have surely made an ally from heaven. We shall hear more of your story at the banquet."

Kamori Liberators. Loran considered the name for a moment. Gwaharad apparently had the mandate of his people and commanded an army, not to mention having possession of an impressive fortress. He probably had enough funds to keep his people fed too. The only thing he lacked was sovereignty over his land. He had every cause and the means to call himself king and wage war against the Empire.

She wondered if she should confer with the dragon again. Loran's fingertips brushed against Wurmath's hilt.

"But perhaps we should refrain from calling you 'princess' for the time being," said Gwaharad, and he clapped his hands to summon his soldiers on duty. "Take Mistress Loran to her quarters."

This sudden demotion to "mistress" seemed to surprise the soldiers more than Loran. They quickly recovered, nodded to Loran, and led the way out of the room.

The quarters set aside for Loran were more spacious than she had imagined. Loran removed her leather armor, still covered in dirt and damaged from her battles in Dehan Forest. The wound on her side hadn't been as painful as she'd expected in the hours she'd traveled with Gwaharad and Emere, and when she inspected it now, there was only a scar that looked as if it were from a long-ago burn rather than the blade of a Powered sword just that morning.

Laid on the simple yet comfortable-looking bed was a change of clothing. A simple tunic, and thin trousers under a skirt with a slit up one side, the kind Kamori women wore. The green lion of Kamori was embroidered on the skirt. There was even a strip of red cloth to be used for an eyepatch.

Just as Loran was about to change, there was a knock on her door.

"Who is it?" she called in surprise.

"Emere, Your Highness."

"Just a moment."

Still in her leather trousers, Loran quickly slipped on the tunic and tied her eyepatch in place before opening the door. Emere had combed his hair, trimmed his beard, and changed into a fresh set of clothes; he looked like a completely different man from the one she had met in the forest. On his tunic was the green lion so common in this palace. Only his wrists, where the ropes of the Imperial army had bruised, reassured Loran that this was indeed Emere.

He bowed deeply. Loran noticed that in Emere's left hand was something long, the length of a sword, wrapped in a fine piece of cloth.

"May I enter?"

This is your palace, and the door is already open. What more permission do you need? Still, Loran went through the motions of nodding and gesturing for him to enter. Emere closed the door behind him and bowed to her once more.

"I have been lightly reprimanded by my brother the king for introducing you to him as a princess without having listened to your story first."

Loran blushed. She bowed and apologized.

"I'm sorry. All because I said something foolish—"

Emere waved his hands. "Not at all! On the contrary. I have come to apologize for my brother's rudeness. With the way the Empire rules the world, who is to say which is a real king or princess? There is only the Senate and the prefects. I have . . ."

Emere looked back to check if the door was well and closed. He stroked his beard and lowered his voice.

"I have not told my brother the king about the princess's . . . transformation."

He meant, no doubt, the business with the scales and the burning eye. She had told him of the pact she made with the dragon and of Wurmath, but she could not explain the strange change in her appearance. She could not blame him if he talked about it to everyone he met. Had it happened to someone else, she would have.

"King Gwaharad is a great man, but he can be a little too prudent, perhaps, and jealous. For now, it may be a better recourse to let him think you are an ordinary warrior who happened to come upon an extraordinary sword. Indeed, I have a feeling that he does not fully believe what you have told us."

Emere bowed again.

"I beseech you to forgive my brother once more, and on behalf of my brother and the Kingdom of Kamori, beg Your Highness when she ascends to the Arlander throne to fight alongside your brother nation of Kamori."

Loran appreciated Emere's kind words, but couldn't help feeling that Emere was too generous to her, when she had nothing to her name.

"His Majesty said nothing wrong," Loran assured him. "Kings must have the right to rule. For someone like me who is not of royal blood to call herself a princess, it would be strange not to think she is acting above her station."

Emere sighed.

"But Your Highness, you have made a pact with the dragon

and received the dragon's sword. I have heard this is exactly how the first king of Arland ascended to her reign."

"Only when the Arlanders accepted this. I have no such support. If anyone with an extraordinary sword may become king, wouldn't that mean the Empire with their Powered legions have more legitimacy to rule over all of us than anyone else?"

Emere vigorously shook his head.

"The people choose their own king, and if the king is found unfit to rule, the king is banished by the very same people. This has been the way all over the world, since time immemorial, ages before the arrival of the Empire. But what presents a king to be chosen is not the people; it is destiny. The dragon has been imprisoned in the volcano for two decades, yet you were the only one in all those years who dared to go there and came out with its fang in hand. This is why I do not hesitate in calling Your Highness the Princess Loran of Arland."

She didn't know where this conviction sprang from. The very word "destiny" made Loran squirm in discomfort.

"All right."

Emere bowed once more, and as if suddenly remembering, carefully presented the cloth-wrapped thing to Loran.

"This is a gift from me. It is not fine enough to befit you, or your sword, but I took the liberty of picking one from our armory. Please consider it a token of my gratitude, for your bravery at the forest."

Loran took it with both hands and, glancing at Emere for his permission, unwrapped the cloth. It was a scabbard, blue fabric with subtle patterns covering its wooden structure. It reminded Loran of the blue flame of Wurmath. As she was admiring the craftsmanship, Emere added, "A sword needs a scabbard, as fury needs restraint."

Loran repeated the words under her breath, then smiled. "Thank you." She carefully sheathed Wurmath. It was as if the scabbard was made for it.

"I shall be waiting by the door. Please let me know when you are ready to go to the banquet."

As she changed into the set of unfamiliar clothes, Loran kept thinking about her conversations with Gwaharad and with Emere. The Kamori king had told her, even through his masked contempt at her lineage, that she could be king through her people's recognition. Emere believed she had a destiny to be king. Maybe they were both right, but she did not have the conviction of either. What had the dragon seen in her, in that dark gray cavern lit by blue dragonfire?

Loran drew Wurmath from the scabbard and stood. If she could not believe in herself, she had to believe in the ones who did. She whispered to Wurmath, the dragon's promise, and to the scabbard, Emere's gift, the same words that she had said in the volcanic cave.

"I am a princess of Arland. And I shall become king."

10

CAIN

Cain left Arienne under the care of Lucretia, madam of a local pleasure house. Lucretia owed Cain—he had solved the murder of one of Lucretia's women last year. The patrollers dismissed the death as no great loss to society, but locals had suspected the death was part of a series of prostitute killings all over the Capital. Lucretia had called upon Cain to find the one responsible.

It had taken Cain almost a fortnight to deliver the culprit to her. He made no special mention of the pains he went through, including a rooftop confrontation where he was stabbed with the knife that had presumably been used to mutilate the victims' faces. Lucretia had not asked after his wound either, only telling him softly that she owed him a great favor as her bouncers took the whimpering man away. To this day, Cain did not know what kind of end the murderer had met. He remembered only admiring the look on the madam's face, of something that reminded him of relief.

Cain had known from a young age that it was advantageous to

have people around the market square indebted to him, and that even small favors could create large debts over time. He also understood that the effect was greatest when he wasn't keeping track of who owed him what.

Helping a fugitive sorcerer escape was quite a large ask, though, and even with what she owed him, Cain had been uncertain if Lucretia would be willing to help. But the madam took in Arienne without a word.

Cain did ask himself what he hoped to gain from helping Arienne, but came up empty. Still, Fienna hadn't taken in a twelve-year-old boy and fed him and taught him to read and write because she had some grand design in mind.

There was a wide array of shops near the pleasure house, which wasn't far from the market square. Cain liked coming to this square, one of the larger marketplaces of the Capital, because there were so many kinds of people buying and selling. Each shop and stall reflected its proprietor's origins, making the whole area more vibrant and chaotic than the drab, austere stone buildings native to the city.

Cain loitered in the bustling winter market under the overcast sky, exchanging wordless greetings with the shopkeepers and street vendors. Although many of them had received Cain's help over the years, he understood that any one of them would have no choice but to inform on his movements if pressed by the likes of Septima.

Cain knew one of the new hires at the travel and outdoor goods supplier had recently moved here—a man who didn't know him and spoke little Imperial. That was the best he could do if he wanted to make a discreet purchase. When the owner left for his midday meal, he stepped into the shop.

A cheerful man not much older than Cain greeted him with a smile. "Welcome, buyer!" Cain did not recognize the clerk's accent, but judging from the worn fur coat he was wearing while right next to a stove, he must have come from a warmer province.

Cain chose two sets of dark blue travel clothes that looked like they would fit Arienne, a pair of leather boots, bedding, and some food. He asked the worker to recommend a sack for travel, and was presented with a leather rucksack, the clerk singing its praises in a broken yet confident Imperial that only the people of this market and the merchants by the docks would bother to decipher.

"From Bachria, buffalo leather-skin. Very endure. Very light. Your good benefit!"

He held up a thumb.

Cain knew some Bachrians living and working in the market square. They held feasts for the entire neighborhood at least once a year, per their custom. Cain made it a point to attend them all bearing gifts. He remembered them complaining that it was impossible to get good buffalo meat in the Capital, a situation he had helped rectify by introducing them to a trader who dealt in Tanvalian bison.

He held the sack up and pretended to be astonished by its excellence, adjusting his spectacles. It was indeed light, and soft as well. It was the right size for Arienne, enough for her to carry what she needed in what was certain to be a long journey ahead for her. He gave the clerk a nod of approval and proceeded to pick out other supplies for Arienne. He reminded himself that whoever was pursuing her would be looking for a girl with neck tattoos. She could use a scarf to cover her clan markings.

At the same store, he bought a coat for himself, the tan one he had on being completely unfit for wearing to a funeral, not to mention stained with blood from the night he was attacked, as well as from when he'd met Devadas in the alleyway. There were other, fainter stains, each reminding him of a job turned violent. The new coat was black, hopefully preventing the problem of such obvious stains in the future. It had a hood attached, convenient for covering his face from both the cold weather and recognition by others. After some haggling, he sold his bloody coat for store credit, then stuffed the things he had bought for Arienne in the leather bag.

He paid. The pouch he had received from Septima showed no signs of getting lighter. Putting a few extra coins in the shop clerk's palm, he asked for a delivery to be made to Lucretia's place.

"Before the sun sets."

"*Gaita z'bak*," said the clerk, his smile widening even further.

If the goods arrived early, Arienne might just leave before dark against his advice, without saying goodbye. Come to think of it, he hadn't asked her where she was going. He wondered if she even had a destination. She was a sorcerer after all and could probably take care of herself, but seeing as she'd been shivering from cold in a dress more suited to be worn *under* proper clothing than *as* proper clothing, maybe she couldn't.

Now in his somber new coat, Cain headed for Fienna's funeral. The capital of the Empire was surrounded by no walls or gates. It had grown so fast that the old city walls ran in a circle only around the heart of the city. As he walked on, the buildings started decreasing in number until he was out in the fields. Fienna was to be buried in a cemetery east of the city, the place where most of the people from his neighborhood were buried.

Arlanders cremated their dead. In their homeland, family and friends would bring fire from the volcano to light the death pyre where their loved ones lay. But here in the Imperial heartland, where almost every acre of its flat and fertile land had been cultivated long before the Empire came to be, using wood to light a body on fire was far too costly.

It took a long time to get to the cemetery, but Cain still arrived early. Snow flurries fell silently from a moody gray sky. Tombstones of all sizes stood in neat rows. The cemetery keeper pointed Cain to where an old gravedigger sat resting on the edge of Fienna's coffin, a freshly dug grave beside it. As Cain approached, the digger rose quickly from the coffin and sat on the ground next to it. The coffin was inexpensive but still made of good material. The dye shop owner, when he had dropped by, mentioned she had paid for the funeral costs. She wasn't going to be present today, however. Perhaps because her only worker had turned up dead. She had seemed very busy when he'd passed her storefront on the way here.

Cain had not had the chance to go to his parents' funeral. He had no idea if there had been a funeral at all. Even as they were being pursued for treason, they made sure their son at least could escape the clutches of the prefect. Cain didn't know what to think of such parents. He could resent them or feel grateful, but either way, they weren't coming back. And Cain could never return to Arland.

At Fienna's gravesite, there were still only Cain and the gravedigger. From somewhere across the cemetery came the strains of a funeral dirge, in a language he didn't know.

"You family?" The gravedigger seemed unable to stand the awkward silence.

"I am not."

"The plot and the coffin, they were bought by the shopkeeper this girl used to work for. Doesn't look like anyone is going to show up, does it? We can start if this is it . . ."

Cain didn't answer. For the first time since her death, he was remembering what Fienna was like in life, rather than trying to solve her murder. Her hands were always this improbable color or that, depending on the day's work at the dye shop, sometimes the dyes staining the knots on her braids, or the corner of her smile. She had always been tired when they met, but she always spared the time to listen to Cain. The rare times Fienna asked for favors, he was more than eager to grant them. But all the things he had done for her, all the stories he had told her, seemed like they were for naught, as they were useless in preventing this outcome.

He should've given her more of his time. He should've been more concerned with what was going on with her. He was too busy trying to make her laugh with trivial stories of his daily life, rather than asking what troubled hers. There had been so many more important things, but he had wasted their precious time together talking about old Agatha or olive oil or new infatuations. He should've thanked her more. Listened to her more.

As he stood there, the folds of his new coat accumulating a white dusting of snow, he noticed people in small groups approaching the grave from the cemetery entrance.

Cain wiped his spectacles with his sleeve and looked again. Scores of people, it looked like, murmuring as they approached.

"You there! The young man! Are you family of Fienna?"

This was shouted at him by an old gentleman walking with a cane. Not answering, Cain took a closer look at the people coming toward them.

Some were wiping away tears, others looked angry. Some kept clearing their throats, and still others were consoling one another. Cain recognized none of their faces.

Soon, they were surrounding the grave and Fienna's coffin. The mourners did not seem to know one another very well.

"She was a healthy young girl, how could she all of a sudden . . ."

"And her family? Where can they be, did she have no one . . ."

Some leaned on the coffin and burst into tears. Cain was unsure of what was going on. The mourners kept arriving, and soon the crowd was several concentric circles deep, with Cain finding himself in the very middle, along with the gravedigger, who looked confused. Cain surmised that he was regretting how he had sat down on the coffin.

The old man who had arrived first hooked his cane on his wrist. He gripped Cain's hand.

"Three years ago, when my family first arrived here, we didn't have anything to get started with our new lives. But Fienna was very generous to us. I had hoped our business would succeed and I would repay her, but then this sudden tragedy . . ."

The old man seemed to have decided Cain was a member of Fienna's family. Swept up in the moment, Cain returned the grip of the old man's hand.

Others followed.

"She set me up with an apprenticeship to a healer, and told me to be a good healer myself . . ."

"I had fled the prefect and came here with nothing. I took to drink. Fienna bade me to stop drinking and start working. She gave me money while I learned my trade . . ."

". . . and that child who was at death's door, now she is going to school. If it weren't for Fienna . . ."

"Who did this to her? If I ever get my hands on him . . ."

In his inadvertent position as head mourner, shaking the hands of those who came, Cain realized that everyone or almost everyone gathered here had clan markings on their necks. They were Arlanders, who had come from all over the city. Which meant there were plenty of others who had not yet heard of Fienna's death, or those who couldn't attend the funeral for one reason or another. The people who mourned her could number in the hundreds. Septima had said Fienna received money from Gladdis. He was beginning to understand where that money had gone.

There were a few who asked what he was to Fienna, but Cain didn't know how to answer. Nobody asked after a while, perhaps sensing his distress.

Soon, everyone had said a few words, and a few young and strong among them stepped forward. Six in all, including Cain. The gravedigger tied rope to all six handles of the coffin, and they slowly lowered the coffin into the grave. When it rested on the dirt below, they tossed in the ropes first, then took up spades to cover the coffin with the freshly tilled earth beside it.

"And the tombstone?" asked the old man who had first talked to Cain. "Why is there no tombstone ready?"

The gravedigger shrugged. "One never arrived. Nor is one expected to."

The old man looked aghast as he turned to Cain, who was busy shoveling dirt into the grave. He then turned to the people behind him.

"There's not a single one of us who hasn't received succor from our late friend. To think she must be buried in a grave without a marker! What will the world say of our people if this is so?"

The old man took out money from his pocket, put it in his hat, and passed it to the next person. The hat jangled as it was passed from person to person, and by the time the hat was returned to its owner, it was over half full of coppers and silvers. The man handed the hat to Cain.

"Erect a good stone for her. One my grandchildren can look upon and remember her . . ."

Cain said he would and accepted the hat now heavy with coin.

The snow thickened. The wind was stronger. Still, the mourners would not leave. They stayed by the graveside and talked. Some sat in a crouch, some stood, and some who rather lacked in decorum leaned against the tombstones. They all, however, spoke of the same things, of how kind Fienna had been and how she had helped them. Cain gave the gravedigger some money and asked him to bring the mourners drinks. The gravedigger grumbled about the need for making such arrangements before the funeral, but he was silenced when a few more of Cain's silvers landed in his palm.

Why hadn't Fienna told him that she was taking care of so many of them? Cain had been avoiding Arlander immigrants ever since he ran away from that country, so he wasn't surprised that he didn't know a single soul among the crowd in the cemetery. Still, it astonished him that he had been so ignorant of the extent of Fienna's reach.

The old man, tapping his cane on the frozen ground, started singing in Arlandais in a low voice. The mourners followed suit, some weeping midway through the song. Cain recognized the mournful melody, but not the lyrics. They contained a mention of the dragon of the mountain helping the dead to their eternal rest, that lay beyond the blue veil of the sky. In Arland, the smoke from the cremated went up into the sky, much like the white plumes of the volcano. But here, Fienna was being buried in the earth . . . and the Empire did not believe in an afterlife. In the brief silence after the dirge ended, Cain wondered if in death he would meet Fienna again.

"Since you're all from back home," said a tall, older woman with a black headcloth, "did you hear the rumors? That Its Excellency the fire-dragon has taken the form of a woman and come down from the volcano to slaughter the Imperial legion?"

"I did hear that a princess in hiding has come out into the world to fight against the Empire."

"I heard that, too. Last month, it was. News of this princess has even reached Kamori and Ledon."

"They say she carries a flaming sword."

"Father, does Arland have princesses?"

"Don't you suspect it's all rumor? There was one like it awhile back . . ."

"But I heard it, too. They say it's real this time."

"Then there might be another massacre, like the one twelve years ago . . ."

"That's not what it feels like in Arland, they say. The prefect isn't like he used to be. The legions are about to change shifts in the three provinces of Lontaria and he is scared of being replaced . . ."

Cain had almost succeeded in forgetting about Arland. As a son of convicted traitors, he was better off without ties to his old country. Since he ran away, Lukan and Fienna were the only reminders of the homeland that he no longer belonged to. But at this news, of an Arlander princess standing up to the Empire all by herself, Cain felt a muscle pulse somewhere inside him, one that he hadn't realized he had.

Cain remembered what Septima had said about how an outpost near the border between Kamori and Arland had been ambushed and its Powered legionaries slain. He listened in silence. The voices of the Arlanders around him, which a moment ago had sounded so sorrowful at Fienna's death, were now infused with a kind of vitality, or hope.

But he wasn't the only one listening.

There was a man who hadn't talked or mingled with the other mourners, who stood by himself even now. Cain assumed this was Gladdis's man, the one Septima had told him about. He took care not to seem interested in the man.

By the time the gravedigger returned with a cask of wine, the silent man had left. Cain hadn't noticed him leaving, but that was fine.

He followed the man's footprints in the snow as they led him out of the cemetery.

11

ARIENNE

In this place, both the men and the women, and even the walls and the furniture it seemed, wore a thick coat of makeup. The brothel owner, Lucretia, was a heartlander beauty whose age was difficult to determine. She never said a word to Arienne, only led her to her room in silence. Cain had said Lucretia owed him something. She didn't ask what that debt might be.

The room on the third floor was small but comfortable. The bed was plusher than the one she'd had in the dormitory, and was covered in a bedspread with an intricate design, of men and women entangled in passionate embrace. There were a table and chair by the window. The carvings on the table legs and the back of the chair rivaled the bedspread in their scintillating depictions. Lucretia brought up sheets and sleep clothes, and a simple meal. It was a rich stew of meat and potatoes.

Lucretia wordlessly showed her the escape route out the window. A sturdy ladder was already in place. Arienne briefly wondered why the room should come with a way to escape it, but her interests quickly turned to the food.

Arienne carried the small tray to the bed before starting on the stew. She was feeling almost relaxed. The potatoes were hot enough to scald the roof of her mouth but tasted utterly divine in her hunger. Before Lucretia left the room, she tapped the bolts on Arienne's door. Arienne got up from her stew and slid the bolts shut behind her.

Eldred then spoke from the room inside her mind.

"When can you make it to the Senate?"

"I have to take care of myself first, I told you. And what business do you have with the Circuit of Destiny?"

"I'll tell you when the time comes. But first, I would appreciate it if you could unravel these bandages. I can't move my arms."

"Only if you keep your promise."

The bandages that wrapped the Power generators were to prevent leakage of the Power. It wasn't mentioned in her studies, but they also seemed to have a restrictive function against Eldred himself. She was afraid to imagine what would happen if she unwrapped Eldred's bandages in the room of her mind.

"Just my head then? I can hardly see in front of me."

Arienne didn't answer.

". . . All right, then. For now. I shall teach you the magic I promised you."

He was acting as if he were doing her a great favor. As if he escaped his coffin and the Academy all on his own. Arienne went on eating her stew.

"My magic is the magic of memories. The principle is to re-create in the mind something one has previously experienced."

"Like the room you're in?" asked Arienne between mouthfuls of stew.

"Exactly. My expertise was in reanimating the memories of the dead and making them live again. Doing this inside one's mind is mere imagination; making it happen in the outside world is magic. That you created this room and were able to move me from the real world into it is a great feat for someone with as little experience as you have."

"You're saying I can learn how to make whatever I imagine come to life?"

Eldred made a sound like a scoff.

"Imagining it is not enough. You must really believe in it. If it's not a memory, it will not work. And you're not creating something out of your imagining. You are using an image in your mind to gather your focus on the spell."

"What's the difference?"

"It would take years to explain that to you. Today, you cast off your robe in the market, did you not? Do you remember the spell you used?"

"I . . ."

Why hadn't she noticed until now? It hadn't been a spell she'd learned before.

"You were applying something you had learned when you made this room. To think of cutting the thread of your robe, you must've learned how to sew back home."

Arienne nodded, chewing her potatoes. It had nothing to do with sewing. No seamstress would make a garment that would unravel at the snap of a single thread. She had imagined a thread that did not exist and cut that instead. Despite what Eldred insisted, that hastily and instinctively wrought spell had worked with just her imagination. As she opened her mouth to contradict him, something told her it was a good idea not to let Eldred know.

"I shall teach you what's immediately useful, the things you need to know to protect yourself."

Eldred spoke a few words, syllables her tongue was not used to. Arienne repeated them. A kind of strength swirled on the tip of her tongue, summoned by the incantation from an unfamiliar realm of sorcery. She didn't have an inkling as to what language the words were, or even if they were human words.

"This is a spell that ends the life of your enemies. Just a few words and any man or woman would die where they stand."

Arienne was aghast.

"Of all the . . . Killing someone with just words? With no ingredient or ritual?"

"The incantation itself does nothing more than call the attention of the universe to the matter at hand. Trying to recall something as vividly as possible and convincing the universe that this is a fate that must absolutely happen is a difficult thing. You have talent, but if your images are not clear, it will not take effect. Now, try to remember a time when you killed someone. Try remembering it as vividly as possible. Try recreating the scene here in this room."

Arienne almost spat out a piece of potato. "I don't have such vile memories!"

Eldred made something of a sigh.

"How easy the lives of sorcerers are today! In my time, we . . . Well, you were trapped in that minuscule school since an early age, studying things far from real magic, I suppose it isn't surprising this should be so. What about beasts, then? Sheep or chicken? You must have struck a sheep's head with an axe or twisted the neck of a chicken."

"Never."

"You, the daughter of a farmer?"

"I've cracked an egg or two."

She put another spoonful of stew in her mouth.

"Cease this eating and pay attention!" Eldred had raised his voice. The bandage around his mouth fell, revealing two shriveled lips. Arienne almost flipped the tray in her revulsion.

"Before I ended up this way, there was a line of young sorcerers going out the door begging me to accept them as apprentices, you ungrateful—"

"You keep talking about killing this and killing that, but it is odd that you're the one who ended up killed."

Eldred fell silent.

"I escaped because I *didn't* want to end up like you," Arienne added.

She was beginning to feel angry. She had expected him to be a poor, tortured soul of a noble sorcerer, but from the moment they escaped the Academy, he had been saying nothing but the vilest things. And he had been a murderer as well! She couldn't forget the skeleton with its broken neck.

"Are you saying you refuse to learn sorcery from me? That you will not listen to anything I say?"

"You should say something *worth* listening to!" she shouted. "What have you done so far to help me? I don't know what grand country you were the great sorcerer of, but ever since we left the school you've behaved more like a murderer or a slaver! If we hadn't been lucky enough to meet Cain when we did, we'd both be in the dungeon of the Office of Truth right now!"

Eldred grew silent. His head was bowed, and so was his waist. Arienne realized her voice had been too loud and was about to open the door and peek out, but the sight of the sliding bolts sapped the energy from her. She sat back down.

It was deep into night now. She could hear coquettish voices and laughter and music seeping in from the outside, reassuring her that no one was paying attention to her. Arienne closed the door to the room in her mind. She finished the stew, put on the sleep clothes, and crawled in between the sheets. She was asleep as soon as she closed her eyes.

When Arienne woke, she heard no music or laughter. Drawing back the thick red drapes brought in sunlight that almost blinded her. She closed the drapes and looked down at the shoes and dress she had cast aside. They were dirty from the street. The shoes she could clean, but the dress was torn in places.

Someone knocked at the door.

"Just a moment."

Arienne drew back the bolts and opened the door. Lucretia stood outside with a wooden basin and towel in her hands. Steam rose from the basin. There was also a leather sack on the floor resting against the doorframe.

Lucretia's attire was plainer and looked more comfortable than yesterday's. She was wearing nothing on her face, but her age was still difficult to tell. As Lucretia set down the basin on the side table, Arienne carried in the sack. Lucretia tidied up a little and left the room with the empty bowl from last night's stew. She didn't speak, but her smile was warm and her movements respectful, which went far to reassure Arienne. What had Cain done for Lucretia, that she should be like this to her?

Along with the rucksack, there was also a pair of sturdy-looking boots, tied together by their laces. They fit comfortably on her feet. The rolled-up bedding on top of the sack was fastened by string. Inside the bag were two pairs of trousers and two tunics made of thick, tough blue material. They were patched in the elbows and knees with leather. Arienne, when she'd come from Arland to the Capital, had worn such clothes. There was an undyed woolen scarf, perfect for wearing over the *t'laran* on her neck. At the bottom was some dried meat and hard bread, enough for three days, or even four if she was frugal. There were plenty of places to get food and drink along the Imperial highway, so these were just for emergencies.

Arienne suddenly realized she hadn't given Cain any money. He had done this for her on his own coin. Would she ever see him again to pay him back? Regretfully enough, that would be difficult. She needed to get as far away as possible. Like in a book, she could choose to have adventures around the periphery of the known world. Maybe somewhere down south where it was never cold. Or stow away on a ship at shore and sail to an island in the middle of the Great West Sea where no one would find her. Kaya, the girl who taught Arienne the sleeping spell at the Academy, had confessed that she learned her spells from a witch in hiding, back in her homeland. Perhaps Arienne could learn Eldred's sorceries and become such a witch herself . . .

She changed into her new clothes. It was good they were a bit loose, but the chafing of her skin against the rough fabric could become a problem. Arienne took them off again and washed her face and body with the hot water in the basin, careful not to splash too much on the floor. She then washed her dirty dress in the luke-warm water. It was torn, but it would be enough to wear underneath her new clothes. She draped the wet dress on the table and chair, pulling open the curtains so the wintry sunlight fell on it. She made sure the bolts on the door were drawn shut once more and went back underneath the covers.

After midnight, when the lower floors were still too loud and bustling for anyone to notice, she would take the window exit Lucretia showed her and slip into the unlit back alley. But she still hadn't decided where to go from there. Well, she would have to leave the Capital and the Imperial heartland, and then she could go on to think of what was next.

She thought more about being a hermit sorcerer in some far-away place where even the Office of Truth wouldn't bother to look. To do that, she needed to learn sorcery; she couldn't move forward into the dark with the candle-lighting spell as her only weapon. Hoping Eldred wouldn't hold her harsh tone from the night before against her, Arienne drifted off to sleep once more.

12

LORAN

Loran was eager to continue her fight alongside the Kamori Liberators, but Gwaharad seemed to be a more cautious leader, as Emere suggested. Initially she was content to wait. Having allies, she felt like she could finally see a way forward, out of meaningless destruction.

Then a fortnight passed in the underground palace. Loran had done almost nothing but practice her swordsmanship out of habit and eat the food they brought her. She found her patience dwindling. She had volunteered to teach the Kamori soldiers, but Gwaharad refused her offer, saying her style of swordsmanship would conflict with their training so far. He seemed, in truth, reluctant to let her come in contact with his soldiers. Loran recalled Emere describing his brother as the jealous type.

Since that conversation, she had almost no occasion to have an audience with Gwaharad. As Loran was also not one to seek the company of others without having a clear reason in mind, she did not make up excuses to do so. Only Emere visited her. He came by every day for lunch and conversation in her room.

That afternoon, over tea, Emere told her about a woman named Gladdis.

"Do you mean the one who left a little after I arrived here?" said Loran. "I only know of her by name."

"She is a great merchant who comes and goes between the Capital and the Three Kingdoms. She is affluent, and well-connected. A generous sponsor of the Kamori resistance."

"Ah. A formidable compatriot to have."

This explained how an army of hundreds was being maintained.

"Yes, I didn't have much chance to talk to her, but my brother holds her in great esteem . . . Not only does she support us with her funds, she also aids and unites our people living in the Capital. We call her the Liberators' prefect of the Capital, in jest."

"I see." Perhaps Gladdis was more of a king than herself, Loran thought.

Emere took a sip of his tea and continued. "The king tells me that her sisters had been priests of the Tree Lords of Kamori, who all burned with the Lords in the conflagration of our sacred groves. Perhaps that is why she does what she does, even after becoming so successful as a licensed trader."

Loran knew that the people of Kamori had once worshipped ancient trees that walked, much as Arlanders venerated the dragon of the mountain. Everywhere the Empire went, gods died and the faithful with them.

After a short lull in the conversation, Emere looked at her in amusement.

"What song is it that you are humming? I have never heard the tune."

She was indeed humming to herself over the tea. Embarrassed, she stumbled to answer.

"My . . . my husband was a poet. This is something he wrote to mourn the victims of the purge in Kingsworth, on the tenth anniversary of the event." She hesitated, then added. "My daughter sang it. They were killed for it, along with several others who organized the remembrance."

Apologetic, Emere sighed.

"Princess, I am sorry to have pried. You have my deepest condolences."

Loran forced a smile, then changed the subject.

"From what I understand, there are Arlanders in the Capital as well . . ."

During the purge, quite a number of Arlanders had taken refuge there, perhaps thousands. Because the Imperial Capital was home to people from all over the Empire, it was considered the best place in the world to start anew.

"Yes, and Gladdis is working to bring the Arlanders together as she has done for our own but . . . I haven't heard much on that front so far."

Loran imagined how many Arlander exiles must be living in the Capital now, what sorts of people they might be, whether they could be persuaded to fight against the Empire. "I'm sure such a person is a great help to our cause."

"Of course, Gladdis exacts no small a price in return. What we did in the forest recently, that was also by her request."

"You mean the metal box you took from the legionaries."

Emere just smiled.

The two sipped their tea without saying anything. Perhaps bothered by the silence, Emere glanced back at the closed door and whispered as if telling a secret, "Have you heard of the weapon called the Star of Mersia?"

"Of course. I should be hard-pressed to find someone who hasn't. It's difficult to believe such a weapon can exist, but I cannot deny what happened to Mersia . . ."

The ultimate weapon of the Empire, that could sweep away an entire country. No one knew what it looked like or how it worked. There were only rumors.

"I cannot help but believe it exists! I was in the Mersian Wastes ten years ago. It's difficult to imagine the green steppes that once stretched across the country. All you can see now is red desert and some ruins." He shivered.

"But why do you mention the Star of Mersia now?"

Emere smiled bitterly. "Because if Kamori or Arland wish to be truly free of the Empire, we cannot but think of it. Mentioning the weapon in this palace at all is forbidden because it can bring down the morale of the soldiers, but I thought Your Highness and I at least could have a conversation about it."

"You've called me Your Highness again, but I do not call you Your Highness in return. Please, call me Loran."

After her conversation with Gwaharad, Loran no longer called herself a princess in front of others. And an order from Gwaharad seemed to have gone down as all the soldiers called her "Mistress Loran" from the second day onward. Only Emere did her the courtesy of referring to her as Her Highness, a princess of Arland.

Emere shook his head.

"I have traveled much since I was a child. All the way to Hyberia in the north, and the very edges of Cassia in the east. I have met many great men and women. I believe I know them when I see them. There is something in Your Highness that seems destined for the title, in my eyes."

Loran could not help but laugh. "You jest again!" she said. His words were not unpleasant to hear, but she felt an inexplicable, bone-deep anxiety whenever Emere mentioned destiny. They say that one can't avoid destiny, but the more time she spent inside this place, the more it felt like destiny was avoiding her.

The door burst open. Emere jumped up like a little boy who had been caught doing something naughty. He shouted at the soldier who stumbled inside, "How dare you enter the princess's chamber without permission! What's the meaning of this!"

"Prince Emere, there is trouble! Mistress Loran must know as well," said the soldier, panting.

"Well, speak!"

"The Twenty-Fifth has sent troops to Arland, vowing vengeance for Mistress Loran's destruction of the outposts and the death of the legionaries."

Loran got to her feet as well. "Does the king know?"

"He does. He ordered me to summon you both."

Loran and Emere followed the soldier out of the room. She was still unused to the structure of the underground palace. She was so nervous she wanted to outpace the soldier, but there was no way of knowing where she was being taken, and she doubted she would be able to find the way on her own even if she was told. Emere said nothing as they walked, but his grim expression told her everything she needed to know about the seriousness of their situation.

After a few turns, they came to a room she had never seen before. The door was open. There was an ancient-looking round table made of stone in the middle of it, engraved with the ubiquitous lion emblem that the nation of Kamori still used today. The room was filled with soldiers. Gwaharad sat at the table, flanked by two advisors whose faces she recognized. There was also a soldier who was covered in scratches, a scout no doubt. There were two seats left at the table.

Gwaharad saw them enter the room and nodded his head.

"You're here, Emere. And Mistress Loran. We were waiting for you to begin, as it concerns Arland."

Loran bowed and took her seat. Emere took the remaining one.

"Now that Mistress Loran is here, make your report," said Gwaharad to the scout.

"Your Majesty, as I have spoken before, the Twenty-Fifth Legion has entered Arland and sent a century to Kingsworth to declare that they will see to it that whoever destroyed the outpost and killed the Powered legionaries is held responsible."

Everyone seated turned their gaze to Loran.

"A century, he says. A hundred legionaries are not a large force," said Emere in a placating tone, glancing at Loran as well. "It would be a tough battle, but we could raise two hundred . . ." In truth, the Kamori forces alone would not be able to take on such a force even with twice the number. But if they included Loran and Wurmath, that was a completely different proposition.

Just as Loran was thinking they might have a chance, the scout added, "My lord, this is no ordinary century. They have the Powered chariots, Scorpios class."

The room broke into murmurs.

"How many?" asked Gwaharad.

"At least three. But it seems likely to be four."

"Four would overwhelm us," said the general sitting to Gwaharad's right, as if it weren't true that even one would likely have been enough to decimate their small force. Her shaved head was covered in scars, and Loran recalled that her name was Belwin. A seasoned veteran who had joined Gwaharad's cause before even Emere had.

"Do we have any weapons that can break through their armor?"

"If we had, we would have won the war by now."

"Our only recourse is to use our siege weapons and pray for luck . . . Or pour all our soldiers into making a stand."

"In Selvetica, they had success using a weapon called the firespear."

"What use are stories from so far up north to us?"

The soldiers went on for a moment like this until Gwaharad raised a hand for silence.

Loran could scarcely contain herself. In mere days, the chariot century would reach Kingsworth. Maybe they had already. She could picture the massacre that would happen when they did. This was not a time to debate the presence or absence of Powered chariots. She gave Gwaharad an imploring look.

Gwaharad looked back at her, seemingly lost in thought, until he said, "We have no way of fighting armored chariots. The best we can do is wait for word from our compatriots in Kingsworth. It will be an opportunity to find out how different the Twenty-Fifth Legion is from the Hundred and Seventy-First."

"Your Majesty!" Loran was on her feet.

"Mistress Loran," said Gwaharad firmly, "you must forgive us, but this affair is Arland's, not Kamori's. A neighboring country to be sure, but a separate one no less. We here have gathered under the great cause of Kamori's liberation. I cannot have such brave men and women run into the path of armored chariots for foreigners' sake."

"Your Majesty. Do you not understand what the Empire means by holding people responsible? It means to take whoever they can and make an example of them. Whether the people they kill are responsible for their ire or not is none of their concern. Their only objective here is fear. Has Kamori not suffered the same way? Is there anyone here who has not lost family or friends to such indiscriminate methods? Is there not a single man or woman among you who vowed to rise against the Empire because of this?"

A somber mood returned to the war room. The memory of her dead husband and daughter never left her mind. If Gwaharad chose not to fight, it would be like her family dying twice, or even ten more times. She would not see that happen.

"What do you propose I do, Mistress Loran?"

Looking directly into Gwaharad's reluctant eyes, Loran drew a long breath, then spoke.

". . . I shall take care of the chariots myself. I only ask that His Majesty and his army keep the citizens of Kingsworth safe."

Belwin stood up, looking incredulous.

"You? Fight four Powered chariots alone? How will you do this? I have heard, from Prince Emere, that you have killed several Powered legionaries, and I know this is not something an ordinary warrior can do. But I have also heard you barely escaped with your life. Their chariots are built to fight monsters and columns of soldiers. They are nothing like Powered infantry. If you fail and get caught or killed, how are we supposed to fight them by ourselves?"

Had she been a monster, could she fight legion chariots? In this moment, Loran wished that she were. But all the gods and monsters that used to roam the world hadn't been able to stop the Empire from conquering it. Now most of them were dead, exiled, or captured. Kamori's Tree Lords were incinerated in their sacred groves. Arland's dragon was imprisoned in its own cave.

Emere raised his hand.

"The legions are made up of men, flesh and blood just like us. They have their metal boxes, but we have the element of surprise. If it ever becomes known that Mistress Loran asked for help and we did not give it to her, we shall never raise our heads high again. I shall accompany her with a hundred soldiers. A century with chariots will not have many legionaries on foot."

Gwaharad stroked his beard. "A hundred, you say."

"Arland's prefect Hesperus is old, and according to Lady Gladdis, the senator who was backing him is dead. There is a rumor that the Senate sent the Twenty-Fifth Legion here so that its legate should take over the prefectship, by force if necessary. A common game played in the Empire, is it not? If my judgment is sound, the prefect's guards will not come to the aid of the legionaries. If Mistress Loran could dispatch the Powered chariots, a hundred Liberators will be more than enough."

Emere looked determined. Loran observed Gwaharad's countenance closely. He still seemed undecided.

"If Kamori risks the lives of its people for Arland, what will the Princess of Arland do in return? How can you repay our soldiers?"

So now she was a princess. Loran forced the corners of her

mouth not to curl into a sneer. She had no time for anger or sarcasm. But she didn't have anything to offer Gwaharad either.

As she hesitated, Emere spoke.

"Your Majesty. Kamori once ruled all the Three Kingdoms. King Uter had made it so because he showed generosity far and wide. If we do not use this chance to earn the goodwill of Arland, who in these lands will follow us into the battlefield against the Empire? I beseech you to show your magnanimity by aiding our neighbor in their hour of need."

Gwaharad's eyes grew wide at Emere, but any sign of his displeasure quickly melted back into the façade of his usual kingly manner.

"Make it so, Emere."

Gwaharad stood.

"I shall also step forth into battle. Gather a hundred. It will take three days to reach Kingsworth, if we hurry. Let us pray that we get there before the Twenty-Fifth does."

"Your Majesty has my eternal gratitude." Loran bowed so low that her head touched the table.

Gwaharad raised his hand and said, "And Loran. Do not forget what we do for you today. This day, in which Kamori embraces Arland in its suffering."

Kingsworth used to be Loran's home. She had lived in a small house that doubled as her school, not far from the old king's castle. The castle was now the prefect's office, and the square before it where the market and festivals used to be held was now kept empty to convey the grandeur and authority of the Empire. There were many other squares within the city walls. Near the western gate was Fire-

Dragon Square, where there used to be a beautiful statue of the dragon. After it was carted away to the Capital, the first prefect renamed the place Liberation Square. Only the pedestal where the statue had been remained.

Loran had climbed up the high southern wall and was looking at Liberation Square to the west. Today, there were four Scorpios chariots of the Twenty-Fifth Legion's Third Armored Century in Liberation Square. Through the buildings between, she glimpsed a blue banner that had a beast that looked like a mix of a lion and a bird.

As Emere had predicted, the prefect's guard had retreated. There was also not a single guard watching the city walls. Clearly, the prefect's intention was to make himself blameless for whatever was about to happen that day. Then he would hold the Twenty-Fifth solely accountable for the atrocities, strengthening his position in the eyes of the Empire and the citizens of Kingsworth.

Even Loran, who knew nothing of politics, could understand that the Twenty-Fifth let their spite get in the way of their legate's bid for the prefectship. She briefly wondered if the same was true for herself, before shaking her head and refocusing on the battle ahead.

Emere and his soldiers were hiding in wait near the gates, but there were likely no guards there either. As a lifelong resident of Kingsworth, Loran knew that the prefect's guards normally were very lax about the city's security anyway, barring the immediate environs of the prefect's office.

Loran returned to inspecting the armored chariots. Each had six legs. The body was box-like, and there was an articulated tail arching forward, like a scorpion's. At the end of each tail was a

Sung-il Kim

heavy automatic crossbow. There were also a pair of large arms with pincers. Three out of the four chariots had cannons on top. The one that did not instead had the upper body of a man coming out from the inside. Loran assumed this was the centurion in charge. He wore the same Powered armor the centurion Marius had been wearing in Dehan Forest. A dozen legionaries in ordinary armor were blocking the entrances to the square, their swords and spears drawn.

About a hundred citizens were corralled inside the square. She spied even some children among them, and bit her lower lip. Earlier in the day, Loran had found it odd that such clear skies were bringing thunder, but the real source of the noise was revealed to her as she looked on—cannon fire from one of the chariots. The nearby bell tower had no top, and rubble was scattered at the foot of it.

"None of you know the culprit? Truly none of you has helped the pretender princess of Arland in her despicable deed?"

The centurion had a device that could amplify his voice using Power. It was so loud that Loran could hear it clearly all the way up on the city wall. Loran had heard such a voice years ago when she had seen the 171st Legion's parade with her daughter. Loran's heart gave a squeeze, before she pushed away the memory.

She quickly scaled down the wall. Even a second too late, and an innocent would die. It was a long downhill path from the southern wall to Liberation Square. Half the city, including a part of the square at the very bottom of the path, was in her view. Ignoring the puzzled looks of the passersby, Loran ran down the path, as she had twenty years ago, when the King of Arland fell from the back of the dragon.

The cobbled street veered north, a large inn occluding her view into the square. She ran faster, knowing that just around the corner she would be able to see into the square again. Someone shouted from behind her, but she could not pay heed. As she made the turn, the amplified voice thundered again.

"None? Then we shall have to ask you one by one."

As he said this, two legionaries dragged a young man from the crowd. He looked tall and strong but it would be impossible for an unarmed man to fight off two trained, armed men. He was thrown in front of the lead chariot. The thunderously loud voice began its interrogation, despite there being people in that square who did not understand Imperial. Just as Loran's daughter had not.

"Do you know who this thief and murderer claiming to be the princess of the Imperial province of Arland is?"

"I don't know!" The young man's voice was full of fear, but just as loud as the centurion's.

"Do you know who violated the Imperial outpost?"

"I don't know!"

"Do you know who it is that murdered Marius, high centurion of the Twenty-Fifth Legion, in such a cowardly manner?"

"I don't know!"

The half-visible centurion made a gesture with his chin. The two legionaries on either side of the man drew their swords and plunged them in his back. The young man did not even have the chance to scream. A gasp rose through the crowd, and then a murmur of discontent. Parents held their children tight and covered their eyes. When the centurion made his gesture again, one of the cannons of the chariots swiveled and took aim at the crowd.

"This is what comes of liars. Now bring me the next person. Of course, if there is one who should want to speak up, they are free to come forth now instead."

Loran was running. She was on the verge of tears. If only she had arrived a little faster, if only she had not attacked the outpost with no thought of what would happen afterward, if only she hadn't gone around saying she was a princess of Arland . . . At the bottom of the hilly street, the square was no longer visible. The centurion's voice, however, boomed in her ears.

"Do you know who this thief and murderer claiming to be the princess of the Imperial province of Arland is?"

"I do not."

It was the trembling voice of an old woman.

"Do you know who violated the legion outpost?"

"I do not."

"Do you know who it is that murdered Marius, high centurion of the Twenty-Fifth Legion, in such a cowardly manner?"

"I do not. But how I wish I did, so I can throw a banquet for her!"

The woman's voice rang out brazenly as she said this, so that the entirety of Kingsworth could hear. Nervous laughter rippled through the crowd in response.

Still running, Loran drew her sword as she approached. The legionary guarding the square entrance must have heard her footsteps and turned toward her. He raised his shield against Loran's blow but too late—his shield and his arm were sliced in two. The shield caught fire as the legionary grasped his burnt stump of an arm and screamed. Loran raised Wurmath again as a nearby legionary lunged toward her with his sword, out of reflex more than bravery it seemed. But his sword split like firewood to an axe as it landed against Wurmath's blade. The legionary backed away with fear in his eyes, and Loran did not bother pursuing him. Instead, she stepped into the square and shouted, "It is I. I burned your outposts. I killed your Marius. I am the Princess of Arland."

The sight in her missing eye returned in a rush, and she threw off her eyepatch, which had caught fire from the heat in her left socket. She touched her cheek. Scales. The crowd parted, giving her a path to the centurion.

Loran spoke to the people in the square as she walked forward.

"Return to your homes. The Twenty-Fifth Legion has no more business with you."

A moment of hesitation, then compliance. Hurriedly collecting the children and the elderly, the citizens vacated the square. The legionaries hesitated, not knowing whether to stop the crowd or not. The centurion spoke.

"Let the rabble go. We have what we want."

Loran was awash in guilt as she sensed the eyes of the people on her. *It's my fault. I should've kept my anger at bay. I was foolish, and these people paid for it. Buildings were destroyed. A young man was killed.*

Loran stopped once she was within throwing distance of the defiant old woman who had been dragged out of the crowd. She stood before the Powered chariot still, two legionaries holding her in place for the centurion's questioning.

The square was otherwise empty, save for the massive Scorpios chariots now taking up defensive positions around the square. The legionaries on foot stayed close to the chariots and kept their shields raised. A few readied their crossbows.

The old woman seemed to be missing an arm. A gust of wind made her empty sleeve flutter.

Loran heard the voice of not the centurion but the old woman.

"You are the one claiming to be a princess of this land?"

"I am."

"And you are the one who burned down the Imperial outpost?"

"I am."

"And you are the one who slew that centurion, Marius, I believe was his name?"

"I am."

The old woman with great difficulty straightened her back and shoulders.

"This crone you see before you followed the king to the battlefield twenty years ago when the Empire invaded. I lost my right arm then. My husband was killed at the king's side as well. And twelve years ago, during the purge, my son and his wife . . . I do not know where my grandson is or what he is doing. Countless people have fought the Empire and lost their lives. If you are truly a princess of this land, the one who will be our king, the burden you bear will be heavy and the road you travel long. So promise me this: that you will see the end of this tyranny."

Loran's throat had closed, she could not answer with her voice. She only managed to nod.

A smile spread on the old woman's wrinkled face. Her remaining arm shot into the air, and she shouted, "People of Arland!" Her amplified voice shook the city. "Come forth and bear witness! Behold, our future king!"

The centurion, who had been listening with his arms crossed, finally nodded to one of the legionaries. The legionary plunged his sword into her back. The old woman fell to the ground, her left arm still raised.

Loran stifled a scream and began to walk forward again. Her grip on Wurmath tightened, and the sword gripped back. Her left eye heated up, flaming with an intensity she had never felt before.

The centurion raised his hand in a signal. The chariots took their positions and trained their crossbow tails toward Loran.

Loran leaped forward like an arrow, and the crossbows fired at her in unison. Not one managed to hit her, and the bolts glanced against the flagstones instead. Crossbows reloaded, clicking all around her. Loran charged the nearest chariot, Wurmath swinging above her head.

Her arm and the blade were one. Red scales covered her right hand and arm. The blade was so hot, it seemed to shine like a small sun.

The chariot was more agile than it looked, stepping quickly out of her sword's path. She managed to land a blow to its side, taking off one of its legs, but that wasn't enough to make it fall. Its pincers swung to hit Loran, who found herself rolling on the ground of the square from the force.

Another rain of bolts. This time, they didn't come at once, the Scorpios chariots shooting in waves as they repositioned and recharged. Loran took refuge behind the stone pedestal in the middle of the square.

A shot had found its way into her left shoulder. Loran gritted her teeth and scanned the square, taking in the position of the chariots and the legionaries once more.

Then she saw the people.

The citizens of Kingsworth were spilling from the alleys. Even more than had congregated in the square before. They came armed with kitchen knives, sewing shears, and garden hoes. In Arland, non-Imperials weren't allowed to possess weapons without a permit, but evidently if the people were angry enough, almost anything could be a weapon.

The centurion realized what was happening.

"Do not approach the square! If you do, we will shoot!"

The formation momentarily took its focus off Loran, and this was her chance. Loran charged the chariot that the centurion was on, and with a swing of Wurmath, the lead chariot lost one of its pincer arms.

With the one it had remaining, the Powered chariot attempted to grab Loran's waist, but she leaped backward, avoiding it. Her body felt light, as if she had sprouted wings.

The nearest Scorpios chariot fired its cannon at her, a weapon reserved for monsters, fortress walls, or massed infantry. An ordinary man hit by a cannon would die an unspeakably mangled death, but the cannon was a slow thing and Loran had already been tracking the movement of the turret; instead of hitting her, the cannon created a large hole in the blacksmith's shop behind her. Thankfully the blacksmith was not inside—he was already in the square with his largest hammer in hand.

Loran found herself grinning, baring her new sharp fangs. The roads and alleys slowly filled with the Arlanders of the city, and the enemy had less and less room to maneuver.

Emere had told her that the chariot that held the centurion would also be carrying the Power generator, its Power being sent out to the other chariots. If she could destroy that, all the chariots would be helpless, and she would have a chance at victory. Loran brandished Wurmath as she charged the lead chariot once more, a veil of sulfuric smoke from the sword cloaking her. Her left eye could see clearly through the smoke; the centurion was shouting orders, growing ever more frantic.

Loran did not know where the Kamori army was, but it did not matter. The people rising up with their tools and even broomsticks to resist the Empire were Arlanders, and this was their home. The battle waging in these streets was not just between the Twenty-Fifth Legion and Loran but between the Empire and Arland. Loran realized she was no longer an ordinary woman. She was now a true princess of Arland. A representative of the fire-dragon.

Two cannonballs missed Loran by a hair as she soared into the air. Crossbow bolts that were shot blindly into the smoke grazed her cheek and thigh midair. But when she looked down at her leg, she saw only unharmed, pristine scales through the tear in her leather armor. She grinned and showed off her fangs once more.

The centurion in the lead chariot drew his sword and struck a defensive pose. His sword and gauntlet glowed violet as Marius's had in Dehan Forest. But at this moment, such things were meaningless to Loran. Landing on the lead chariot with a heavy thud, she raised Wurmath, staring down the centurion.

The centurion was a northerner, perhaps from as far north as Hyberia, his hair as white as snow. He was cowering, murmuring in a guttural language she did not understand. She looked into his scared eyes. They were the color of the sky on an overcast day. For a very brief moment she pitied this man, who was taken from his homeland only to die in this unfamiliar country. Then there was something else, her fury, her grief, and her thirst for vengeance tightly lumped into a savage red thing. It decided the matter for her. She sliced the centurion in two, along with his sword.

Loran then pierced the hull of the chariot and summoned dragonfire. Black smoke issued from the puncture, and violet light seeped out. Just as Loran flung herself off the lead chariot, it exploded, fragments deflecting off the scales on Loran's face and body. The Power generator destroyed, the remaining three chariots went limp.

The square was now filled with people. With their Powered machines rendered useless, and with a woman before them whose left eye was blue fire and whose sword was the color of the sun, the remaining legionaries put down their weapons and raised their hands in surrender.

Kingsworth roared.

13

CAIN

Cain followed the silent observer from the graveyard past the cabin-like houses and frost-crusted gardens that made up the outskirts of the Capital. There was nothing remarkable about the man's appearance. He seemed middle-aged and wore a nondistinct black coat very much like Cain's own. He blended effortlessly, changing his gait and posture to match whatever crowd he was moving with. A part of Cain admired his quarry's craft, while another part cursed it as he summoned up all his skills to keep up with the silent man.

It was a long pursuit, and the bustling streets were tinted blue with Powered lamps under the evening sun by the time they neared the city's central port. Walking along the docks, Cain wondered if they were heading to Gladdis's house. But the silent man took a different turn and entered the port's popular food street instead. Cain avoided this area—too many pickpockets hovering to prey on newcomers looking for a peck after a long sea journey. Half of the broad street was taken up with food stalls, the smell of spices from all over the world mixing in a strange yet mouthwatering bouquet that never failed to slow the movement of the crowd. Cain struggled around pedestrians who stopped without warning to buy or even just smell the food, but the silent man walked on as if nothing had changed.

Then, without slowing his pace, the man looked over his shoulder. They almost met eyes, but Cain managed to sidestep into a tented food stall, nearly knocking over the smoking grill. His spectacles slipped off, but Cain reflexively caught them before they could hit the ground. The silent man looked ahead again and walked on. The startled Cassian woman in the stall selling the mysterious skewered meats shouted in an unfamiliar language, but Cain could tell that it was likely curses. He put his spectacles back on, apologized in what few words he knew in one of the Cassian languages, and quickly left the stall.

There was quite a lot of distance between them now. Still, Cain doggedly pursued the man, going against the river of the crowd. People bumped into him and occasionally he had to fight through an especially thick eddy of passersby, but the man from the graveyard moved as if he was melting and flowing through the crowd, almost as if he could predict the motion of every person within the current. Did he know he was being followed? If he did, thought Cain grimly, he could have shaken Cain ages ago. Cain felt a swell of anxiety every time the silent man turned a corner. Was this where he would lose him? Or worse, would the man be standing there, facing him, expecting him?

Something in Cain's guts whispered that if Gladdis had a killer doing her bidding, it would be a man like this.

They had reached a remote end of the city docks when the

man finally stopped, miles away from the nicer side of town where Gladdis's house was. The man went inside a run-down house, and after making sure no one was watching, Cain approached the house himself. He crept around the side, looking for an alternate entrance, afraid at any moment he would turn around to find the silent man staring at him with piercing eyes.

Cain spotted a ventilation window that opened into the basement, but not only was it too small, it was also locked shut.

Suddenly, the door to the front creaked open again. Cain dropped to the ground in the alley. From where he lay, he could see the man walking away from the building and back toward the market. Cain sighed.

The dagger he had used to stab Devadas of the Ministry had never been returned to him, and he felt its absence keenly. Were there other people inside the house? It would be prudent to retreat and come back later, but perhaps this was the perfect time to break in, as he was sure the silent man at least was not there. Cain intuited that the man was not one he could win against in a fight or fool with his wits. Despite the cold, he could feel nervous sweat soaking his tunic.

Cain got up, tiptoed to the front, and looked closely at the door. There was a large lock attached to the latch, one that looked more like the kind that would be used in a warehouse, and one that Cain was certain hadn't been there a moment ago. The silent man must have put it there. Cain looked around again before taking two pins out of his pocket and sliding them into the keyhole of the lock. A lock like this, that could be opened only from the outside, suggested that there was no one inside. Within a few moments, he had picked the lock and stepped inside the house.

It looked like an ordinary, working-class house inside, exactly what you would expect from how it looked on the outside. The living room had lime-painted walls and the attached kitchen was narrow. On the second floor would likely be two bedrooms, perhaps a third.

Just in case there was someone there, Cain took off his shoes and carried them in one hand as he explored the ground floor. The place was covered in dust. In the living room there was an old, large, red rug, but no other furniture. There was nothing at all in the kitchen either. He checked the outhouse in the backyard. There was no smell. No sign that anyone lived in the house.

Cain went back into the house with less caution. Up the steps were two rooms after all, and neither of them had beds or wardrobes. In one was a shelf with a small plate about the size of his palm with a candle that had been burned almost to a stump. The sun had set. Cain prodded his coat and made sure he had his flint box with him. He took the dish and candle.

He sat at the bottom of the stairs and thought about where he might look next. It occurred to him that despite there being a ventilation window outside, he had seen no steps leading down to a basement. He got up and looked for an entrance in the back lot. Nothing.

Back in the living room, he noticed again the only piece of furniture in the whole house, the red rug. There was no dust about its edges. Cain peeled the rug back, revealing a trapdoor. He hesitated for a second, then lit the candle with his flint. He opened the trapdoor and descended.

The smell of mold pierced his nostrils. In the corner of the basement was a wooden box, about as long as he was tall. Fienna's coffin this morning flashed in his mind. He moved the candle closer to it. The planks of the box were unpainted. There were holes along the edge where it had once been nailed shut.

His answers must be inside this box—answers as to why Fienna had been murdered, and what, exactly, the Ministry of Intelligence was after.

He carefully opened the lid.

Inside was another box, this one wrapped in chains. A coffin made of lead. Cain had never seen a Power generator with his own eyes, but the soft violet light seeping out of it could be from nothing else. He gently pressed the right leg of his spectacles in place with his hand and bent over to look at the writing engraved on the coffin, a low hum reaching his ears as he did so. THE 25TH LEGION, CLASS 4 POWER GENERATOR, FREDERIKA. There was a griffin engraved on the coffin as well. It was perhaps the symbol of the Twenty-Fifth Legion.

A military Power generator. Cain remembered what Septima had said about a Power generator going missing in Arland.

All generators belonged to the Empire. Everyone knew this. It was common for a large private business to license the use of Power generators to assist in the running of a factory or farm, but there was a strict application process and each generator had a designated sorcerer-engineer attached, with unannounced inspections by the Office of Truth inquisitors. What lay before Cain was a military Power generator to boot. There was no explanation as to why it would be in the basement of a civilian house, other than that it had been stolen.

Just looking at this box might constitute a crime.

He closed the wooden lid. The answers he'd been hoping for

had not all been inside the box. In fact, it only contained more questions. The candle on the plate went out, and the sudden tang of smoke reached his nose. Cain felt his way out of the basement and opened the trapdoor. Thankfully, he was still alone. He returned the nub of the candle to its place on the shelf on the second floor, slipped out of the building, relocked the door, and made his way into the night.

The Power generator. He couldn't stop thinking about it. Why did Gladdis have it—if the person he'd followed was indeed Gladdis's man? And why did she bring it into the Capital? How did a merchant, however rich and well-connected, even manage to get ahold of it? And what did *any of this* have to do with Fienna?

He wondered whether he should tell Septima of what he saw today. If Septima got wind that a Power generator stolen by provincial rebel forces was hidden in the heart of the Empire, the Ministry of Intelligence—and the Office of Truth that controlled the use of all Power generators—would turn the city upside down looking for the culprits, and Gladdis would either go into hiding or be caught. Then the case would be beyond Cain's reach. He would never know what Gladdis had been trying to do or why Fienna had died. Compared to the interests of the Ministry of Intelligence, the Office of Truth, and the rebel movement, Fienna's death wouldn't even amount to an afterthought.

The Capital was the most powerful city in the world. In contrast, Fienna was only a worker at a small dye shop. People died every day. Compared to the immensity of the Capital, Fienna's death was a negligible one. She would be forgotten soon. Such things were inevitable in this city of millions. His heart felt the heavy grip again.

Cain, however, remembered. The Arlanders at the funeral also remembered. And more than anyone else, the culprit remembered. Whether it was Gladdis or the silent man or anyone else who had killed Fienna, Cain would not allow them to forget.

But if something happened to him—which felt more and more likely with every new secret he uncovered—there would be no one to do something about what he'd just learned. These secrets were too big for him to shoulder alone. He thought of Arienne. As a sorcerer, she was the closest thing to an expert that Cain knew. Had she left already? Maybe she had even been caught. But his meeting with Septima wasn't until midnight, so he had time. He made his way to Lucretia's.

14

ARIENNE

Arienne had been afraid her long, exhausting day might cause her to oversleep, but she woke up just as the sun went down as she'd intended. She felt well-rested. It was cold outside the covers, and she dressed quickly. For six years, she had worn only her school robes. Summer robes for the summer, winter robes for the winter . . . Her new tunic and trousers were still stiff and a bit uncomfortable, but she supposed she would break them in with time. She rubbed the leather patches that covered her elbows and knees.

It was snowing outside. Not the best day to begin a journey. Not the best season, in fact. But it wasn't like anyone could set a convenient date to leave their old life behind. This was her destiny, so to speak. It made her a little sad thinking of this.

Eldred had remained silent after Arienne had talked down to him. It was better this way. She wanted to stop hearing about his penchant for killing people, to say goodbye to the past six years in peace.

There was a knock at the door. She froze, unsure of what to do, until she heard Cain's voice.

"If you're still inside, let me in."

She withdrew the bolts and opened the door. Cain was standing there, the pair of spectacles on his face. A forced smile was on it as well.

"You're still here. I'm glad. You should wait until later in the night before setting out."

He was wearing a new coat. It was black.

Arienne nodded. "That's my plan. Thank you for the clothes and the bag."

This man had bought her clothes and also a meal at Lukan's. The money she'd brought with her from the school was in the sleeve of her old robe. The very robe she had left behind while running away from Duff. The few silver coins Lukan had given her were the only money she had.

Her cheeks flushed. She hoped he wouldn't think she was taking any of this for granted. She had intended to repay him, before she realized that she had lost the coins. Though even a brick of solid gold wouldn't be enough for most people to aid a runaway sorcerer.

"I'm sorry. I thought I had money to pay you back, but I don't." She bowed her head. How pathetic she must seem to him.

Cain didn't answer. He went over and sat in one of the two chairs in the small room. Arienne sat down opposite him.

"When I first came here to the Capital," said Cain, "I was twelve. I couldn't speak the language. The man I came with had left me to fend for myself . . . If my—" His voice faltered for a moment. "If Fienna hadn't helped me then, I don't know where I'd be right now."

"Who is she?"

"A woman, about five years older than me . . . And kind. *Feigere. Arleshe.* You remind me of her a little." Arlandais had crept into his Imperial.

"Your girlfriend?" She immediately regretted asking him.

"No."

"Just a friend then?" Why did her mouth insist on asking these questions, she wondered.

"Yes. She died. I'm trying to find out who killed her."

Arienne nodded. There was no tea to sip or biscuit to nibble to punctuate the silence. But this was not an easy topic of conversation to maintain.

As if reading her mind, Cain changed the subject. "Have you thought of where you might go?"

"Anywhere. I'm a sorcerer, so . . . I think I can manage wherever I go."

That was not true. She did not know any sorcery that could protect her, especially from the dogged manhunt of the Office that would inevitably ensue. But she couldn't bring herself to tell Cain that she needed even more help, for the fear that he might give it.

Eldred was still silent. She was glad he wasn't whispering to kill Cain before he could sell her out to the Empire.

"Well, it's just that some years ago I had a friend who was hired to help a runaway sorcerer . . . I'd assisted him with it. I think I understand what's involved."

Oh. She nodded.

"It was about five years ago, but the runaway never showed up . . . If you don't have a route in mind, I can tell you what we had planned for that boy back then."

She nodded again.

"The most important matter is to leave the Imperial heartland as quickly as possible. Four days at sea and three days across Ledon on foot will bring you to Arland. But there are clearance procedures on the docks before boarding, and records are kept . . . If you walk the eastern roads instead, you will arrive in about a fortnight. The road isn't that dangerous either. It took me twenty days to walk from Arland to here. I was very little then, and slow."

"I haven't decided if I want to go back to Arland . . ."

Cain shook his head. "If you speak such perfect Imperial outside of the heartland, you will attract attention. Unless you speak a third language fluently, hiding in Arland will be the safest for you. What's more . . ." He smiled. "I went to Fienna's funeral today and heard a very interesting story. There's someone claiming to be a princess of Arland who is fighting the occupying legion there. They say she was sent by the dragon and wields a flaming sword."

Arland's last king had died some years before Arienne was born. He had left no progeny from what she could recall, but had a daughter been hidden away all this time? Arienne imagined a young woman wearing a golden crown and shining armor, riding a dragon as she held aloft a fiery sword. In Arienne's imagination, the princess resembled herself.

"If she continues to do well, the Empire will be too busy to concern itself with a mere rogue sorcerer."

That made sense; what few runaway sorcerers there were would benefit from the Empire having something other than them to occupy its attention.

Cain named a string of passes, roads, inns, and villages, where she should go and where she should avoid. Arienne committed all of them to memory. It seemed that the sorcerer Cain had mentioned had also tried to run away to Arland or Kamori. Since that was five years ago, she knew why he likely hadn't shown up—he must have been that skeleton in the basement of the Academy.

"Thank you."

"And . . ." A shadow crossed his face. "Not to say I expect a favor in return, but I do have some questions for you."

Arienne straightened her back, her face attentive.

"How strong is a Class Four Power generator?"

"They're fairly uncommon. Any number lower than five is military grade, I should think. There might be a few in important buildings or very large factories." She had learned as much in school early on. It felt odd to think this was extraordinary knowledge to ordinary people.

"Is there a place one can be used without the help of a sorcerer-engineer?"

"Even the weakest Power generator requires the skill of a sorcerer-engineer. They need one to forge the control chains, distribute the Power output, and design the machines that would use it. The generators are useless on their own. Worse than useless. They're dangerous."

"Dangerous how?"

"With a Class Four, even a relatively stable one, you could blow up a large house if you aren't careful."

She could recite the precise Power output range of each class, but she doubted Cain would understand what they implied.

Cain was silent for a while, seemingly lost in thought.

Arienne became curious. "Why do you ask?"

"This is a secret. Perhaps an even more dangerous secret than your flight."

"Are you going to share it?"

"That's why I'm here." Cain looked very serious.

"Why with me?"

"Because someone other than myself should know this. Preferably someone who knows about such things better than I do." Cain bent closer to her and whispered, "In an empty house near the docks, someone has stashed away a stolen Class Four Power generator."

Arienne gasped. "A military Power generator? Who would do that? *How?*"

It occurred to her in a flash that she herself was, in fact, doing what she was so surprised at, as she was stealing Eldred, a Power generator, and herself, a future generator, from the Empire. She understood why Cain would share this with her, even if he didn't know the full extent of Arienne's actions. He needed to tell someone who would never go to the Office of Truth with this.

"It must be the rebels in Arland or Kamori . . . You know Dehan Forest, yes? The woods on the border of Kamori and Arland? The generator seems to have been stolen during a rebel ambush there. I found it, but I don't know how it would be used."

"Why were you looking for such a thing in the first place?"

"I wasn't."

Arienne thought quickly. Hiding a Power generator itself was easy; hiding a facility that used a Class Four Power generator would be like hiding a windmill. Maybe in a remote mountain it would be possible, but not in the Imperial Capital, where there were millions of eyes and ears. The best one could do with a stolen Power generator would be to lock it away from prying eyes.

"There is one *use for it."*

Arienne was startled by Eldred's voice suddenly speaking in her head.

"There is one very good use for a Power generator within the Capital. Unravel these bandages."

Arienne peered into the room of her mind. The withered lips that had been exposed were smiling. A smile that seemed to say, *I will give you what you want, if you do this one thing.*

She wanted to help Cain. But to do so, she needed to share a secret of her own.

"I also have something I want to show you. But you must prepare yourself."

She spoke calmly, but she couldn't help the beating of her heart.

Cain looked at her. "What is it?"

Arienne unraveled the bandage until Eldred's desiccated head was revealed in the room of her mind. His eyebrows were missing, and his eyes had deflated and were sunk deep in their sockets. He had no nose to speak of anymore. Eldred's mouth was little more than a ripped gash that revealed two rows of yellowed, sparse teeth.

Using the bandage, Arienne made a circle in the air that was large enough for a person to step through. Violet fragments of light kaleidoscoped inside. At the same time, in the room on the third floor of Lucretia's house, an identical ring appeared, the inside of it swirling with the same deep violet patterns. Cain looked surprised and bewildered.

"Step inside."

Even as his feet hesitated, his hand was already reaching into the ring, reappearing inside the room in Arienne's mind. Arienne watched Cain as he ran his fingertips along a leg of his spectacles, hesitating only a moment before stepping into the ring.

15

LORAN

". . . As you well know, I did not authorize the atrocity you saw in the square. To execute citizens without a trial, in the middle of a public square no less. Such a thing would be untenable under Imperial law and all that is good under heaven."

It was the morning after the battle in the square. Loran and Gwaharad were paying a visit to Prefect Hesperus's office. Officially, they were there as representatives of the citizenry to petition for redress, but the prefect knew as well as they did that the real reason they were there was because a hundred Kamori soldiers were holding the surrendering legionaries prisoner. The prefect's hair was grayer than Loran remembered, and his face more wrinkled. He was wearing a deep red doublet with gold buttons.

"Seeing what has transpired since then, I expect the Twenty-Fifth's Legate Aurelia to also blame it on some rogue element in her legion. That legion is mostly comprised of Phaidians. Unruly barbarians accustomed to pillaging for their supper. The legate is still on her way from Rammania with the main contingent of her command, which makes it difficult to accuse her of this heinous act."

The prefect's office had long drapes with a pair of falcons embroidered on them. Symbols of the Empire. Furniture made of luxurious dark wood, imported from who knows where. On the wall was an elaborate portrait of the prefect, painted in vibrant pigments that also had to be imported from afar.

". . . The right to resist unjust force is the natural right of any citizen of our Empire. Even if the orchestrator of this violence be an Imperial officer, these deeply illegal, unsanctioned actions . . ."

The scales had fallen from Loran's face and the light had gone out in her left eye. Her fury, however, would not subside. Hesperus was the prefect who had ordered the deaths of countless citizens, then had her husband and daughter killed for mourning them. This man, who had refused to grant her an audience no matter how desperately she had petitioned him, was now sitting in front of her and Gwaharad, spewing ridiculous excuses and acting like he cared about the citizens of Arland. He simply would not stop talking.

". . . The presence of the legion is, of course, wholly necessary to the security of Arland and the entire Lontaria region, but such things do happen on rare occasions. To mediate in such cases is also my duty as the prefect . . ."

Loran wanted to grab this man by his lapel and put Wurmath's tip on his throat, demanding an explanation for the murder of her family. It was as if her blood were boiling in her head. But she must not show it. Gwaharad had asked her not to cause trouble, had told her Hesperus must not be antagonized. That only the prefect could convince the Empire to blame the legion for the incident at the square. That they must use the friction between the Twenty-Fifth and the prefect as an opportunity. That it was crucial they did not put the legion and the prefect on the same side.

". . . And although there is talk of calling your people a rebel force, I have seen no evidence of such. You may call yourselves king and princess, but that in itself is no crime. Then we would have hanged 'the Salt King' or 'the Shipping King' who work in the market as pretenders. I myself know several women in Kingsworth who are often referred to as princesses." He laughed.

Loran did her best not to burn the prefect to a crisp.

"But what would you do in my situation? If, for example, you retreated at this point, I can make an official report to the Senate that will keep both you and me safe from blame."

"That is the right thing to do," Gwaharad said. "But my army suppressed the rogue legionaries' riot, and brought peace back to your city. Surely there must be some compensation for this."

Loran's head quickly turned to Gwaharad. Whether he hadn't seen her or was ignoring her, he continued to stare at Hesperus.

"Of course. How about ten thousand denarii?"

"Thirteen thousand. In gold, not silver."

"Then eleven thousand."

"Arland is lucky to have such a wise prefect."

They were talking like merchants at the market. Despite Loran's glare, Gwaharad didn't even give her so much as a glance. The prefect's eyes darted toward Loran a few times, but that was it. The two were acting as if they made such transactions every day.

Loran could not stand to be silent any longer.

"Your Majesty, what's the meaning of this?"

At her calm yet firm voice, the prefect and king stopped talking and turned to Loran.

"Two innocent people were killed, and the legion has wrecked Kingsworth. Are you to do nothing but accept his money and retreat?"

Hesperus, disconcerted, gave a polite cough. Gwaharad softly clucked his tongue to himself and said, "You've heard it yourself, Mistress Loran. The affair was not the responsibility of the prefect. It was the legion that was responsible. There will come a day when they answer for what they've done."

"This division between the legion and the prefect is the Empire's, not ours," Loran growled. "It does not concern us! How could there be a prefect without a legion, or a legion without a prefect?"

Losing her last scrap of patience, she drew Wurmath from its scabbard. Hesperus gasped and ran toward the window, but tripped over a rug and ended up grabbing the drapes, almost ripping them.

Loran's voice grew deeper and louder. Smoke issued from her new eyepatch, her left eye regaining sight. "If I slay this man, will the legion not retaliate? Then how is it you consider them as separate?"

Gwaharad, panicking, raised his arms toward her. "Princess, please be calm!"

Now she was a princess again? Loran did not turn away from the prefect.

"You know what will happen if you persist in this manner!" Gwaharad continued.

She knew. She also knew that the reason they were having this conversation with the prefect at all was because the people of the city were still riding high on their triumph, and Hesperus wanted to make the incident go away by blaming it on a rogue element of the legion. Had this been a real war, the prefect would have locked himself inside the castle and waited for the Twenty-Fifth Legion to arrive. Loran and Gwaharad were still in the shadow of the Empire.

She lowered her sword. Gwaharad assumed a persuading tone.

"The matter concerns not two, but hundreds and thousands of lives. What are we to do if the entirety of the Twenty-Fifth overwhelms Kingsworth?"

Her left eye lost its sight again. Wurmath stopped issuing smoke. Gwaharad took a step toward Loran.

"Liberation cannot be achieved in a day," said Gwaharad placatingly. "Do not forget that a moment of foolishness can cost us everything we've gained."

His voice was soft. The prefect, still petrified, would not let go of the drapes.

"Prefect Hesperus. Forgive us," Gwaharad said, turning back to the prefect. "The princess is still unused to the ways of the world and seems to have momentarily forgotten herself."

Loran sheathed her sword. Hesperus coughed again and leaned against his chair to stand up. A few guards burst into the room, but Hesperus dismissed them with a wave of his hand. He gave Loran a sidelong look before straightening his doublet and sitting down once more in as dignified a pose as he could muster.

"When will you give us our compensation?" Gwaharad asked.

"You shall have it when you leave. Will you join us for our midday meal?"

While the prefect and the king exchanged more pleasantries, Loran stared up at the golden falcons on the red drapes. The Empire was strong. No matter how strong Loran herself was, no matter how hot Wurmath might burn, it wasn't enough to stop the legion and drive the Empire out of her country. She needed to take what she could when she could; perhaps Gwaharad was right.

But there was still one thing she could not accept.

"What are you going to do with the gold?"

Their conversation interrupted, the prefect frowned. Gwaharad hesitated before answering.

"We will use it for the Liberators, of course. You need not worry about it, Mistress Loran. I will make sure my staff do not waste any of it."

"This is coin gathered by taxing the hard work of Arlanders. Why should it be spent on the Kamori army?"

Gwaharad smiled awkwardly. "As I've said before, the Kamori Liberators fight not only for ourselves but for the good of all the Three Kingdoms. I hope you come to see it that way as well. The princess shall have her turn—"

"That money is the price of the lives of two Arlanders," Loran cut in. Before Gwaharad could speak again, Loran continued. "The old woman in the square had lost her husband, son, and the wife of her son at the Empire's hand, and now her own life as well. You wish to fill your own stomach with the money made from that injustice?"

Gwaharad looked appalled. "How dare you speak to me this way?!"

Loran's vision filled with blue. Her burning eyepatch fell to the floor. She smothered the flame with her foot, then took a step toward Gwaharad.

"To be sure, Arlanders are not your own people. But even so, your lack of qualms is astounding. You dare call yourself a king? Much less speak for all the Three Kingdoms?"

Gwaharad's eyes were wide, his trembling hand on the hilt of his sword.

Loran drew Wurmath and swung the blade. But not at Gwaharad—at the prefect. Half the room was suddenly engulfed in blue dragonfire.

Hesperus screamed, but the sound soon disappeared with him into the fire. Gwaharad stared at Loran, dumbfounded, before running out of the door.

Loran stood where she was, watching as the red drapes went up in blue flames.

16

CAIN

Cain found himself in what looked like a child's room. Everything looked normal—there was a small bed, a shelf full of books, and a dresser with some drawers. But then, sitting on the edge of the bed was a dried-up cadaver wrapped in bandages. The bandages constrained the cadaver's arms to its body. Its legs were also tied together. Cain couldn't tell the body's age or gender. The only thing he could say for sure was that it was dead. Its withered lips surrounded a mouth that was torn at the sides, revealing teeth.

He tried hard not to be alarmed. He sensed this was not a space any ordinary mortal could understand, and there was no reason to understand it. Cain tried not to pay too much attention to the body but instead looked at the small shelf above the drawers. The books were mostly adventure stories featuring heroes of the Empire. Cain rarely read such books, but he recognized most of the titles of the books here. Among the smaller volumes, there was one larger book. *The Sorcerer of Mersia*. He had never heard of it, but he knew Mersia as the steppe country that was rumored to have been destroyed in a single night. Just as he stretched out his hand to it, Arienne's voice came from nowhere.

"This is not a real room. I imagined it using the memories of my childhood bedroom back home . . . You are inside my mind."

The window by the shelf looked out into the pastures of Arland, but the open bedroom door looked out into darkness. The darkness trailed into the room like smoke as Arienne walked through the door, but was sucked out through the cracks of the door as she closed it behind her. She pointed at herself. "This isn't really me either. The real me is outside, sitting in the room at Lucretia's. This is me as I think of myself."

"I am physically here but you aren't?" Cain asked.

Arienne shook her head. "I haven't attempted it, but I don't think I can go inside myself."

It was an imaginary space, created with logic that was beyond Cain's own understanding. He had no idea what was possible and what wasn't. Cain eyed the cadaver at the bed.

Arienne explained. "That man . . . Well, that's a Power generator. His name is Eldred."

Cain waited for her to continue.

"I stole him from the Academy."

"Why?"

"He asked me to. He promised me he would help me escape and teach me sorcery."

"Do Power generators normally speak and use sorcery?"

"Eldred is special. He can't cast spells, though. At least, not in this room. Probably."

Cain widened his eyes at Arienne. "Probably?"

"If he could, he would have done something by now."

The mouth on Eldred's face grew wider. The smile was reminiscent of another smile, one that had been carved onto the murdered woman's face at Lucretia's last year. But it also reminded him of the grin on the killer's face when Cain had confronted him.

Cain had never liked sorcery. When people came across something too difficult to comprehend, they would place the blame on a broken Power generator or some hidden sorcerer, choosing to ignore facts that were right in front of them. Cain considered such attitudes lazy, but still, sorcerers and sorcery existed in this world. If this was a room of Arienne's imaginings, anything could happen in here. The walls could collapse and monsters could appear, and none of that would be out of place. Cain hated the powerlessness it made him feel.

"Why did you bring me in here?"

Arienne looked taken aback by his tone and hesitated. Cain asked again, more gently this time. Arienne relaxed her shoulders.

"Because Eldred knows what that Power generator you found might be used for."

"Couldn't you just tell me what he said instead?"

"You're not the only one who wants to share burdensome secrets with others."

This was understandable. Cain nodded and turned to Eldred. He wanted to hear what he had to say and leave this place as quickly as possible.

Eldred spoke. "Then I shall tell you." He let out a long sigh, a small cloud of dust escaping from his lips with the sound. "You must be aware that the Empire uses something called the Circuit of Destiny?"

Cain nodded. He had heard of it. Something to do with pre-dicting the future using Power generators. It had greatly contrib-uted to the Empire conquering the world, but such things were beyond Cain's interests. Until now.

"It is perhaps the greatest of the Empire's treasures. The last testament to their ingenuity, before they devolved into the current sorry state where a sorcerer is only taught to barely light a candle." Eldred glanced at Arienne with his desiccated eyes. "They are go-ing to smuggle that generator into the Senate and connect it to the Circuit."

"To do what?" said Arienne. "Isn't it made of scores of Power generators? A single Class Four generator can't control all of that."

"Precisely," replied Eldred. "There are three hundred and twenty-seven Power generators in the Circuit that are at least Class Three."

Arienne looked surprised. "How do you know that so well?"

"I just do."

Cain watched them closely. Arienne seemed to distrust El-dred. She must've been fooled by him once or twice already. Maybe he had even tricked her into stealing him away from the Academy. Eldred, on the other hand, was enjoying this lack of trust. He rel-ished the power that came from keeping secrets.

Cain spoke up. "He knows because . . . Eldred was probably the sorcerer-engineer in charge of maintaining the Circuit of Des-tiny."

Eldred's shriveled eyelids trembled a bit.

"This one isn't completely empty in the head," Eldred mocked. "But he's wrong."

"Then you were part of the Circuit," Cain said immediately.

Arienne looked back and forth between them in surprise.

Eldred's grimace widened. "That's not what's important now. Think harder. If the Circuit can't be controlled, what can they do with it instead?"

Arienne said, "With over three hundred Power generators? They can't do anything except . . . overload the Circuit to make it explode? But that would mean the whole city would . . ." She gasped, her eyes darting to Cain.

Not meeting her gaze, Cain considered all he had learned in the days since Fienna's murder. He thought of Gladdis, who was being investigated for treason by the Ministry. Of the Power generator, stolen by the rebels. Of the silent man who went in and out of the house the generator was hidden in. Of this so-called princess of Arland. Of the Circuit of Destiny. Where did Fienna fit into all this? Was it a coincidence that he had encountered Arienne and Eldred?

"Not an unlikely plan, if inelegant. But there is another possibility," said Eldred. "Have you ever heard of the Star of Mersia?"

Everybody has, Cain thought. Mersia had declared independence and was devastated by the Empire as an example to the world. The Powered weapon used then was called the Star of Mersia. A weapon of absolute power, one that no one knew anything about, but at the same time one that everyone feared, whether they believed in its existence or not. Eldred did not wait for Cain's answer, as his expression made it clear that Cain had heard of this infamous weapon.

"An overload of the Circuit may take out the Capital. But in Mersia, nothing lives, not a blade of grass, not even worms. There are just ashes, dust, and dead things. So shall the Imperial heartland be, if the Star shines on it. For the Circuit of Destiny does not simply predict the future; it creates destinies. The Star of Mersia is one of the ways the Circuit can be used. A way the Empire will never use again."

Cain didn't understand. "What do you mean, never use again?"

"Well, you see, they weren't trying to use it that way in the first place. The Star of Mersia did not happen because the Empire wanted it." Eldred paused, as if savoring their shock. "In fact, Mersia had always been a faithful lapdog of the Empire. They had never declared independence."

Arienne said, "But then who brought Mersia to ruin, and why?"

Eldred's grimace returned.

"Indeed."

Since exiting the room in her mind, neither Cain nor Arienne had spoken. She sat on the edge of the bed. Her leather travel sack, packed and ready, leaned patiently against the bed as well. Cain sat next to it, on the floor, ignoring the chairs.

Eldred could be lying; the thought had crossed Cain's mind. But what else could be happening here? It sounded like a fantastical piece of propaganda concocted by the Ministry of Intelligence, of provincial rebels plotting to destroy the Empire and all it stood for. But that only made it feel more real somehow.

"Should we . . . tell the patrollers at least?" said Arienne finally, a look of disbelief still on her face.

Cain was supposed to meet Septima of the Ministry at midnight. It would make more sense to tell her instead of the patrollers. But was that the right thing to do?

To many people, the Empire was the world itself. It just existed, the way the earth existed or the ocean. What was about to happen would be like an earthquake or a tidal wave. But different. An artificial calamity. If that were so, the Empire also was not like the mountains or the rivers, for it was also artificial, built and maintained by the hands of people as well. Before the Empire conquered them, the Imperial provinces never would have imagined their kings or parliaments falling either.

"I will try to speak to the one orchestrating this. To hear what they have to say."

"You know who it is?"

Cain sighed. "I have a feeling."

Gladdis. Maybe there was someone behind her, but Gladdis for now.

"I'll leave the Capital as planned," said Arienne, "and maybe I'll learn more when I'm in Arland. Maybe if I met that princess . . ."

Cain nodded. Even if she never got to meet the princess, someone outside the Capital needed to know what was going on, or about to happen.

Arienne added sheepishly, "I'm on the run . . . I wouldn't be of any help to you. And even if I wasn't, I don't know how to do anything that could help in this situation."

She got off the bed. Cain looked up at her.

"Do you think if the Capital is destroyed, Arland will be free?" he asked.

"Maybe the whole world will be free. But what would it matter?" Arienne answered in a soft voice. "Hundreds of thousands would have died in the Capital alone. We've both lived here for a long time. Everyone we know would be dead. Maybe it's silly of me to say such things when I'm trying to leave everything behind, but . . ."

Well, not everyone would die, thought Cain. But many would, and the survivors would lose their homes and their work. Old Agatha, Lukan, Lucretia, even the shop clerk in the square who spoke awkward Imperial so confidently. And everyone who had come to Fienna's funeral, the people she took such care of . . . The pressure gripped his heart again, but in that moment of distress, pieces fell into place in his mind. Fienna, too, must have known about all this. She must have felt the same thing Cain was feeling right now.

And he finally understood why Fienna had been murdered.

17

CAIN

Cain knocked on the door of the agents' safe house near the docks. He still couldn't quite grasp the magnitude of the situation he found himself in. Gladdis was planning to set off a chain reaction of Power generators to destroy the Capital and bring down the Empire. Or perhaps even trying to re-create the Star of Mersia, which according to Eldred could erase all life from the entire Imperial heartland. He had never heard of anyone even attempting such a thing. But that princess of Arland was said to be bold enough to take on an entire legion alone. Maybe this sort of plan required someone just as bold.

But it did not seem likely to him that the hero said to be facing an entire army by herself with only a sword would be plotting indiscriminate mass murder in a faraway city.

He found himself rooting for the princess before he'd even realized it. He hoped she would have nothing to do with what Gladdis was planning, so he could continue to root for her.

The door opened.

Septima wore her black stola. She was not wearing a different gown of the same color, but the exact same stola—the almost invisible spot that had appeared when her wineglass had been shaken by Lukan's wiping of his bar was still there in the fold near her chest. There was a hint of powder under her eyes, perhaps to cover signs of exhaustion. She no longer smelled of perfume. A few strands of hair had come loose from her previously immaculate coiffure.

Devadas and the stout man looked similarly worse for wear. The stout man straddled a chair as he hugged its back, glaring at him with eyes full of suspicion. The giant Devadas leaned against a wall. Cain couldn't tell whether he was dozing off or just had his eyes closed.

"You made it on time. Did anyone of interest come to the funeral?"

That hint of fatigue in her voice. Cain nodded.

"Was it someone you know?"

He shook his head. "Black coat, medium height, medium build, thick hair. It's hard to describe. I never got a good look at his face."

"You can throw a rock in the market square and hit someone with that description," jeered the stout man. Cain still didn't know his name.

Cain shrugged. "It's hardly my fault he looks like everyone else."

"You think because we paid you you're Intelligence, too? You little—"

If it hadn't been the stout man who called him "little," Cain would have kept in his laugh. Something flew toward him and he ducked, hearing a shattering sound behind him. A jar had been smashed behind him. Not mad enough to get up from his seat, it looked like. Just as Cain was wondering what he had thrown at the jar, Septima said, "Look."

"What?"

Septima didn't say anything at first. She bit her thumb, thinking, before taking a step toward Cain.

"Was there anything else?"

"What?"

"Was there anything else that happened, at all?"

"Not really—"

"The badger is lying," said the stout man with a sneer, using a pejorative reserved for people from the northwestern provinces. "We know you bought a load of things in the market this morning. We thought you were going to make a run with the little money we gave you, but then you sent it off to a whorehouse instead?"

Cain was annoyed at himself; he hadn't thought they would be following him. Why would they? The money had been a generous sum, but not enough to change a whole life. Even if Cain had made a run for it, the amount would have been nothing to Ministry agents. Why were they surveilling some minor informant like him when they were so busy they had no time to rest their bloodshot eyes?

Maybe that was the wrong way to think. Maybe to the agents of the Empire, a provincial informant was a mere tool. And an artisan should always know where their tools are.

Devadas was now leaning against the only exit out of the room. His glowering eyes were now open and trained on Cain. Who knew what these three would do to Cain if he misspoke. His spectacles slipped down, just a little, along his sweaty nose.

Cain felt the urge to tell them everything about the silent man and the squirreled-away Power generator. But not yet—he had to find Gladdis first, he had to find out for himself first. He looked for something convincing to say, quick.

"You're not as smart as you look," said Septima. "How disappointing."

"Maybe the headquarters would get more out of him," said the stout man menacingly. Cain knew of a few people who had been dragged into the Ministry headquarters in the old city and released. One of them was still able to walk on their own.

Septima turned to Cain again.

"Think carefully before you speak. Lying has costs."

Cain sighed.

"I know someone who is from Arland. She can't be here anymore, so I am helping her leave the city."

"Who is this?" asked Septima.

Cain decided to risk it, as they would have surely already heard about a runaway sorcerer. "A girl named Arienne."

Septima and the stout man exchanged looks. It made Cain sure his lie would work.

"She said she was in debt with some dangerous people."

"Do you know her well?" asked Septima.

"No. We're both from Arland, but we've only just met."

"Where did she say she was going?"

"Why do you want to know—"

Septima put the point of her index finger on Cain's face, this time pushing up the spectacles that were sagging precariously on the tip of his nose.

Trying to seem hesitant, Cain said, "She wants to go back to Arland and become a farmer."

Septima grinned. The stout man burst into laughter.

"Something we can finally sell to the Office of Truth."

"The Office of Truth?" said Cain.

The stout man came over and slapped the back of Cain's head. "You fool, do you know who you've just helped? A runaway sorcerer from the Academy!"

Cain summoned all his skill to look as surprised as possible. "I . . . I had no idea! She never mentioned anything like that to me!"

Septima tilted her head, looking at him. *Really?* She was asking this with her eyes, not her mouth. Her eyes looked like they could bore through his lie. Cain tried not to resist her gaze. He concentrated on believing what he was saying.

Her gaze finally faltered. With a voice that was softer and more placating than before, she asked, "Think, Cain. Which route did she say she was taking?"

There would be no room for mistakes here. Cain said, "The docks would be watched by debt collectors, so she was going to take the land route . . . I didn't hear which."

"She'll take the boat for sure," said the stout man.

"What?" Cain said, as if he couldn't understand what the man was saying.

"No one is foolish enough to share her plans with someone she's only just met," explained Septima patiently.

"But what if she was lying about going home?" said Cain, feigning innocence.

"A child who was practically imprisoned in the Academy since she was ten? Where else would she go but home? She only speaks Imperial and her native tongue. She would be noticed wherever else she goes. The Office of Truth already have their people looking for her in that direction."

The very advice Cain had given Arienne.

"What are you going to do with me?" He no longer had to act scared. He was begging the heavens in his heart they would still find him useful. If he was handed over to the Office of Truth, it was all over.

Septima smiled. "You should be glad you told us about her. The Office of Truth . . . Who was in charge of this case?"

"Grand Inquisitor Lysandros," said the stout man.

"That ancient monster himself, over some runaway . . ." Septima trailed off. "The Office of Truth requested we look into this, as discreetly as possible. We haven't slept at all. If you'd said what you just said to anyone else besides us, you'd be dragged off to the dungeons by now. They don't know how to do anything besides torture," Septima finished with a roll of her eyes, looking somewhat relieved.

"I still don't understand why they wouldn't let us enlist the legions in the search, if this runaway is so important . . ." the stout man grumbled, crossing his arms.

"You know that if they want to issue a legion bulletin, they have to file a formal request to the Board of Legates. The Senate *will* find it suspicious, and the Office of Truth is clearly trying to keep this quiet."

"A runaway sorcerer is so important that she must be kept secret from the Senate?"

"The Academy has also been given a gag order. Have you ever heard of the Office of Truth making a request to us? This is serious . . . Of course there is more to it than meets the eye. But if we play nice and dig a little deeper, we may find something useful to us down the line."

In that moment, it came to Cain: The Imperial offices and ministries were not as omnipotent as everyone assumed. They needed each other to do their jobs. They had things to hide among themselves. The Ministry of Intelligence didn't know everything. The Office of Truth, with all its infamous inquisitors, needed help catching Arienne while keeping things secret from the Senate. From this new perspective, Septima and the others seemed less like a force of fate, and more like ordinary people trying to do the jobs they had been assigned to.

The stout man looked at Cain, his face more relaxed. "You're an unlucky one. Getting caught up in all this."

Septima picked up a glass of wine from a dusty side table, took a sip, and said to Cain, "Let's talk about your mission, shall we? Black coat, medium height, medium build, thick hair? Anything else?"

Cain shook his head. "Only that he slipped through crowds like a ghost."

"Did he catch you following him?"

"I don't think so. But he really did move in the crowd almost like he was dancing. Like a snake . . ."

Devadas took his back off the door. Septima and the stout man looked at him. Cain also hadn't expected him to respond.

"Safani," said Devadas.

Cain had never heard this giant say a word. His voice was deep, and he had drawn out the name into three slow syllables.

"Safani is dead." But the stout man's voice lacked conviction.

"We've thought he was dead before," said Septima in a low voice, "and we got Aquilla killed because of that."

171

"Who is Safani?" asked Cain.

"A mercenary often involved in provincial rebellions," answered the stout man. "Ten years we've been dealing with him on and off, but we still don't know his name. Safani is a code name Devadas gave the man. It means 'snake' in Varatan."

Septima sipped slowly from her glass of wine, thinking for a moment before saying, "Did you see where he went?"

"Gladdis's house, near the docks."

Giving them the most believable lie was Cain's only option, as he couldn't talk about the empty house yet. Septima spat a tut.

"We can't go in there. Why is the Senate always protecting her?"

The stout man answered her: "Because Senator Juliana is close to Gladdis—"

"It's not just Juliana. That badger merchant has at least seven senators in her pocket. To think of all that money she bribes them with!" Septima eyed Cain, as if regretting the slur.

Fienna's death was now connected to Imperial politics. Cain felt frustration at how the case was slipping out of his control. He cleared his throat, and the three of them looked at him again.

"Why don't I go? Isn't that why you're paying me in the first place?"

Septima gave a satisfied smile. The stout man gave the smile a puzzled look, turned his head to Cain, and said, "All right. But watch out. If Safani was really the one you saw, he'll have the likes of you for supper if you get caught."

18

ARIENNE

Arienne knew nothing of what an agent of the Ministry of Intelligence might look like, aside from what she had gleaned from adventure books. They wore sleek black clothes, knew strange ways of fighting learned from distant lands, were beautiful to look at, and always had a witty quip on hand in the face of a dangerous situation. Their day-to-day job involved saving the Empire whenever it was in peril. Then they would go on a vacation in a fantastic locale with other beautiful people.

There were no adventure books at all when it came to the inquisitors of the Office of Truth. In her mind, an inquisitor was a muscular, potbellied man with a black veil over his head who carried torturing implements. He'd be the sort to look right at home in a dungeon with some poor sorcerer's blood on his face.

Which was why, on the morning of the fifth day of her escape, she could hardly believe Eldred when he told her the very ordinary-looking man and woman sitting at the middle table in the inn's dining hall were inquisitors of the Office of Truth.

There were many people in the hall. Arienne lowered her voice. "How do you know?"

"I can smell their master's stench. They are the minions of the wretch Lysandros."

"Who is Lysandros?" It was not a rare name in the Capital.

"Their superior, who else? Unlikely they're here to do anything to you. Their mission is probably to keep you in sight until Lysandros arrives. Turn your head toward them as naturally as possible."

She did. In the corner of her eye, both quickly looked away from her and at their bowls of porridge. The two of them looked like mundane travelers in their thirties. The knives they wore on their belts might attract attention in the city, but they were crucial tools for anyone on the road. Their gray clothes and leather shoes were also typical. The medallions they wore around their necks, however, were distinct. Arienne turned her eyes back toward her own bowl.

Why had they followed her all the way here? Arienne had safely left the Capital and passed several guard posts without incident. No one seemed to be looking for a runaway sorcerer. Only thieves, murderers, or traitors, their likenesses drawn on broadsheets and plastered on the billboards along the road. Arienne had begun to hope for the past few days that the Office of Truth had been completely thrown off her scent.

Eldred said, *"If you were alone, the Office of Truth would have issued bulletins, and a hundred legionaries would be looking for you at every legion watchpost. And you would have been caught. But Lysandros is being careful not to let too many people know about your escape, as I am his little secret."*

Arienne was only a runaway sorcerer. But Eldred was a Power generator who had maintained his sense of self. Perhaps the only one that had in the whole world. It was a secret that must be kept from the legions, evidently. Maybe that was why he had been buried so deeply at the Academy.

But that would mean the Office of Truth knew the truth about Eldred.

". . . Then do they know you're in my mind right now?"

"Maybe not those miserable underlings. But Lysandros might have an inkling. He knows what kind of sorcery I'm capable of."

"Who *is* this man?"

Eldred ignored her question. *"Now might be a good time to lose them. Since you can't function as a proper sorcerer."*

"And you can?" Arienne scoffed into her food, but he was right. She had to lose them.

Arienne forced down the breakfast she was suddenly too nervous to eat. The sausages, porridge, bread, even fruit and vegetables, grew odder and stranger in colors and shapes the farther she got from the Capital. What had food tasted like in Arland? Would it also feel strange on her tongue?

She rose from the table and took the steps up to her room. It was impossible not to feel the eyes of the two inquisitors once she became aware of them, but she forced herself to act normal. Locking the door behind her once she was in the room, she picked up her sack and looked out the window. The building was a low two stories; she figured she could safely land a jump from this height, though breaking a leg while the Office of Truth agents were this close would be a death sentence. She spotted a drainage pipe next to the window.

The windowsill was just wide enough to support her foot as she stepped up onto it. The copper pipe was blue green with rust, and the wooden pegs that fastened it to the wall hardly looked strong enough to sustain a good wind, much less her with her traveling pack in tow. Hoping she had perhaps lost some weight the past five days on the road, Arienne slowly gripped the pipe and eased her body off the window ledge. The pipe creaked, but it did not tear from the wall and send her crashing to her capture. Gripping it lightly with her hands and knees, she slid carefully down the side of the inn, holding her breath until she reached the ground.

The inquisitors had no doubt ridden here on horses. Leaving by the main road now would guarantee her capture. But going too deep into the woods risked meeting wolves or getting lost. As she was thinking through the best course of action, she noticed a tower rising above the forest pine.

A sorcerer's tower. Before the arrival of the Empire, many sorcerers cloistered themselves in such towers. They had been built all over the world, and maybe sorcerers somewhere did still live and practice their arts in them, but not here. Some of the towers right outside the Capital housed Power generators now, but this one looked dark and quiet.

Arienne crouched low, and with as much stealth as possible—another thing they didn't teach at the Academy—she stole away into the forest.

The tower was farther away than she'd thought, and it was just past noon when she arrived. No one seemed to be following her, but there was nothing she could do about her footprints in the snow aside from using bare rocks as stepping stones or crossing streams she did not need to cross. Not having spent much time outdoors, she wasn't sure whether such methods would be effective. The stream water that seeped into her boots had her feet aching with cold.

The tower was narrow, but it was taller than any tree in the forest. There wasn't a single inch of it not covered in ivy. Each block of stone was outlined in lichen. The door had crumbled to the point where not even fragments of it remained. The tower had been abandoned for a long time.

The inside was dim, but there was some sunlight filtering through the ivy that covered the windows. The staircase that spiraled up the interior connected the floors of the tower, or at least the floors that hadn't caved in from rot. The stone stairs themselves, however, were intact.

She climbed it up and up, reminded in reverse of when she had gone down deep into the underground of the Academy to steal Eldred.

The topmost floor had not caved in. Mysterious metal instruments were scattered about, smashed into pieces. There was a half-burned tapestry hanging by a single rusty nail. She took it down and unfurled it to reveal a star chart.

"This was an observatory . . ."

At the upper end of the broken ladder was a skylight. Arienne pictured whoever lived here having gone up the ladder to observe the stars and augur the future. Maybe from the stars, that sorcerer had learned the fate that awaited them, had foreseen the arrival of the Empire that would conquer them.

There was a wooden bookcase lying broken on the floor, surrounded by books that had turned to mold from the winds and rain that had made it inside the chamber over the years. Arienne tried to lift the bookcase upright, but it refused to budge. She sat on it instead. It was less cold than the stone floor. She took off her boots and wrapped herself from the neck down in a blanket. She couldn't risk lighting a fire, but even just drying her feet made her feel much warmer.

She found herself idly thinking of the soft bed and the thick sheets she had at the dormitory. There at the school, her life had been comfortable, safe, and predictable . . . Then she shuddered at the thought. She was not the kind of person to trade freedom for a bit of comfort. At least, she was determined not to be.

Eldred said, *"What do you plan to do now?"*

"Hide here until tomorrow morning and go out onto the main road through the forest once the sun comes up. In two days, I can cross the river and enter Marthia. There we can take the smaller local roads to lose whoever follows us." She answered promptly, recalling the escape route Cain had explained to her.

She could see Eldred nod in her mind. *"They probably expect you to be going to Arland. Lysandros is sure to try something overwhelming in the coming days. But we'll deal with that when it happens."*

"You keep talking about him. Who is he?"

Eldred didn't answer but lowered his head. Arienne imagined herself into the room in her mind. Nothing had changed with Eldred since the bandages wrapping his head had come off. He spoke when he wanted to and was silent otherwise.

She approached her bookshelf. *The Sorcerer of Mersia* was not a book she had owned as a child. It had come here with Eldred. And when Cain had entered this room at Lucretia's, the book had been there as well. Arienne had no recollection of putting it there. Eldred couldn't have either, as he couldn't move his arms.

The book wasn't on the shelf. Nor on the bed. After a moment of thought, Arienne got on her knees and reached below her bed. Ten-year-old Arienne had hidden her diary there. Her fingers brushed up against something. It was *The Sorcerer of Mersia.*

She gripped the book in her hands. Here was a story that was inside her mind, but a story she did not know. She closed her eyes and concentrated on the texture of the book against her fingertips, imagining the shape of the book. Remembering the impressions in the leather cover. The glint of the gilt lettering. With the book in her hand, she stepped out of the room.

There, sitting on the fallen bookcase on the topmost floor of the tower, Arienne now drew a book from underneath the blanket. It was *The Sorcerer of Mersia.*

19

LORAN

Loran's thoughts were endless as she left the prefect's castle. The citizens of Kingsworth shouted her name, calling her their princess. But she was awash with dread, not for herself, but for the cheering people.

Gwaharad looked more afraid than furious and was silent as they took the streets toward the city's exit. When he finally spoke, as they were passing through the south gate, his voice was trembling and low.

"Mistress Loran, a legion has six cohorts, a cohort ten centuries. You vanquished a single century out of sixty such, and saw it fit to execute the prefect. Do you understand what kind of calamity you have brought upon all of us?" Gwaharad threw his right hand back, in the direction of Kingsworth. "To all of *them*?"

Of course Loran understood. It was all she could think about since the moment she set fire to the prefect's office. She also knew that once the feeling of victory waned in the city, the people would realize the same thing.

A hand rested on her left shoulder. It was Emere. He had his eyes fixed on the road, with a grim determination that Loran had never seen on his face before.

Why had she done it? Had it been to avenge her family? If so, had she succeeded in that? Could a person become king solely through acts of vengeance? Was what she had done something that was needed to become king?

She looked back at Kingsworth, where her empty home was, where they were still chanting her name. She, a self-proclaimed princess and future king, had betrayed her people to their doom. She could not bear to stay there a moment longer.

Emere whispered, in his calmest voice, "Your Highness, perhaps it would be best if you were to collect your thoughts back at the palace."

She nodded. At least Emere would be there. She had nowhere else to go.

For the three days it took them to get back to the underground palace, few words were exchanged. Despite the heavy air, a few of the Kamori soldiers tried to congratulate Loran, but the others silently discouraged them.

Once back at the Kamori's underground base, she didn't leave her room. Gwaharad didn't summon her, and only Emere continued to see her, coming by every day for their midday meal. He would tell her the news, but even he avoided talking about the prefect. Loran's thoughts kept her awake as she lay alone in her bed each night.

The Kamori Liberators declared the battle at Kingsworth a

victory, but morale was not high in the underground palace. Reports of the Twenty-Fifth Legion's movements raised tensions even more. The legion force currently in Arland, having lost a chariot century, had holed themselves up in their fortress, but the main contingent of the Twenty-Fifth was due to arrive any moment. Kamori scouts relayed rumors that a gigatherion was on its way from the Imperial heartland.

Five days after they had returned, Gwaharad declared a feast would be held in honor of their victory. Loran was strongly requested to attend, as the celebration would be awkward without the greatest warrior in that battle.

The mood at the table was far from festive, though, the air full of dread and anxiety. Gwaharad, as if painstakingly curating this mood himself, looked grave throughout the evening and ate almost nothing.

Loran was seated at the far end of the table, away from Gwaharad. The food was of excellent quality considering they were a rebel army at war hiding underground, but Loran was not in the mood for delicacies either.

The banquet wore on, and as the evening grew late, Gwaharad tapped his glass with a spoon. The murmurs subsided.

"The Kamori Liberators have garnered a great victory. We have gone to the aid of our neighbor Arland, driven the Imperial curs from Kingsworth, killed the prefect Hesperus, and raised our glorious name as the true guardian of the Three Kingdoms. We must celebrate!"

It was a self-serving version of the events, but the hall was awash in applause and even some cheers. Loran raised her glass as well. Gwaharad waited until it was silent again to speak.

"As you all are aware, it was Mistress Loran who was most instrumental in bringing about this victory. Her sword sliced through the Empire's Powered chariots as if they were turnips. She saved many Arlanders who would have otherwise died at Imperial hands. It was also Mistress Loran who passed judgment on Arland's prefect Hesperus, who had been weaseling out of his complicity."

More clapping and cheers. Loran nodded in acknowledgment, out of courtesy more than anything.

"But even victories have their price. Even in this moment, the main contingent of the Twenty-Fifth Legion is on its way here. Legate Aurelia is losing sleep in her thirst for vengeance, no doubt. If we do not prepare for this, the world shall remember us as fools who insisted on starting what they could not finish." Very briefly, Gwaharad's gaze fell on Loran.

The banquet hall filled with murmurs of assent. The doors opened, and some soldiers brought in kegs and goblets. As everyone took a goblet, Gwaharad looked at Loran from his place across the room and spoke in a voice that sounded almost humble.

"Princess, what say you—will you surrender yourself to the Empire?"

The almost hundred people at the banquet fell completely silent. Loran turned her face to Gwaharad. His eyes avoided hers, instead darting among his staff. She had expected something like this to happen, but actually hearing those words, in that placating tone, made her heart ache and veins burn.

Gwaharad continued, almost pleading, "That is not what I myself wish at all, but they will not be satisfied until they have you. Think of Arland, of all of the Three Kingdoms. Lay yourself down for the good of all."

Some looked back and forth between Loran and the king, their expressions incredulous. Others were nodding silently. While she wasn't surprised by his request, she didn't answer right away. She needed to hear every word Gwaharad had prepared for this audience.

"It's a matter of time before the Twenty-Fifth Legion arrives in full force," Gwaharad continued. "How noble would it be to save a whole country with just one life? You have already done more than one person possibly can. Having burned down the prefect's castle and destroyed an entire Powered century, you have ensured that the Empire shall never again attempt the kind of tyranny that they had undertaken in your land."

He sounded almost convincing. Loran tried to keep the mockery out of her voice as she said, "I am honored by His Majesty's great concern for Arland."

"This is not merely a matter for Arland. We aided in what happened, so the Empire's ire will extend to Kamori."

"Is that what you fear, Your Majesty?"

The banquet hall, already quiet, somehow became even more silent. As if the world itself had stopped breathing.

Even Gwaharad seemed momentarily taken aback. Loran could feel her left eye beginning to see once more. The silence in the room was a thunder of fear.

"It is," said Gwaharad. "There are two hundred brave men and women gathered here. I cannot throw away their precious lives because a guest overreached herself."

Murmurs again. Emere, sitting beside Gwaharad, kept his head down and his eyes trained on his plate.

"And for what purpose, then, have these two hundred people gathered?"

"Certainly not to die because of your recklessness."

"Then have they gathered here so you can play soldier, Your Majesty?"

Belwin, also sitting next to Gwaharad, leaped to her feet. The scar on her shaved head had turned bright red.

"Do you mean to insult everyone here?"

Several other officers stood. Loran also stood, and bowed deeply. She turned to the room.

"There are two hundred gathered in this palace to fight for Kamori. I have not heard of even ten Arlanders gathering to fight the Empire. Because Hesperus had massacred innocents based on suspicion alone, nobody dares rebel. Kamori is truly a country of warriors." Loran paused. "But I did not know any of you existed. Nor did I know there was a King Gwaharad until I met him in Dehan Forest."

A few people made to stand but sat down again. Uncomfortable coughs.

"The day I returned to Arland, two people died by the hands of the Empire in the square. But because of those two people, four chariots were destroyed, and that heinous prefect was finally killed. Those two murdered people were precious lives. But with such precious lives . . ."

Her husband and daughter . . . Her right knee almost buckled. Perhaps she was too agitated. Loran placed both her hands on the table to steady herself.

"Such precious lives were being bargained on the prefect's table for a few gold coins. I could not stand there listening to such things. I may not be the child of a king, but I have styled myself a princess. Many may scoff at me for doing so, but as long as I have, there are things I would rather die than do."

Her legs were about to give way. She tried to lean on the table again but her hands were limp; she could only grip the tablecloth with her fingernails as she fell to her knees, bringing down the tablecloth and some of the plates with her. The plates shattered around her. She tried to stand, but her legs were too weak. Her hand gripped the hilt of her sword but her arm was not listening to her. More murmurs. Shouting. Soldiers approaching . . . five? Seven? A dozen? Her vision was blurring. Loran stared at Gwaharad. He had stood up and was looking down at her from his seat.

". . . You've poisoned me? Because you feared the legion's retaliation? Because I might not agree to surrender?" A bitter, weak laugh escaped Loran. "Why do any of you pretend you fight?"

Even speaking was difficult now.

The soldiers, waiting for a drug-induced opening, were creeping up to her. Emere had grabbed Gwaharad's arm and was shouting at him, but Loran could no longer distinguish words.

Her left eye ignited.

Her whole body suddenly grew hot and the poison coursing through her dissipated, not virulent enough to withstand the heat. Strength returned, tears threatened. Loran stood, and the soldiers approaching her instantly fell back. There was no longer anyone sitting in that banquet hall. They had all risen from their seats and were staring at Loran.

The poison subsided, but Gwaharad's words remained. She had barely defeated a single armored century. There was no way she could fight an entire legion by herself.

"I *will* surrender to the legion."

"That's suicide!" shouted Emere. "Please, Princess, heed not my brother's words!"

"Be quiet, Emere!" Gwaharad shrieked.

Loran smiled. "It is not his words that moved me so. I had a mind to do it for days now. He is right in that it is the only way to stop the Twenty-Fifth from retaliating against Arland."

There was surprise, shame, and something like guilt in the eyes of those gathered. Gwaharad spoke, suspicion in his tone.

"And you expect us to believe what you say? That you will walk to your death on your own two feet?"

"*You* may not be able to believe me, Your Majesty," said Loran, "but there are many in this hall who will willingly lay down their lives for their family and their neighbors. *They* will not find it strange there is one more such person among them."

A look of incomprehension crossed Gwaharad's face.

"I shall put it in terms you might understand," said Loran. "I could kill everyone in this hall and take this palace, so why would I bother lying to you? Make way."

The poison still lingered. Her steps were a little unsteady, her head still swimming. But when Loran drew Wurmath, everyone gave her as much room as they could. She walked out into the hall. Soldiers were gathered there as well, but they only watched her pass, their backs close to the walls.

How small and suffocating this place seemed now. Perhaps it was the poison; perhaps she was just tired. The Princess of Arland silently resheathed Wurmath and stumbled her way through the dark tunnels of the underground palace.

20

CAIN

The Capital's winter tended to turn strangely warm this time of year, and the docks were packed with pedestrians and carts alike, everyone trying to get as much work done as possible before it inevitably turned freezing again. Around sunset, Cain was sitting at the end of an alley on a discarded wooden crate, watching five children walk toward him. He put on his spectacles, which he'd taken off to avoid standing out, and took a few silver coins from his pouch.

"We're here."

It was the oldest girl, who was also the smartest. Her name was Ayana, and she looked about fourteen. There was a spiral scar on her left cheek, made with great care. Ayana had negotiated shrewdly with Cain on their pay, but Cain was even more impressed with her insistence that he pay the coins in multiples of five, so that she could divide equally among the children.

"How did it go?"

"The money first."

Cain had already taken out half the promised amount from his pouch. He handed it to her.

"You'll get the rest when you tell me how it went."

"It's only half," said the boy next to her in a heartlander accent. The girl counted the coins.

"It's all right," said Ayana, "we'll just tell him half, then."

Cain raised his spectacles with his fingertip and said, "If there's no trust in a transaction, the whole business becomes very tedious." Cain sighed with slight smile. "Tell me, and you'll have the rest."

"You're joking?" Ayana said with a cock of her eyebrow. "If there was *trust*, you would give us *all* the money. This isn't your first time with us."

She had a point. He handed her the rest. Ayana quickly counted it, put it in her pocket, and looked around her. Satisfied no one was listening, she said, "We did what you said and watched from a different place than last time."

"You weren't seen?"

Ayana shook her head. "It was easier this time, the scary one wasn't there."

He had put the children on surveilling Gladdis's house by the docks for six days now. They learned that the man Devadas called Safani came and went from there as if it were his own home. Whenever the children reported that Safani was at the house, Cain had slipped into the run-down house to check on the Power generator hidden there. It had disappeared from the basement yesterday, as if it had never been there. Whatever was going to happen, Cain's time was running out.

He had been preparing to infiltrate Gladdis's house for almost twenty days, which flew by on account of his having had so much to do. He had to convince the local thieves that his suspicious-looking activities did not pose a threat to them. He had to make deals with the dockworkers and patrollers. Then there was the actual casing of the joint, for which he had enlisted the children's help. It was the longest time and the most effort he had spent on a single job. Everything had to go right. He could not afford to be careless in any way; the stakes were too great.

During all that time, he spoke not a word to the three Ministry agents about the hidden Power generator or his suspicion of Gladdis's plan to destroy the Capital. He rationalized his silence by telling himself that the information was not reliable, coming from a cadaver of a sorcerer, and that Arienne might get into even more trouble if he revealed how he came by it.

"And we saw something you might like."

"What did you see?"

Ayana looked up at him and held out an empty palm.

Cain frowned. "I told you I'd give you more once the whole business is done. Unless you want to get some now and much less later."

Ayana looked peeved.

"Well, an old woman with expensive clothes was there."

Gladdis was finally in the city? That was somewhat reassuring. They wouldn't blow up the city if Gladdis was in it. If that was what they were going to do . . .

"What did she ride in on?"

"Carriage."

"Was it dusty?"

"Dust, dirt . . . A lot. And that cloth hanging on the side . . ." She mimed its shape, moving her hands up and down.

"The dust screen?"

"The dust screen was torn a little. It had the same emblem as the one on the house gates."

"And the horses?"

"Covered in mud."

Gladdis had come a long way, then. Maybe she just arrived from Lontaria. Which meant today was his perfect chance.

"What was she wearing?"

"A fluttering blue dress." She mimed the motion again. It looked like dancing.

It reminded Cain of when he'd first come to the city. Not knowing the language, he had used every gesture he could muster. Even after Fienna had taught him the language, it took awhile for him to drop the habit of gesturing. He had a sudden memory of watching Fienna's lips move as she taught him words.

"Was her dress ripped as well?"

"No, it was like new. Not dirty. Very pretty, and shiny."

Cassian velvet. It didn't stain or wrinkle.

"And shoes?"

"Shoes . . ." She turned to the others, who all shook their heads. "We didn't see her shoes."

Cain nodded. "It's okay. Not important."

Ayana continued to report on the security and the general feel of the place. There didn't seem to be much change, even with Gladdis's arrival. That was a good sign.

"Good. Well done. Come back here tomorrow and I'll give you your prize."

"Then we're finished?"

"We are."

Ayana looked a little disappointed. "Why tomorrow?"

"Because I need you all to not tell anyone until then."

"How will you know if we told anyone or not?"

"Because if you do tell anyone, I'll be dead before the sun comes up tomorrow."

He couldn't help feeling a little disgusted with himself for saying this, since it was a form of threat, an attempt to manipulate the children using the prospect of being responsible for his death. Ayana and the children had done well so far, and there was no sign of them having ever talked to anyone about him. But he needed to make sure this continued.

Ayana was solemn. "All right. We won't tell anyone. And you won't die."

Cain quoted a Bachrian proverb: "Silence and care catch lions."

Ayana made a big smile and replied, "While loose lips and inattention lose buffaloes."

He dismissed them, and stood up from the crate. He took off his spectacles and put them away in their case again, and left the alleyway.

Cain went to the shop where he'd purchased the new clothes and pack for Arienne twenty days ago. He needed supplies of his own now. Cain knew the shop clerk had leaked his whereabouts to the agents after his last visit, but either he did not recognize Cain today or he simply did not understand the magnitude of what he had done to him. The man only smiled warmly and said "Your good benefit!" about the hooks and ropes he recommended to Cain.

Gladdis's house had only two entrances: the front and the back. Both doors had guards. But there was a possible point of entry in the small gap between a toolshed and the outer wall. He could hide in the gap and cross the unlit yard to approach the side of the main building. Ayana had told him about it when she'd climbed to the top of a bell tower to peer into the property. The wall was high. It required ropes and hooks to scale, but thankfully it was by an alley that rarely saw passersby. If he went over that part of the wall quickly and silently, he would land behind the shed without being noticed.

As it was the season for the last of the year's Dalosian olive oil to come in, the docks were busy day and night and the patrollers were mostly concentrated near the off-loading areas. As long as he was dressed like a dockworker, it would attract no suspicion to be holding a sack full of equipment.

It wasn't as if he had never broken into a home in the middle of the night before. Before Fienna got him the job at the oil shop, Cain had committed almost every crime a child could possibly commit. He had also been lighter and faster than other children, which allowed him to become adept at breaking into homes on the second floor. Like Ayana, he had also done surveillance jobs for adult burglars. But all that was years ago. Could he scale this wall without getting caught? If the silent man Safani was inside, he could be watching this very gap on the other side for all Cain knew. Or the ex-legionary from the dark alley that night. Sneaking in was one thing, but he had never learned how to fight properly. There were so many ways this could go wrong, even after so many days of preparation.

But no one was there to do it for him. For Fienna . . .

Later that night, Cain approached the alleyway next to Gladdis's house. He was dressed in dockworker's clothes, with his new black coat over them to guard against the cold. On the limewashed outer wall, right at the bottom edge, was a mark Ayana had left with her sandal. This was where the shed would be when he climbed over the wall. Not even Ayana could determine what the security situation was like inside the main building itself, but crawling into a window should have the least chance of being discovered. No one would leave a window open in this cold, but he had a crowbar in his sack that, properly used, could quietly dismantle windows, in case it was not possible to simply open them.

He stuck a lead panel on the base of the streetlamp in the alley. The light blinked for a bit before going dark completely. Days of reconnaissance had established that this was a common enough occurrence in this part of the city.

He tied his sack to his shoulder and threw the grappling hook over the wall, which was about three times his height. It lodged firmly in the iron spikes on top. The clang of the hook was louder than he'd expected; he looked around him one more time and adjusted his spectacles so that they were secure on his face. He climbed the rope, almost bounding up the wall. At the top, he loosened the hook, and lowered himself over the side of the wall until he was hanging with his arms fully extended. He let go and landed on his feet against the dark ground. It was soft earth and weeds; he staggered a little, having expected a firmer surface.

The shed smelled of rot from its damp planks, thanks to the warmer weather melting the snow. Careful not to make any sound, he walked sideways through the gap. The yard was quiet. The three-story main building had no open windows, as expected. There was almost no light seeping from the windows on the upper floors. A lamp shone by the front door. From there, the guards' shadows reached almost to Cain's feet, stretching toward him like giants in the sliver of light. He could see at least two of them standing at the front door. There could be more patrolling the grounds.

Cain skittered across the yard until he was hugging the side wall of the house. He clenched and unclenched his freezing hands a few times to get his blood circulating, then skillfully climbed up the side of the house. Decorative divots in the brick wall served conveniently as hand- and footholds; with the high outer wall and guards, intruders weren't expected to make it this far.

As he climbed, he thought over what he might encounter in a moment's time. In a three-story house, the master bedroom was typically on the second floor. If the woman Ayana had seen that day was indeed Gladdis, that was where she would be at this hour.

He steadied himself against the wall, holding on to the windowsills. A gap in the drapes of one of the windows allowed him a glimpse into a corridor, though it was too dark to properly see anything. But that darkness also meant there was likely no one in this hallway. He pulled the crowbar from the sack on his back and carefully wedged it between the window and window frame. There were no bolts. Only a small creak announced his success.

Cain parted the curtains and slipped into the house.

21

ARIENNE

Arienne felt a chill as she looked down at the book. There was a subtitle on the cover, its gilt peeled off but the words still legible, revealing the full title. *The Sorcerer of Mersia: The Grim King's Fall.* The prospect of Eldred's memories leaking into her own made her skin crawl.

The book in her hand looked older than it had in the room of her mind. Arienne was exhausted from all that had happened since spotting the inquisitors that morning at breakfast, but her curiosity revived her. She had to know what this book was. As she carefully opened it, Eldred spoke with irritation in his voice.

"Where did you get that?"

His tone was different than she'd ever heard it. He almost sounded appalled.

"I brought it from the room," she said, her voice casual, though in truth she did not know how she'd been able to take the book from the room. The thought had simply occurred to her that she could, and she had done it.

"You may not read it. Burn it. Now."

"Why? It was in my mind, it's mine." She was enjoying his agitation.

"That book contains my private life. It is not for your eyes or for anyone else's."

Arienne blithely turned the first page. "Your private life? There's a publication date here. And the name of an author."

It had been published 170 years ago. No wonder the book looked so worn. The author's name, Lysandros, was followed by his title: Inquisitor of the Imperial Office of Truth.

"That Lysandros man wrote this book?"

But if this was the same man whose lackeys had been following her up to the inn, he had to be about two hundred years old. The name wasn't uncommon, so this must have been a different person. Right?

When there was no answer from Eldred, she quickly glanced into the room in her mind; the sorcerer was sitting on the edge of the bed with his head down again. Arienne turned to the first chapter.

And the printed letters began squirming on the page. Startled, she threw down the book. The spider-like letters continued to scatter across the ivory expanse of the opened pages, becoming illegible. Arienne realized that Eldred wasn't merely bowing his head, he was reciting something.

"Stop that!" she shouted. Eldred stopped reciting. The letters returned to their proper positions.

"Since when were you able to do this?"

"Who knows." Eldred's withered lips stretched sideways, revealing the gaps in his smile. Even with no real answer, Arienne knew. It was the bandages. Unraveling the bandages around his head had loosened his power.

Arienne thought back to the skeleton below the Academy building. She had only a vague imagining as to how Eldred had thrown them down the stairs. How he must've blinded them, made them stumble, or pushed them—*So this is how he did it.* She felt her bile rise.

But that poor student never managed to bring Eldred's body into their mind. He must've killed the student even while inside the lead coffin. Arienne had never learned of what might happen when a Power generator was inside a person's mind. There probably wasn't anyone who could teach her that, anyway. What if she had committed an irreversible mistake? The prospect frightened her.

Regret was useless, though. Living at the Academy only for the purpose of dying had still felt more terrifying than this new path she was on, even if she had not a single inkling of what might lie ahead. And no matter what did come from all this, she would always feel this way.

Seemingly oblivious to Arienne's feelings, Eldred spoke.

"Must you do this, even when it is clear I protest against what you're doing?"

"I'm doing it *because* you protest so much! Why shouldn't I read the book?"

It didn't matter if she was being unreasonable. No matter how trivial, if she wasn't allowed to do something because Eldred said so, it was no better than being pushed down the stairs and breaking her neck.

Eldred, after a silence, spoke.

"Read it, then, if you must. It's not any kind of pleasurable story."

Arienne was taken aback. She had not expected him to relent. As she hesitated, Eldred continued. *"But you must keep this in mind while reading that tripe. You are a sorcerer, just as I am. You are of my world, not theirs. You must never forget that. Before the Empire conquered the world, it was a wondrous time when magic was grand. And we ruled supreme under many strange names, alongside gods and monsters. You hold in your hands a version of history, the one written by a spear tip of the Empire as it spread over the world like a flash flood in the grasslands . . . destroying true power and wonder wherever it encountered them, whittling down the world into a paltry thing their ambitions could grasp and therefore control. Do not forget that it is to the Empire that you have lost your birthright."* Eldred's voice was softer than ever, almost nostalgic. *"But I recommend that you at least peruse it later and not now."*

"Why?"

"The inquisitors at the inn are near the tower. I can smell Lysandros's stench from here."

"How did they . . . ?"

"Following your tracks, no doubt. He wouldn't send utter incompetents all the way here."

As careful as she was, Arienne was no expert in erasing her tracks in a forest. The only things she knew to do were what she'd read in adventure books. She might have fooled the custodian Duff, but the inquisitors of the Office of Truth were a different matter altogether.

"Why didn't you tell me earlier?"

"What would you have done earlier? I, too, assumed they would search the highway first. That if we managed to stay hidden here for a day, the snow would erase our tracks overnight . . ." Eldred sighed. *"What will you do now? If I'd known this would happen, I would have pressed you harder to learn my sorcery."*

"Shut up," Arienne snapped, looking around the room. "I'll have to make do."

There wasn't a suitable weapon in sight, aside from a rusty poker in the fireplace. It had a tine on its side. Would it be enough to defend her against the blow of a sword? Arienne almost laughed at the thought. These were inquisitors she was dealing with. Infamous throughout the Empire for hunting down sorcerers.

Outside the window, she could see the man and woman from the inn walking toward the tower. What did Lysandros smell like, that Eldred would have detected it? The man and woman now had weapons other than the knives on their belts—the man carried a bow on his back, and the woman held an axe.

Without hesitation, they disappeared into the entrance of the tower. There was hardly a likelier place someone would be hiding out in the vicinity, but it was also probably because Arienne's tracks led right to the doorway. Their footsteps rang through the tower as they made their way up the stairs. They were in no rush. If they'd indeed tracked Arienne through the woods, then they also knew she was still in the tower and had no way out.

"What do I do?"

"Do not ask me."

Eldred did not sound at ease either. Arienne looked inside her mind's room again. There was no expression to be read in his parched face. The only thing she could be sure of was that he was not smiling.

There had to be a place to hide in the room, but nothing looked like it would do. The footsteps were louder now, closer. One of the crumbled lower floors had something like an intact wardrobe in it, but going down the stairs now only meant getting caught sooner. Hanging from the window was an option, if she thought she had the strength in her fingers to do so for more than a minute, which she didn't. Even if she managed to hide herself, she had left too many fresh traces in the room for them to not notice she was immediately about.

She imagined being bound in lead manacles and chains. She imagined being dragged up the center path of her school, countless people lined on either side, jeering at her. Rotten vegetables and eggs flying at her, hitting her head. The stench. The green yolk of an egg gone bad flowing down the side of her face. Duff was in the crowds, her boyfriend Felix, the prodigy Magnus, Kaya who had taught her what few spells she knew. And Eldred.

Maybe dying would be better, to say goodbye to the Academy, to the Office of Truth, to this Powered parasite in her mind. Never to see Cain or Lucretia again. Arienne looked out the window and down. Jumping from here would mean instant death. The skeleton in the underground staircase at the school—the hapless student killed by Eldred. Whom no one had found, whose eye sockets were now home to mice . . .

Arienne imagined this student, whom she had never met, being fooled by Eldred into going down the spiral staircase. A boy, ordinary height, slightly heavy, wearing spectacles with buffalo-horn rims and the school robes. He comes all the way to the door of the Power generator chamber, where no one has ventured for many years, before getting scared and turning away. And almost at the top of the staircase, merely a few steps from the door that would lead outside, he sees something so horrifying that he screams. He falls backward, down, down, *this can't be happening* writ on his face, frantically reaching for handrails that are not there . . .

Arienne turned to the stairs. She imagined it happening, firmly engraving the details in her mind, just as she had when she created her inner room. She thought of it again and again. The boy she had never seen fell to his death, over and over.

The man from the inn had finally reached the top of the stairs. The bow he'd been carrying on his back was now in his hands, the arrow already on the string. A smile on his face, like a hunter who had just spotted a deer in the woods.

The boy in her mind vanished, replaced by the man with the bow. The killing incantation Eldred had taught her at Lucretia's house came to her lips.

The man looked as if he'd seen a ghost. He started walking backward, then stumbled and fell backward toward his doom, the same expression as the boy in her imaginings on his face.

"Nerius!" screamed the woman.

Arienne turned to the woman, whose face was filled with rage as she ran up the stairs with her axe raised. The falling man in her imaginings turned into the woman before her.

Arienne recited the incantation.

22

LORAN

Snow fell on the westward road. Loran had only a cape covering her leather armor and Wurmath hitched to her side as she walked for days. She did not rush, nor did she tarry. Whenever she stopped to eat or rest her legs, though, she would ask herself if she truly needed the break or if she was giving in to fear and deliberately prolonging her journey.

As she left Dehan Forest to enter Arland, the scenery became more familiar. The horizon was faint through the falling snow. East, west, and south, there was not a single hill or mountain in sight, just scattered copses and groves on the plains. North, there was always the huge volcano, a faint plume of smoke whispering from its mouth. And here and there, in every direction, hamlets and villages, peaceful farming communities.

The highway laid down by the Empire followed the Finvera Pass to enter Lontaria from the south, first passing through Kamori, and veered west from the gates of Kamori's capital, Karadis, toward Arland. It ran through her homeland and along the black cliffs overlooking the Great West Sea toward the north before twisting again midway through Ledon and going toward the shores.

This road also led to the fortress where the Twenty-Fifth Legion's Arland detachment was stationed.

Bringing her waterskin from her belt to her lips, Loran took half a mouthful of the cold water inside. Beside the road was a stream fringed with ice. Kneeling, she knocked the ice loose with her gloved fist until the babbling of the water came through, then dipped the canteen into the freezing water. Tiny fish darted away from her hand.

She sat and stared into the flowing water, listening for the footsteps of the people who had been following her for the past hour or so.

"What do you want?" she shouted over her shoulder.

The footsteps paused. She turned her head to find a cluster of people, perhaps ten. They stopped, maintaining the distance between them and her. While they were mostly dressed in the typical winter garb of farmers, one woman, perhaps over fifty years of age, stood out. Her clothes were of high quality, but they were torn and stained in places. Her hands were tied in front of her, and the clothes she wore weren't suitable for winter. She was shivering. Loran saw no *t'laran* adorning the woman's bare neck, signifying her to be an outlander, probably an Imperial.

Were the rest bandits? Loran stood, brushing off the snow and dirt, and walked up to the crowd.

"What is it that you want?" she asked again.

The group exchanged glances before a man near the front replied.

"Are you . . . You don't happen to be . . . Are you the princess?"

Should she say yes? That the princess of Arland was walking down a road alone to surrender to the Empire?

"Maybe it's not her," said a woman in the crowd. The woman in the expensive, dirty clothes said nothing. She still shivered, whether from cold or fear. The other end of the rope that kept her bound was held by the man who had asked Loran who she was.

"I am," she finally replied. "What business do you have with me?"

"It's her . . . she says it's her," the man holding the rope stammered.

"Should we kneel?" another man said, looking around as if seeking advice from others.

Twenty years had passed since the last king of Arland had been killed, and these were simple peasants who would not know the ways of the court. In reality, Loran was no different.

"Do not trouble yourselves," she said, "but why have you tied up this woman?"

A tall young woman stepped forward and pressed the end of the staff she carried into the prisoner's shoulder until the tied woman fell to her knees. Then she too knelt before Loran and lowered her head before speaking.

"We farm the lands here in the village of Azaley. We've been holding this criminal so the princess could pass judgment on her for us, and we happened to hear that someone who resembled the princess was passing through."

"She is a criminal?"

"Her name is Metela. An Imperial landowner in these parts, who had Esmund from our village beaten to death while she was trying to steal his land. Raise your head, woman."

Metela did as she was told. Her skin was pale but flushed, her name an Imperial one.

But why me, Loran almost said. They were in the middle of the road, hardly an appropriate place to hold a trial. And she was on her way to surrender to the Empire, most likely to be hanged somewhere in a few days. She had no right to preside over a trial, if she ever had. But it felt wrong to just send these people away when they had sought her out.

"What is your name?" she said to the woman with the staff.

"I am Wilfrid, Princess."

Loran turned to Metela. "Is what Wilfrid said true?"

"I hadn't meant to kill him," she answered listlessly, "I paid the fine and my servant was sent to the quarries—"

"But here you are, still alive and rich!" Wilfrid struck the back of Metela's head with her large hand.

"Do not strike her, if it is a trial you wish from me," said Loran.

The tall woman lowered her head once more.

"But I've already had a trial . . ." Metela sobbed.

"A trial you bribed the prefect for!" shouted someone from the back. A thrown stone hit her. Metela screamed as if she'd been pierced with a sword, collapsing forward.

Loran raised her hand.

"Everyone, please be silent."

A conundrum. The prefect was burned alive, the main contingent of the Twenty-Fifth had not arrived yet, and until they did, the advance detachment was holed up in the fortress. There was no one to represent the Empire in Arland. This had happened only very recently, but the people were already drunk with liberation.

They couldn't be blamed. This very liberation was what they had craved for so long, none more so than Loran herself. But her rash actions had turned those hopes into a fleeting daydream.

"I am sorry. But I cannot hold a trial."

Wilfrid looked up. Surprise was writ on her face.

"Why . . . why not?"

Loran spoke as gravely as possible. "I am on my way to the legion fortress."

Wilfrid lowered her head again and said, "We are aware you are much occupied with ridding our lands of enemies. I have come here as well with my weapon to join you in the fight." The staff at her side, no doubt. "But this woman's crime is very clear, and if you would delay for only a moment for the sake of justice for our village . . ."

Loran sighed.

"I am not on my way to fight. I am on my way to surrender. By killing the prefect and the legionaries, I have placed Arland in peril."

"What?" Wilfrid shouted, her eyes wide. A murmur rose among the gathered people. "How can this be! If you go, they will kill you. And the Empire will return!"

"The Empire will return whether I am here or not. The Twenty-Fifth Legion's main body is arriving as we speak. As long as I am alive, Arland will be in danger."

Some slumped their shoulders in disappointment, others burst into tears. Still others made fists, anger in their eyes.

Metela, from the ground, looked up at the others and slowly got to her feet. Proving her shivering before was from fear and not cold, her manner was now calm.

"Look here. I have done wrong. But the Empire is returning, and should an Imperial heartlander such as I be harmed, what would come of all of you? I will compensate Esmund's family well. Let us return to the village now and we shall consider the past few days forgotten."

Her words were careful, but there was a note of confidence in her voice. Even scum who would murder another for their wealth held their heads high when they expected power and authority to be on their side. Loran's anger made her head spin, but there was no other way. She nodded.

The man holding Metela's rope reluctantly untied her. Metela patted the man on the shoulder and began walking back to the village with two others. But the rest of the villagers did not turn away.

Not wanting to see the back of Metela, Loran turned toward her destination once more.

"The day is cold. Please go back home."

"No!" shouted Wilfrid.

"There is nothing to be done," said Loran, calmly.

"I shall at least remain to see you on your way." Wilfrid's tone was equal parts stubbornness and disappointment. Loran was not cruel enough to drive the people away from her. They did not seem like they would go, regardless.

She turned to Wilfrid and said, "Then do so."

Wilfrid got to her feet, and four people came forward to stand with her. They held their farming implements like spears.

"We shall also see you on your way."

Two others standing behind them holding rakes gave each other a look, bowed deeply to Loran, and headed off in the opposite direction from the other leaving villagers, crossing the stepping stones of the stream.

"Where are they going?"

"They are from a different village," said Wilfrid, "and they were the ones who came to us saying the princess was passing through. They are returning to their village now."

And once they did, no doubt they would spread the word that the self-styled princess who had killed the prefect was now on her way to surrender to the Empire. That it had all been a pointless mess, from beginning to end. How disappointed they would be, and everyone in Kingsworth . . . Loran gritted her teeth.

The five who had not gone back stood by, their faces immobile and serious. The fortress was two more days away. Loran began to walk once more. Heavy footsteps followed her.

23

CAIN

Gladdis's house was huge compared to most residences in the Capital, but the halls were empty and dark. The light of the city seeped in from outside, but Cain could see only the faint outlines of the doors lined up on either side of him.

The floor was of expensive marble, so there was no need to worry about creaking. Cain stuck close to the wall, his every sense on high alert. He hoped that one of the identical doors before him led into Gladdis's bedroom.

Every time he passed a door, he checked to see whether there was light in the cracks before placing his ear to it. Halfway through the long corridor, he had not heard a single sound from behind any door, not even breathing. Cain took his new dagger out of his inner pocket and held it in his left hand, the blade pointing downward, its double edges longer than a man's hand. A copper wire was wound decoratively around the hilt that fit into Cain's hand perfectly.

The dagger was for threatening Gladdis. Cain had no chance of winning a fight against Safani, or the ex-legionary woman that had presided over his beating in the alley. The best thing he could hope for in this situation was to find Gladdis and hold her hostage. He briefly thought of what he might do if "the best thing" became impossible, but nothing came to mind.

At the sixth door, he heard something—the sound of liquid flowing. Taking care to keep his spectacles from knocking against the door, he brought his ear to it. Another pouring sound, like wine filling a goblet. There were at least two people in the room. He tried to breathe as silently as possible.

". . . unsure if he's trustworthy. I could do it . . ."

The voice inside was low, but recognizable. The ex-legionary. He'd felt relieved to find there were no guards in the corridor, but he realized now that meant Gladdis's bodyguard was in her room with her.

"Your priority is to keep me safe. This plan must not be disturbed in any way."

A middle-aged woman. Not a voice he knew. The hairs on the back of his neck stood up. That had to be Gladdis.

He concentrated his whole being into his right ear against the door. There was a sound of pouring again, but neither seemed drunk.

"Branwen sends word," said the bodyguard.

"The sorcerer-engineer? What does she say?"

"She needs more time to get the generator into the Circuit . . . to avoid her colleagues finding out."

An exclamation of frustration followed.

"I'd thought this was the perfect time, with the changing of the legions in Lontaria," said Gladdis. "How long do we have to wait?"

"She says two more days."

"And there have been other delays . . . If we waste any more time, Legate Aurelia's Twenty-Fifth may just take Kamori for themselves once the Capital is in ruins. Just the thought of that hag taking over my homeland . . ."

"But if the Senate wanted her to replace the prefect of Arland, would she not settle there in Kingsworth instead?"

"The Twenty-Fifth will be the only legion in Lontaria and the Senate will be in no position to keep the legions in check once the Capital is destroyed. Do you think she will settle for just Arland? We have to finish the job before the whole of the Twenty-Fifth enters Lontaria. Only then can His Majesty have the chance to rise, don't you agree?"

"I do."

"We can't leave this up to Branwen. That sorcerer-engineer girl may be our surest way to the Circuit of Destiny, but I can indulge her anxieties no longer. I must allow that man to go ahead with his plan. We must force things in motion. Immediately."

A silence. By "that man," she must mean Safani. After a sound of the wine being poured, the ex-legionary broke the silence.

"And how is King Gwaharad?"

A name he had never heard before. The title of "king" was one he'd only read about.

"His Majesty is well." Gladdis sounded morose.

"But still refusing to emerge from his underground palace?"

"We gave His Majesty enough money to do whatever he wanted.

And he did go to the site himself, as we asked, but the actual deed was done by Prince Emere."

"So His Majesty is still reluctant to take the next step in the liberation of Kamori."

"Our great undertaking will surely spur His Majesty to action. If he decides to do so, and the Capital is in chaos by then, Kamori will have hope."

"Does His Majesty know of our plans?"

"The king is too prudent. He would have objected if I told him. But I trust he will act once the world knows of our deed."

Another silence. Cain wondered who Gwaharad was. Septima and the others might know, perhaps.

Gladdis said, "And there's that woman, Loran."

"The one they say is a princess of Arland?"

"So you've heard of her."

The Arlander princess was named Loran, then. The same as his mother's name.

"Recent arrivals from Kamori talk of nothing except her," said the bodyguard. "She felled four or five Powered soldiers by herself. That's how the prince managed to secure the generator before even the Liberators arrived. As long as I have served in the legions, it is unheard of in my time."

"She has even destroyed a few chariots on her own, since we left."

"The Scorpios class of the Twenty-Fifth?"

Her voice was almost a shout. Cain thought of Arienne; it had been wise to tell her to go back to Arland. Nobody was going to worry about a single runaway sorcerer while Loran was going on a rampage.

"Does it seem like anyone has caught word of our plans?" asked Gladdis.

"Not at all, my lady."

"Septima and her minions?"

"Not that we can tell."

"I see. And that . . . that . . ." Gladdis hesitated. ". . . Fienna, she . . . well . . ."

"I made sure the whole matter has been taken care of. No one suspects."

Cain forgot to breathe. He was so quiet he could hear them gulping their wine.

"Were there many mourners at the funeral?"

"I heard fifty Arlanders at least, my lady."

"I see. She would have been an excellent addition to our efforts. It is truly regrettable. But all of our lives are but brief flecks of snow before the fire of the cause. Do not berate yourself too much."

Cain wanted to bash the door down. He gripped the dagger tighter in his hand. The copper wires wrapped around the hilt bit into his palm.

"There is a man going around asking questions about her. But we caught up with him and shook him up a little—"

"Who is this?"

"A young man from Arland . . . I believe his name was Quine or some such? A friend of the late Fienna."

"Will he prove to be a problem, do you think?"

"If he hasn't by now, I do not think he will. The great deed is close at hand, anyway."

They paused once more. Taking his ear off the door, Cain looked

214

around. There was still no one in the hallway. Just the occasional sound of the wind rattling the windows.

The ex-legionary would leave the room soon, and there was no place for him to hide. The only way was to ambush her with the dagger when she left the room, jump through the door, and get ahold of Gladdis. Or what if the bodyguard did not come out? Then he had to enter when at least one of them was asleep. He had to get Gladdis before the sun rose. It was too late to turn back now.

The sound of a chair being pushed back. At the same time, the sound of a metallic goblet upending on a table before rolling off to the floor.

Something was off. Until now, he hadn't heard the cups touching the table. Which meant they were both holding them in their hands. Then whose was it that had just rolled off?

Slipping his spectacles into his pocket, he peered through the keyhole. His naked sight was blurry, but Cain made out the two women holding their goblets, and an empty one rolling around on the floor. There were only two of them in the room, but there had originally been a third.

"Oh! I didn't see that there."

"I shall pick it up, my lady. It's a good thing his cup was empty."

"What is taking that man so long?"

"Perhaps he is checking the whole building."

It was then that Cain realized someone had been watching him from behind this whole time. He rolled forward, wasting no time to look at the silent watcher in the dark, deftly transferring his dagger from his left hand to his right, but in that moment, as if predicting his movement, something sharp stabbed his left thigh. The fiery pain was the only thing that registered in the pitch-blackness.

Suddenly there was someone before him. His face was hidden by the gloom, and he made no sound. It had to be the silent man he had been pursuing since the funeral, the Safani that the agents talked about.

He touched his thigh. There was a skewer-like dart embedded there. A smell of honey that hadn't been there before. His left knee buckled on its own, and he fell. The fiery sensation in his wound was now numb, and the darkness turned even darker.

The door opened. A candle burned. The face of Gladdis and the ex-legionary woman, with recognition lighting up the latter's eyes. And Safani, as well, standing over him and looking down expressionlessly.

The candlelight went out. Or it didn't; it was his eyes that were closing. He tried to open them but they wouldn't move. The three were saying something to one another. Cain tried to concentrate on what they were saying. But soon, he could hear nothing.

24

ARIENNE

Since they had fled the tower, Eldred had bombarded Arienne with questions, but the main one he kept coming back to was how she managed to use that spell on the inquisitors when she had no experience of ever having killed someone. Arienne did not answer. Who knew what he would say if she told him about her imaginings of the skeleton underneath the Academy.

If Cain was correct, it would take a day and half to cross Finvera Pass and walk into Kamori. A harsh climb, especially in this cold weather, but at least it wasn't snowing anymore. It was daytime now with no cloud in sight, and the only sound was that of light wind rustling past the trees. But the dark green monotone of the forested scenery reminded her of the stories of Finvera Pass she'd heard as a child, which had always featured a night blizzard, with owls and wolves screaming among solemn firs that filled the mountain.

The only open inn by the pass was large but shabby. This part of the road had seen better days since the Empire took over

Lontaria and established a port on the west coast of Ledon. It used to have many inns, but most of them stood abandoned by the roadside now.

Arienne found shelter in one of the closed ones and waited for morning. She would have gotten a room at the working inn and enjoyed a proper meal, but after having killed someone—after having killed *two* people—she feared being seen by other travelers. Even though it had all happened in that forest where no one could have seen, she felt like her crimes were written all over her face.

The abandoned inn was derelict, as if no care had been taken of it for a decade or so. Its fireplace, however, was still sound. Arienne used parts of broken furniture for firewood, and found a dented pot in the kitchen. She filled it with snow and boiled the hard bread and dried meat she had, hoping it would result in something resembling meat porridge. The wind coming through the cracks of the building made the flames dance and throw monstrous shadows on the walls.

"Why not stop reading that," said Eldred.

"Books are meant to be read," she answered without looking up.

Arienne had been reading *The Sorcerer of Mersia* every moment she had a chance since fleeing the tower, and she was almost at the end. It was the story of how the sorcerer king Eldred, who had ruled Mersia through fear and death, had been vanquished by a young inquisitor of the Office of Truth named Lysandros. A tale so old it happened decades before the devastation of Mersia a hundred years ago.

"What an evil bastard you were. I see why you did not want me to read it."

"Have you already forgotten what I said about that book? Think of

who it was that wrote it. The wretch Lysandros, as befits an agent of the Empire, conquers through lies."

Arienne scoffed. "This book doesn't read like lies. I'd say the author's tone is very sincere."

"Nobody conquers the world with insincere lies."

Arienne remembered her history classes at the Academy. Neither her textbooks nor her professors had mentioned Mersia, much less a sorcerer named Eldred. But they were unequivocal in describing the pre-Imperial world as barbaric, superstitious, and impoverished. She had always assumed such descriptions were heavy with propaganda and were to be taken with many a grain of salt . . . But what had the old days really been like, before the Empire took over, if they were a time that the Grim King of Mersia could reminisce fondly about?

Arienne turned her eyes back to the pages.

"Is it true you sat on a throne made of a hundred skulls?"

Eldred had no answer.

"You also kidnapped the son of this Lysandros and murdered him."

"I did not kill him."

"But you did kidnap him? As a hostage?"

"No, I wanted him as my apprentice."

"A baby?"

"I could sense the talent in him, even while he was in his mother's womb. And I tried to save the child."

In the room of her mind, a small cloud of dust formed as Eldred sighed. *"Now he will never grow up to be a proper sorcerer. He could have been so much more!"* Eldred paused. *"Little sorcerer, listen to me. A Power generator is an abomination."*

Arienne nodded in agreement. "I know. That's why I—"

Eldred interrupted, *"I do not mind abominations. Some might even say all sorcerers are abominations."* His face twisted in a wry grin before it dropped into a sneer. *"However, the piece of magic that creates Power generators is a degradation of all sorcerers. It is not just how our bodies are used, but how our lives are designed to satiate the hunger of banal, ordinary men. That I cannot abide, whether the damned things are made of a powerful old witch or a small boy who hadn't learned a spell in his months of short life. That is another reason that I chose you. You share that sentiment with me."*

Eldred drew breath as if he was going to say more, but paused instead. Arienne, quick to understand, perked up her ears as well. Nothing seemed out of the ordinary, but the outside was shrouded with darkness except for the light coming from the windows of the inn down the road.

"I smell him."

Arienne stopped breathing. There was only the crackling of the fire, and the winds raking the crumbling walls.

Closing the book and slipping it into her tunic, Arienne stood. The boards creaked beneath her feet.

The fire in the hearth suddenly died, leaving not even an ember. There was no time to panic, but her chest felt tight, as if her heart and lungs were being slowly squeezed by an invisible hand. Inside her mind, the room groaned and twisted like an empty paper box. The walls were bending and the windows cracking. The floor was tilting and the books on the shelf were falling. Eldred remained on the bed. For the first time on his shrunken face, there was feeling.

"He's here. The wretch is here . . ." Eldred moaned. Was he upset? Perhaps he was anxious to meet his old enemy after all this time.

This was not the top of a tower. She couldn't use the spell she had used to deal with the inquisitors. Even if she could, she doubted that it would work on this man that even Eldred seemed to fear. She had to run. But as soon as she stepped into the narrow corridor leading outside, the door opened with a loud creak. She stopped in her tracks.

Standing at the door was a man holding a lantern, which spilled a blue light like the streetlamps in the Capital. No, he wasn't holding a lantern. The light came from one of his eyes. He wore a hooded cloak, and half his face was covered by an iron mask. Not a mask either. His lower jaw and the entire left side of his face *were* metal. The man threw back his hood with his left arm, revealing a head of thinning hair. There was a very quiet ticking sound, like a clock's.

"Are you Arienne of the Imperial Academy, the Eleventh College, Division of Sorcery?" His voice was mechanical, not like a human's at all. "Where is Eldred?"

He stepped forward, and his feet made a scraping sound as if there were iron studs on his soles. Arienne took a step back.

"I am Grand Inquisitor Lysandros. Are you the one who killed my underlings?"

Eldred whispered, *"Do not let on that I am inside you. He will know it soon enough, but we need to buy as much time as possible."*

Her inner room was about to collapse from the pressure Lysandros exuded. Just as Arienne tried to concentrate on maintaining its integrity, Eldred said, *"Unravel the bandages around my arms. If you do not, we are both done for. Hurry!"*

Resisting the force squeezing her heart, Arienne whispered, "What will you do if I release you?"

"What did you say?" said Lysandros. Arienne waited for Eldred's reply.

An invisible force slammed against her front. Arienne was knocked off her feet and sent flying along the corridor. Eldred said something, but she couldn't hear.

Lysandros said, "Where have you hidden Eldred? Give him to me. Then this will all be forgotten, and I will allow you to return to the Academy."

Lysandros's voice did not go high or low; it was all a single tone.

Eldred shouted, *"The bandages, now!"*

Her head pounded, and not because she was hit, but because Eldred was excited. She stretched an imaginary hand into the room and undid the bandages securing his arms with one pull. His emaciated torso and arms became exposed. As Eldred unstuck his arms from his sides, there was a stiff sound of tearing flesh so gruesome that Arienne winced.

Eldred's bony hands waved in the air. Red runes separated from the bandages and formed a line in the air. They transformed into different runes, ones Arienne had never seen before. But somehow, she knew how to read them. Their sounds and meanings were clear.

"I cannot teach it to you in words. This is the only way to transfer my memory to yours."

222

"So that's what you're . . . You're making me do this, too?"

She stood up. Lysandros, finally understanding, gave a gasp.

"You've hidden Eldred in your mind. To witness this trick again after all these years! Do you know who this monster truly is? Did you learn his magic knowing that?"

"He's Eldred, the Grim King of Mersia. And I had the pleasure of reading your book, *Sorcerer of Mersia*."

She needed time to prepare the spell she had just learned. Just a little more time . . .

"If you only read the book, then you've merely learned half the story. You don't know what happened decades later, because of him."

"Then tell me the other half."

Even as she spoke, she focused on the room inside her mind, which was still crumbling under the mental pressure Lysandros was applying to her. Then imagined it being completely crushed—no, not crushed, but crumpled—into the size of a fist. She stepped backward as Lysandros advanced.

"Have you never thought of why such a monstrosity would be kept hidden away in a mere school, where no one would think to look? Why a Class One Power generator should be locked away in such a place?"

Eldred shouted, *Why are you dawdling? Hurry! Do it now!*

"After I executed Eldred and made him into a generator, we connected him to the Circuit of Destiny. Do you know what that is?"

Arienne nodded.

"The real problem occurred long after that. It was more than

223

one hundred years ago now, but I remember it like it was yesterday."

She was desperate to hear more, but Lysandros was only steps away from her. She could delay no longer.

Arienne concentrated on the room that was collapsing in her mind. The rafters were bending, the floor was splitting, lime fell from the walls. She imagined herself in the room and she was there. She heard the creaking, smelled the dust, touched the splintering wood and lime powder.

She imposed those senses of collapse on the derelict inn around her, and imagined the inn collapsing under that pressure. Arienne spoke the incantation Eldred taught her, leaping backward with all her might.

A rafter fell directly toward Lysandros's head. He grabbed it with both hands. Arienne realized with a start that his arms were made of metal. With this motion, his cloak slipped from his shoulders, and Arienne could see the gears turning and pistons firing within his body. Everything except the top half of his head and the right side of his face was machine. He carried a wooden box on his back, which looked out of place next to his metallic form.

The humming of his machinery suddenly rose to a keen; the weight of the rafter was too much. Then, the roof collapsed on top of him. Lysandros tried to get out of the way, but the floor came up from under him as the roof came down.

In the scattering dust, the pressure on Arienne's heart disappeared. The inn lay half in ruins before her.

Eldred said, *"We do not have time to wait until the sun rises. You must cross the pass now."*

"But Lysandros is dead, isn't he?"

"*Did you not see his body of metal? This will not be enough to destroy him. We must keep him at as much distance as possible.*"

More lights were coming on at the open inn. The sound must've woken the guests there. The edge of the eastern sky was tinting red, the sun just under the far away hills. Arienne quickly grabbed her things and set off toward the pass.

25

LORAN

"No, Your Highness, we shall not! We shall not let you go!"

Three people had lain down on her path, preventing Loran from going forward. One was a man who looked at least seventy. The other two seemed to be his daughters. Behind them were about a dozen others with determined expressions.

"Why must we give up?" one of the women on the ground cried. Her face was wet with tears, soon to freeze on her face. It was a cold winter, even for Arland. What if they should get sick? She remembered how difficult it had been that winter when the winds seeped into her house and her daughter became bedridden for much of the season.

There were nearly a hundred people following her now. They had beseeched her not to surrender herself, and then joined her in her walk, saying they would at least see her off. Many more had turned back when they heard what Loran was going to do.

To the three people lying in the road in front of her now, pleading with her to stop, Loran spoke as gently as possible.

"You say you cannot give up," she said, "but I have only been fighting since late autumn. It has been less than a season. You shall forget me soon enough."

"Late autumn? We have been awaiting Your Highness's arrival for twenty years!"

A woman in the crowd behind her shouted, "I sell fruits and greens in Kingsworth. Do you know why I am here in the country every winter with my relatives? It's because my whole family was killed by that prefect! I cannot bear the cold, empty house in the winter."

Loran knew this feeling all too well. The only difference between the woman and herself was that she had gone to the volcano instead of her relatives' house.

"But the prefect is dead," Loran said, almost apologetically. "Perhaps this is justice enough—"

"They will send another to take his place! I no longer have a family they could murder, but what about those who do?"

"But surely the new prefect would not be as cruel as Hesperus?"

Another shouted, "How can we know that? What if he's worse? Then who will fight for us? Why must we live under such fear?"

Then why don't you rise up instead of asking me to do it, she almost said. But she'd been the one who set out trying to become king. No one had asked her to do it. It wouldn't do to complain about it now.

Who else will emerge to unite the people of Arland? How many people would have to die to take down one Powered soldier or a single chariot?

She hesitated in her answer. And in that hesitation, the shouting came in waves.

The old man lying down in front of her rose to a kneel before Loran with his head bowed.

"We who block your way know you will not change your mind because of us. But please, consider our words. When the princess defeated the legion and killed the prefect, we became full of hope! And we have been preparing to accept Arland's new king with joy in our hearts. I know many who have been sharpening the spears they have hidden in farming sheds, ready to fight under your command. Please think of them."

A harsh wind blew down the road. Loran approached the old man and tried to help him to his feet, but he refused her hand and lay prostrate instead.

"But if I do not surrender, many will die," Loran pleaded.

"Is there anyone here who would regret such a death!" shouted Wilfrid from behind. A murmur of assent rose from the crowd.

Loran gripped the old man's arm and said, a little louder, "There are a hundred of you. What of the many who did not come? There must be those in Kingsworth and the hamlets who fear the Empire's reprisals, who resent me for spoiling their peace. It is not your place to speak in their stead."

The old man who lay prostrate righted himself and stood. He trembled with cold.

"But who was first to do as they willed with our lives?" he boomed.

It was herself. She had nothing to say to that.

"The princess blames herself," said the old man, "but this is not so. It is not the princess who wants to decide if we live or die. It is those who threaten to kill us if we do not obey."

The woman from Kingsworth spoke once more.

"That day when Your Highness came to Liberation Square . . . no, Fire-Dragon Square, as it had always been called. In Fire-Dragon Square, I was there! Did the people not rise with their tools from home, ready to fight by your side?"

Loran could give no answer. This was not an opponent she could convince or vanquish. Wordlessly, she went past the people who stood before her. Some of them rushed to lie down in front of her farther along the path, but she simply walked around them.

A voice called from behind. "Princess, we still shall follow. If we do not beseech you for the remainder of your journey, we shall live to regret it for the rest of our lives."

That much, she owed the people. Loran nodded and walked on.

Loran's progress slowed as her followers grew. She did not spend her nights in inns, preferring roadsides and empty fields. The dragon's power made her oblivious to cold, and she was afraid wherever she entered, people would overwhelm then follow her. She urged the others to seek comfortable shelter, but the people were determined to sleep where their princess slept.

That night, it was especially cold. The sight of the shivering people huddled against one another on the fields shorn of their harvest made her sad. There were about three hundred gathered now. Some of them were the elderly and children.

Loran had settled down a distance away, not wanting to be a bother. Wilfrid approached her. Whether it was her manner or her prodigious size and build, Wilfrid was often tasked with conveying messages to Loran, who sometimes heard the others refer to her as "General Wilfrid" in jest.

"Princess. Many are cold. We're trying to gather kindling."

Why was she being told this?

"I see."

"There are only empty fields here around us. We were hoping to ask some nearby farmhouses for straw."

"But straw burns so quickly."

"Indeed, it doesn't last long, but . . . The harvest wasn't long ago, they ought to have much of it."

Loran was not a farmer. She did not know much about the land, but there was something that bothered her.

"Would they not require the straw for themselves?"

"People freeze. They should be able to spare some meant for their cattle and thatching to save lives."

"If it were ours to use, certainly. But we cannot ask the people every night to give it up for us."

Then Loran had a thought.

"Well. You have followed me here, so I shall do something about it."

She stood and walked to where the people sat huddled and freezing. They gathered around her, thinking she was about to make a speech, and shook awake the ones who had gone to sleep.

Loran drew out Wurmath. The long blade glowed and began to heat up. The people gasped.

"This was a gift from the fire-dragon of the mountain."

"You have met Its Excellency?" said many.

"I have." The locals referred to the fire-dragon as "Its Excellency." Those in Kingsworth had not. Perhaps all Arlanders had in the past.

Until now, she had told only Emere how she had come upon the sword. She took off her eyepatch and staked the sword into the earth. Her left eye began to heat. Through the darkness she saw each shivering face. All hoping for freedom. All putting their hopes into Loran.

"Princess, your eye . . . !"

Loran said, "Do not be alarmed if I shift in appearance."

Her left eye burned blue. The heat of Wurmath grew. A fire burst forth from the soil. Dry stubs of stalks burned, and the earth melted. It reminded Loran of looking down over the lip into the volcano. Soon, the heat was so intense that no ordinary person could stand next to it. The people that had been crowded around her backed away a little from the pit of lava.

"How could it . . ."

"A miracle!"

"I have heard rumors, but *this* . . ."

Faces that had been ashen only a moment ago glowed warmly by the light of the molten earth. Hands thrust into armpits now extended toward its heat. Loran held the hilt, trying not to let the lava pit grow too large nor let it cool too quickly. Wurmath gripped back.

Their surroundings brightened. The eyes of the people getting warm grew wide as they started to rise to their feet. They were staring at the sky. Loran raised her eyes as well.

A bright white-and-blue pillar of light had pierced through the clouds as if all the stars in the sky had gathered above her and burned, making their surroundings as bright as day.

As they made a turn around a hill a few days later, the Arland fortress of the Twenty-Fifth Legion came into view. An Imperial building made of stone and slathered in lime. To Arlanders, it symbolized their conqueror. She glanced back toward Kingsworth to the north, hours away from this eyesore of a fort. If she had been alone, it should have taken three days to get here; instead, it had taken her seven days.

No one in the fortress would think she was there to surrender. Thousands were now following her, many of whom had seen the pillar of light in the night. They were mostly country folk, but there were also not a few from Kingsworth.

Wilfrid approached. She now held not a staff but a sturdy spear, courtesy of two blacksmiths and a leatherworker who distributed weapons and leather armor to whoever was trained in the fighting arts. Some also carried the arms of the prefect's guard, whether former guards themselves or having stolen them off a rack. Loran counted some of her neighbors and former pupils of her own small sword school. But somehow, they did not seem to recognize her.

"Princess. Do you still wish to surrender?"

Wilfrid sounded almost amused.

Emere had said he had seen her destiny. Loran saw something like it now, in everyone gathered here. Even if the Twenty-Fifth would end Arland, or the Star of Mersia turn the country into ash, it would all be part of the destiny of this land.

"I do not," Loran said quietly to Wilfrid with a smile. Then she unsheathed Wurmath from its scabbard and held it aloft as she turned to address the crowd. "We shall attack the Empire's fortress. Those who wish to return may do so. But all are welcome to join the Princess of Arland in the liberation of our homeland!"

A deafening roar answered her.

26

CAIN

A lantern with a shade. Sight blurry. Spectacles in the pocket. The floor shaking. Two people in front. He could just about make out their outline against the light of the lantern. One of them was rowing. His body would not move. The cold air was mixed with the stench of dirty seawater around the docks. His thoughts refused to cohere. Safani's poison burned in his veins. The poison, or his helplessness, pressed down on his chest.

"Cain." It was Fienna, standing in front of his weak, unmoving body. She was dead. She couldn't be here, however desperately Cain wanted her to be real. Everything was dim, except for Fienna. As if the moon shone only on her.

"Fienna." His mouth didn't move but the name came out regardless.

"You're dying."

"I know."

"Do you know where you are?"

"The sea. Near the docks. A fishing wharf, from the smell. On a small boat."

Fienna gestured to the side with her chin. "And you know who those two are?"

"Gladdis. I don't know the name of the other one. The ex-legionary bodyguard."

Fienna nodded.

"Good. Keep thinking. Don't let your mind slip away."

"I had to know who killed you. I . . . needed to."

Fienna nodded and stroked his hair. He wanted to cry but the tears wouldn't come.

"I know. You did well. So, did you find out?"

It took great effort to weave his thoughts to words.

"You were receiving money from Gladdis to help the Arlanders living in the Capital."

Fienna nodded.

"You may have gone to her, or Gladdis may have had her own plans and come to you, but that was the gist of it. She probably wanted to create an Arlander dissident group in the Capital. So that they could have an ally. But Gladdis came up with a plan to destroy the Capital. With the Circuit of Destiny."

"Yes." Fienna's voice was calm.

"I don't know why she wants to do that. Or how you found out about her plan. But she does and you did, and you tried to convince her otherwise. Because it would mean the Arlanders here would suffer."

"Not only Arlanders," said Fienna.

"You were so against it that Gladdis was afraid you would leak her plan, so she silenced you. That's what you wanted to talk to me about that night, right? And she thought you were going to report her to the Ministry of Intelligence or whoever else."

"But you could've reported the plan yourself," said Fienna. "Why didn't you? When you were introduced to not only one or two, but *three* Ministry agents. Why didn't you tell them what you knew?"

"I don't care about independence or freedom, but I don't want to get in the way of those who do . . . I wanted to know for sure before acting."

Fienna smiled. "Did you, really?"

At her smile, heat rose in his eyes. Somewhere, tears were rolling down.

". . . No."

"Then why?"

"I wanted to avenge you by my own hand."

"Yes. That's my Cain."

Fienna leaned forward and kissed him on the forehead. He trembled. Gladdis glanced his way and said in a low voice, "Did he just move?"

The ex-legionary woman stopped rowing and looked in his direction and shrugged. "Impossible. That man uses no ordinary poison. If he's not dead by now, he must be very near it."

"Is it so?"

"I brought you here because you insisted, my lady, but is it wise? Should you be seen—"

"No," said Gladdis firmly, "this young man is not a lackey of the Empire, and he came to me only because he was angry for his friend and wanted answers. He does not deserve to be thrown into the sea like this, and I will not ask someone else to do the deed for me. I regret not being there when Fienna had to be dealt with. At the very least, I can see this man off."

Fienna stared at Gladdis. "Despicable" was all she said.

"It is rich coming from someone who's about to kill hundreds of thousands of people," agreed Cain.

Fienna turned back to him.

"No, she's not."

"She's not what?"

"She's not going to kill hundreds of thousands of people. You're going to stop her." Fienna's face was gentle as ever.

"Fienna, I am hallucinating right now from a poison so strong that I can't even lift a finger. I'm tied up in something, a rope or a chain, I can't even tell. How do you expect me to stop her?"

Fienna leaned so close their noses almost touched.

"Do you remember when I first found you on the streets? When the fruit seller caught you stealing an orange and I begged and begged him to let you go if I paid him? You were shouting in Arlandais."

Cain nodded. His neck moved.

"Why would I save a twelve-year-old child like that? Was I made of money then?"

"No."

"That girl you helped . . . What was her name?"

"Arienne."

"When you gave Arienne your bread, did you expect something in return? Did you help her run away because she would do something for you?"

"No. Not any of that."

"Do you think I gave that woman's money to Arlanders because I wanted something in return?"

"No."

"Then why did you do it? And why did *I* do it?"

"Because we could."

He could now feel the tear rolling down his face.

Fienna smiled.

"Since you've found out what I tried to do, you'll do it for me, right? You'll take over where I couldn't finish? Because you'd done everything I asked for. My clever and kind Cain."

Fienna stroked his cheek. His eyelids fluttered on their own. The night breeze brushed the back of his hand.

The rocking of the boat lessened. The ex-legionary had stopped rowing.

"This looks like a good spot, my lady."

"Is that so?"

The two were rising, but Cain was not paying attention to them. He was gazing at Fienna. Her braided hair glowed as if she were wearing a crown of light. Cain looked up at the night sky. The overcast sky was dark as ink, with no moon shining down.

"The Capital may look shiny and bright, but the people there live a hard life. When this is all over, I want you to take care of them."

"The Arlanders?"

"Everyone. Everyone you can help."

His body felt warmer. A headache pulsed in his temples. The cold from the chains bit his flesh where they connected. But they had been fastened with sinking in mind, not restraint. There was no lock he could discern, and while his arms were fastened tight to his sides, the chain was looser below his elbows.

"What about me? Who will take care of *me*?"

His vision was blurry, but from tears, not poison. And perhaps his lack of spectacles.

"You're clever and kind. You'll be all right." Fienna caressed his face once more. "So get up. Avenge me. Vanquish the villains and save the world. If not the world, then at least the people I once looked after."

"Like a hero?" Cain smiled for the first time. Fienna smiled back.

"Like a king."

Gladdis was looking down at him. Cain had never actually gotten a good look at her face before. Her white-streaked hair framed her small and wrinkled face. She wore padded clothes made from red Cassian velvet. Her expression was quizzical.

"Why is his face wet?" She touched his cheek. "Are these tears?"

"Still alive, I see. Move aside, my lady, I shall take care of this."

The ex-legionary let go of the oars and stood up.

Fienna held out her hand. Cain gripped it, and got to his feet. But that was only a hallucination of the poison-addled head. What actually happened was that, all of a sudden, Cain sprang to his feet of his own accord and slammed his head directly into Gladdis's face.

Gladdis screamed. The ex-legionary woman, with surprising calmness, drew her sword and swiftly sliced at Cain, but the blade merely scraped against the chains wrapped around him, causing sparks.

Cain stretched out his hand through the loosely tied chains

and grabbed Gladdis's side, feeling a handful of soft Cassian velvet. With a strength that would have torn any other fabric, Cain pulled at her as if bringing her into an embrace.

He spun, his legs wrapped in chains, Gladdis's body helpless against the weight of Cain's and the heavy chain. The ex-legionary took a step back to avoid colliding with the two of them, and Cain, still grabbing the older woman's clothes, threw himself overboard.

Just before his body hit the water, the ex-legionary shouted something. He did not understand Kamori.

The sea engulfed them, and Cain was chilled to the bone within seconds. The weight of the chains dragged him and Gladdis down, pulling them toward the inky depths. Gladdis clawed at the water as if it could give her purchase, but soon she stopped moving. Cain released his grip and watched as the woman who had killed Fienna and planned next to take the lives of a hundred thousand more sank to the bottom of the ocean, her once-struggling hands and feet motionless.

His own air ran out. He tried to loosen the chain around him, but he didn't think he could make it to the surface even if he did. He'd been too optimistic about his chances of survival.

But this was enough. He had avenged Fienna. Without Gladdis, the plot to use the Circuit of Destiny was over. The pressure that had been gripping his heart since Fienna's death finally lifted. He hoped death would come before this feeling of freedom left him.

The last breath from Cain's lungs became a bubble in the water and floated up to the surface.

27

ARIENNE

By the time she had climbed up to the middle of Finvera Pass, it was past noon. The steep passage was covered in pristine snow, evidence of sparse travel in this severe season. Fir trees shook off snow whenever a sudden gust of wind blew down along the slope to chill Arienne's face.

Since burying Lysandros alive under the old inn at dawn, Arienne had walked along the highway then the narrow road through the pass without a moment of rest. Having been a desk-ridden student her whole life, she was unused to a climb as sharp as that of Finvera, but she could not afford to take her time. Lysandros would catch up to her at any moment. Even if she managed to reach Arland, who knew what would happen to her there. A Grand Inquisitor of the Office of Truth was sure to have a backwater prefect at his beck and call, and possibly the legion as well, to aid in his hunt for the rogue sorcerer.

But even the tension and fear couldn't keep her going forever.

Arienne had to stop at a rock overlooking the shaded valley below and catch her breath. She was hungry and thirsty. She had some food left in her sack, but there had been no time to grab her waterskin when she left the ruins of the inn. There wasn't a sign of a river or stream nearby.

"Why are you dawdling?"

Ever since the bandages around his arms had come undone, Eldred had been running his fingers over everything he could in the room as if he had just discovered the sense of touch. He stroked the bedsheets and massaged the pillows. Everywhere he touched, he left a black smudge. It made her uneasy, but she didn't want to know what it was.

"I need to rest a bit. I'm so thirsty—"

"Why not melt some of that snow and drink it."

"Isn't it dirty? I can't boil it now like I did before."

Her tinderbox was buried at the inn along with Lysandros.

"There's snow on the branches, if it bothers you so."

She came down from the rock, went to the firs on the side of the road, put her coat down on the ground, and knocked snow onto it. She shoveled it into her hands and brought it to her mouth. Her head hurt. She was surrounded by snow, and there was plenty untrodden by people or animals, no less clean than the snow on the branches. She recalled herself drinking from streams and picking berries to eat on the spot when she was a little farm girl in Arland. Perhaps years of living in the Capital had made her squeamish.

"Now unravel the bandages from my legs. Who knows when he will be upon us again? Only when I am free can I even hope to defend us."

Arienne glanced at the black stains on the bed and pillows.

"No."

Eldred shrugged. Something he couldn't do before his shoulders had been freed.

I know you will, once you realize that only I can save you. I only hope it is sooner rather than later.

His torso, even more so than his face, was rotted. The shriveled skin was torn in places, revealing muscles that looked like dried meat. Arienne suppressed the impulse to ask him if he hurt and said instead, "That book, *Sorcerer of Mersia*, it ends with you being killed by Lysandros and being turned into a Power generator. Did something else happen after that?"

Listen not to what Lysandros says. Did you notice what he carried on his back?

"The wooden box?"

A Class Two Power generator.

"If it's a Power generator, why is it so small?"

The body itself is small.

"What, is there a baby sorcerer in there or something?" Arienne almost laughed at the ridiculous idea, but her breath caught in her chest as she remembered that Lysandros had had a newborn son, whom Eldred had tried to make his apprentice . . .

Lysandros thought I had corrupted his son. So he killed him, drowned him with his own hands. He calls me a monster, but to murder his own child and turn him into a Power generator to prolong his mechanical life—that is truly monstrous.

Somehow Arienne knew this was true. It chilled her colder than any northern winter could.

She carried the coat with snow back up to the rock. The late-afternoon light made the snow shine bright. Not a cloud was in the sky. Pretty soon she would make it to the top of the pass. A smoke plume was coming up from there. There must be people there.

Back the way she'd come, far down, she could make out the shape of a person, only one. Lysandros? She didn't want to know. She could do nothing but push onward. Eldred said nothing.

Before the Empire took over, Finvera Pass was inhabited by elves who exacted a toll for those who wished to use it. It was also said they would bring out their hounds on winter nights and steal human babies.

Arienne knew Finvera Pass had a large clearing on top of it, where the elves' palace had once stood, but she had never seen it. She had taken the sea route from Ledon when she left Arland, so this was going to be her first time seeing Finvera Square with her own eyes. But she did know that the Empire had massacred the Finveran elves prior to conquering Lontaria. She also knew that they knocked down the ancient palace, laid down a road right through it from south to north, then erected an Imperial square, leaving no trace of the former residents except for strange elven markings on the fir trees that surrounded the square. Maybe identical squares dotted all the conquered lands of the world.

Once she reached the top, Arienne stopped, surprised at the sight of the square. There were fifty or so armed people. She almost turned herself around. She was far from that forest tower where she had killed the two inquisitors, but what she had done haunted her still. She drew a steadying breath and walked on, ignoring the impulse to hide herself in the shade of the fir trees. There were tents and fires here and there, people gathered around each in fours and fives. Were they mountain bandits? She felt eyes on her as she stepped into the square, and heard whispering among the small groups as she passed. She was halfway across the square when some of them stood up to block her. There was no other choice but to stop in her tracks.

The one who stood closest to her was a tall man in his forties. He carried himself in a way that gave Arienne the impression he was the leader. She eyed the trees surrounding the square like walls, and thought back to the spell she'd used that dawn to collapse the derelict inn. Could she use it now? There was no roof here, but she could imagine the trees falling on these people the way the walls of the inn did.

Then Arienne realized that she was thinking so calmly of ways to kill fifty people at once. She shuddered. She'd spent too much time with Eldred.

The man spoke in slightly accented Imperial.

"We apologize for disturbing you. We are not bandits, I assure you. We simply have a few questions that we hope you'll answer before going on your way."

He was polite, but Arienne doubted they would let her go if she happened to not like their questions, or they her answers. "If you're not bandits, who are you?"

"We are the Kamori Liberators. I am Emere, the younger brother of King Gwaharad."

The only way through the square was the exit on the other end. The trees were dense on either side, and just behind them were steep, snow-covered peaks. She didn't see a way around them, nor could she make a run for it through this encampment.

"What would you like to know?"

"Only if you have seen any legion forces coming this way."

"I have not." She took a step forward, but Emere did not give way. Apparently, his interrogation wasn't finished.

"Not at all? And no rumors of the Twenty-Fifth Legion approaching?"

Time was of the essence, and the faster she got down from the pass, the better. Any moment now, Eldred would be whispering in her ear that he could smell Lysandros.

"Not at all. Is that why you've blocked the pass with all these men? To ask whoever comes by that question? Aren't Imperial legionaries all over the three provinces of Lontaria, anyway?"

Emere smiled.

"There is a changing of the occupying legions, which means their numbers are much fewer than usual. And what few there are have holed up in their outposts, waiting for the main contingent of their legion to arrive. Thanks to the Princess of Arland."

The princess Cain had mentioned. Curiosity reared its head.

"What happened?"

"It is quite a long story," said Emere, whose smile widened. "She vanquished an armored chariot century on her own, killed the prefect of Arland, and gathered thousands of Arlanders to overtake the main Imperial fortress outside Kingsworth. I have no doubt she has even more soldiers at her command now."

A gasp escaped Arienne. Emere nodded.

"It is indeed surprising. But this is why we are here, standing guard. Blocking the passage of Imperial spies and gathering news on the legion's movements."

There was one thing Arienne didn't quite understand.

"You said you were the Liberators of Kamori? Has Kamori allied with Arland to fight against the Empire?"

Emere's smile faded. His eyes darkened, and he did not reply. No matter. This was not a priority to Arienne. The important thing was for her to go down the pass undeterred.

Eldred whispered, *"Arienne, I smell him. Just kill these useless nothings and be on your way."*

Above her, the peaks to the either side of the pass were covered in fresh snow. She could use the collapsing spell to set off an avalanche. But to kill all these people just to walk past them was completely absurd.

"Well, I'm not a spy. Let me pass."

"A spy would say they are not a spy."

"And one who isn't a spy would also say the same."

"Which is why we need to keep you here for a short while longer. Until we can make sure."

Irritation rose in her. "Look, I am being pursued by the Empire. There's no time to waste. If I do not pass, all of you may die. And you should hide as well. Even if for just a moment."

Emere frowned. "You said you hadn't seen any Imperial soldiers."

"He's not a soldier, and he's only one man. But that one man—"

Emere, and the men around him, laughed.

"My lady, there are fifty-three Liberators in this square. We are well-settled and there is only one route through here, narrow and quite steep, which means we can defend this square against several more times the men. You need not worry over a single . . ." He suddenly gripped his chest.

The pressure in her chest that she'd felt in the old inn returned to Arienne as well. The birds around them suddenly fell silent.

In the square, soldiers were also gripping their chests, their eyes wide, falling where they had stood. Their mouths moved but made no sound. Behind her came the sound of footsteps coming up the path she had just taken.

All the fires in the square flickered in unison, then died.

28

CAIN

Water spewed from Cain's mouth as from a drain suddenly un-clogged. He coughed and hurled up the remaining water in his lungs onto a wooden floor. His mind was still underwater. Was this the boat or the docks? It wasn't the bottom of the sea, at least. Lying strewn to his left was the chain that had been around him only a few moments ago. His soaked coat was clinging tightly to his body. Even in his delirium Cain wondered if his spectacles were still in it.

"Disgusting."

The stout man's fingers were entwined and resting on Cain's sternum. He wiped his face with his sleeve.

Septima, in her black stola and a lantern on her knees, sat at the side of the boat. Cain was on the same boat he had come in on. Another, empty boat of similar size was bobbing next to theirs. Devadas, soaking wet, was hunched over and searching the body of the motionless ex-legionary before him. It was difficult to tell whether she was alive or dead.

"He really lives again," said Septima, arching an eyebrow.

"We don't know that yet," the stout man said with a sideways look at him. "In my sailing days, I've seen many a man dragged out of the waters who revive to die anyway or become useless for life."

The feeling of lightness and peace that Cain had felt in his last moments of consciousness in the sea was gone, and the crushing weight in his chest was back. He took the stout man's extended hand but his grip failed and he fell back down on his rear. The poison still lingered.

Septima stood up and looked at him closely.

"Devadas fished you out instead of that woman," said the stout man. "Don't make us regret that."

All he could answer with was more coughing.

"What happened?" Septima asked.

Cain just about managed to catch his breath. "How did you get here? How did you save me?"

"We have our ways," said the stout man.

Devadas, apparently coming up empty on the ex-legionary, looked at them and shook his head, even as he continued his search. As the boat rocked, the woman's arm beneath him moved lifelessly like a puppet with its strings cut. Her chest on the lower left-hand side had caved in as if hit by a hammer. Devadas, done with his search, wrapped the body in chains and threw it into the ocean, making a loud splash. Foam rose to the surface, and then nothing.

"What happened, I said." Septima looked impatient.

Before answering her, Cain rifled through his coat and found his spectacles. As he put them on, everything came back into focus. With a calmer head, Cain thought carefully before opening his mouth. What could he afford to tell them?

"That man . . . Safani. He poisoned me with a dart."

He wanted to show them his thigh but to do so he would need to take off his trousers. Devadas stared at him with wide eyes.

"So you survived that too," said the stout man. "You almost died twice tonight."

Septima took the bait. "Tell me about Safani. Where is he now? I thought he'd be here."

"You were right. He's working for Gladdis."

Cain told them everything he knew about Safani. He didn't need to lie about that at all. He still didn't know what exactly he did for her, only that he was at Gladdis's house. This was where the stout man interrupted with a whistle of amusement.

"You went inside her house?"

Septima glared at the stout man, who immediately shut his mouth. Thanks to this, Cain confirmed they hadn't been following him the whole time. Or perhaps they were trying to make him think so, to see if he would lie? Who knew where this chain of suspicions would end.

"What was Gladdis's plan?"

Cain had to think for a moment. That Gladdis wanted to destroy the Capital using the Circuit of Destiny under the Senate was not a plan he had heard this evening, but something that Eldred creature had told him, in the room inside Arienne's mind. Did he believe this was true? If he did, should he tell Septima? But now that Gladdis was dead, he couldn't see the point.

"I don't know."

Septima frowned. "Then what do you know? What have you been doing this whole time?"

"The woman is dead. Doesn't that mean whatever she was planning is over?"

"Safani is the kind of man who will follow through on a job, whether the one who hired him is dead or alive."

Fienna had bidden Cain to save the people she cared about. It was a hallucination from the poison. But it was also something the Fienna Cain had known would have said. Wouldn't telling Septima now be the best way to save them? But the words wouldn't leave his mouth. His vengeance was over, so why was he hesitating?

Devadas began rowing them back toward the docks.

Maybe, somewhere in the shadows of his heart, he wanted to see the Imperial Capital go up in flames. Many heartlanders believed that all provincials deep down wanted to harm the Empire. Cain was beginning to think this might be true.

"I don't know what the plan is, but it's soon. She said something about two days of delay . . . But also that two more days would be too late. And that she would have Safani do it to stay on schedule."

The part about the Capital turning to ash was conveniently left out. How could he trust Eldred, Cain thought, justifying the omission to himself. Still, he couldn't think of a good reason to have left out the stolen Power generator in the empty house.

"There's nothing we can use here," muttered Septima.

"Knowing Safani, I'd venture a guess it'll involve an assassination or five," said the stout man.

"It would be most welcome if it were simply that, as nothing is more replaceable than people in the Empire."

But could the Empire replace hundreds of thousands? Would they just bring in people like olive oil was brought in through the docks? As the boat crossed the black waters, Septima and the stout man swapped theories while Devadas, rowing, stared at Cain without speaking.

The boat made it to the docks. Devadas went up the ladder first and took a quick look around before signaling the others to follow. The stout man quickly climbed the ladder. Septima turned to Cain and said, "You're going to our headquarters."

"But I . . . Didn't you hear? I almost died twice tonight."

"And two people actually died, one of them a great merchant with connections to the Senate. We need to write something in our report, you know."

They had two days at most before the Capital blew up. Sooner, if Safani did his job . . . *He has to be stopped.* But he could not find the words to say it.

A short distance from the docks, a black carriage waited for them. A driver in a dark cape nodded in their direction. He woke the horses with a shake of his reins, their hooves clacking on the cobblestones. Septima sat next to the driver, and the stout man got inside. Cain was very conscious of Devadas standing right behind him, blocking any chance of escape. There was an air of skepticism coming from him that Septima and the stout man did not share. Cain climbed into the carriage and took the seat behind the stout man. Devadas sat next to Cain.

Along with the other central offices of the Empire, the Ministry of Intelligence headquarters were in the old city. The carriage briefly paused by the wall that surrounded the area, permits being required to enter this part of the city at night. The guards signaled over the wall, and the gates opened. The first thing he saw were the dense rows of streetlamps, which turned the old city a different color from what it was in the day. Pale blue, running on Power. The carriage ran through a street that was as blue as a river.

The stout man was talking. "Have you ever been in the old city?"

"A few times, to deliver oil," said Cain, looking out the window. Almost no provincials lived in the old city, and even people from the other six cities of the Imperial heartland were uncommon. As the district where the Senate, the Commons, and almost all the headquarters of the Imperial ministries and merchant houses resided, this was the true center of the world, the place where the Empire was born. Buildings were grander, lights brighter, shops more extravagant. Even the leaves of the ubiquitous trees planted among the streetlights and the buildings gleamed.

"Take a good look, because you won't be seeing the outside for days."

If Eldred was correct, the 327-body Circuit of Destiny would overload, causing an explosion big enough to destroy the Capital. Even worse, a Star of Mersia could be unleashed to destroy the entire heartland; if either happened while he was in the Ministry headquarters, he wouldn't be seeing the outside ever again.

Cain realized Devadas was still staring at him, which made him so uncomfortable he finally just met his gaze directly and asked, "Why are you looking at me like that?"

Devadas said, in a low voice, "You weren't alone on that boat."

"Of course not. The ex-legionary woman was there, and Gladdis."

A strange look came over Devadas's eyes. Something like a look of sadness. He pointed his finger at Cain's sternum.

"No. There was one more. I can see it in your face."

Cain felt his heart stop. He didn't answer. How could he know what Cain had seen in his poison-addled state?

Devadas lowered his voice. "You have a task, right? A burden you inherited from someone great."

The stout man scoffed. "Truly a Varatan, no question. If you say something superstitious like that too loudly, the Office of Truth will come and take you back."

Not responding, Devadas turned away and closed his eyes.

Cain remembered Fienna's last words to him. To avenge her, to vanquish villains, and to save the world. Or not the world perhaps, but at least the people she had taken care of. As if he was their king. She was only a figment of his poisoned mind, but those words had been ringing in his mind ever since.

Cain finally understood why he had not told the agents about the Circuit of Destiny conspiracy. This was not a job for the Ministry of Intelligence, or any other organ of the Empire. This was a job for Cain himself.

But the realization had come too late. He should've made a run for it before he got in the carriage. Devadas and the stout man made it impossible for him to escape, and to do so from the Ministry of Intelligence, one of the most guarded places in the world, was unimaginable.

Outside the window on the right, he could see the hill of the Senate, the stately white-domed building of the highest political power in the world. And buried somewhere inside that hill was the Circuit of Destiny that would devour the whole city. Cain knew that Safani was in there, trying to create the disaster that would bring down the Empire. He felt the weight in his chest keenly.

The lights of the streets began flickering like stars on ocean waves. Devadas stirred. The stout man frowned and looked out the window.

Suddenly, all the lights went out.

"What's—"

Before the stout man could finish what he was saying, all the streetlamps lining the street suddenly shattered, raining sparks. Power, having lost its vessel, flowed down the poles, and the pale blue of the street was now lit with violet lightning.

Septima shouted, "Hold on!"

The horses screamed. The world itself seemed to shake, and Cain was soon bouncing in his seat. The carriage leaned violently to the left, and Cain's body was thrown to the opposite side. He could hear the stout man shouting. Just as Cain turned his head toward Devadas, a huge impact struck his body.

29

ARIENNE

In the square at the peak of Finvera Pass, Arienne slowly turned around to face Lysandros. He had not put his cloak back on, the busy gears and pistons of his body apparent to all. He must've come up the pass at great speed but did not seem tired in the slightest. Would a machine body even understand fatigue?

Lysandros, in his single-tone voice, said, "Do you now understand that you cannot run from me?"

Arienne gulped.

"Follow me and I will allow you to return to the Academy. It will be like nothing happened."

Lysandros looked and sounded different—more monstrous, more horrifying, now that Arienne knew that the box that he carried on his back was his infant son's coffin. She wasn't sure if the tiny baby's cry underneath the humming of the Power generator was real or imagined. His strides were huge as he approached her.

The pressure on the room in her mind was greater than what

she'd felt in the old inn. What would happen to Eldred if the room collapsed? She had not an inkling as to the answer.

"Did not I tell you that you would lose this way?" said Eldred. *"Unravel the bandages of my legs. Then, I shall use all my power."*

That must never be allowed. She had not forgotten what had happened when she had first tried to read *The Sorcerer of Mersia*. What Eldred had manipulated wasn't the ink on the page but her very vision. That was before his arms were free. She had no way of knowing what he was capable of doing to her now. Better to not find out what freeing him completely would do.

"Why do you not answer?" said Lysandros, pausing in his steps. "Is the corpse speaking to you?" His gaze lifted from her face and he seemed to look at someone behind her. "You fool a mere student into doing your bidding and yet lack the shame that would keep you silent. You have made a murderer of this child. All you do is bring misery to those around you."

Suddenly, her lips trembled. Her tongue moved on its own. A terror much like when a hand enters the mouth to rip out a rotted tooth came over her. Arienne tried to cover her mouth, but her arms only came up to her chest. From Arienne's mouth, in Arienne's voice, came Eldred's words.

"Have *you* forgotten the misery you caused Mersia?"

"Misery *I* caused?" Lysandros did not seem surprised Eldred was talking through Arienne.

"Did you not play Mersia's subjects against their king? Was it some other Lysandros who lied to all of Mersia that if I were gone, freedom and prosperity would come, that they would be free of fear?"

"Lies? You were the one called a tyrant by all. You turned the dead bodies of your own subjects into unliving soldiers. You took what you wanted and destroyed what you did not. Do you know how grateful Mersia was to the Empire after your death?"

"This Mersia, does it still feel gratitude toward your Empire? Does a pile of ash send letters of thanks to you every year?"

"You monster—"

"*You* call *me* a monster! You must be two centuries old by now. Creating a Power generator out of your own child and living beyond your natural time—if this does not make you a monster then what will? What are you *all* but monsters for turning Mersia into fields of dust and ash? Your Empire's lot is to diminish and consume the world, until nothing of worth is left. Has the Star of Mersia not revealed that about your vaunted destiny of conquest? I failed to stop you once, but you will not rob me of my second chance."

Arienne was not concerned with the argument at hand. She burst into the room inside her mind, where Eldred sat as usual on the edge of the bed.

"Give me back my body this instant!"

"Silence. Children should not interfere in the talk of adults. Loosen the bandages of my legs. Or I shall kill you."

Eldred and Lysandros were still sparring with words, but none of it reached Arienne's ears. Fifty-three soldiers were dying of suffocation in the meantime, but even that was not important to her in this moment. She was most afraid of losing control of her body forever.

"Give back my body! *Now!*"

She threw a punch in Eldred's face. It felt like desiccated bark against her knuckles. Dry leathery particles dropped off his cheek. Outside, Arienne's mouth stopped talking in midsentence. Inside the room, Eldred stood from the bed, pushing himself up with his arms.

"You little—!"

Lysandros took a stride forward. As he came within an arm's reach, Arienne tried to back away, but Eldred still controlled her body. Something whirred in Lysandros's machine arms, and his toneless voice spoke over the noise.

"Why, Grim King, do you have nothing more to say?"

In the mind's room, Eldred gripped Arienne's shoulders as he hissed, "Do not regard me as a mere cadaver, I am Eldred. I am the Grim King! Not one the likes of you can place their hands on!"

"Decrepit *corpse*!"

She pushed him with all her might, but Eldred's bone-thin hands only gripped her shoulders tighter.

Lysandros's voice came through from the outside.

"I am sorry for you, student girl, but we are now out of time. I sentence you to death for running away and stealing a Power generator. This is a risk you were aware of when you left the school. We shall lose Eldred as well, but perhaps we have gone past the point where he could be reclaimed."

With lightning speed, he extended his machine hand and grabbed Arienne's throat.

In her mind's room, Eldred's hands were now gripping Arienne's throat as well.

"I may not have my legs, but once you're gone . . . You useless waste of a failed sorcerer, you don't deserve to crawl this earth. I will take your body. I will kill your mind first and then that inquisitor." His hands squeezed harder. "You shall become the vessel of the great king's rebirth."

The view outside the window vanished, replaced with Lysandros's face. His expression was impossible to read, as half of it was metal. There was something of an expression on the withered visage of Eldred, but she didn't know what it meant either. Whether her neck broke in life or in this room, she was going to die. Her mind was a rush of what would be her final thoughts.

She remembered her parents back home. There was not a shred of longing in this memory. Ever since entering the Academy, she had not written a single letter to them, nor received one from them. The room in her mind was probably gone in the real world. Perhaps they had had a new child since and were raising them in it.

She thought of her friends in the Academy, especially Magnus, who had offered to tutor her, and her boyfriend Felix, and the professors. The custodian Duff. Their lives must be upside down by now. She felt nothing about this. She had fled the school without a single look back.

Cain. Who hid her only because she was from his homeland, who risked danger and used his own money to help her escape. But Arienne knew she would never see him again.

Arienne realized she was completely alone in the world. No one cared if she lived or died. She had left everything behind, severed all her ties. Except with Eldred and Lysandros. Who ironically were both trying to kill her.

The breath was leaving her body. In the room and in Finvera Square, her tears were welling. How silly her school robe should come to mind in this moment. The sorcery she used then . . . the thread that didn't exist, how she cut it to unravel herself from Duff's grip and escape . . . Eldred hadn't taught her that.

That's it. What she had done all along, what she was best at. Arienne imagined the Princess of Arland whom Cain had told her about. She is on the back of the dragon of the mountain, wearing a shining suit of armor. She has the graceful dragon markings surrounding her neck, signifying her royal heritage. She holds a flaming sword in her hand. The princess in her imagination solemnly hands Arienne the sword. Its hilt feels hot in her grip.

A word slipped past her lips. The word she had forgotten since that day in the market with her robe. Her mouth filled with strength—and she swung the flaming sword through the four arms that strangled her.

In the room of her mind, Eldred's arms—and outside on the Finvera Pass, Lysandros's arms—fell to the ground. Breath rushed back into her body.

Eldred screamed, a sound almost as injurious as the suffering it protested against. He fell onto the bed as violet smoke flowed from the stumps of his forearms. Arienne, sword in hand, left the room.

Lysandros was looking down at his sliced-off arms, seemingly unable to comprehend what had just occurred. Arienne gave him no pause as she concentrated on the cord of Power that secured the generator to his back, a cord made from thousands of knots. There was no such cord, of course, and even if there were, it would not be visible. But the imaginary sword easily slashed the imaginary cord.

The machine sounds ceased as the gears and pistons in his body stopped. He stood motionless. The human half of his face showed panic. He moved his lips, but no words came out. It was not only his limbs but his lungs that relied on Power.

With all her might, Arienne kicked Lysandros in his stomach. The metal body fell backward. The wooden coffin on his back smashed open, and a small sarcophagus of lead rolled out.

30

LORAN

Loran sat in a large chair, listening to the others talk of whether to defend the fortress or Kingsworth, how they would gather more troops, and how they would procure the necessary provisions. Among the dozen people, there were none that Loran had picked herself. Either they were representatives of their villages or the guilds of Kingsworth or they had experience serving in the legions, and Loran had only assented to their presence. There was also a man who had worked for a long time as a low-ranking clerk at the prefect's office who seemed to know everything about the city.

She eyed the *t'laran* on the necks of the people debating in front of her. She had forgotten many details about the traditional meanings in the intertwined patterns that showed which clans they had come from. But she still remembered the dragon design that had adorned the necks and banners of the old kings. Two of the councillors showed parts of that design, being perhaps a generation or three away from the royal house. Loran herself had none, but there was no challenge to her about it. It amused her that she hadn't expected any, and that she was only reminded of her common birth by the vestiges of royal markings on others.

The task at hand was more difficult than laying siege to the fortress. Wilfrid, who stood by Loran's side but had only listened so far, finally leaned toward Loran and whispered, "Princess, I think making a decision is the only way to end this long prattle."

"Perhaps."

Loran knew little of war or politics. Her only work had been that of a local swordmaster. Her intention in hosting this discussion had been to listen to those who knew more than she did and wait until they had come up with an answer. But the Empire's forces would be overwhelming regardless, and she had a feeling it was no use planning or preparing anyhow. The only thing they could control was how they would act on the day of the battle.

The fact that no one mentioned the gigatherion was proof enough of this. No matter how many soldiers of flesh and blood they had, they would be nothing against a Powered weapon the size of a castle. Everyone knew this. Still, they did not give up, and tried to think of what little there was they could do. Which meant that what they could not do, she would have to do herself.

In the back of their minds, they were probably thinking about the Star of Mersia as well. Emere had spoken to her of Mersia, of how the once-green grasslands were now a barren red desert where nothing lived. The Empire might turn Arland into such a wasteland. But that was to fear the unknown. And nobody, not even Loran, could do anything about the unknown. It was better not to think about what they could not know or anticipate.

But there was one part of the discussion that weighed heavily on Loran's mind.

"What concerns me the most in this moment is our scout's report of the Ledon northerners crossing the border," she said to Wilfrid in a low voice.

"Yes, but we've been talking mostly about what to do when the Empire arrives instead," whispered Wilfrid.

The raider tribes of Ledon, which was north of Arland, had been the country's biggest concern before the invasion of the Empire. Were they using the unrest in Arland and the absence of a real legion presence as an opportunity to raid again? But the soldiers reported the Ledonites were bringing their musk oxen. It was unthinkable they would stage a raid with cattle in tow.

The discussion had reached a lull. They seemed to have decided that the food in the prefect's granaries belonged to Kingsworth and that the militia should not touch them, but that they would ask the city's richer citizens and the landowners in the country for provisions, and that they would send out recruiters to all corners of the land to strengthen their numbers. Loran raised her hand to stop further discussion.

"Your suggestions have been noted. As for my decision . . ."

Loran's consent was a matter of form. As long as a consensus was reached with the people's circumstances in mind, she needed only to voice her approval, and that was that. At least, this had to be the way things were done for now, when she knew so little of ruling.

But before Loran could give her approval this time, a soldier burst into the hall, out of breath.

"Princess! The barbarians are approaching the fortress."

The hall became awash in murmurs. Why had the Ledonites made their way so deeply into Arland? Loran had assumed that their goal was border raids, but perhaps she had underestimated the wild folk. She couldn't help but feel that voicing her worry aloud to Wilfrid had somehow summoned them.

Loran stood. "I'll see to them. Wilfrid?"

Wilfrid grabbed her spear, which had been leaning against the wall next to her, and followed Loran out.

The fortress, in truth, was not the most defensible of buildings. It was more of a monument to the military might of the Empire than a true fortification. This was why its towers were unnecessarily tall, although it did afford a good view.

Loran made her way up to the tallest watchtower.

Kingsworth was visible to the northeast. Its castle, once so beautiful, was charred. Loran had done that. Perhaps it was better burned than preserved as an office of the prefect.

She looked northwest. A large horde of people and beasts were approaching.

Wilfrid leaned forward and narrowed her eyes. "I should say they are about five hundred, Your Highness. And two hundred heads of musk oxen . . . But why do they not wear their tunics in such cold weather? They seem to be carrying something long on their backs."

"Swords, no doubt," said Loran. Five years ago, she had fought a match against the wild folk from the north who had visited her school.

"Their swords are that long?"

"Ledonite swordsmen believe they've lost if they fail to slay with the first swing, breaking through their opponent's defenses. That's why they insist on such heavy and long swords."

"And not wear armor, as well?" said Wilfrid, her eyes still fixed on the horde.

"That is so."

"But it is winter, and to have only their fur cloaks to shield themselves from the cold . . ."

Loran smiled. "Well, there are limits to my knowledge." She paused, thoughtful. "This fortress is difficult to defend, they say, but we are still five thousand strong. If a battle happens we will still suffer losses, but I have a feeling they do not come to fight. I shall go to them and hear what they have to say."

Loran was not used to riding a horse. Wilfrid had offered to lead it by the reins, but she was afraid the northerners would look down on her for it. With a hundred soldiers following, Loran rode out to meet the horde.

One hundred soldiers. In Gwaharad's underground castle, Loran had to beg for one hundred of his Liberators. But now, at her call, several times more were putting themselves forward to help her. Perhaps this was what it meant to be a king.

Just when she had come to this thought, the horde had stopped their progress, about three hundred paces away. Loran raised her arm to stop her own soldiers and continued forward with Wilfrid. The musk oxen herd had a pungent smell that carried all the way to Loran, wholly different from cows of Arland.

From their side approached a lone man as well, a giant of rough skin and grizzled hair and beard. He looked at least seven feet tall. As he was taller than the others, the sword on his back was also longer. The red war paint on his face looked like congealed blood. Wilfrid, tense, knocked the ground with the bottom of her spear as she walked.

About ten paces apart, Loran and the giant came to a stop.

The giant spoke first, in a loud and cheerful voice. He spoke not Ledonese or Imperial but fluent Arlandais.

"The new king of Arland is in that fortress, I hear? The king who destroyed four chariots with a dragon's sword?"

In times of turmoil, rumors traveled quickly. It seemed the tale of Loran and Wurmath had already spread to the north.

"I am not a king yet, but I believe you are speaking of me."

The giant gave a short laugh. "You are smaller than I imagined."

He was armed, and his voice gruff, but his eyes were kind. Loran smiled back. Wilfrid, still tense, gave a little groan.

"I am Griogal, warrior-in-chief of the fifteen tribes of Ledon. If you are not a king, how must I address you?"

"You may address me as a princess." She felt no compunction in using the title anymore.

"I ask to be called Griogal. We are here to convey a message to the princess."

"A message that requires an escort of five hundred warriors and two hundred musk oxen?"

"The cattle are a gift!"

Griogal opened his arms and approached. Wilfrid, still nervous, trained her spear at him, but Loran gestured to her to stand down. Carefully—if she fell on the ground here, it would be disastrously embarrassing—she dismounted the horse.

"Our windboats sailed out to the Great West Sea and saw the

Twenty-Fifth's blue griffin banners. They should have landed on Ledon's coast by now."

Loran did not know what a griffin was. Perhaps the beast on the banner at the forest, a mix of a bird and a lion. And what were windboats? She didn't know that either, but it wasn't important in that moment.

"If they are indeed in Ledon . . ."

". . . Then they will be here where we stand in as many as six or as few as four days," Griogal said, picking up where Loran had trailed off. He looked intently at her face. Loran tried not to look surprised.

"Ever since the arrival of the Empire," Griogal went on, "the fifteen tribes were treated as no better than beasts."

Southern Ledon was under Imperial rule, just like Kamori and Arland, but the northern part of Ledon was not even afforded that. The Imperial forces made sorties against those tribes regularly, killing and driving out the people who lived there, a tyrannical move even Loran was aware of—one the Empire was eager to make known, in fact, as it made Arlanders feel grateful to the Empire for protecting them from being raided by the northern "barbarians." In truth, Loran, insomuch as she thought of it at all, had been one of those people until today.

"When we heard the princess had vanquished the legion forces, we were determined to fight by her side. There was no time to send emissaries. Please forgive our impudence for barging into your realm."

Griogal extended a large hand toward Loran.

Loran did not hesitate. She stepped forward, closing the gap between them, and grasped it.

31

CAIN

Cain came to. How much time had passed? The carriage had fallen on its right side after a downward tumble, probably off the street itself considering the incline. He could see nothing outside. He dragged his hand over his face, checking for blood or pain; miraculously, his spectacles were intact. Something cushioned his back; it was the belly of the stout man, who was unconscious.

Cain heard a sound of chaos from outside. Maybe it was an earthquake, but he had never experienced one or heard of one happening since he arrived in the Capital. There was also that blinking of the streetlamps right before the earth moved. Something had happened to the Power generators in this part of the city.

Had Safani finally done something to the Circuit of Destiny? That would mean Gladdis was winning, even in death.

His limbs were fine. There was dizziness from the shock, but he could move. The roof of the carriage had a door with a latch, which he could just about reach, but it was jammed in its twisted frame.

There was a warmth on his side. His fingertips touched his seawater-drenched clothes there and came away with red blood. It didn't hurt. He looked up. Devadas was holding his long arms against the walls, a human rafter. His great bulk and immense strength had prevented the carriage from being crushed and killing everyone inside. A piece of wood had speared itself through Devadas's stomach, and his blood was dripping from the tip onto Cain's coat. He was looking down at Cain, eyes wide open in pain.

Devadas spoke, only for the third time since they had met. His voice was low.

"Get out of here. Do you not have a task at hand? A burden you inherited?"

Cain was daunted. "What do you mean?"

"I am the last of my order. My own burden is heavy. I know the look on your face. I see it in the mirror every day." He said this with a grimace, perhaps from the pain of his wound. He made his left hand into a fist and, with a great roar, punched the roof door. It flew off into the night like a bird.

Cain glanced back at Devadas and the stout man before maneuvering his legs out of the wreckage. Once outside, he found the carriage had fallen into a large pit that should not exist in the middle of a city street. Using the protruding rocks on the walls of the pit as handholds, he pulled himself up.

The Capital was on fire. Just in front of him, a shop full of expensive clothes had turned into a raging bonfire. He had heard that fires followed earthquakes, and at night, when lanterns and candles blazed, such fires seemed even more likely. The shouts and screams of the injured and the afraid mixed with the ringing bells of the fire carriages. The streets had erupted in places, leaving gaping holes that made it impossible for carriages to cross.

Standing at the edge of his own such pit, Cain looked up toward the Senate hill. It was usually brightly lit by Powered lanterns, but now there was only darkness. As if the entire Senate had vanished. Cain was dizzy, and everything felt like a dream. The buildings surrounding the hill were on fire. Violet lights of Power threaded through the thick smoke. Inside the pit, the three whinnying, struggling horses seemed to have broken their legs. The carriage was irretrievably damaged, but the yoke was still intact, strangling the still-alive horses. Cain took in every bit of the horrific scene while emotions he struggled to name raged inside him.

However, his own yoke was broken. No longer was he a puppet of the Ministry. Nor was he a tool for anyone else. The grip he had felt on his heart had loosened.

He'd only taken a single step forward when someone shouted his name from behind.

"Cain!" Septima stood at the other side of the pit, her stola torn and her hair disheveled. "Where do you think you're going!"

Without answering, he turned and ran. He was sure to get caught again if he hesitated.

The streets were full of people and carriages trying to escape the chaos. They looked impassable, and he did not know how the alleys in the old city were laid out. He started climbing the wall of a stone building that wasn't on fire.

Septima was approaching fast, her body low and her face ferocious. She looked like a completely different person. There was something in her right hand that glinted in the firelight. Cain quickly made his way up the wall onto the roof.

The old city had turned orange with flames. Quickly, he scanned the layout of the streets for a path to the Senate. He couldn't make out any route that didn't go through burning buildings and smoke-filled streets. Septima had probably spotted him on this building, and if he dawdled, he would be caught. Breathing deeply, he took a few steps back, and leaped onto the roof of the burning building next to him.

He was thankful his clothes were too soaked with seawater to catch flame, but the heat was already unbearable. The next building was higher up. He leaped to a window covered with wooden bars. A small grunt of pain escaped him as his bruised body collided with the wall of the house, but his hands gripped the bars firmly. The bars weren't heated enough to really burn his hands, but the air itself felt like it would burn his lungs. Even breathing the smoky night air outside the buildings made his throat and his chest ache. The legs of his spectacles felt like they were searing themselves into his temples. Gritting his teeth and letting go with one hand, he carefully removed them and put them in his pocket. Then, shifting his grip on the bars, he began climbing the wall once more.

When he got to the third building, Septima shouted at him.

"Come back this instant!"

He turned. Septima stood on the roof of the burning building, staring at him with a long dagger in hand.

"You'll die if you stay there," he said. "You're a public servant. Shouldn't you be helping the public by putting out the fire or something?"

"Are you somehow involved in all of this?"

To anyone else, this would have seemed a natural disaster. But not to Septima. Just like Devadas, she must have harbored a feeling there was something Cain had been withholding from them all this time.

Instead of answering, Cain leaped to the next building. Septima screamed something at him, but he was already flying through the flames, jumping between buildings.

At the last building, Cain slid down the drainpipe into the alley, the pipe so hot that he had to pull his sleeves over his hands to do it. Without a proper grip on the pipe, it was almost like falling. He rolled on the ground when he landed.

Stepping out onto the main road, he found himself surrounded by a sea of fire.

Even with his unaided eyes, Cain could see the slightly different tint to the fire here. In the red-and-yellow flames, and even in the black smoke, was a sheen of violet. Cain avoided the fire as best he could, walking in the center of the street, but still, he could feel his skin burning.

Now he was at the foot of the Senate hill, the Senate itself a building built before the Empire had named itself so. Underneath it, apparently, were 327 Power generators linked together to form a circuit.

A disruption in the Circuit of Destiny must have caused this night of terror, spreading somehow to other Power generators of the city. Cain knew nothing of sorcery or Power, but that cadaver Eldred in Arienne's mind had said the Circuit was going to explode, or a Star of Mersia would extinguish all life in the Imperial heartland. Which meant this fire was only a preamble of what was to come.

He went up the hill along the road. There were no people about, everyone having died or evacuated. Only the buildings burning in eerie violet, with even the stone buildings billowing fire from their windows, kept him company as he made his way to the Senate. It was so difficult to breathe that he covered his nose and mouth with his coat. His clothes were now almost dry. But as he climbed the hill, there were no buildings to burn. It became less smoky, and he could soon breathe easier.

It was forbidden to erect buildings near the Senate, in order to preserve its grandeur. Instead, there was a garden filled with sculptures of dead senators. He crept through them to the front entrance of the Senate.

It was night and no senators would be about, but there were sure to be guards. There weren't any he could see. Just when he was about to be glad for it, he found a woman in a guard uniform lying on the ground. Cain approached, sneaking from sculpture to sculpture. There were two more people on the ground.

Gulping, he cautiously made his way to one of them. They weren't breathing. A faint smell of honey . . . There were dots on the neck of the guard, the skin around them turned dark blue from poison. Safani's poison. He squinted his eyes to see no dart in the wound, which meant Safani must've stabbed them from up close. Cain remembered Safani standing behind him at Gladdis's house, materializing as if from thin air.

He entered the main doors, which were ajar. It was dark inside. From somewhere came a heavy, irregular hum of machinery. He walked down the dark corridor, following it.

Just when he noticed the cloying smell of honey once again, something grabbed his ankle, almost making him shout. It was a fallen guard, a weak moan escaping his lips. Cain bent down and listened.

"Who . . . who are you?"

"Cain, from the Ministry of Intelligence," he lied. "What happened?"

"A man wearing black . . . appeared from nowhere . . ."

"Where did he go?"

"Stairs . . . underground . . ." He let go of Cain's ankle and pointed.

Half of the guard's neck was discolored, a fact obvious even to his blurry vision in the dimness. The puncture wound itself had widened to the width of a coin and his flesh was rotting inward. Cain lied again.

"You will be fine. Rest."

He then took the guard's sword from his belt. The guard reached out to him as if to object, but his arm fell lifelessly before he could grab Cain's ankle again.

Cain passed through the darkness. There was a door where the guard had pointed. He took his spectacles from his inner pocket and leaned toward the sign posted on it. Under the open-eye insignia of the Office of Truth, it read, NO ENTRY.

32

ARIENNE

Arienne could sense that Emere feared her. Most people feared sorcerers. Having seen her slay a machine monster with an invisible sword was likely to have added to the intimidation. Arienne didn't dislike this state of affairs. If he hadn't seen her do it, he never would have asked to escort her to Arland himself. Once she removed her scarf and revealed her clan markings to show that she was from Arland, Emere insisted she meet Loran.

"But why?"

"Princess Loran faces a tremendous challenge."

"The invading legion you've mentioned."

"That is so. As you are also a thorn in her enemy's eye, there should be much you can do to help each other."

It was true she was being pursued by the Empire, but to describe her as a thorn in their eye seemed a bit much. But thinking back, she was now far, far from having an ordinary life. She had hidden the infamous Eldred in her mind and had just killed the Grand Inquisitor

277

of the Office of Truth and taken his Class Two generator. She was a thief, murderer, traitor, and rogue sorcerer, arguably a mortal enemy of the Empire. All that and she was only sixteen. Not disliking this notion either, she smiled to herself.

Since she left the pass, Eldred had sat on the edge of the bed, saying nothing. Violet smoke continued to trickle from where his arms had been cut. Arienne did not speak to Eldred either.

What was she going to do about him? It was unforgivable that he'd tried to steal her body. But she didn't know if it was wise to get rid of him either. While she could try to remove him from her mind, she was hesitant to let him out into the world, having seen what he could do within the confines of the imagined room. But perhaps Eldred, having tested Arienne and lost, would prove more docile in the future?

The former legion fortress looked more like an office of the Empire than a military fort. Instead of the imposing, impenetrable walls she imagined, it had almost what might be a fence. The keep and towers were tall and impressive, though. Other than the decrepit tower in the forest, she hadn't seen a building taller than two stories since leaving the Capital, which made the fortress feel more dominating before her now. When the wind blew, there was a smell fouler than a stable before cleaning.

From Finvera Pass, it had taken her six days to reach this place, and each step made her more nervous about meeting the princess. In Arienne's mind, the Princess of Arland was not named Loran. Because she had imagined her so vividly for the purposes of her spell, she had already preconceived the princess's voice, appearance, and manner. A part of her did not want to meet the real princess.

There was something that bothered her about overwriting the one in her mind.

The guards did not know Emere by sight, but readily opened the gate when they heard his name. Soldiers came forth and escorted them both inside. Arienne was given a high-floor room with a good view. The princess was said to be in talks with the Ledonite allies who were camped near the fortress and would return in the evening.

Arienne unpacked. The first thing she took out of her sack was the lead sarcophagus. The baby's name, apparently, had been Tychon. It was heavy, but she couldn't bear to leave it on Finvera Pass. Not just because it was a Power generator, but because it was the resting place of an innocent child. An infant son who'd been murdered by his own father. Since her travels with Eldred, she could no longer regard the beings inside Power generators as mere corpses, if she ever had.

Arland had not felt like home to her when she arrived, and it was only in this room that she began to feel her journey was at an end. Ironically enough, the building was in the Imperial style. Its interior reminded Arienne of her old dormitory and of Lucretia's house.

She had intended to lie down for just a moment on the welcomingly familiar Imperial-style bed, but the sun was setting when she was startled awake by a knocking at her door.

"Who is it?"

"It is Loran. May I enter?"

Who was Loran? Recognition jolted her out of her stupor. The princess had come to her room, in person.

"Wait, please wait a moment!" Arienne frantically put the clothes she had scattered on the floor back on, clothes she hadn't washed throughout her journey. Her body and hair were also filthy. How could she meet royalty in such a state?

But it wasn't as if she could do laundry while the princess stood waiting at the door.

Arienne opened it.

In her imagination, the princess had been a woman in her twenties and worn shining armor and a crown. The woman who stood before her was older, perhaps late thirties, with a serious yet kind face. A red eyepatch covered one of her eyes. Her hair was cut neatly, and she had a sword slung on her belt. She wore worn leather armor. Like the imagined princess she had her clan markings on the neck, but none of the patterns resembled the royal dragon design. Arienne touched her own tattoos.

Loran smiled awkwardly as she entered the room and sat down at a table by the windows. Arienne also sat down, across from her.

"I hear you're an Arlander from the Capital."

"I am." It felt less like an audience with a princess and more like a talk with one of her younger professors at the Academy. Arienne knew nothing of royalty except for what she had read in books.

"And that you're a sorcerer."

"Yes." She couldn't find anything to say except to answer questions.

"How do you find your homeland after all this time?" She seemed genuinely curious.

"I don't really remember what it was like."

"You haven't reunited with your family yet. Maybe it'll seem more real to you when you do."

"I don't . . . think I'll see them."

Loran looked a little taken aback, but a sadness settled on her features.

"I see. I'm sure you have your reasons."

There was a brief silence.

"I hear you're fighting the Empire," ventured Arienne.

Loran raised her eyebrows. Arienne was inwardly aghast; had she made a mistake? But Loran's expression returned to normal as she spoke.

"I am."

"Will you win?"

Loran turned her gaze toward the window.

"They say a legion of the Empire numbers ten thousand soldiers, but it is smaller than that. More like six thousand, including noncombatants. On top of that, a small part of the Twenty-Fifth Legion is divided between Ledon, Kamori, and Arland, and the bulk of their forces are coming by sea. In terms of pure numbers, they are not an insurmountable foe. And every day, we have men and women coming to this fortress, pledging themselves to the cause. You may have also noticed our Ledonite allies camped outside. However . . ."

"Yes?"

Loran turned to Arienne and looked her in the eye. Her gaze was so firm it made Arienne uncomfortable.

"It's the Powered weapons that are the real problem. Especially the gigatherion."

Arienne had once seen two gigatherions, on a parade day in the Capital. They had been too large to fit inside the city, and instead stood at the outskirts like massive sculptures. One was a human-shaped giant that looked like it could touch the sky, the other took the form of a four-legged beast.

"The Twenty-Fifth Legion," continued Loran, "has a gigatherion named Clarios. It is being shipped here as we speak. I wonder if it's made it to the shores of Ledon by now."

"Then it'll be here soon."

"That is so. Which is why I wish to ask . . . Would it be possible for you to help us?"

Fear rose in Arienne. It wasn't the call to arms that frightened her but the prospect that in the end, she would have nothing to offer.

"But I know nothing of war—"

"I would not ask you to fight in battle. You've studied in the Empire's school of sorcery, have you not? You know how their sorcery works?"

". . . Somewhat." What Imperial sorcery she was aware of was only the bare fundamentals of Powered machines.

"Have you ever seen a chain engraved with runes?"

"I have. They are used to control Power generators." She was glad to share something she knew.

"I see. I didn't know that."

Arienne wondered what Loran would ask of her. The princess seemed to be hesitating as to whether it was something that could be asked.

"To fight the Twenty-Fifth's gigatherion, there is one thing that I absolutely require."

"What is it?"

"The fire-dragon of the mountain. Only the dragon can fight the gigatherion. But it lies bound in black chains in its cavern inside the volcano. I need you to break those chains. This may be our only chance, as the Empire's reinforcements have not arrived yet, and I have the support that I have. Will you do it?"

It was disconcerting. "But why would you entrust *me* with such an important task?"

"I was a mere teacher, a neighborhood swordmaster, before all this. I taught those who sought amusement, or exercise, or employment in the legions or the prefect's guard. Still, I have some confidence in my skill with the sword. But I do not know how to break the chains forged in the Empire's sorcery."

Loran unhitched her sword in its scabbard and placed it on the table.

"I have slain the Empire's Powered soldiers and even destroyed their Powered chariots with this sword. But the sword is made from the fang of the dragon. I cannot sever the chains that bind the dragon with its own fang. And the only one here who knows Imperial sorcery is the young lady Arienne."

But I don't know either. The words had almost left Arienne's lips. But Arienne had severed Eldred's arms, and the machine arms of the Grand Inquisitor Lysandros as well. She had killed Lysandros by cutting a cord of magic that did not even exist. It had been in that moment that Arienne realized cutting and severing were indeed her greatest talent. And as Loran said, there was no one who could do it in her stead.

Gathering her courage, she nodded.

"I shall try."

Loran sighed softly, looking relieved.

"It is some distance to the volcano. I know you've just arrived from a long journey, and it pains me to ask you to do this so suddenly,

283

but the fate of our kingdom hangs in the balance. Please be on your way as soon as possible. Fifty of our soldiers and Prince Emere himself will travel with you and help you on your way."

Arienne wondered if she was meant to be here from the beginning, when she had decided to leave the school. Perhaps everything from that moment had happened in order to prepare her for this purpose. She stood up. Loran picked up the sword from the table.

"This sword is called Wurmath. I received it as a sign of my promise to the dragon. There are two paths into the volcano. One of them is untenable." Loran seemed to be remembering something as a small smile rose to her face. "For the other one, you will need this sword to pass. Please keep it safe for me."

"But what if the legion arrives while I am gone? What will you do without the sword?"

Loran smiled again. "I don't need it anymore."

Arienne received Wurmath from Loran's hand. The hilt was hot. She remembered the scene in her mind at Finvera Pass, where the princess with the golden crown had handed her a sword of fire.

She felt exactly now as she did then.

33

LORAN

Loran was alone in the officers' exercise hall on top of the hill that the fortress was built around. She had never fought in a war. If she hadn't met her husband and married young, maybe she would have tried to become a legion officer.

She looked around the spacious hall; the floor was of rough granite, and there were no walls. Twenty pillars erected on the edges of the square floor supported a thin roof. On one side was a weapons rack with several kinds of spears and swords. The sculpture of two falcons, once hung by two chains, had been torn off the roof without any instruction from Loran.

It was a full moon. There wasn't a single lit torch, but the moonlight shone brightly into the hall. It was by arrangement that Loran was here alone. She had been so busy since taking over the fort that she had hardly any time to practice her sword skills. Not since that brief period before and after giving birth to her daughter had she rested her sword for so long.

She slowly drew the sword at her hip. It had a different balance from Wurmath. The tip was lighter, making it closer to the blades she would use as a swordmaster instructing her pupils.

Turning her body so her right arm and shoulder came to the fore, Loran trained the tip of the blade between the eyes of an imaginary opponent. She had always been small for her age, which meant she had almost never sparred with an opponent her size. This put her in the habit of holding her sword somewhat higher than others would do. A bad habit her grandmother and her mother had decried her for, but Loran knew from her own experience that this was her best stance given her height.

She sliced the air from upper left to lower right, took a step and thrusted, parried with a short sideways swing, and took a half step back. A basic practice form that her school taught for generations. Repeating these moves until she was sweating and warmed up was the beginning of her practice routine. She had put a small wooden sword in her daughter's hand and made her do the same. She was to take over the swordmaster practice when she grew up. If she had no talent for it, Loran would have eventually pinned her hopes on a future son-in-law, but Loran had so wanted her daughter to take to the sword and follow in her footsteps.

The wind was cold. Her sweat evaporated almost as soon as it appeared on her skin. Wiping her forehead with her sleeve, she went to the edge of the hall and looked down at the fortress grounds. Torches were lit here and there, and strains of an old song were being sung together. Northeast of the fortress were scores of bonfires where the Ledonites were encamped. Loran had invited them into the fortress, but Griogal had demurred, citing the need to avoid unnecessary friction.

"You look like you are enjoying yourself."

Loran knew whose low voice it was that spoke to her. Her left eye grew warm. She took off her eyepatch and opened her closed eye.

"If you could have shown yourself to me all along, why haven't you spoken to me before now?" she said.

Her left eye caught the faint outline of the fire-dragon.

"I do not know the affairs of the human world well. Is it my place, then, to interfere with you?"

"I had hoped to see you again when I was sleepless for those many nights in Kamori after killing the prefect."

Her words had an edge of resentment to them, but that wasn't how she actually felt. Loran turned and walked back to stand in the center of the hall. She posed again, aiming for the middle of the imaginary eyes. The dragon was right. She was enjoying this moment.

"Those sleepless nights were what made you leave the underground palace. There are some things one must come to conclude on one's own."

"Did you foresee all of this?"

"I knew you would become king the moment I laid eyes on you. But not how you would." She was reminded of Emere's words in the underground palace. *What presents a king to be chosen is not the people; it is destiny.* Maybe the dragon saw her destiny, as Emere did.

"But I am not king yet. I may die before I am. Along with the six thousand here gathered with me."

Loran swung her sword diagonally five times in the air. She advanced twice and retreated twice as she did so.

"I have sent a sorcerer to you," Loran said. "She carries Wurmath."

"I know all that you know," the dragon replied. *"But can such a child sever these chains?"*

"I have a feeling she can."

"You, too, like that boy Emere, have seen the hand of destiny upon another then."

Maybe she had.

"Will you come help us if she severs the chains? There is no other way I can think of to fight the gigatherion."

"Who am I to refuse a royal decree?"

Loran laughed. She switched stances to raise the blade in a high position.

"I am not a king yet."

The dragon laughed its terrifying laugh. Loran stopped in midthrust as she winced.

"When you first came to me, you said you were not a princess. But you earned the title, as well as the right to my audience, the moment you threw yourself into the mouth of the volcano. And now you are a king, but claim you are not. What will it take for you to know what you are?"

"No one calls me king. I've never had a coronation—"

"To say that you, who have called yourself a princess without ever having been the child of a king, are not a king only because no bit of gold decorates your head, that *is to laugh. Listen, Loran."*

The outline of the dragon became clearer in her left eye.

"You are king. And much more deserving of the title than that mole in the caves of the Kamori forest. You held the lives of two people more precious than gold, and killed a prefect of the Empire when you could not bear the anguish of it. You offered your own life as sacrifice when you feared the wrath of the Empire would further harm the people. It is not I who recognized you for these deeds. It is the people of Arland. In

this bitter winter, they who would sit trembling in their houses, afraid the Empire would destroy their lives, rose up to fight when they heard of your presence in their midst. The people to whom you gave warmth when they shivered in the ice and snow are gathered there in the fortress on which you stand. Do you still say you are not king?"

Loran spoke gravely. "But that changes nothing. Once the legion arrives, we will likely be defeated."

"Even if I appear in the skies?"

But you were defeated by a gigatherion, twenty years ago. Loran did not say these words, but her tact was unnecessary. The dragon knew all too well the reason for its chains.

"Even if we win this battle, the Empire has a hundred legions. If one does not defeat us they will send two, if two does not then three, if three does not then . . ."

Loran stopped herself before she mentioned the Star of Mersia.

"You believe," said the dragon, *"that Arland will fall in the end. That it will never escape the grip of the Empire. Then why do you persist in your fight?"*

The dragon's tone was more curious than accusatory.

"Because it is what the people of Arland desire the most. To fight for freedom is our destiny."

"And is defeat at the hands of the Empire also your destiny?"

Loran answered slowly, thinking as she spoke, "Victory or defeat matters less than the fact that we fight. For there to be a next time, Arland must survive, but our spirit must also. If we abandon this battle, there will never be another. But if we fight, maybe one day, when . . ."

The dragon roared in satisfaction.

"That is right, Loran. But that is why you must know you are king.

So that the title of king may befit whomever follows in your steps. That even if you are felled in battle and die, the people of Arland shall remember that there was a king who rose up. Destiny may offer men and women who would be kings, but only the people may exalt them.

"But I do not feel this battle will end so. I see this country again through this eye of you who have become king. I see a different future for Arland. I also believe that you shall not die in this coming battle."

It still felt like empty encouragement to Loran. She corrected her grip and continued to practice. A silence flowed. After a few repetitions, the dragon spoke once more.

"Your sword . . . Can you fight without my fang?"

"I realized it first when I fought the Powered soldier in the woods, but Wurmath contains only a little of your power. As you first told me, the sword is merely a symbol. What you have given me is far greater than the weapon."

She focused on her warm left eye. It shone brighter; heat circulated in her body. Scales budded on the back of her hands. Her fingernails sharpened, the sword in her hand heated too, and smoke began rising from the blade.

Closing her eyes, she calmed herself. The blade cooled quickly. The scales on the back of her hands fell to the floor. Her left eye dimmed.

"And if I am truly king, as you say, then I need the sword even less."

"Your power is not a thing I have given you. It became your own as you became king. I only provided the spark." There was satisfaction in the dragon's voice. *"I am accustomed to slumber through the season of ice and snow, but this winter, you have made sleep impossible. I shall rest a little now. Perhaps that will lessen the fright of the sorcerer child."*

Loran had one final question. "You said that you saw the future of Arland. When the Empire invaded this land twenty years ago, what did you see then?"

The dragon hesitated before speaking again.

"I saw the Empire's forces trampled beneath me, never to cast so much as their shadow on Arland."

"I see." Loran smiled.

"I was young then." With this final quip, the dragon vanished from Loran's vision. Her left eye was blind once more. She fastened her eyepatch. Then, from the weapons rack, she chose a legionary's shortsword and gripped it in her left hand.

34

CAIN

The downward passageway was like the inside of a well, with winding steps protruding from the circular wall. It was bright with a light from an unseen source. The passage had to lead to the Circuit of Destiny. Cain had the feeling he'd seen these stairs before. It was a memory as faint as someone else's dream. Why was he imagining there would be an old skeletal body at the bottom of these steps?

The steps were endless, the common lime-painted wall seeming to go down into the depths of the earth. It was uncertain how far down he had come, or how far he still had to go. His shoes were in his left hand to lessen the chances of Safani hearing his approaching footsteps. In the deep silence of this place, the squelching of his boots had seemed mercilessly loud even to him. Taking off the shoes, though, only made him more aware of the sound of his breath.

In his right hand was the sword of the guard who had just

died. He had never held a soldier's weapon before. It was heavy and awkward in his grip, but since he'd lost his dagger, he had no other weapon to use against Safani.

Finally, the bottom. There was an iron door. The lock lay broken on the floor, looking as if it had been struck with something heavy, leaving scrape marks. The marks were too deep and wide to be from a knife or a sword; did Safani carry an axe? He tried to recall what little he had seen of Safani. There was his stern expression, but Cain's memories were all very unclear. There was something about these quiet stairs that made it so . . .

Carefully, he opened the door slightly and peered around it. It was completely white inside, and so bright it was almost impossible to tell the walls from the floor. Safani was nowhere to be seen. Cain adjusted his spectacles and entered the room. The iron door shut behind him.

It was even quieter inside. Not only could he hear his own breathing, he could hear his very pulse when he held his breath.

Behind him, the crude iron door stood as if floating in an infinite expanse of white space. There was something that resembled a door in front of him as well. Approaching it, he found it was not a door but something like the iridescent sheen of a soap bubble. His light touch sent ripples through it.

Putting his shoes back on, he slid three fingers under the left glass of his spectacles to cover the eye. He was adjusting at least one of them to the dark. This room had been so bright, his eyes had trouble adjusting to it, and if the next room was darker, he would be essentially blind for just as long—enough time to decide whether he lived or died. Cain had learned this trick from an old sailor who frequented Lukan's bar.

Then, holding out his right hand, he stepped through the bubble-like barrier.

Cain had imagined the chamber to be dark. A library of death, with 327 cadavers stacked over one another in their coffins like books.

But the chamber was not dark. It was also hardly a chamber at all. And there were not rows of coffins. Instead, over a vast red wasteland, cocoon-like figures floated in a sky splotched with violet. Cain didn't need to count them to know what they were. He uncovered his left eye.

Like an audience looking down at a stage from above, the 327 Power generators wrapped in their bandages were leaning toward the earth. Each generator seemed to emit an irregular vibrating sound, slowly adjusting and harmonizing with the others.

Their eyes, though obscured by the wrappings that covered their faces, seemed fixed on a lead coffin that looked out of place here, beside which was the back of a man wearing a black coat like Cain's.

Cain, stepping as softly as possible, approached Safani's back. The legionary's sword in his right hand was uncomfortably heavy. His back and hip hurt, perhaps injured when the carriage overturned. His fingers ached from scaling walls. There were blisters from the fires he had braved, bursting and throbbing with pain. But more than these trivial pains, it was the presence of cadavers above that gripped his heart, made him feel the weight on his chest again.

When the scattered hums became one, it turned into the sound of hundreds of voices whispering at once. Cain froze, feeling something was about to happen, but Safani only gazed upward. As Cain took another careful step ahead, Safani suddenly threw open the lid of the lead coffin. The lid fell upon the red earth and rang like a dull bell. Bright violet fumes unfurled like fern fronds from within.

"Now I can have my revenge."

This was the first time Cain heard Safani's voice. Not a high- or low-pitched one, but the voice of an ordinary man, yet soaked in hatred and glee. It sent chills down his spine. He had to stop this man.

The whispers stopped. Three hundred and twenty-seven cadavers, the Circuit of Destiny, turned toward Cain. Through the whispers that rose once more, he heard one distinct proclamation.

". . . He is here, the man who would be king . . ."

Sensing their attention had shifted, Safani also turned. With all his might, Cain raced over the red earth toward him. Something flashed, and a dart cracked one of the lenses of his spectacles. Cain didn't hesitate but raised his sword as he ran. Safani drew his dagger but Cain was already in the air as he lunged at Safani. A red, hot liquid splashed on Cain's face. Both of them tumbled to the ground as Cain collided with Safani.

Safani got to his feet first, holding his left shoulder with his right hand. Between his fingers gushed a considerable amount of blood. Cain managed to hold on to his sword, but Safani's blade was lodged between Cain's ribs. Blood had splashed on his spectacles and made everything even more red.

Betraying not a hint of pain on his face, Safani kicked at the still-prone Cain, reminding Cain of when he was assaulted by Gladdis's men. But accepting any blows here meant death. He rolled out of the way, his hand still firmly gripping the sword hilt, his weight pressing the dagger's blade farther into his side. He bit back a scream. The tip of Safani's boot grazed Cain's back. Safani deftly regained his balance and looked down at Cain.

"You're the boy from earlier tonight. Weaseled out of death to live another day, I see."

Earlier tonight. Cain couldn't believe everything that had happened in less than a day. The stout man from the Ministry had said Cain had almost died twice in one night. Counting the carriage, it was three times. Soon, it might be more, if the dagger between his ribs didn't kill him.

"Do you know what's going on outside?" said Cain. "There's been an earthquake. Power generators everywhere are overloading. The Capital is on fire."

A leer broke through Safani's still mask of a face. "How droll. A fitting foreshadow of the judgment ahead."

"What are you about to do?"

"Only what the Empire deserves. Ten cities like this going up in flames wouldn't be enough for all the lives they've destroyed."

Cain struggled to stand. This was not the time for this conversation. He felt the stare of the cadavers above him. Their whispers, their incomprehensible whispers . . .

"Don't get up, or I'll kill you," threatened Safani. A slight panic had slipped into his voice. He seemed weaker. This was not the same Safani Cain had confronted in Gladdis's house.

Cain did not heed his words, instead carefully pushing himself off the ground to stand. Safani's dagger dug farther into his ribs. He bore it out with a pained groan. Safani, as if in the inverse to Cain's motion, stumbled then and fell to the ground. The blow Cain had landed to his shoulder must have been more effective than he'd thought.

Cain wiped the blood from his lenses with his sleeve.

"I don't know what you're trying to do. Just tell me how I can stop it."

"Why stop it? Once the Empire falls, the world will rise. All its oppression will fail. Without the support of the Capital, its many legions will disintegrate sooner or later. The majority of legionaries are province-born, after all. There will be rebellions! Don't you see what this means?" Safani's careful mask was crumbling. He grimaced, as if speaking caused him pain. "Think about it. Why give up this chance?"

Cain slowly approached Safani.

"I have no interest in the world. But this city is Fienna's kingdom, and that kingdom is in my care now. Your poison allowed me to realize this once and for all. *That* is why I came for you."

"Who is Fienna?"

He doesn't even know, Cain scoffed bitterly. Fienna was just a name to this man, no more a person to him than she was to the Empire and the Capital.

Cain limped ahead. Safani frantically dragged himself away from Cain with one working arm, blood gushing from his shoulder as it lost the pressure the wound needed. The amount of blood told Cain that Safani's artery was pierced, and that he was as good as dead. The dying man asked, in a weaker voice that resembled a sigh, "What kingdom are you talking about?"

Cain replied, "The one you didn't bother to see." He plunged his sword into Safani's chest.

35

ARIENNE

Arienne was crossing the snow-covered valley on a chestnut horse. She was clad in light armor according to Emere's suggestion. Lysandros's Power generator—his son, Tychon—was in one of the bags hanging from the horse's side.

White smoke rose from the volcano. With the smoke came an unbroken sort of buzzing, an invisible but palpable tension. It reminded Arienne of a working Power generator.

Arienne stopped the horse before a small stream. In the water's reflection, her eyes were violet and glowing slightly. Whether because the dragon was near or perhaps Eldred's Power was spilling from his wounds and into the world, she didn't know. She splashed her face with the cold water. Behind her, fifty soldiers waited at least ten paces away from her. Farther away, Emere led the way on his horse. They all feared Arienne. She still didn't dislike this.

Just a little bit more, and she would come upon the mouth of the cave, the secret entrance into the volcano.

"That sword is a dragon's fang."

It was Eldred. He spoke for the first time since the fight at Finvera Pass.

Arienne looked over her shoulder, making sure the trailing soldiers were too far to hear her speak. "I know. The princess told me so."

"That princess is no ordinary woman."

"Neither am I."

She'd been dragged to the Capital for being a sorcerer. She'd had to run away, hide, and be chased after for the same reason. But being a sorcerer did not mean she was a slave. Sorcery was strength, and sorcerers had that strength. Arienne had come to realize this on her journey.

Eldred made a sound that was something like a laugh.

"And I, myself, am not an ordinary man."

"You're not a man at all."

The stumps of Eldred's arms still leaked violet smoke, which by now should've overflowed the room but somehow hadn't. The windows of the room in her mind were twisted from Lysandros's attack, the books from the bookshelf scattered on the floor.

From ahead, Emere raised an arm and shouted, "Lady Arienne! I have found it. A marked wall. But it does not seem to be a door. I see no cracks or seams . . ."

Arienne squeezed her legs twice, and her horse trotted forward.

Emere had come down from his horse to inspect the wall. Just as the princess had told Arienne, there were deep sword marks on the stone.

Arienne dismounted and shouldered her bag, its strap biting into her body with the weight of the Power generator.

"Thank you. Please wait here with the other soldiers. I shall enter alone."

"Will you be all right?"

She nodded and drew Wurmath, the fang of the dragon, from the blue scabbard on her belt. The wall of rock melted at her approach. As soon as she was inside, the wall reappeared behind her. It was dark here, but Wurmath's slight glow gave enough light for her to see the way, and its warmth calmed her fast-beating heart.

It was not long before she came to another wall, which also vanished when she approached with Wurmath held toward it. A chamber of gray rock walls, larger than any hall of her school, lay before her. And in the middle of the cavern lay something Arienne had never thought to see in her lifetime.

Could such a huge thing be alive? This was her first thought at the sight of the chained, sleeping dragon. Dark red scales covered its enormous bulk; it was the size of a large house. Spear-like teeth overlapped its closed lips. Its many eyes were closed. The folded wings looked like they would cover the whole sky when spread. Each claw of its front paws, upon which its head rested, looked almost as long as she was tall.

To think a human army won against such a creature was incredible.

"It sleeps," said Eldred.

"I see that."

Her curiosity overcoming her fear, she took a few steps forward.

"Do you know why it is bound in chains?" Eldred asked.

"Because the Empire couldn't kill it, so they had to imprison it instead?"

"No. A dragon is like a living Power generator. The Empire stole secrets from many places to concoct its method of sourcing Power. A dragon's heart is one of these. Gigatherions were created by the Empire in the dragon's image, and Arland's fire-dragon is kept alive in case a time comes when it will be more useful."

Was the humming from the volcano the sound of the dragon's heart? "They let such a dangerous thing live just in case it might be useful someday?"

"Would you be so afraid of an enemy you've conquered once before?" Arienne stared at the chains entwined over the dragon's bulk. Eldred sneered.

"I shall not distract you. Go ahead. Try severing those chains."

Arienne rehearsed the cutting spell a few times to loosen her tongue and concentrated on the black chains. She imagined them snapping in her mind. She remembered how Eldred's and Lysandros's arms had been severed. She recalled the images she had used when she had severed Tychon from Lysandros. She uttered the incantation. The Power blossomed on the tip of her tongue.

Sparks flew as the imaginary sword bounced off the chains, leaving not a dent. A wind blew past Arienne and hit the wall behind her, leaving a deep gash in the rock.

It didn't work. And there was nothing else she knew of to try.

"How regrettable. Why not try again?"

Arienne by now had spent enough time with Eldred to recognize when he was mocking her.

Still, she tried again. This time, she swung Loran's sword Wurmath on the chain as she cast the spell. The blade got caught in it. Her right arm and hand screamed in pain. The dragon groaned in its sleep. She pulled at the sword, trying to dislodge it, but it refused to budge. In her struggle, her hand slipped from the hilt. Arienne fell backward on her behind.

"Those chains were forged by the greatest of the great sorcerers of the Empire. They will not break for the likes of your little tricks."

"You taught me this magic!"

"First, that spell is one you made up based on my magic, something akin to a baby's babble. Second, you are simply too ignorant of true magic to understand the depth of it."

"That babble sliced off your arms."

"Then you should know, if you could do that after only a little of my guidance, I can more than break that chain myself. Release my legs."

And there it was, the request she had been expecting to hear again for some time. She hadn't expected, however, that her answer to Eldred would determine whether she would return to the fortress as a success or a failure.

"You defeated me once. Do you still fear me?"

Arland had never felt like a true home to her, but ever since she'd met Loran, she had felt a conviction that this task was something she had to do. All she had done until now was run away. Which was necessary then, but now she needed to accomplish something else. She needed to break the chain. She needed to do this if she did not want to have to run and hide ever again. If that meant having to face Eldred outside her mind's room and defeat him again, so be it.

She looked in the room of her mind. It had been close to collapsing ever since Lysandros's attack. Eldred was already standing and was facing her as she entered. She could see the discolored teeth in his face.

Imagining herself inside the room, Arienne unraveled the bandages from his legs. She cringed at the wet sound of skin being ripped as the bandages came off.

"Good," Eldred said, without a hint of pain or discomfort. "I shall keep my promise."

The unraveled bandages floated in the air and made a circle. A violet whirlpool ensued. Eldred limped toward it, perhaps the first steps he had taken in nearly two centuries.

Arienne immediately regretted what she had done.

She was trying to grab him when something exploded, and her consciousness was thrown out of the room of her mind.

Through a sudden, splitting pain, she gripped her head and tried to see what was happening before her. There was the dragon. The chains. And Eldred. He stood on his two feet, on the cavern floor. And behind him was the violet whirlpool.

His arms had regenerated. Eldred noticed Arienne's confusion.

"These arms? You see, that thing only happened in your mind. That was just imagination. I am no longer at the mercy of your mind." He turned to the dragon and said, in a satisfied voice, "Now I shall have my revenge."

A face she had seen before, words she had heard before. Perhaps in a dream.

"The chains?"

"They will be severed, as I do what I must. Do not worry, little sorcerer. I will not let such a magnificent beast be kept in chains . . . And now that I am free, the world will be unchained as well, its wonders restored. I will rule as a god-king, as I had so long ago." Arienne recalled what Eldred had said, back at the tower in the forest, before the inquisitors came. *It was a wondrous time when magic was grand, and we ruled supreme* . . .

Eldred placed a hand on the sleeping dragon and spoke a long incantation. Another violet whirlpool appeared in the air.

"How simple the mind of a dragon can be! But deep. Very suitable, for me to create a room within it."

"What are you saying?"

Eldred didn't answer as he stepped into the whirlpool. Arienne hesitated only a moment before trying to follow, but she was too late. The whirlpool disappeared.

Then the dragon suddenly raised its head and roared.

Its body shook. Its wings spread wide. A hazy violet aura filled the dragon's many eyes like a grim omen. The cave seemed to shrink in comparison. Arienne stumbled backward, trying to get away.

Chips of volcanic rock fell from above. The dragon stretched its four legs and stood. It folded its wings. It spoke in a voice too heavy to be misunderstood as human.

"I am finally received by a vessel worthy of a king!"

It fluttered its left wing, then its right. The resulting wind made it difficult for Arienne to remain standing.

"This magnificent strength of flesh, Power as if containing a generator of its own . . . Behold, Arienne, what a true sorcerer is!"

Eldred, with his dragon mouth, recited Arienne's incantation of severance, but with a foreboding of Power far beyond what Arienne had thought was possible. There was a sound so loud it felt like her eardrums would split. The runes on the black chains shone and screamed at once. They snapped in a hundred places and listlessly slid down the scaled hide of the dragon to the cavern floor, before the dragon turned its many eyes on Arienne.

"You have done well. In return, I shall bestow upon you the honor of being the first sacrifice. I have always wanted to know what a human tasted like to a dragon."

The dragon's tongue slithered from its mouth, red as lava and split into three prongs.

36

LORAN

The skies were clear and the wind was cold. From the top of the tallest fortress tower flew the red dragon banners of Arland.

"What say you?" said Griogal.

Loran, standing on the fortress wall, looked out at the main contingent of the Twenty-Fifth Legion approaching. The snow had begun melting on the plain, which stretched before them yellow with patches of white.

"Legate Aurelia of the Twenty-Fifth Legion demands the surrender of the rebel Loran. You cannot hope to stand against the might of the Empire."

It was a Power-amplified voice, like the one she had heard in Kingsworth. Only this time, the speaker was an older woman of grave seriousness. She had repeated this warning several times since the Twenty-Fifth arrived.

"The enemy seems to have everything but cavalry," Loran commented. On her side, they didn't even have archers, much less cavalry. Many had trained with bows since arriving at the fortress, but they had not made significant progress.

Griogal grunted. "And three thousand strong."

"You have deceived the people of Arland," said the amplified voice, *"and confused them into rebelling against the just rule of the Empire."*

Loud as it was, the voice was merely a nuisance.

"They have many Powered chariots. Why don't they attack?" Loran wondered. Four sets of five Scorpios chariots stood in wait.

Griogal answered. "Probably because they don't know for sure how powerful our princess is."

"If so, they're biding their time until the gigatherion arrives," Loran said.

"Then we must fight now!" said Griogal, pounding his chest with his fist.

"The other side must expect us to do that, but . . . it seems we have no choice."

"And Griogal of Ledon," the loud voice went on. *"Aiding the treasonous is also treason. But if you capture Loran and bring her to us, we shall extend the hand of mercy to the tribes."*

Griogal scoffed. "The warriors of our fifteen tribes shall be the vanguard. Not to put too fine a point on it, but most in the Arlander army have never lifted a weapon until mere days ago. They will never break the Imperial formation."

"You are correct, but the vanguard will be decimated by the chariots. Your five hundred warriors will fall before they even reach the enemy formation. I urge you to wait for your moment and attack from the flank, as we previously discussed."

"But if we do not break their formation with the first charge, I am afraid that we shall lose even before the gigatherion gets here."

Loran was reminded of the Ledonite sword doctrine.

"The undefeated gigatherion Clarios is on its way," shouted the loud voice. *"You cannot win."*

Loran wanted to scream at them to be quiet, but they wouldn't be able to hear her from that distance.

"I shall lead the first charge," she said instead.

Griogal cleared his throat. "Has the princess ever led an army into battle?"

"I have not."

"The vanguard will be struck by the Empire's cannons, as you yourself mentioned just now. Many will die before they even reach a stone's throw of the enemy. The warriors of the fifteen tribes came ready for that sacrifice, but what of the farmers and the merchants? Do they understand what that would mean for them and their families?"

"Put down your weapons and surrender your leader. The blameless and ignorant people of Arland shall be left unharmed. Only the ring-leaders shall face judgment."

Loran smiled despite herself. It was the very "blameless and ignorant people of Arland" who had prevented her from surrendering in the first place. She looked down the fortress wall. None of the gathered seemed to pay the words of the Twenty-Fifth any mind. Many of them had joined her on her way to surrender, dissuading her every step of the way. She had witnessed their determination firsthand.

She said, "I believe that all those gathered here understand what it would mean."

Griogal nodded. "Then only say the word. We five hundred are at the princess's command."

Ready to do so, Loran turned her head—and glimpsed a soldier on the wall opposite waving a red flag. There were two accompanying bursts from a bugle. Something had happened on that side.

Coming down the ladder, she said, "What is it?" Only after asking three more people as she rushed to that side of the fortress did she receive an answer.

"An army approaches from the east."

A legion pincer attack was impossible. She had hunters roving those forests and hills as scouts, keeping an eye on the movements of the enemy. If there had been a detachment going around the fortress, they would have sent up smoke signals.

Crossing the fortress, too hurried to respond to the parting sea of soldiers bowing to her, she climbed the ladder on the other side to see this approaching army. She removed her eyepatch and concentrated on her left eye. The wriggling lumps in the distance began focusing into people. About a thousand of them. The banner was just about visible now.

The green lion. Kamori.

Loran shouted down the ladder, "Ready my horse! And a hundred soldiers to greet our reinforcements!"

Gwaharad came. Despite what happened, a thousand-strong Kamori Liberators came to aid Arland. Had he learned of Loran's capture of the fortress, and changed his mind?

She quickly mounted and went galloping out the gate before a hundred soldiers had managed to gather. She kept looking back, wanting to go full speed to meet the Kamori, but the foot soldiers could not follow her so quickly.

The Kamori force finally came into full view. A young man in chain mail holding a long spear led the other soldiers. He seemed to recognize Loran and came swiftly ahead on his horse.

But something was off. Gwaharad was not leading this force. Nor did she find any others that she recognized from the underground palace. Had they sent a new commander? She was glad enough to be sent help, but couldn't help feeling a little disappointed Gwaharad had not come himself.

The man on the horse spoke in Imperial.

"Are you the Princess of Arland?"

"I am."

The man dismounted, planted his spear on the ground, and knelt before her.

"I am Gwedion, a teacher of the spear and bow. Hearing that a hero has appeared in Arland to fight the Empire, I have gathered as many of my people as I could and came to fight with you. We may not be many, but we implore you to accept us into your ranks."

Loran dismounted as well.

"When you have come to aid your brothers, you should not have to be kneeling before them." She helped him to his feet and dusted the dirt from his knee. "How is King Gwaharad?"

Gwedion looked surprised. "Gwaharad . . . ? Whom do you speak of, Your Highness?" He looked behind him, as if this man he had never heard of might be among the crowd. But no one there knew of Gwaharad either.

The disappointment melted away in Loran's heart. Of course. Gwaharad was, indeed, the king of his own nation. Which was not Kamori, but a rabbit warren out in the woods.

"Never mind. I was simply mistaken. I cannot express how

grateful I am that you should all be here. Please come with me to the fortress. The enemy has already—"

An earsplitting whistle interrupted her words. Loran turned back toward the fortress and saw dust rising above its walls. Another whistling sound. With a crash, one of the towers crumbled like a sandcastle.

It was a weapon she had never seen before. She had worried over the gigatherion so much that it hadn't occurred to her that the Empire would have a weapon that could destroy the fortress from such a great distance.

The eleven hundred troops of Arland and Kamori around her gazed in shock at what had just happened to the western end of the fortress. Loran mounted her horse, urging it into a gallop before even settling into the saddle. The horse neighed sharply as it darted forward, its head aimed straight for the fortress.

Scales covered Loran, to the point where her leather armor felt like it was in the way. Atop her horse, she shed her armor piece by piece. The sight in her left eye grew as clear as her right. There were two more whistling sounds, as well as the yells of the Ledonite warriors. Arlander soldiers poured out of the gap created by the fallen wall.

Griogal would have found it impossible to wait for her order after such a fearsome attack. The terrifying sound of the cannons that she remembered so well from the battle at Kingsworth followed. Arrows rained down on the charging alliance.

Only Griogal and a handful of his warriors had made it to the enemy lines, but they swung their greatswords, fighting like lions. The Arlanders, meanwhile, struggled to make progress across the battleground in the rain of arrows and cannon fire.

She had almost made it to the enemy lines but her horse slowed, panting roughly. She spurred again, but her mount had reached its limit. An arrow struck the horse on its shoulder. It fell forward, but Loran took her feet out of the stirrups and leaped into the air. Her heart was heavy, but her body was lighter than it had ever felt. In the air, she drew her own sword with her right hand and a legion shortsword with her left. The two blades turned white with heat.

Loran descended like a meteor into the massed enemy. She spun, her blades creating blue flames all around her. Perhaps the Imperial soldiers screamed, but the melee was already awash in screams, shouts, and the clashing of blades.

Through the sulfuric smoke and the fire, she searched for a glimpse of Griogal. The muslin clothes she had worn underneath the leather armor were on fire. She didn't feel the heat at all. From behind her someone screamed.

"Dragonfire!"

"The princess is here!"

As much as she wanted to show herself to the Arlander soldiers, she needed to save Griogal first. Despite her powers of the dragon and his unusual height, Loran was still shorter than most and she could not see her ally in the crowd. Slashing away with her blades, she searched and searched for the man, creating columns of smoke wherever she went.

A Scorpios chariot suddenly blocked her way, swinging a pincer at her. Not even flinching, Loran sliced off the pincer with the shortsword on her left and pierced the chariot in its torso with the sword on her right. The chariot collapsed, ceasing all movement.

The enemy began to give her a wide berth. As her horizon widened, she spotted a bloodied giant twenty paces away, fighting for his life. His blade was red with blood from tip to hilt. Loran, slaying anything that came into her path, made her way toward the giant.

"Griogal!"

Her own voice surprised her, as it came out like the growl of a great beast. Griogal turned to her, and his eyes grew wide. He had been gamely fighting off twenty men at once without letting on the slightest of discomfort, but the sight of Loran made him look like a frightened man.

"Princess . . . Loran . . . ?"

Loran chased away the enemy swarming around him with the fires blasting from her swords. "I apologize for being late."

"Never mind *that*, Your Highness . . . *What of your body?*"

She looked down at herself. Her body was covered in red scales. Her armor was completely gone, but the scales protected her better than even the strongest armor could. There was nothing wrong with her, it was only that Griogal had never seen her in this form.

"There is no need for alarm. But please, come with me to—"

She was hit hard on the side, strong enough to knock the breath out of her for an instant. Had a soldier snuck up on her with a hammer? Not the most Imperial of weapons, but she had heard that many in the Twenty-Fifth Legion hailed from Phaidi, in the far north. Judging from the blow, however, this was an opponent of formidable strength, which was why she turned toward the attacker with some keenness in learning whom it might be.

A group of Imperial soldiers, mouths agape, were backing away. One had even dropped his sword on the ground. Next to her was a cannonball the size of Griogal's fist. And there it was, the cannon it came from, mounted on a Scorpios chariot, violet smoke issuing from the muzzle.

"A mon . . . a monster!" the legionaries screamed.

"I am Loran. *King of Arland*. You cannot harm me, and Arland will not surrender!"

Loran roared. The sound, as if amplified with Power, spread far and wide across the battlefield. Her left eye saw fear spreading among her enemies, a violent ripple soaking them in sickly green. Her heart thumped like a drum.

Behind her, the Arlander soldiers roared as well.

"Follow the king!"

"Behold, our king!"

"Long live the new king of Arland!"

Griogal bellowed, "A thousand congratulations on your ascension, King of Arland! The enemy is in disarray, this is our chance to win the battle before the gigatherion gets here!"

Only then did Loran realize she had called herself a king for the first time. But she didn't regret it; the title felt right.

Arrows flew over her head onto the enemy. They had come from the fortress side. Gwedion had arrived with his archers. The legion's morale was broken, their soldiers falling to the ground as they were struck.

Thousands of Arlanders descended on the remnants of the Twenty-Fifth. Loran made the way for them with her swords. With the two forces entangled, the cannons on the chariots could not attack as easily as they had before. Griogal was right; they could win this battle.

That was when the sound of a bugle ripped through the air.

It was accompanied by the voice that had demanded their surrender all morning, only much, much angrier.

"Clarios has come. Now you shall all be nameless corpses on the bat-

tlefield, and Arland shall be a graveyard without a tombstone. I gave you the chance to save your lives. But you cast it aside and chose death."

Far away, a giant machine approached on four legs, its lower body reminiscent of an ox. Its upper body was upright, like a man's torso, with four thick arms. On top of it all, there was a huge trumpet-shaped head. The obsidian monstrosity, gleaming in sunlight, was as tall as any of the watchtowers of the fortress. It was even larger than the fire-dragon of the mountain.

The soldiers of Arland stared at Loran. Loran looked toward the volcano. She could only hope that Arienne had arrived in the dragon's lair and succeeded in breaking its chains.

37

CAIN

Safani convulsed, and finally fell forward. A dark puddle formed as blood gushed from his chest and shoulder, filling the grooves in the rust-colored dirt around them. Cain stared, thinking how he had killed two people in one night. He had been in alley fights before, injured many, even seriously to the brink of death. But he had never killed anyone by his own hand. It didn't quite feel real to him, whether from shock or the unnatural quality of this place.

The whispering of the Power generators increased. Now it sounded like a song with no words. The bandages that the 327 Power generators above him were wrapped in unraveled in unison, and they fell to the red ground like snow.

And suddenly, Cain was standing in a field where snow was melting. Something about the scenery was familiar. Before him, thousands of people were in a raging battle. There were even Powered chariots, the kind he had seen in military parades. Blue flames erupted. A woman covered in dark red scales was swinging a sword in each hand. At some distance, a metal giant with four arms and four legs approached.

Far away to the left was a volcano, the sole mountain in view, a white plume of smoke issuing from it. Cain somehow knew what was going on inside there. He blinked and was suddenly inside the volcano where a dragon stood, its many eyes filled with violet light. Arienne was looking up at it. Under a light layer of armor, she wore the clothes he had bought her, which were now rumpled and faded from her long and arduous journey.

The withered corpses that comprised the Circuit of Destiny were looking down at this scene. Just as he was about to approach Arienne, a voice addressed him.

"Good of you to come."

He turned.

Beneath the 327 withered corpses stood Fienna. Her long braided hair moved slightly in the breeze. It was hard to see through all the blood and cracks on his spectacles. Cain wiped them with his coat sleeve, but he knew very well this was not the real Fienna.

"Where am I?"

"If you're talking about your body, it's in the chamber of the Circuit of Destiny underneath the Senate. What you're looking at, however, is the inside of the volcano in Arland. It's where the dragon of Arland once lay trapped."

"'Once'?"

"It's free now. The chains . . ."

There were chain fragments scattered about the dragon.

"*We* are inside that dragon," said Fienna. "The thing that used to be us, that used to be our king."

Cain asked, "This is happening right now, in Arland?"

Fienna tilted her head. "Now . . . It will happen, very soon. But everything feels like 'now' to us."

He didn't understand. "Why do you look like Fienna?"

"Because it's the most comfortable for you." The Fienna who wasn't Fienna reached out and stroked Cain's hair. Cain wanted to step back, but somehow, he couldn't. Her fingers lightly combed through his hair.

"You hardly ask anything. When you've come all the way here, looking for answers."

"I hate things like this," said Cain.

"What things? Scenes from your homeland?"

His surroundings changed once more. Fienna now stood in the middle of the battlefield from before, the woman in dark red scales fighting right in front of them. Even though the battle seemed to be between a ragtag Arlander army and an Imperial legion in all their battle regalia, the legion seemed to be losing. But the approaching gigatherion had the heavy air of inevitability.

"This is going to happen in the future as well?" Cain asked.

Fienna nodded. "Yes, very soon."

Cain felt a twitch inside, of the muscle that had been atrophied for so long that he had forgotten that it existed. For the first time in as long as he could remember, he cared for his homeland. These were, however, faraway affairs. This was a battle being fought by Loran and Arienne. Cain gazed at Fienna's face, a face he knew he would never see again after this, and tried hard to say the thing he needed to say.

"Arland may be my homeland, but it has nothing to do with me now. I want to leave here."

Fienna's eyes turned a shade darker.

"It's not so simple. There's still one more thing you need to do for us."

"What's that?"

Fienna turned toward the battle scene and pointed to where the gigatherion, as large as a castle, was coming from.

"That is gigatherion Clarios, Powered by the Class Two generator Hadiya. Not something Arland's militia can do anything about. Loran's fortress will likely fall, and then Kingsworth would be devastated."

Cain bit his lower lip. "Is there a way to stop it?"

"Not by you. But King Loran is ready to fight to the death."

Their surroundings once more turned into the cave in the volcano. The fire-dragon with a glowing violet haze in its eyes was roaring at Arienne. Cain almost screamed.

"He was once one of us . . . Eldred, our former king, is inside the fire-dragon of Arland. Arienne is trying to bring the dragon to the battlefield, fighting alone against the archsorcerer that has possessed the dragon."

Cain sucked in his breath. "Is there anything I can do to help her?"

Fienna shook her head. "There's nothing you can do. You are very far away from Arland."

He bit his lip. "Then why are you showing me these things?"

"Because there is something *we* can do. We can let Arland fall, or we can force the Twenty-Fifth Legion to retreat. But we can't do it alone."

Far above him, the song of the three hundred Power generators reached a new intensity. Cain stared upward.

"Those two people," said Fienna, "are at a crossroads. They have to decide not just their own fate but the fates of countless others. Like kings. And such moments fill us, make us . . . We have power. We have knowledge. We are history, but we are not future. Our purpose must be given to us." Fienna's eyes darkened more. "By someone like you."

Cain drew a long breath and said, "You want me to decide for you."

Fienna nodded and reached out to him. "Take our hand. Come inside us. A throne awaits you. Every moment of destiny will be your subject. You are worthy. You can be king. You can save your homeland. And your friend." Her voice was pleading. The real Fienna had never spoken to him like this. He suppressed a flinch.

"Then everything I wish for will come true?"

"As long as destiny allows it."

Cain scoffed. "And Mersia. Was that also allowed by destiny?"

". . . That wasn't our fault." Fienna looked sorrowful. He could not stand seeing her so sad, even though she was not truly Fienna. He couldn't ask her what she meant. It wouldn't matter to him, anyway.

"What happens to Arland if we leave them alone?"

"Not even we know. We are at a king's crossroads. Arienne could still come to the battlefield with the dragon. The King of Arland might vanquish the gigatherion on her own. Or everyone might die and Kingsworth will end up a mass grave."

Cain made his decision.

"What I really want, what frustrated me because it was never in my hands, was not the fates of the people from the place I left, but the people here, in Fienna's home. I must go back to take care of them now. I have no desire to steal for myself what Loran and Arienne are fighting for."

Fienna looked as sorrowful as ever.

"You are a sleeping king after all. Perhaps you aren't ready yet to rule. But there will come a time when you awaken."

Fienna vanished. Cain suddenly stood not on the plains of Arland or a land with red earth and a violet sky. He was instead in a narrow, dim chamber filled from floor to ceiling with large, coffin-sized drawers. He felt his way out.

He climbed the spiral staircase and got to the hall of the Senate. The sun was rising in the east. Seeing as the sky wasn't covered in smoke, the fires seemed to have been brought under control somehow.

Just as he stepped outside, Septima came walking through the forest of statues. The stout man limped along beside her, and Devadas brought up the rear, no sign at all of having been wounded in the crash. Their faces were sooty, their clothes filthy. Only Septima's green brooch still sparkled.

"You!" Septima shouted, and increased her pace. But Cain didn't run. He stood calmly by the doors of the Senate, his back straight.

"You . . . !"

Oddly enough, Septima was having trouble finding the words. Cain looked down at his person. Was his being covered in blood throwing her off? Perhaps an explanation was in order.

"Safani's body is in a room filled with drawers underneath the Senate."

"Safani was there . . . ?" This was Devadas with his low, thick voice.

"I killed him. I took care of the problem."

The three of them looked at one another, and then the stout man said, "I don't believe that. We've been unable to find for him for a decade. No way a badger informant has done what we couldn't."

The stout man came up to Cain, his hands balled up into fists. Cain took a step forward, coming face-to-face with him. "*You* had a job. *I* had everything at stake."

The stout man opened his mouth halfway as if to speak. As Cain stared down at him, the man took a step back without saying anything, his fists loosening up.

Silence fell on the Senate hill.

Cain met Septima's eyes. Her displeasure from a moment ago was replaced with something like amazement. As he further studied her face, she averted her eyes from him. The stout man was staring at his feet as well, unwilling to challenge Cain again. Devadas lowered his head for a moment, as if he was paying his respects, then looked at Cain. There was a glimmer of appreciation in his normally expressionless face.

Cain was surprised, not at the change in their attitudes, but that he had somehow expected all of this.

Septima finally spoke again.

"So . . . what . . . what happened? What happened in the end?"

"I ran after Safani and killed him. I don't know what he was trying to do. I trust you aren't going to find fault with me for going into the Senate."

"Well . . . as long as you didn't touch anything . . . I suppose it won't be a problem."

There was the matter of the dead guards beyond the door behind him.

"If something is amiss, blame it on Safani."

". . . Fine."

"What about the fire in the city?"

"Something went wrong with the Power generators, but they are working again. The fires are almost out, and there are fewer casualties than was first feared."

"That's good news."

He walked down the steps. The stout man came up to Cain and reached for his arm.

"Still, you should come with us to the headquarters—"

He stopped. When Cain turned around, Septima had her hand on the stout man's shoulder. Confused, the stout man looked from Septima to Cain and to Septima again before taking a step back.

Leaving the three behind him, Cain made his way down from the Senate hill. Wisps of black smoke hung above the city vista ahead, while white smoke rose from the chimneys of the houses around him.

Cain would commission a good tombstone for Fienna's grave, as the Arlanders who had come to her funeral had asked. Ayana and the children who had surveilled Gladdis's house also deserved more money for their troubles. He needed to find out exactly who Fienna had been helping all this time and continue her work. He needed a new job. He also had a feeling he'd be seeing the three agents again before long. There were busy days ahead.

A winter wind blew up the hill, but Cain found his heart warmer and lighter than ever. He hugged his coat tighter around himself and went on his way.

38

ARIENNE

Arienne could not take her eyes off the slithering tongue of the dragon. She could feel Eldred's Power in the violet haze over the dragon's eight eyes. As much as her mind screamed at her to run, her legs refused.

This was a primal fear. She had beaten Eldred once; she was not afraid of him. But the fire-dragon of the mountain was a creature of legend, the guardian of Arland that went toe-to-toe against an Imperial gigatherion. There was nothing she could do.

The claws of the dragon swung toward her.

Arienne closed her eyes and waited for death.

But the dragon only left a deep scratch on the floor before her. Was he going to toy with her before killing her? But then, the dragon's voice bellowed Eldred's words. "This beast persists in its useless defiance."

Arienne could feel two waves of Power colliding. The awakened dragon was battling Eldred inside itself. The dragon was more powerful than Eldred, but the sorcerer had already created a room inside the dragon's mind and settled in like a parasite. If half of what Eldred boasted about his sorcery was true, the room would be a veritable fortress. And Eldred, free of his constraints, would eat away at the dragon from within.

All Eldred needed to do was breathe fire once or strike her with the dragon's claw and she would die, instantly. With all her might, she willed her feet to move.

"Where do you think you're going? Do you really believe you will leave this cave alive?"

The door to the valley had melded back into the wall, and the key, Loran's Wurmath, was wedged in the chains. She was trapped.

But there was one other place to hide. Eldred had left the portal open in the room of her mind; without a second thought, she jumped into it.

She had been to this room many times. But this was the first time her body physically entered her own mind. The room was in disarray from Lysandros's attack. She ran to the window and crouched beneath it before carefully peeking out of it. The window showed not a pastoral scene of Arland but the interior of the cave.

"Hiding in one's own mind . . ." The dragon, or Eldred, smacked its lips. "You truly are a rare talent. Only one other student of mine survived what you just did . . . But how long do you think your mind can withstand the contradiction? What do you think will happen if you linger there too long? Do you know what happens when a bag tries to go inside itself?"

With the portal closed, Eldred couldn't enter this room. But Arienne still needed considerable courage in looking out the window.

The dragon's movements were awkward and slow. Eldred was still fighting the dragon from within.

Around her, Arienne felt a pressure like the one she had in Lysandros's presence. The room was collapsing again. The doorframe creaked loudly as it leaned into an improbable angle. Eldred was doing the exact thing Lysandros had done. He was crushing her mind with the immense power he now had at his disposal.

If she didn't do something now, everything was done for. She would die, and Loran and Arland would be pulverized by the Empire's gigatherion. Eldred would roam the world in his dragon body. This room was her last bastion. But even that was falling apart.

Eldred shouted, "We must still be connected, I can see you cowering like a rat in that room with the stink of manure! How I long to be rid of you forever. Now that I am free, you have finally learned to fear me! Look outside the window!"

Arienne did as she was told. The window no longer showed the cave but a room of obsidian with a throne made of a hundred white skulls, where Eldred sat. He wore black robes, and on his head a crown made of bone and gold. His eyes were still sunken and his flesh was withered, but he looked more alive than she had ever seen him.

This was a true sorcerer. Fear washed over her like a wave. Trying to ignore it, she looked around the room for anything she might use. A mess of a room collapsing in on itself, but a room she knew intimately by heart. A room where she'd lain in bed on her stomach, drinking warm milk, reading and rereading her books. A room she had cried all night in when she received her decree of entry condemning her to an eternity of serving the Empire.

Something lay on that very bed now. A small bundle, wrapped in bandages.

The sack on her back had felt light. What had happened to the Power generator she had carried? When she saw the bundle on the bed, she knew.

Even smaller than the pillow it lay next to, the bundle was covered in runed bandages. Power generator Tychon. Arienne leaned over the bundle and whispered the name.

"Tychon."

Outside, an anguished roar was followed by a maniacal laugh. Arienne undid the bandages, revealing the dry corpse of a newborn inside. This was the child Eldred had kidnapped and Lysandros had murdered to be made into a Power generator. Next to the baby lay Arienne's decree of entry to the Imperial Academy.

She undid the last of the bandages. In an instant, the shriveled corpse became a plump baby with bright, blinking eyes. The bandages became a blue blanket that swaddled the baby. It had white flowers embroidered on it. The baby was quiet as if asleep, but he was audibly breathing. Who had his mother been? There had been no mention of her in *The Sorcerer of Mersia*. Violet lights swam deep within the baby's eyes.

A tiny hand protruded from the blanket. Arienne placed her index finger in its grasp. Something flowed into her, a shock that went all the way to the top of her head. The room filled with violet light.

Blue fire hit the window. Even if it was dragonfire, nothing on the outside could harm this room. But this pressure, applied to Arienne's mind by Eldred in the body of the dragon, even more powerful than Lysandros, would crush the room soon enough, if the contradiction of her body being inside her own mind did not obliterate her first.

Arienne finally understood what she needed to do.

She picked up the baby, who cuddled against her as he would to his mother.

Holding the baby in her arms, she stepped out of the room.

The cave was full of scratches and burnt rocks, casualties from the turmoil inside the dragon. The sulfuric fumes made breathing difficult. In Arienne's arms was the lead sarcophagus containing Tychon.

The dragon turned its many eyes to her. "Wait only a moment longer, Arienne. Soon, it will be your turn."

The dragon whipped its neck, slamming its head against the wall. It stumbled but regained its balance. A pained roar. Eldred's laughter. The dragon seemed to have lost control of its body completely.

"Now we shall see the end! You have talent. But what use is talent that I can't control? You should have been more obedient."

The dragon turned its head toward her. Its jaws opened wide. Down its cave-like throat glowed a hot blue flame.

Arienne glanced once more inside the room in her mind. It was a complete mess. Her mother would have scolded her had she left it like that as a child. But there was no way, now, that she could explain why the room was in such a state, not in a way that her mother would understand.

Arienne stared at the fire in the dragon's throat.

"Eldred! Remember my room? The room you were trapped in when you were bound by your bandages?"

Even the dragon's scoff was hot enough for her to barely withstand.

"Do you think I would miss that hole of a room that stinks of cow dung?"

"On the contrary. I'm going to stop missing it myself."

"You'll miss nothing when you're dead." The dragon opened its mouth once more. What would come out of it was death. Or destiny.

Arienne closed her eyes. Tychon, who had been a baby in a swaddling blanket in her mind, was again a corpse in a lead sarcophagus when she walked out. But she could still feel the clasp of his small hand on her finger, and the Power that coursed to her through the connection made in her mind's room. It bypassed the lead as if there were nothing between her and Tychon. Her professors at the Academy had said that a sorcerer could not draw Power from a generator. The human body was not designed for it. How it was now possible for her, Arienne didn't know. But there was an undeniable feeling of symmetry between them. She had never felt so *right*.

She recalled Eldred's room, the one he had shown her outside her window. His black regalia, his crown of bone and gold, the throne of skulls, the smooth obsidian walls.

And upon the image of Eldred's throne room, she overlaid her own collapsing room, as she had done at the tower to kill the inquisitors, and at the abandoned inn to bury Lysandros. She stretched out her left hand, reciting an incantation she had never spoken before.

Her mind's room, the one that might still exist on the second floor of her childhood home, started to pulse with her heartbeat. Eldred's surprised shout escaped the lips of the dragon.

"This is . . . this . . ."

He shouted something, an incantation, a scream, Arienne couldn't tell. Her room twisted violently, warping everything inside it, the books, the bed, the patchwork dolls, the shelf her mother made, her decree of entry.

Arienne was destroying the last good memory of her childhood. Just as a bag could not enter itself, a room could not exit itself. It was flipping inside out. But there was no outside for this room of the mind. The room began to compress itself, to collapse inside her. And at the same time, the room Eldred had made in the dragon's mind, the skulls and obsidian and all, collapsed with it. The Power flowing from Tychon to Arienne to Eldred's destruction made her feel as if the very blood in her veins were on fire.

Eldred screamed. It was not the dragon's voice but the insidious voice she knew from inside her own head. The screams did not last long. The dragon collapsed in an avalanche of red and black. Its wings covered the floor like falling twilight.

Her mind's room was now completely inside out. Somethingness had entered nothingness. She retched a bit, but nothing came up. There was, however, the feeling that a heavy thing had finally left her. Arienne stroked the lead sarcophagus in her embrace.

"Lovely boy. I'll make you a new room soon. Just you wait."

The fallen dragon lay on the ground as it came back to itself. Its eight eyes were open, and the violet aura around them had disappeared. One of the eyes reminded her of Loran.

Arienne straightened her back. Something within her had changed. She was no longer afraid of the dragon. Was it because she had defeated Eldred, or because she had destroyed so much of her own past when she collapsed the room? She couldn't be sure. Arienne walked up to the dragon, with no hesitation or fear.

39

LORAN

Gigatherions were never meant to be used against mere people, only the likes of dragons or gods. But with the Empire's conquests continuing for two centuries, even such enemies had become scarce, and there were almost no more instances of deploying the giant war machines in battle. Now they were simply paraded about as symbols of the Empire's absolute military might, and that was enough.

From the moment she heard rumors that the gigatherion was on its way, Loran had wondered if the Empire, or at least the Twenty-Fifth Legion's Legate Aurelia, likened her to a dragon or a god in their minds. She almost felt proud of it. She had also thought, in the back of her mind, that if this was how they thought of her, maybe there was nothing stopping her from battling them as equals.

This thought vanished from her mind at the sight of the machine giant. Clarios was a fortress walking on four legs, each like a tower. Loran felt more afraid of it than she ever had of the dragon.

No doubt the Arlander militia was even more frightened. And

not just their side. The legionaries were fleeing the battlefield without carrying off their injured with them. Even the chariots were making a hasty retreat. Loran stood firm. If she showed fear now, everything would be over.

But maybe everything was already over.

"Stand as far away from Clarios as possible!"

Even as the Twenty-Fifth Legion heeded Aurelia's warning, they could not help looking back at the terrifying gigatherion towering over the field. Perhaps they had never seen it in actual battle themselves.

Wilfrid's voice rang out. "Do not retreat! If we run now, why did we prevent the princess, no, the king from surrendering before?! We are the ones who compelled King Loran to battle! How can we run now having done so?!"

On the contrary, Loran wished that they all just retreated. She could not, however, order it. The decision to stand their ground or to run would affect their futures more than whether they won or lost this battle. This was not, Loran thought, a decision even a king was allowed to make.

She looked behind her. Gwedion's Kamori army of a thousand were no longer shooting arrows. There were no human targets in range. Shooting at the gigatherion would be like shooting at a hill. They had slung their bows on their backs and brought out spears, but their doubt at the effectiveness of their weapons was palpable even from where she stood.

Griogal had lost most of his Ledonite warriors in the first charge. Those who survived were busy gathering their wounded. Wilfrid, noticing this, ordered the Arlanders to tend to the wounded as well.

Loran began walking toward the gigatherion Clarios. Her greatest fear now was that the people behind her, unable to move forward but unwilling to retreat, would waver in their resolve because of her.

"Your Majesty! Your Majesty!" Wilfrid's voice beseeched. Loran turned her head. There was a long cut on Wilfrid's face. She worried that if her general did not get it cleaned and dressed, the wound would fester.

"Where are you going, Your Majesty?"

"Something must be done about that monster."

"Well, if this is the end, then we shall end together!"

Wilfrid was a farmer. Such words did not suit her. What had made her into this? Was it Loran herself, the Empire, or something else?

"If you refuse to retreat now," she said, "there is nothing I can do to stop you. But at least let me be the one to face that . . . Clarios first. I die, then there will be no one to stop you from doing as you wish."

"And Its Excellency? Will the dragon not come?"

"I do not know. But I can wait for the dragon no longer."

The dead filled the battlefield. Among them were legionaries burned by Loran, and Arlanders who had been killed by arrows. There was a Ledonite mangled beyond recognition by a cannonball during the initial, fatal charge. Broken blades, banners, and arrows were strewn about. Violet smoke from the cannons and Loran's own sulfuric smoke mixed into each other, casting a pall over all.

Clarios caused the earth to quake with each thunderous step. Loran turned from Wilfrid and continued walking toward the gigatherion. There before her was her destiny, the king's destiny as Emere had told her. It would be enough for her to have reached it. Her pace quickened. Soon, she was running. The bloody battlefield, the melting snow, the yellow ground beneath it all blurred into one. Only the gigatherion Clarios remained in clear sight.

Something burst from the gigatherion. They seemed to number in the hundreds. To Loran, they seemed almost suspended in the air. Small metal pellets. Turning, she avoided all but one that hit her chest. It hurt. The pellet was of considerable power. But it did not pierce her scales. If Loran had not approached the gigatherion, that attack would have rained down on her Arlanders. She ran on.

About twenty paces from the gigatherion, she ran up a boulder jutting from the ground and sprang from it—pellets raining down on her once more. She twisted in the air but could not avoid so many of them at this close range. They hit the right side of her waist, her neck, and her left arm. One grazed a part of her cheek that wasn't covered in scales, leaving a tear that bled. She paid it no mind. A common enough thing that happened even in sword practice. Loran flew through the scattering of pellets and plunged her white-hot swords into the front left knee of the gigatherion.

This wasn't to disable the machine. Loran pulled herself up by the hilt and stepped on the flats of the two embedded blades to climb Clarios. There had to be a point of weakness somewhere. Maybe a door of some sort that led to the Power generator. Then maybe, just as she did with the chariots at Fire-Dragon Square, she could destroy the generator and stop Clarios.

The gigatherion had seemed slow from a distance only because of its size. Being right up against it freed her from this illusion. With every step Clarios took she felt like she was hanging from the pendulum of a giant clock. As she found whatever handholds her claws could in its rivets and seams, Loran almost lost her grip many times.

The volcano in the distance, as always, continued to send up white smoke. The dragon had said to her that it would come when summoned. *Who am I to refuse a royal decree?* Had Arienne failed? Loran had seen the girl only that once, after all. A sorcerer she might be, but Loran knew nothing of Arienne's abilities. But she had sensed that the young sorcerer would pull through. She still felt this now.

With her draconic strength and speed, Loran clawed her way up without a moment's rest. A single stop to catch a breath could mean the difference between victory and massacre. She didn't even stop to look around until she had made it to the shoulder of the giant machine beast. Perhaps because it couldn't find a way to attack her, it was moving its large bulk toward the alliance. Just a few showers of those pellets from before and they would be decimated.

Loran had hoped Wilfrid would have ordered a retreat, but her general was simply too stubborn. The main contingent remained, refusing to take a single step back. Only a small band of warriors led by Griogal was moving now, carrying the wounded to the fortress.

Etched into the gigatherion's shoulder were different writings and symbols. She searched for the words "Power generator," focusing her sight through her left eye as much as she could. Then a strange violet ripple became visible in the air around her. She crawled against it, hoping to get to the origin.

The winds were strong, from Clarios walking so briskly. She crawled until she could see that the violet ripple was emanating from the back of the neck. As she gripped the seam beneath her, hanging on as best she could, Clarios came to a stop.

And then it roared, a sound so loud it almost pierced Loran's eardrums. She screamed. The scene before her undulated as if she were looking at it through a distorted lens. The Powered force that warped the very air shot forward at impossible speed. The fortress in the distance exploded. Towers and walls turned to dust.

There had been at least a hundred people left in it. Children and the sick among them. Speechless, Loran stared; there was a hiss from her left eye, the sound of a tear evaporating.

She could not stop here. Turning her gaze from the fortress, she continued to climb to the source of the aura.

There it was, right in the middle, a steel hatch. CLASS 2 POWER GENERATOR HADIYA. She needed to smash this and enter. Retracting her claws and making a fist, she brought down all her might upon the hatch—but her fist was stopped before it even met the hatch.

Where her fist had stopped shone a rune she couldn't read. It gave off bright violet waves like light reflected from a pond. Desperately, she punched it again and again. She tried piercing it with her claws, scratching at it. Even stomping on it. But the rune continued to shine intact, emitting the violet waves. A sorcerous protection. Much stronger than what protected the Powered armor the centurion Marius had worn in Dehan Forest.

The strength left her shoulders. Now there was truly nothing she could do. Was *this* the king's destiny? Was her final act to accept this ending? The gigatherion knew not of, nor cared for, her turmoil. It continued to move forward.

And then, her heart gave a huge thump.

Something was coming from behind her. The smoke from the volcano was black now, and a white cloud above it scattered into nothing. There was a rumbling, and then a sound like thunder. The gigatherion stopped. The volcano erupted, spewing a gush of lava into the air above.

From the smoke, something black and red leaped forth at incredible speed. Loran focused her left eye with all her might. The fire-dragon. And someone was holding on to its scale-covered back for dear life. Arienne, with Wurmath at her side. They were flying toward her. So fast, she wondered if the rider could hold on, but with a flap of the dragon's wings, they approached even faster.

Clarios turned. Loran held on to a handle by the hatch, but her eyes never left the dragon. The gigatherion's head was also trained on the approaching dragon, as if in anticipation of its new adversary.

The fire-dragon closed in at an unimaginable speed. Not slowing at all, it slammed directly into the gigatherion. Loran was flung into the air, the shock breaking off the handle in her hand, and she fell, spiraling toward the ground far below.

"Are you all right?"

Arienne's voice. Loran's shoulder blades ached—she must've landed on them. Despite having fallen from a great height, she wasn't injured.

"Lady Arienne?"

"I have brought the dragon, Your Highness." She bowed.

There was something different about Arienne. The violet ripple Loran had seen on the gigatherion's shoulder was also surrounding the sorcerer.

Above her, the fire-dragon battled Clarios, attacking it mercilessly with its claws. Perhaps remembering its battle from twenty years ago, the dragon did not waste its fire on the gigatherion. It flew in and out of Clarios's range, striking more nimbly than one would expect of a creature of its size. Clarios had already lost an arm. It tried to grab or strike the dragon whenever it swooped down for an attack, which only resulted in flailing its remaining three arms in the air.

"You have risen, King of Arland."

The dragon's greeting rumbled in the sky.

Loran shouted, "I was never asleep!"

"The young sorcerer accomplished her task admirably. I am now free! And I am here to fulfill my pact by serving the king." The dragon's voice was buoyant with joy.

Loran had only known it as a creature trapped in a cave, but the beast that crossed the sky before her was more like a beautiful sleek bird than a gigantic monster. The dragon was finally in its true element.

"Princess," said Arienne, "we must get you to safety. If we get dragged into those two giants' fight . . ." Her voice trailed off as her eyes grew wide.

"What is it?"

"Princess, your . . . back . . ."

Loran looked over her right shoulder. There was some kind of red membrane behind it. Her left side as well. They seemed to extend from her shoulder blades, which had ached a moment ago.

"Wings . . . ?"

This had never happened before. She tried moving them. She couldn't.

Arienne was looking Loran up and down, fascination in her eyes. All of Loran's clothes had either been discarded or burned off her, with only the dragon scales covering her. This would be the first time Arienne was seeing her in this form.

Loran said to Arienne, "I cannot leave the battlefield. Lady Arienne, you must find shelter."

"But it's dangerous, even for you!"

"I am King of Arland. Now that I have called forth the dragon, I must fight by its side."

"Only if the fight is one that humans can partake in!"

"Please, you must retreat. The gigatherion makes a sound that can easily destroy your ears. It is dangerous to be near it."

Arienne looked from Loran to Clarios and back again. She nodded, reluctantly.

"I see. This place is indeed where the princess . . . I mean, the king should be. I hope to see you again soon, Your Majesty."

Arienne unhitched Wurmath from her side and held it up with both hands, offering it to her king. Loran smiled, nodded, and accepted the sword. Giving her one last imploring look, Arienne, her heavy sack on her back, turned and fled.

Loran drew Wurmath in her right hand. Straightening her back, she turned toward the fight between the fire-dragon and Clarios.

Clarios was much stronger, and larger, but the dragon was superior in speed. Unlike the one from twenty years ago, this gigatherion did not fly. The dragon smashed into another of Clarios's arms with its claws, creating a shower of sparks and the sound of metal bending and tearing. The arm fell off the monster, leaving only one on each side. Armor plates were also coming off here and there, revealing the inner workings of the machine.

Perhaps they would indeed win this battle, Loran thought. Perhaps losing it was not in their destiny.

The dragon made a half-turn to attack Clarios's back. Its speed was incredible. Its aim was seemingly to decapitate the gigatherion. This was when Clarios made its earsplitting sound once more.

"Get away from it!" shouted Loran. The upper half of Clarios's body swiveled around, a movement no living thing could execute. The rippling force that had devastated the fortress launched from the gigatherion's head and hit the dragon squarely in its chest. Like a bird struck by a stone, the dragon spiraled to the ground at Clarios's feet.

Clarios lifted one of its massive legs. The dragon tried to get up, but the gigatherion stomped on one of the dragon's wings. The fire-dragon of the mountain, the guardian of Arland, gave a wretched cry of pain.

Clarios's head swiveled, no longer minding the crippled dragon. It was turned to the fortress. No—it was looking toward Kingsworth beyond.

The Empire was truly powerful. There was no way to deny it. This was the guardian's second defeat at the hands of the Empire. Hope was futile.

But wasn't despair even more so? All that was left for Loran was to do whatever she was able to, at this moment. That was what she had been doing all along, ever since she left home for the volcano.

Loran was walking toward Clarios, Wurmath lowered to her side, when a voice shouted to her from behind.

"Your Majesty! Your Majesty, King Loran!"

Wilfrid. And not just her. All of Arland's soldiers. Aside from the injured, they were all here before her. The battle between the fire-dragon and the gigatherion had kept her from noticing their approach. Arienne was among the crowd as well, half hidden among the soldiers. Loran had a feeling it was Arienne who had brought the people to her.

"Why have you come?" said Loran. "You will all die if you linger here. Please, escape with your lives!"

Shouts of adamant refusal from the crowd. Wilfrid spoke up.

"The Twenty-Fifth Legion has vowed to make Arland into a grave with no tombstone! Where would be left for us to flee?"

Loran raised her voice so that it would carry through the crowd. "There is nothing more foolish than to think death is glorious. You must return home. And bide your time until our next chance."

"Our dying here will not mean the end of Arland! Those who come after we are gone shall fight their own battles. But it is indeed those who come after us who must be able to say one day, 'Here was our king, and here the people fought by her side'! If we abandon you now, who will take on the mantle of the king ever again?"

Loran remembered the days and nights she had walked with the intention of surrendering to the Empire. They had told her, then, much the same things as they were telling her now. This was, perhaps, the destiny of the people before her as well.

Then she herself must follow her own destiny. Loran now understood why the wings had sprouted from her back, as well as what she could do. What she *must* do.

"Wilfrid."

"Yes!" Wilfrid stepped forward.

"This battle was never to defeat the faraway Empire. The day may come, but today is not that day."

"But—"

"I am not saying we should not fight. Only that today, even if we should win, the Empire also has its tomorrow. That is what you need to prepare for. If we only take up arms and fight, we shall always lose."

"We can win? You are saying, there is a chance we may win?"

Loran smiled. "That is the only part of my words you have heard! But please, whatever happens, remember today. I shall always be with you all. And I shall let the Empire know that as well."

Loran took a step forward.

"Are you aware that, in the olden days, there used to be something called knights in Arland?"

"I have heard of them."

"And I have read that a king may grant knighthood on the field of battle."

Wilfrid did not seem to understand.

"Please kneel."

Wilfrid knelt. With her sword in her hand, Loran lightly tapped Wilfrid's right shoulder, then her left.

"With the authority invested in me by the people of Arland and the fire-dragon of the mountain, I dub you a knight of Arland. A knight serves her king, protects her people, and defends her country. Rise, Sir Wilfrid."

Wilfrid stood.

"I am the King of Arland," said Loran. She could barely remember how it had happened, but she could feel the truth of it.

"I have thought of you as so since I first saw you," said Wilfrid, holding back tears. Loran sensed Wilfrid knew what her king was about to say.

"Sir Wilfrid, should I not return from battle, I bid you to look after this country. That even if we are once more under the foot of the Empire, today shall not be in vain. That all the hopes and dreams gathered here today shall not be rendered meaningless."

"Your Majesty . . ."

Loran forced a smile. "But I shall do my best to return."

She thrust the blade of Wurmath into the earth. Heat rose from beneath her feet. The pillar of light that had blazed that one cold night on her way to the fortress ascended once more into the sky. This time, it reminded Loran of the eruption of a volcano.

Her whole body felt warm, as if immersed in a hot spring. Loran's heart was thumping like a drum. The sound was not dissimilar to the sound of the sleeping dragon in the volcano.

She spread her wings. They gracefully fluttered as if she had used them her whole life. Loran flew up, her heartbeat louder than ever. Too loud, it seemed, to come from so small a human body.

Bathed in the blinding light, she was crying over the bodies of her husband and daughter. She was at the edge of the volcano. All her sorrows, all her deeds, came back to her, happening for the first time. She held her newborn daughter, lying in the bed of her family home, and saw her husband looking both happy and worried for his beloved wife. She whispered the names that she had dared not speak for a long time.

Had everything been to prepare her for this moment?

Soon, the column of light obscured Clarios, the fire-dragon, Wilfrid, and the people of Arland, until she could not see them anymore.

40

ARIENNE

It had been a chaotic year.

The repairs of Arland's royal castle were nearly completed, and Arienne had been given a room there with a good view. It wasn't much more luxurious than the inn she had lived in until then, but it was much better suited for her to focus on her work, away from the well-meaning attentions of others.

Following the battle of the past winter, a people's council had been formed, and Arienne had been working with them. There were many ongoing issues in Arland aside from the oppression of the Empire, from conflicts between guilds of Kingsworth to irrigation feuds going back centuries between villages, and land disputes between families as well.

The sun was setting. Tomorrow, a new prefect would be taking up position. A reception banquet was planned for tonight. She took out the blue dress the tailor Cedric had made for her for this occasion. Cedric had been among those who, along with Arienne, had last seen Loran on that day.

Many on the council had also been in the field that day. Most of the makeshift army returned to their previous lives, while still others, enamored of the soldier's life, joined the militia. But there was one thing they all had in common. Whenever they got the chance, they would talk about that day.

The story of how King Loran had defeated the Empire's gigatherion and saved the fire-dragon of the mountain varied from person to person, sometimes by a little, sometimes a lot. Even when it was witnessed by thousands, the discrepancies increased a year after the event. Arienne wondered why so many others were contradicting what they experienced firsthand and so clearly re-membered, as each and every one of them did as well.

There was a knock on the door. Arienne gladly ran to open it.

"Wil!"

Wilfrid wore a formal Imperial suit, its black tunic and skirt setting off the accents of golden thread. There was a long scar on her face, a souvenir from the previous year's battle. Even tired from her long journey, she smiled and embraced Arienne.

"How have you been?"

"The same as always. And how was the Capital?"

"The Senate is filled with old men who keep talking their talk. The Commons is a bit better . . . But how large the Capital is! You lived there for so long, Kingsworth must seem very small to you. And I never knew there were so many different kinds of people!"

"And the language?"

Wilfrid nodded. "My Imperial is as bad as ever, but the Arlanders of the Capital helped. A man named Cain somehow knew I was arriving and came to see me. We exchanged news. There are many who wish to return to Arland. Especially after hearing of King Loran—"

"Wait, Cain? Did he wear spectacles? About twenty-five?"

"Yes. Do you know him?"

"He helped me once."

She couldn't quite remember his face. Ever since she destroyed her inner room during her battle against Eldred, Arienne had trouble remembering details of her life before coming to Arland.

"A young man with considerable reach among the people. Not just among Arlanders . . . Even the Ministry of Intelligence agents are said to tip their hats to him. Well, enough of that, I have some things to confirm with the council. Can you look at them before others do?"

"I forbid you from starting work before tomorrow, Prefect Wilfrid."

Wilfrid grinned. "Well, I've nothing to do the day after and the day after that as well. I'm merely a puppet of the council!" She stretched out her arms, pretending to be one. "The important decisions must be made by the council. I will speak when needed, of course . . . But my first duty is to what the king told me." Wilfrid brushed her shoulder, where Loran had touched with Wurmath to make her a knight of Arland. "What needs to be confirmed are the requests of the Arlander member of the Commons."

"And how long is his remaining term?"

"Until summer next year."

"Then we shall have to think of who will take over."

Wilfrid handed her a folded document. "Cain made some suggestions to that end."

"You must be joking? The argument we've had with the Empire in allowing us to make that decision!"

"Well, he is asking for this person to be put forth by the council. I did meet the candidate, and he seems well-suited. Strong ties to the immigrant communities from many provinces. Cain mentioned the needs of the Arlanders in the Capital must be considered as well, as whoever sits in the Commons will affect them more than us. There is some sense in that."

Arienne narrowed her eyes at Wilfrid. "You traitor."

Wilfrid laughed. Arienne took the document from her.

"Let's bring it up at the council meeting tomorrow morning, then."

"Thank you."

Wilfrid had changed much in the past year. Once a country-woman working a farm in Arland, then a general under Loran, and then a knight, this last change being the most dramatic. She had learned to read, and the way she dressed and carried herself changed. Loran had, after all, personally entrusted her with the future of Arland.

"Has King Loran made an appearance since I've been gone?" asked Wilfrid.

Arienne shook her head. "Still nothing since that day. Nor do we know where the fire-dragon has flown . . ."

"How I wish we could see her again, just one more time . . ." Wilfrid said somberly.

Arienne was secretly glad of Loran's absence. Had Loran stayed in Arland, the Empire would have done everything it could to rid themselves of her, sending wave after wave of their legions. On the other hand, if Loran had died, they wouldn't have felt the need to make the current compromises. Even as the Empire breathed a sigh of relief that Loran had disappeared, they could not ignore the fact that somewhere, the King of Arland who had destroyed one of their gigatherions was still at large, which was why they had been the first to open negotiations with Arland.

The negotiations did not last long. All the Empire's wrong-doings were to be pinned on the late Prefect Hesperus and the Twenty-Fifth Legion, and Arland was to remain a province of the Empire. But Arland was, for almost all intents and purposes, self-governing. Had Loran known this would happen?

"I still wonder from time to time," said Wil sadly, "whether what we did was the right thing. Whether this was indeed what Her Majesty would have wanted . . ."

"Well. We did not have to continue fighting, the Twenty-Fifth Legion was sent away far south, you are prefect now, and we have the right to send whomever we want to the Commons . . ."

"But this is not true independence. We still send taxes to the Empire . . . Not that it's anywhere near as staggering an amount as under Hesperus. Still, I may have the title of prefect, but there is nothing I can do should the Empire refuse to hear no for an answer."

"That is true. Our fight is not over yet. There are still other battles to come."

Wilfrid nodded. "What of the new occupying force? Are they any trouble?"

"The Eighty-Second? Unless there are extraordinary circum-stances, they are to stay in the fortress and never leave. We never see them. That's good for them as well as us."

"And I saw that the wreck of the gigatherion still stands on the battlefield."

"We've forbidden the Twenty-Fifth from removing it. Only the Power generator and some other important parts have been returned to the Empire."

Perhaps sensing Arienne's displeasure, Wilfrid said, "I'm sorry, I know you were against the Empire getting their hands on the generator."

Arienne sighed. "I've made peace with the council's decision. I knew the Empire wouldn't give us that . . ."

The Empire would also continue to test for children with magic and take them away. The council tried to convince her that this had to be the way things were for now, but she suspected that the matter was merely a bargaining chip to them. *How our lives are designed to satiate the hunger of banal, ordinary men,* Eldred used to say, of the sorcerer's fate.

Sometimes, when the whole thing didn't feel like a victory to her, she would remind herself of what Loran had told Wilfrid: *Even if we should win, the Empire also has its tomorrow. That is what you need to prepare for.* Prepare she would. At the Academy, a classmate had taught Arienne a spell learned from a witch in her homeland. Now it was Arienne's turn to be that witch, teaching the sorcerer children of Arland all that she knew—Eldred's magic, and her own.

She would have to find them. She would have to get a place to teach them in secret. She couldn't speak of this to anyone, not even to Wilfrid. Arienne changed the subject.

"The council wants to make a memorial there, but I wonder how useful such a place would be, hours away from the city." Arienne suddenly gave a start and clapped her hands. "How rude of me! I didn't serve you anything to drink. I was simply too happy to see you!"

Wilfrid laughed and waved her hand in refusal. "It's fine. I have many other people to see."

"If I'd known you were just arriving today, we would have delayed your banquet, so you could rest."

"I could've come earlier, but when I was passing Ledon, Chief Griogal had come out to greet me. He insisted on me staying for three days. I must confess I have grown rather weary of banquets of late."

"Ledon doesn't seem to be doing well in their negotiations . . . Kamori as well."

"*Their* prefects are alive." Wilfrid nodded thoughtfully. "But at least the Ledonite tribes will not be so terribly harassed as before."

"Speaking of Kamori, Prince Emere told me he was about to take over his sister's seat."

"Kamori's Commons seat?"

"Yes. His sister is getting on in years, apparently . . . As for dealing with their prefect, Gwedion will take over, as he is quick of mind and used to the ways of the city."

"And the other one . . . What was his name, the second eldest of the Kamori royal house?"

"Gaharas, or something? I don't quite remember either."

"Does he still live in a rabbit warren in the forest?"

"I don't know. Emere never talks about him."

"I see." Wilfrid sighed. "Well, I must go. We shall meet again this evening."

"Please do not drink too much tonight. Don't forget to get your sleep for tomorrow."

Wilfrid hugged Arienne once more in reply, then left.

Arienne had a little time before the banquet. She sat in her armchair, resting her back, and paused to look inside the new room of her mind. It was modeled after the room where she had stayed on her last night in the Capital, though without the suggestive sculptures and paintings she considered inappropriate for children.

In the middle of the room, next to the large and soft bed, was a bassinet. Tychon lay inside, her little secret. He was in the form of a baby wrapped in a swaddling blanket. Despite it being a year past, he remained an infant. She looked tenderly into his face. He cooed, and grasped her finger when she presented it to him. He might never grow. He might never become a boy or an adult. But here, in this safe place, he could live without being used for his Power. It would be better for him in here than in a lead sarcophagus.

While she played with the baby, the sun continued to set. Outside, the new banners of Arland glinted in the last light of the day, two red dragons against a white background. One was the fire-dragon of the mountain, the other represented Loran, King of Arland.

After an hour with the baby, Arienne left her mind's room to get ready for the banquet. She put on the blue dress Cedric had designed, undid her hair and retied it neatly. She brushed some color around her eyes and sprinkled perfume. She didn't often bother with such things, but tonight would be a night full of old friends she hadn't seen in a long time, not to mention the foreign emissaries who had promised to come. Care needed to be taken. Especially since a very special guest was to arrive before the banquet. For the sake of that person, she needed to put her best self forward, as she hadn't been able to the last time they had seen each other.

The sun had completely set. Arienne looked out the window. The lights came on one by one, on the streets and in the houses, dotting the cityscape with soft orange colors. The stars covered the night sky. This was a very different scene from the Capital, where the lights from the Power generators made the city glow blue. She opened the window to the cold, crisp air.

The stars of the sky suddenly disappeared and reappeared again. A gust of wind burst into the room, as if deliberately blown into her window.

Someone now perched on the windowsill. Arienne bowed deeply, bending her back and knees, paying the greatest respect she knew how to.

"Your Majesty, I have awaited you. Please enter."

ACKNOWLEDGMENTS

On a very cold day in 2014, when I was days away from turning forty, Lee Kyu-seung of Onuju Publishing urged me to write a novel. He had read a vignette in my self-published TTRPG world setting and liked it so much that he wanted to see the whole story unfold. Drunk on baijiu and the once-abandoned dream of being a writer, I obliged. A year and half later, *Blood of the Old Kings* was in Korean bookstores. I have him to thank for setting me on the path.

By the time the second book of the series was done, I discovered that it had no home. A small publisher, Onuju was not in a position to receive it, nor was anyone else about to publish only the second book of the trilogy. So the Mersia Trilogy, as it was known then, lay forgotten, with just one book on the shelves, another on my hard drive, and the other in my dreams.

Acknowledgments

Years later, as I became more active as a writer, I hired an agency. In late 2022, Toni Kim and Bae Jeongeun of Greenbook Agency started showing the translated sample chapters of *Blood of the Old Kings* to publishers outside Korea. There is a lot to be said for their diligence and persistence. They also have my most sincere gratitude.

It didn't take long until Lindsey Hall of Tor picked up the series. Not only did she want to publish the whole trilogy in English, Lindsey had gotten Anton Hur on board, one of the best Korean-to-English translators, known for such works as Bora Chung's *Cursed Bunny* and Djuna's *Counterweight*. What Anton has accomplished with my original text is tremendous—as a translator myself, I could only hope to do so well. I thank him for his brilliant work.

I can't express enough gratitude toward Lindsey Hall and Aislyn Fredsall, the editors of this book. Kind yet honest, believing yet exacting, they carried the book to the greatest heights it could hope to achieve. They gave me guidance that I needed and encouragements that kept me going. I am excited that I get to do it all over again with them for the next two books in the series.

Even the best manuscript isn't a book. I'd like to thank Jamie Stafford-Hill and Dominik Meyer for the fantastic cover. Gertrude King's marketing team and Caro Perny's publicity team also have my deepest thanks as they make sure that the book reaches as many people as it can. I'd also like to thank Omar Chapa, Dakota Griffin, Jacqueline Huber-Rodriguez, and Rafal Gibek of the production team for making sure the book is as polished as it can be. My thanks also go to Emily Langmade for the beautifully stylized map of the Empire.

Acknowledgments

My wife, Narim, is the first reader and critic of everything that I write, and probably my biggest fan in the world. Every step of the way, she has been excited about my newfound career as a writer and offered me crucial advice. Whenever I am in self-doubt, I remind myself that there will always be at least one person who believes in my stories.

It was my mother, Hyejoon, who taught me how to read with compassion. My late father, Yungmyung, trained me to think with history in mind. Now both are important parts of my writing process. I will always be grateful to them for those and so many other things.

In my adolescence, William Gibson's *Neuromancer* taught me the value of crisp prose, which I am still hoping to achieve. Through his *Count Zero* and subsequent works, I learned what multiple viewpoints and plot arcs could do. He was the first writer who let me see writing as a craft. Whatever I write, it will always have his influence, visible or not.

I'd like to thank Lee Suhyeon and Kim Bo-young. Lee Suhyeon is a writer and translator who has introduced Korean readers to Le Guin, Butler, and Scalzi, among so many others. Kim Bo-young is perhaps the most well-known Korean SF writer in the English-speaking world, with books such as *I'm Waiting for You*. When I had no publisher and was about to give up on the whole thing, they invited me to write for their projects, without knowing me personally.

Finally, I'd like to thank my readers. I often tell my friends that I write to reach people who are like me. If you find this book fun to read, or even meaningful, you are like me, at least in that particular way. I may never know who you are, but I firmly believe that you are out there.

ABOUT THE AUTHOR

SUNG-IL KIM was born in Seoul in 1974. Despite his life-long dream of writing fiction, he only got around to it in his forties. He writes science fiction, fantasy, horror, or some blend of those. In South Korea, he is known for *Blood of the Old Kings, I Will Go to Earth to See You,* and "The Knight of La Mancha," the last of which earned him an Excellence Award at the Korean SF Awards in 2018. He spends most of his time in his downtown Seoul apartment with his wife and two cats.

ABOUT THE TRANSLATOR

ANTON HUR is the author of *Toward Eternity*. He has translated several books, including Bora Chung's *Cursed Bunny*, which was nominated for both the International Booker Prize and the National Book Award for Translated Literature. He lives in Seoul.